Gray Victory

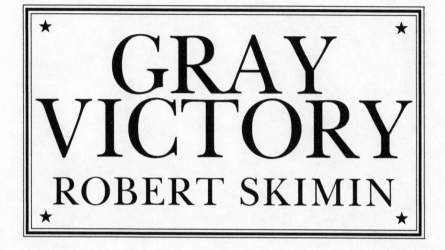

GRAY VICTORY

ROBERT SKIMIN

St. Martin's Press

NEW YORK

Design by Jennifer Dossin

Library of Congress Cataloging-in-Publication Data

Skimin, Robert.
Gray Victory/by Robert Skimin.
p. cm.
ISBN 0-312-01374-4 : $19.95
1. United States—History—Civil War, 1861-1865—Fiction.
I. Title.
PS3569.K49G7 1988
813'.54—dc19
87-27329

First Edition
10 9 8 7 6 5 4 3 2 1

TO SUZANNE

War's End

═══════

I T WAS all so simple—a matter of not replacing a general.

For over three years the great American Civil War had been the most devastating conflict in the history of warfare. Massive battles had been fought with staggering numbers of casualties. But the decision of the president of the Confederacy to retain a defensive wizard at a pivotal point was the key to the war's final outcome.

At no time had the Confederacy sought to win the war in the sense of conquering the North—its goal was simply recognition as a free nation, independent of the union of the United States. Thus, for the South to win the war, the North had to quit. And with the vast superiority of numbers and industry in the North, it was only a matter of time before the rebel armies would be ground into submission.

Of course it was politics that altered the inevitable, politics and that key decision. And just a few insiders in the Confederacy, as well as a handful of astute observers, knew how it had happened.

The vital Northern election was coming up in November 1864, with the incumbent president—Abraham Lincoln—running for reelection on the Republican ticket pledging to preserve the Union and to emancipate the slaves by carrying the war to victory. Opposing him on the Democratic slate was General George B. McClellan, running on the peace plank, which promised a swift conclusion to the war—one that would be favorable to the South. But the North was war-weary. Lincoln's army needed a major victory in order for him to win the election.

Atlanta was the second most important city in the Confederacy, and in July the powerful Union Army of the Tennessee was knocking at its gates. Its fall would give Lincoln his victory.

As the crucial battle for Atlanta continued, President Jefferson Davis of the Confederacy was also listening to the voices of dissent in the war-ravaged South. Win or quit! they cried. Confederate General Joe Johnston, whose forte was plodding, but often ingenious, defense, was in command at Atlanta. It was proposed to replace him with a more aggressive general—the fiery, one-legged John Bell Hood.

But at the last minute, Davis had a premonition that Hood would pull his army out of its Atlanta fortifications and, like a white knight, fall under the Yankee sword.

And that was the crux—Davis did not send Hood, and Johnston held out until the Northern election day. Lincoln was voted out of office, and McClellan in. A cease-fire went into effect the following day.

The South had won the war.

Prologue

═══

COLONEL John Mosby turned his head at the sound of horses rounding the nearby bend in the road. He drew in a deep breath, unable to believe that within the next hour the war would be officially over. Nor could he believe that his beloved South had won.

On the road, riding at a brisk trot, General Robert E. Lee led a small contingent that included his two general officer sons and the bearers of the two bright flags—the colors of the Army of Northern Virginia and the bright red, white, and blue battle flag of the Confederacy. Lee rode erectly on his famous gray horse, Traveler, his trappings gleaming brightly in the early afternoon sunlight.

It was twelve minutes before one o'clock and two large balloons swayed lazily on their ropes in the clear sky above the pasture of the MacIntosh farm. One of the balloons, the silvery one with the red stars, was Confederate. The other, piloted by Professor Thaddeus Lowe, was painted with broad red-and-white stripes, while its basket bore clear white stars against a dark blue background. Both stared down at the MacIntosh farmhouse, a two-story structure that had been a popular inn during the Revolutionary War. It had four thick white columns on its front porch and was located just northwest of Spotsylvania Court House on the Brock Road.

Mosby nodded slightly to Major General Jeb Stuart at his right elbow, never taking his eyes off Lee as the general turned into the lane leading to the farmhouse. "This is the greatest moment of our lives," he whispered.

Stuart nodded, the tall black ostrich plume in his hat bobbing. His eyes shone as he watched Lee. "Undoubtedly," he replied softly, trying to keep the emotion out of his voice.

Nearly two dozen other senior Confederate officers filled the yard around the white columned veranda, all quiet, solemn.

There were no bands to play, and only a few privileged journalists were on hand. Mathew Brady, the illustrious Northern photographer, had been granted the exclusive right to photograph the momentous occasion; his prints would be distributed among the press of both nations and the rest of the world. He slipped under the black hood of his camera as Lee returned the salutes and dismounted.

Lee stopped for a moment on the steps, nodding in approval to those who had been so close to him in the good times and the bad. He seemed to want to say something, but probably not trusting himself to control his emotions, he turned and hurried inside the MacIntosh house.

★ ★ ★

THE gravity of the occasion gripped Mosby. So many times he had thought this day would never come—and that if it did, the tattered and defeated leaders of the Confederate Army would be dragging in on starved horses to hand over their swords in ignominious defeat. But no swords would be surrendered on this magnificent day. . . .

The faint noise of the horses shifting weight, the soft jangling of spurs, and the muted conversation of the waiting officers were the only sounds as everyone anticipated General Grant's arrival. They knew he would be neither early nor late, just as he had never stopped coming at them during the hostilities. The Bulldog, some called him. Others called him worse, hated him as much as Lincoln. But Mosby knew what had finally stopped him.

The politicians.

Mosby stroked his short blond beard, glanced sideways at Jeb Stuart again. It had all started a thousand years ago in brittle sunlight, yet some of it seemed only moments old. The old soldiers' tale—remember the good times, let the ghosts and the rest slip off into a forgetting haze. Battle wasn't rational, why should its recall be?

God! Was it only four years? Could that short but interminable period so dwarf all that went before? Could it truly be over? These Yankee officers standing so close—were they more than a dream, should he draw his revolver and take them prisoner?

Was the magnificent Lee with his white hair and beard actually going to pick up a pen and end it all—finally send his brave boys home for good?

Mosby turned to where the Union flag had been planted on its staff in front of the porch. In an earlier life he had saluted that flag, sung to it, loved it, and had been ever so deeply moved by its richly colored stars and stripes. For four years he had fought against it. Was it now going to be just another foreign banner, no more important than the Union Jack of Great Britain, or the tricolor of France?

He sighed, weighted by the sadness, glanced up to the roof of the porch where the Confederate battle flag moved only slightly in the gentle breeze. It took him back to the smoke of the battlefield: bugle calls sounding, shells bursting, crackling musketry; men crying out shouts of violence and pain; wounded horses screaming, crashing to the ground . . . a flagstaff bearing regimental colors shattered, its tattered standard falling to the dust to be picked up by an eager Yankee soldier.

Flags and honor and death. Save our flag! Capture theirs!

The flag—still the most moving symbol of all to a patriot. And there were only patriots at Spotsylvania today, surviving patriots. Even at this last moment they would die for their cause, for their flag. The Yankees thought they were fighting to preserve their glorious Union and to free the slaves—and they could fight just as zealously as any Rebel boy who ever walked.

The Southern boy—he was fighting for his *rahts*. He wasn't exactly sure what his rights were, but he would wade into cold steel for them. Yankee or Rebel, it didn't matter, they were Americans who knew about Patrick Henry and Benjamin Franklin, Thomas Jefferson, George Washington, and Andrew Jackson. And all were about to belong to one country or the other, foreigners for evermore.

"What are you thinking about, Mosby?" Stuart asked in a quiet voice.

"The flag."

"Whose?"

"Mostly theirs. I was just thinking. . . ."

"I know—if after all this, if we're right."

"Yup."

Stuart wasn't a man of riddles. "We're Virginians," he said more firmly.

Mosby nodded. "I know, but I just kinda' feel like a bridegroom who suddenly remembered an old love. I wonder how much I'm going to miss her." He wondered if Stuart might be remembering ceremonies on the plain at West Point when he was a cadet, or on a small parade ground on a post in Kansas when he was fighting Indians with the First U.S. Cavalry Regiment. Retreat, the flag coming down. . . .

The sudden stirring jerked him back. Stuart nudged his elbow. "Here's Grant."

Rounding the bend in the Brock Road and leading a small entourage of officers under streaming colors, Lieutenant General Ulysses S. Grant rode his big horse, Cincinnati. He rode easily, for he was one of the best horsemen in the U.S. Army. He looked only straight ahead, his expression hidden behind his short dark beard and under the brim of his slouch hat with the tarnished cord. His uniform was plain, everyday undress blue, with only the slightly faded bullion of his shoulder boards and their three stars serving as adornment. His trademark cigar was missing.

"Unconditional Surrender" Grant was coming to the treaty table to sign a paper that, in effect, said he had lost. He seemed to look directly into Mosby's eyes as he dismounted. The gaze was dark, bleak, masking the melancholy. He seemed smaller than Mosby had expected. Behind him were the blank, grim faces of Sherman and Meade, Hancock and the detested Phil Sheridan, two other major generals, and Grant's chief-of-staff, Rawlins. They all dismounted and followed the Union general-in-chief up the steps and into the house to the waiting Lee.

A horse whinnied.

Mosby nodded, letting the excitement take over.

It was finally finished.

If you want to smell hell—
If you want to have fun—
If you want to catch the devil—
Jine the cavalry!

Gray Victory

"**W**UXTRA! *Wuxtra! Read about Jeb's Stuart's joy ride to Gettysburg!*" shouted a teenage newsboy from his favorite spot on Ninth Street across from Capitol Square.

At a few minutes before eight on this soggy Monday morning, the newsboy sold copies of the *Richmond Examiner* as fast as he could handle the coins. Government workers and shopkeepers, a few army officers in their gray undress uniforms, even the driver of a mud-spattered buggy getting a copy for his mistress, swarmed around the newsboy. Anything about Old Jeb made good reading, and particularly if that mud-slinging Pollard had written it.

"Read all about it! Stuart exposé!"

Lieutenant Colonel John Mosby stopped on his way to the War Department building to buy a copy. Just hearing the newsboy's chant made him angry—how could that damned Pollard be bringing up that old trash again? He whipped the paper open to the headline: STUART'S GLORY JAUNT LOSES GETTYSBURG! Shaking his head, he read below the shouting headline:

STUART TO BLAME FOR GETTYSBURG. Three years ago today the Battle of Gettysburg was still flaming without the presence of Robert E. Lee's prima donna cavalry leader. Major General J. E. B. Stuart was just bringing his missing troopers back to Lee's main army after being gone for nine days on a glory jaunt around the Union army. Stuart had elected to pull away and fight independently on June 25th, thus depriving Lee of the vital intelligence cavalry is supposed to provide about the location of the enemy.

Stuart—well known for brash decisions that might bring him glory and fame, regardless of cost—had left Lee's eastern flank open at the most critical time of the long march into Pennsylvania. Had our noble general been doing his proper job, instead of gallivanting off to the tune of his own self-seeking drummer, there may *never* have been a Battle of Gettysburg. And if the battle had still occurred, Stuart's presence from the beginning would have provided a great Confederate victory.

Without a doubt, this would have meant a quick end to the war—sparing the South a hundred thousand additional casualties. How many of our brave soldiers' deaths are directly attributable to this vainglorious general's selfish motives? Why hasn't Jeb Stuart's conduct at Gettysburg been aired officially? Why is the Army—or more specifically, its commander-in-chief—still hiding the Gettysburg dirty linen?

Who else are you protecting, Mr. President?

The Confederacy will be conducting its first national election as a bona fide member of the nations of the world in a few months. Before you ask the voters to cast their lot for you, you had best answer some of their questions.

Mosby slammed the newspaper into his palm. The bastard! Pollard hated President Davis with such venom that he would destroy *anyone* to get at him. And he had sniped at Jeb before, so it was a perfect smear.

He thought of Jeb, and felt a sudden emptiness in his stomach. The man simply could not take a thing like this lying down. It would rip into his gut and twist like an enemy saber. For no man alive had more pride than General Jeb Stuart! But it was more; it also struck at John Mosby.

He frowned as he started across the Capitol grounds, tried to get his mind off the editorial by thinking of the city of Richmond beginning to yawn and shake itself awake—not perceptibly, but by subtle movements like those of a huge cat. A dog barked off to the south toward the river, where a boat's shrill whistle penetrated the wetness. He knew that somewhere close a woman's scolding voice carried to her neighbor's house, and that a doctor hurrying home from an early morning delivery of a new baby probably stopped to gaze up at the leaden sky and remark that all Mondays should begin on a brighter note.

And somewhere in an early opening market, a cook from one of the fine houses on Clay Street, wearing a sparkling white turban and a stern expression on her ebony face, would be selecting fresh vegetables and clucking about their poor quality—while two miles away in Rocketts, her cousin counted out pennies for a pound of rice and a handful of chitlins that would have to feed her family of five for two days.

Richmond, capital of the Confederate States of America as well as the Old Dominion state of Virginia, was still struggling with its identification as one of the seats of world power. And with its peace. Like a new mother, the city was adjusting from its teeming, pulsating, seam-bursting wartime experience to calm and stability. Gone were thousands of young soldiers in gray or butternut. Also departed was much of the flotsam of war: the profiteers, the more brazen of the whores, the gamblers, and the pawnbrokers who gladly traded on misfortune by purchasing family jewels for a pittance and reselling them for exorbitant sums.

Gone were fear and starvation, mutilation and the specter of death.

Richmond's pulse rate had slowed considerably since its hobble-dehoy stage of existence. Trees, walkways, and flowered tree-boxes brightened three sides of City Hall. Fresh from Boston, the "Black Crook" extravaganza with its buxom, tights-clad ladies of the chorus filled the house at the new Richmond Theater.

And the elegant ladies of Richmond no longer had to struggle with redone old fashions, or pay a ransom to blockade runners; their dresses were of the latest style from Paris, London, and New York. Murmuring from behind their fans, or smiling from under their fancy silk parasols as they promenaded on the street or rode in their shiny horse-drawn conveyances, they made one undeniable statement: *the world was theirs*. Notably influential during the war, the ladies of Richmond were proud of their status as one of the powers of the South.

Mosby stopped for a buggy before crossing Ninth Street to the Old Mechanics Institute building that had housed the War Department since Richmond became the capital. Federal posters during the war had described John Singleton Mosby as "slender, five feet nine inches tall, sandy-haired, with keen blue eyes that tended to flash out at one with arresting penetration, having a restless manner usually accompanied by a satirical smile; creative, dangerous." As the notorious commander of Mosby's Rangers, his exciting forays behind Union lines had made him one of the most famous of Confederate officers. Now thirty-two, he was chief of Military Intelligence in the regular Confederate States Army—a new-fangled section that Stuart had recommended when he served on the board that devised the army's peacetime structure. Like Stuart, he had taken a one-grade reduction in keeping with small army austerity.

Entering the building, Mosby told himself that maybe the women of Richmond thought the world was theirs, but it certainly didn't lie at the feet of the Confederacy. The new nation was deeply in debt from the war and did not yet have an adequate tax structure. After all, secession itself was based on states' rights, and already South Carolina and Texas were beginning to grumble. And there was another problem: the poison within.

And as chief of Military Intelligence, he was as familiar with that poison as anyone . . . it was the smoldering dissension in the country's bowels that would someday erupt and devour . . . it was four million negro slaves who had heard about Abraham Lincoln and his Emancipation Proclamation. . . .

Glancing again at the newspaper in his hand, he switched his thoughts back to Stuart.

★   ★   ★

JAMES Ewell Brown Stuart, class of '54 at West Point, had been —hands down—the most romantic and theatrical of the recent war's many flamboyant cavalrymen. He was the ultimate modern knight: a Virginian born to the saddle, prideful to a sin, unafraid of any odds, the quintessence of chivalry. Thickset and broad in the shoulders, he wore no chain mail, but his uniform matched his bearing: high boots above the knees that bore golden spurs a female admirer had given him early in the war, a short jacket of fine gray wool with gold buttons and bullion insignia of rank on sleeve and collar, a bright yellow sash and a light French sword—and on his head the true mark of the cavalier, a dark gray slouch hat to which a large black ostrich plume was fastened with a gold clasp.

Now thirty-three, Jeb Stuart still wore his long mustaches and the chestnut beard that jutted to his cravat. His detractors had whispered that the beard hid a weak chin, but it wasn't so. His nose was large, his blue-gray eyes could range from mirthful to piercing. Above a high forehead, his dark brown hair curled over the tops of his ears to the edge of his collar in the back.

Power seemed to emanate from him.

But Jeb Stuart had a touchy Achilles heel—an acute sense of pride and honor. It could overpower him, eclipsing all other values. When he was severely wounded at Yellow Tavern in '64, he shouted to troopers running back toward him, "Go back! Go back! Do your duty as I've done mine. I'd rather die than be whipped!"

Now, on this wet Monday morning, Jeb Stuart was being sullied.

He was seated alone in his office at the huge oak table that served as his desk. Trying to hold the newspaper still, he stared at the inflammatory article on the front page. His cheeks burned, his eyes had trouble focusing on the accusatory words. His stomach was empty, aching. He tried to fight down the violent anger that was washing over him like a cloudburst.

Letting the *Examiner* drop to the tabletop, he stared past it to the opposite wall where the regimental colors of the 1st Virginia came into focus. That faded battle flag had ridden into many combats with him—when it was his first cavalry command in the early days of the war, when the regiment was part of his brigade, and, naturally, as part of his corps. He had served with Stonewall Jackson under those colors, once even captured a whole company of bluecoats single-handed.

His hand trembled, his whole face was hot.

The shock was still there—as if someone had viciously slapped his face and he was slowly reacting. His eyes dropped to the newspaper again, blinking at the venomous words. Some of them leaped off the page . . . "brash decisions," "self-seeking drummer." But the sentence that most twisted his gut was *"How many of our brave soldiers' deaths are directly attributable to this vainglorious general's selfish motives?"*

No commander had ever cared more for his men! he cried out to himself. He had never asked one single soul—officer or enlisted man—to take any risk he wouldn't take himself. *Never!* He reached for the .44 caliber, ten-shot LeMatt pistol that he kept on his desk as a paperweight. He had shot at least a hundred Yankees with this powerful handgun—and always while in front of his men, or mixing it up alongside them in close combat.

5

The ghost of Gettysburg had returned, the old allegations. He had suffered them once with severe anguish. But then there had been new battles to join, new glories to answer anyone's snide whispers.

"Sir, Colonel Mosby to see you," his aide announced from the doorway.

Stuart nodded. "Send him in."

"Morning, General." Mosby glanced at the newspaper on his desk, then at the huge pistol in his hand. "You thinking about using that cannon on somebody?"

Stuart scowled darkly. "You trying to tell me I shouldn't?"

Mosby sat on a corner of the desk. "I'm damned near as mad about what Pollard wrote as you, Jeb. I just came by to tell you how sorry I am. If it'll make you feel any better, everyone knows that Pollard will do anything to get at the president."

Stuart dropped the pistol with a clatter, grabbed the newspaper. Shaking it at Mosby, he snapped, "This isn't accusing *Davis* of losing Gettysburg! This isn't placing the deaths of thousands of our heroic boys on his head. It's *me*, John—Jeb Stuart, who is being vilified!"

Mosby could only nod in agreement.

"How can this bastard get away with printing such tripe? I oughta call out one of my squadrons and burn his newspaper to the ground! No, I could do it *myself*, and nobody would raise a finger!" He rolled the newspaper, twisting it, struggling against the anger that roiled in his stomach.

"You can demand a retraction. Sue him out of his underwear for defamation, libel—the works. Then he'll have to prove every statement."

Stuart shook his head. "No, the damage is done. I'll have to kill him."

Mosby waited several moments before asking, "In what way?"

"Any way he wants."

Mosby nodded. He understood honor and he knew Jeb Stuart—one defined the other. And it would be useless to try to dissuade him. "Just stay logical, my friend," he cautioned.

★   ★   ★

DODGING puddles from the latest shower, Mosby thought of Gettysburg as he headed back to his office . . . Gettysburg, Pennsylvania—the sleepy little town just across the Maryland line that accidentally became the site of one of the bloodiest battles in history. And one of the most crucial to the war. For if Lee had been able to inflict his will on Pennsylvania in that critical summer of '63, the war would most likely have been shortened by at least a year.

Gettysburg—the disturbing memory that troubled so many. Due to the eventual Southern victory in the war, that sore had been conveniently ignored and was trying to heal itself. But now Pollard had opened Pandora's box, and God only knew what pestilences might occur . . . Gettysburg, with its glories and tragedies, its famous little hills and separate dramas. The South had called the battle a draw, but it wasn't. Lee had been blocked on his Pennsylvania mission, forced to return prematurely to Virginia, and had failed to destroy the Union Army of the Potomac when he had had the chance. Most important, there weren't enough brave Southern boys to step into the gaps his casualties had left—all twenty-eight thousand of them.

Mosby stopped to wait for a buggy to pass, and when he looked up he saw an attractive young woman with large dark eyes watching him with a whimsical smile from the cobblestone walkway on the other side of Twelfth Street. Her eyes held his as he crossed. She was nearly as tall as he, and confident. Most attractive. He touched his slouch hat in greeting as he passed. "Ma'am."

He turned, looked back. She was still standing there, watching him, smiling. He shook his head, pushed his mind to his errand.

★　★　★

THE major mission of his office was keeping track of the underground movement that had sprung up across the South since the end of the war. The cancer of the Confederacy, it was the shining light of the black people. Its goal was freedom for all Negroes, its ultimate method, revolution, either passive or flaming.

It was known as *Abraham.*

And the heart of it was in Rocketts, or Nigger Town, as the southeastern corner of the city was now being called by many whites. Rocketts Landing was the first docking area for commercial traffic coming into Richmond in its early days; later, when other wharves were added and the city began to grow, new businesses and some small factories began to spring up in what became known simply as Rocketts. The district started at Pear Street where Cary Street ended and extended along the James River southeastward until it faded into farm land. Above the Navy Yard and other docks, it was a hodgepodge of houses, stores, shacks, and tents—a part of town where no decent white lady went unescorted.

The firm of A. Y. Morris was located between Lester Street and the river; close by was the Sail Loft, a store that sold and repaired sails and tents. And below that were Gibson's Brickyard, the glass factory, and Brummel & Burns Distillery. Up the hill from Rocketts to the north was Chimborazo—the hospital that had been the largest in the western hemisphere during the war. It was said that enough arms and legs had been sawed off in Chimborazo to equip a division of infantry.

As Mosby walked down Lester Street, ignoring the stares from the many black faces that filled the dirt road, a Negro boy of about nine with hand-me-down overalls and a big yellow dog on a piece of rope, sidled up to him. "Is you a general, suh?" he asked softly, his eyes wide and a touch of wonder in his expression.

Mosby smiled, scratched the top of the dog's head. " 'Fraid not, son. What's your dog's name?"

"Teacup."

"Quite a name for a big boy dog."

"Uh huh. How's come you ain't got no gun?"

"Cause I'm not gonna shoot anyone."

"Huh."

The corner of Lester and Hague streets was filled with loitering negroes, watching him quietly, sullenly. They seldom saw an army officer in this part of town nowadays. Mosby thought about how Rocketts had become a teeming island of black existence in the past year, a place for Negroes to put down even the flimsiest of roots. . . .

Just after the armistice, colored refugees began to stream into Rocketts from not only Virginia, but other parts of the South. A majority were free, many were runaways, some who had belonged to plantations that had gone under during the war were neither. A good number had been free Negroes in Richmond for years—for in spite of the picture the Yankee abolitionists liked to paint, many Negroes in the South had been free for a long time.

Rocketts had become the colored melting pot within the capital of the Confederacy, a place and a people that were pretty much left alone in a nation that was tip-toeing through a world that was frowning harder and harder at slavery.

Unemployment was severe among the Negroes in Richmond, just as it was among free coloreds all over the South, and in the daytime the streets were usually jammed with idle men, youths, and children trying to amuse themselves. Those women who could find work in households without slave "servants" were usually the sole source of support for a large family.

And the usual vices existed—gambling, thievery, childhood prostitution; now and then there was a rape, a murder. But by and large, the residents of Rocketts were religious and hopeful, for they had heard of the Day of Jubilee, the day of freedom for all, when all colored folks would be equal and life would be good.

Just like Mr. Lincoln had said.

The Day of Jubilee had been postponed, but it was out there on the horizon waiting, and to some it was waiting to be taken. Or at least spurred forward. Many residents of Rocketts had served in the Union colored regiments, and some of these trained soldiers exhaled the hot breath of revolution.

One such was Jubilo—the man Mosby was coming to see.

Mosby would never forget their first meeting. He had been down on Pleasant's Wharf, just a few blocks away on the river, looking at a small boat he was thinking of buying. It was a sunny day, with a stiff breeze out of the east. Suddenly, cries for help caught his attention. Downstream, about three hundred yards away toward the Navy Yard, a small sailboat was in trouble. Hurrying along the wharf toward it, he saw that its sole occupant was a woman in a white dress. Suddenly her scream pierced the air as the craft capsized and spun upside-down into the swift-moving current.

He was horrified. It was too far to swim, and he had to dodge around a building and over some bales of tobacco before he could find room to run. Her head went under, came up, went under again. *God, he'd never get there in time!*

He guessed it to be about a hundred yards, and was about to dive in with all his clothes, when he saw the powerful swimmer surging toward her. My, how the man's arms tore into the water! In moments the rescuer had reached the woman and had her in tow. It took him no more than two minutes to get her up to the wharf where Mosby anxiously waited to pull her out of the water.

She gasped, cried from shock, and vomited river water. She was young and quite pretty, in spite of her condition.

Her rescuer was a huge black man.

"Good job," Mosby said. "I'd never have gotten to her in time."

The Negro grunted, wiped water from his face. "Damn fool, out there alone."

A crowd was gathering; one man had a blanket. "We've got to get her someplace out of this sun," Mosby said.

"My store is close," the huge Negro said. He was well-spoken.

The young woman was sobbing incoherently.

"That'll be just fine," Mosby replied. He soothed the girl as the black man picked her up as if she were no more than a feather. They came shortly to a large old house with a sign over the front porch that read, "Jubilo's Store and Bank" in fresh red lettering.

Inside, the young woman was placed on a sofa and immediately tended to by a gentle colored woman in a white turban.

"My woman is a midwife. Missy will be okay," the black man said as the women shoppers in the room hovered around.

Mosby introduced himself. "That was a remarkable rescue you made there. I don't remember ever seeing such a powerful swimmer."

The man nodded, permitting a fleeting smile of pride to cross his lips. He started to stick out his hand, but remembered he was talking to a white man. "Name's Jubilo, Cunnel. Reverend Jubilo."

Mosby shook his hand. "I'm pleased to meet you."

That was his first contact with the man now rumored to be the head of all underground activities in Virginia. With a true calling as a preacher, Jubilo had converted a nearby old schoolhouse into a place of worship. It was called "Jubilo's Church," and not only did the huge Negro rule over a large congregation there, he supposedly operated his Abraham activities from the same location.

In the intervening year, Mosby and Jubilo had met on several occasions and had developed an informal relationship, that while not quite a friendship was at least amicable. Now Mosby had to crack down.

He dodged a big puddle and entered the main room of the store. Jubilo was there, in his cluttered office at the rear of the first floor. A large brown mutt lying beside the preacher's feet growled as Mosby entered.

"Be still, Dog," Jubilo said in his deep voice. "Have a chair, Cunnel." He smiled briefly. "Care for a sarsaparilla?"

"No thanks, Jubilo. Let me get right to the point—I'm here to talk about Abraham."

Jubilo shook his head sadly. "You still think I'm involved in something illegal, don't you, Cunnel? Why, I'm so busy making an honest dollar and tending to my flock that I wouldn't have time for anything that trying. You know that, Cunnel."

"Huh!" Mosby chuckled. "I know damned well your interest rates would make the most usurious banker in Richmond blush. Now let me get on with the purpose of my visit. I didn't come down here in the mud to whiff the fragrance of Rocketts, you know. The word has been sent down from my superiors that the leaders of Abraham must come into the open and work cooperatively with the government toward an agreeable objective—or else the army will have to go after them as enemies of the state. A matter of plotting for insurrection, Jubilo."

The big man sniffed. "I don't know nothing about no insurrection, Cunnel. I wish you would quit hurting my feelins by saying such things."

Mosby leaned forward, looked directly into his eyes. "Up until now, the government has tended to overlook your Abraham as sort of a semi-secret fraternal, or social, movement. But no longer. Spread the word, Jubilo. It's talk, or go to jail."

The preacher shook his head. "I sure wish I could help you, Cunnel, but I just ain't involved in nothing like that. Tell you what, though —I'll mention it in my next church service, and maybe if one of my lambs is involved, possibly he'll pass on the message."

Mosby had to laugh. Jubilo ruled his church with an iron hand, and *no* member of his congregation would be doing anything he didn't approve of. "All right, you do that, Reverend. But don't blame me when they come around and slap the irons on you."

Jubilo held out a box of expensive havanas. "How could I ever blame you for anything? 'Ceptin' for that drowning girl's momma, you're 'bout the only white friend I got."

Mosby took a cigar as he gave Jubilo another even look. "I'd hate for anything to change that."

When Mosby departed, Jubilo's expression hardened. He lit a cigar with a wooden match and looked down through the smoke at the big brown dog. "I think trouble's coming, Dog," he said quietly. "Feel it in my bones."

★ ★ ★

M OSBY had known before he went to Rocketts that the discussion with Jubilo would be a waste of time. But it was an above-board step that he could refer to later when Abraham became more troublesome. For there was no doubt in his mind that it would. The fires of revolution could smolder and take forever to ignite, or, if the blaze were fanned in the minds of a people who had almost reached freedom, it could explode suddenly into an inferno.

The trouble was that nobody in the seats of power seemed to realize that such a tinderbox sat under the Confederacy. He had recently written a ten-page report on the matter, but the only response had been a note from the general-in-chief that said, "Food for thought, Mosby. See if they want to talk about it."

Even those government leaders who did realize the seriousness of the problem didn't want to believe it.

Entering the police captain's office, he said, "Good morning. Is the man ready?"

The captain nodded. "Sure is, Colonel Mosby. Follow me."

The secluded room was down a back hall in the city jail. A scowling guard greeted them at the doorway as they entered. At the plain table, a skinny black man of about thirty-five sat staring at a knot in the worn wooden top. His name was Israel Jones and he was a free Negro. He was charged with stealing a silver-inlaid pistol from the house where he worked as a handyman. A shaft of bright sunlight streamed down over his bowed head from a barred window high on the wall. There was no ventilation in the hot smelly room, and Israel Jones was sweating profusely. The armpits of his patched cotton shirt were large dark circles. He had once served a sixty-day sentence for wife-beating.

Mosby identified himself. "Now, Israel," he began, "I have a prop-osition for you. You know what happens to colored folks who get caught stealing, don't you? Particularly known criminals who have been to jail before."

Israel Jones looked up with wide eyes, nodding his head.

"You did steal the pistol, didn't you?"

The Negro tried to still his shaking hands. "I jes' borreyed it, Cun-nel, suh," he whispered. "I was gwine bring it back, that's a fact. I swear by the Almighty, Cunnel, suh."

"No judge is going to believe you. You know that, don't you, Israel?"

"But Cunnel, suh, I was jes' gonna get a loan on it for a short while. Tha's all. You see, I'se got a sick wife and she can't work, and with three little ones, they just ain't enough to eat on the money they's paying me."

Mosby's voice was detached. "What will happen to them when you go to prison for ten years?"

"But Cunnel, suh, I just can't go to no prison. I just *can't!*" Jones shook his head violently.

"And I don't want you to, Israel. No, I told you I have a proposition for you—one that will pay well enough that you'll always be able to feed your family. There are things I need to know about the goings on in Jubilo's Church—things that could be very important to me. You see, we know very well about Jubilo's activities, but there are still certain elements that could be of value. You could tell me about them. You could sort of be on parole while you were working for me. And then, after a while, you would be pardoned . . . clean."

Israel asked, "But how's I to know what you want?"

"You'll be told all about it."

Mosby had his first informant into Abraham.

★ ★ ★

SEVEN blocks away at the *Examiner* Building on Twelfth Street, Jeb Stuart strode purposefully past the receptionist. Heads turned and typesetting stopped as he jerked open the door to Pollard's office. The editor's startled look instantly turned to a dark frown as Stuart roared, *"Sir, I demand a retraction!"*

Pollard dismissed the reporter who was seated by his desk, telling him to close the door. Glaring up at Jeb, he said, "What kept you, Stuart? I figured you'd be here an hour ago."

Jeb had never liked this skinny, baldheaded newspaperman. No one in the army or the administration did. His acid sniping at the president and his family, combined with veiled, and usually unfounded, charges of corruption, made him a major irritant. And he was arrogant. The *Examiner* was the enemy, and Edward A. Pollard was the *Examiner*. "What about the retraction?" Stuart snapped.

"On what basis, General?"

"Because it's all a dirty lie and you know it!"

Pollard leaned back in his chair, placing his hands behind his head in an open gesture of contempt. "No, General, I'd say it's common knowledge. Fact is, I think you should've been court-martialed back in Sixty-three. If we'd had a man in the presidency, instead of a pompous ass, you'd be out on the street corner peddling toy horses."

Stuart jerked a white buckskin riding gauntlet from his belt and threw it down on the editor's desk. "Sir," he said evenly, "I demand satisfaction."

Pollard glanced disdainfully at the huge glove, smiling thinly. "No, Stuart, if I met every challenge thrown willfully in my face by some self-styled knight, I'd spend all of my time in the gray mists of dawn with a pistol in my hand."

"Then you are either a coward or no gentleman."

Pollard leaned forward, thrusting out his jaw. "Oh, don't be trite, Stuart. You sound like a fop out of a cheap novel. My courage is more than a matter of—"

Stuart's wounded roar cut him off. Before he could react, the burly general lunged over the desk and caught him by his shirt front. He was jerked from his chair into Stuart's flaming face, a powerful hand twisting his collar, choking him, bulging his eyes. "Don't ever blame me for casualties I'm not responsible for!" Stuart ground out. "Because I'll kill you, whether you fight or not."

Pollard was no coward, but he had never looked at such fury so closely. As Stuart released him and he slumped back into his chair, he had to wait a moment for his anger to catch up. "You'll pay for that!" he rasped.

Stuart was still leaning over his desk, hands spread, eyes hard, his voice brittle. "No, *you'll* pay, Pollard—if I have to sue you out of your last inch of filthy type. Print that!"

★ ★ ★

A S AFTERNOON thunderheads promised new showers on this hot and eventful July day, another storm was brewing in the "Court End" of the city, just three blocks north of Capitol Square. There, with its four freshly painted sets of tall white columns facing an immaculate garden to the south, the Davis Mansion exuded the power of its occupant. Referred to by some as the Executive Mansion, and by others as the Confederate White House, the imposing structure at 1201 East Clay Street was where the president held many of his office hours. Inside, in his small study, the president of the Confederate States of America scowled as he discussed Pollard's article with Secretary of War John C. Breckinridge and his general-in-chief, Pierre G. T. Beauregard.

At fifty-eight, Jefferson Davis was as slender as when he graduated from West Point and as erect as when he commanded the Mississippi Rifles during the Mexican War. Tall, with a sharply hooked nose and gaunt, pronounced cheekbones, he reminded the literary of Ichabod Crane. His narrow patch of graying blond chin whiskers seemed oddly droll, but there was nothing amusing about the piercing blue-gray eyes—one of which was quite blind—that glared out from dark hollows when matters did not suit him to perfection.

And he glared fiercely as he slammed the rolled-up copy of the *Examiner* into his left palm. "I ought to do what Lincoln did—muffle the damned press and shut that bastard up!" he said vehemently. "Gettysburg was dead and buried."

"But that was in time of war," John Breckinridge reminded him.

Davis strode around his desk to the side wall where the sword he had worn in the Mexican War hung in its brightly polished ceremonial scabbard. He touched it fondly, as he often did when he was angry. "Johnston and his damned Whigs are going to have a heyday with this. Since he was out in Mississippi and had no part in Gettysburg, he can scream like a wounded banshee! He'll make it sound as if Lee and I aren't fit to command a squad."

The opposition Whig Party had been formed shortly after the armistice and had already nominated General Joe Johnston, the hero of Atlanta and Davis's longtime bitter foe, as its candidate for the presidency.

Breckinridge nodded. "It's a certainty. We'll have to do something to counteract it, something mighty strong." The secretary of War had not only been vice-president of the United States under Buchanan, but also a U.S. senator, and had run against Lincoln for the U.S. presidency. Now he was calling on that extensive political background to manage the upcoming campaign for Davis's reelection in December.

General Beauregard said, "Pollard's article will be picked up all over the South and in the Northern publications as well. I can tell you for sure that Johnston will jump on the bandwagon with both feet. Reviving Gettysburg is perfect for him." He nodded knowingly to Davis. "By the time he stretches the story out over the whole campaign, he will have had you personally standing on Cemetery Hill in full uniform, calling every last Confederate soldier blindly to his death. He'll call it your biggest blunder of the war."

Pierre Beauregard and Jefferson Davis had become bitter enemies early in the war. Only when the president found it politically expedient to mend his fences following the armistice, had he apologized to Beauregard and asked him to become general-in-chief. Therefore, the general could afford as many liberties with the autocratic Davis as anyone in the government. "I must remind you, sir," Beauregard added, "that his criticisms will carry weight because of his reputation as a strategist. This Gettysburg thing can be a bugger!"

Davis slammed the newspaper into his palm again. "I don't need you to refresh my memory, General!" He returned to the rear of his desk, scowled. "Well, don't just sit there. *What should we do?*"

John Breckinridge shrugged. "I don't know, but we have to keep Lee out of it."

"Yes," Davis replied emphatically. "I'll get a note off to him by courier right away telling him that regardless of what takes place, he is to take no part, nor make any statement. But *what*, gentlemen, are we going to do?"

Breckinridge said, "Why don't you do just what Pollard said—air it out?"

Davis's eyes narrowed. "What do you mean?"

"Investigate the battle, make it public well before the election, and then forget about it."

Davis nodded. "Not a bad idea. What about a court of inquiry? That's right—do just what that damned Pollard says. Open it up, package it neatly, then wrap it up and put it away forever. Yes, we could do that."

"A court of inquiry can be an unwieldy thing," Beauregard cautioned. "You never know when it might get into areas that could prove embarrassing. It could backfire, you know."

Davis crossed his arms, pursed his lips. "Not if it's handled properly, controlled by an iron hand." He nodded. "You know, I considered the possibility right after the battle—when there was so much talk. But my generals still had a war to fight . . . yes, the idea is appealing. You're right, Mr. Secretary, hang it on the line, then roll it up in a tight little bundle, and get on with our plans for a dynamic second term."

"How would you approach it?" Beauregard asked.

Davis stroked his chin whiskers. "Well ... Pollard did hang it all on Stuart's neck—even though he was after me. We could convene a court of inquiry to look into Stuart's actions, and kill several birds at once. We show the voters that we are concerned with the truth, that we are willing to cooperate with an opposition newspaper, and we put Gettysburg away for good."

"And what about Stuart? You sacrifice him and half the women in the South will be on your neck."

The president shrugged, smiled thinly. "They don't vote, do they? Besides, who said anything about sacrificing Stuart? The proceedings would be efficiently arranged for a speedy conclusion, and if Stuart is found derelict, we give him a slap on the wrist and go on with life."

Beauregard frowned. "I have to admit I've never been one of Stuart's greatest admirers, but he *is* a brother officer. This could signal that no officer in the Army is immune from politics ... but maybe the people of this country do have a final reckoning coming to them over Gettysburg—enough of their loved ones died there." He rubbed his chin. "What if Stuart balks at being a sacrificial lamb? He's a mighty proud man, you know."

Jefferson Davis didn't even blink as he said, "Then there'll be one less brigadier on the rolls."

★ ★ ★

JOHN Mosby stared at the charred ruins of the house. A couple of the heavier uprights still stood, like ragged sentries, black and dead. What had been the floor was a mass of rain-hardened ashes, more unburned remnants, and a fieldstone outline of the floor plan of the frame house. Woodenly, he wandered inside the ruin, staring harshly at the receipt God had left for him, the receipt for two lives. His eyes blurred, the pain returned.

He hadn't been back to this place of horror in the eleven months and nineteen days since the fire; in fact, he thought he never would return. It was all too grotesque.

She had sent him back, that tall woman at Capitol Square. The one with the dark eyes.

Pauline's eyes had been dark.

He edged inside, poked with a stick in the lengthening shadows of sunset. Something bright, a table fork. A rusted iron skillet that the scavengers had missed, the latch from a steamer trunk. Something dirty yellow, an ear, an eye—part of the head of the rocking horse he had given his youngest son for his second birthday, four days before he was . . . before the tragedy.

He sobbed suddenly, choked it off.

He poked further, where their bedroom had been, where they had . . . something of hers, anything that had been overlooked. Anything, *goddamnit! anything!*

He brought himself back under control, continued to jab the stick around. It had all happened so fast, a hot iron left alone on a flimsy fabric. Maybe. Pauline outside, hanging clothes. Maybe. The tiny, innocent son having his nap. That was how he reconstructed it, that made *some* sense.

There, something else bright, a piece of mirror, her hand-mirror with its pale blue frame. The one she used when she combed her long beautiful hair.

He picked it up, looked into it, and saw her face.

His eyes clouded up again.

He had been barely able to see when he got there. Forty-five minutes afterward—too late. Smoke, the terrible odor, two forms under blankets, one larger, one smaller—fire-ravaged, violated in the most vulgar of atrocities.

He had stared, unable to speak, unable to function.

A hand had touched his arm, and Jeb's voice said, "I'll take care of everything, John." The tone was gentle, like an echo. "I'll bring your mother from Lynchburg, and you can stay at my house."

"Funeral, must have a funeral."

"I'll take care of everything."

"Her family, Pauline's?"

"Don't worry about a thing, John."

"I've seen terrible things in war, but this—"

Jeb's powerful arm came around his shoulders. "Let it go, John. Cry, scream, beat on me. Let it all out."

But the tears had passed.

A week later at the family farm, Jeb rode in just before dusk. "C'mon," he said cheerily. "I've taken a week's leave and you and I are going riding. You'll need a bedroll and your best horse. I'll take care of everything else."

The reply was listless. "Where to?"

Jeb's grin was broad. "Why you and me, we're gonna reenact that first ride around McClellan, just as we did it back in Sixty-two. You know, the one that made me the most famous cavalry commander in the world." He laughed. "And you the most important private in the army—the scout, John S. Mosby."

"No, I couldn't. I don't want to see anyone."

"Just you and me, John."

★   ★   ★

WITH their slickers, blankets, and mess kits, they rode back to Richmond, then north to the South Anna, where they veered east and moved on to the Winston Farm. That was where the column had bivouacked that first night in Sixty-two.

"We'd have more fun over at Wickham Hill," Jeb teased. The Wickham place was a plantation five miles away where Jeb had spent the night the first time.

"No," Mosby replied quietly. "I don't want to talk to anyone."

"A little fiddle music might be good for your savage breast."

Mosby shook his head. "Sorry, Jeb."

Stuart talked until after midnight, recapping the scout movement Lee had ordered. McClellan had his Union Army of the Potomac deployed east of Richmond in position to continue his campaign to take the Confederate capital. Stuart, with twelve hundred troopers and a section of horse artillery, was to ride around McClellan's left or northern flank to determine how strong the Yankee positions were. Mosby had scouted the route only a few days earlier, and it had been on his recommendation that Jeb had gone to Lee with the idea.

The next morning they rode leisurely on toward Hanover Court House. Jeb chattered on effusively, ignoring Mosby's near silence. "It was about here," Jeb said around nine o'clock, "that we spotted the first bluecoat cavalry—'bout a hundred and fifty of them. Remember, John, how we sent them skeedaddling and we rode on until we met some more Yankee cavalry on down the road toward Old Church."

Mosby nodded, recalling the encounter vividly. He'd been right at Jeb's side when Stuart held his sword aloft and roared, *"Form fours!*

Draw saber! Charge!" The column galloped on in chase, until the Yankees finally wheeled to fight, and had been quickly knocked out of the way.

"It was here," Jeb went on a little later, "that the heroic Captain Latané was killed. Bless his noble soul. Remember, he was our only loss on this entire glorious reconnaissance. I—" Catching himself, he glanced sharply at Mosby. "I'm sorry, I didn't mean to talk about death. I got carried away."

"It's all right," Mosby replied, remembering the brave young officer as he was dying . . . and seeing the covered corpses of his own wife and son near the smoking ruins of his house. How could anyone *not* talk about death? It was the terrible end to everything, wasn't it—the brutal burning of a beautiful young mother and her innocent little child?

Jeb rode close, touched his arm. "I won't do that again, John." His eyes were sad and full of solace, his voice low and pained.

Mosby turned away, collected himself.

They rode on, silently, across the Totopotomoy and past Old Church. "It was about here," Jeb said, "that I made the decision to ride on, defy the huge odds, and try to go all the way through McClellan's supply lines and circle his army. Lord, what a chance that was, John. Remember?"

"Like you said, Jeb, it made you the most famous cavalryman in the world." Mosby found a smile. "And it was fun, too. That is, if you consider sleeping in the saddle fun."

Jeb's eyes lit up. "Remember when that gun got caught in the mud down near Tunstall's Station? It was up over its hubs in that hole and those horses couldn't budge it with all the whips and swearing in the world. Then old Von Borcke came up and said, 'Vy don't chew put that damned captured viskey keg on top and let them big boys haf a go at it?' And those big cannoneers, licking their lips in anticipation, waded in up to their arses and lifted the whole thing out—gun, caisson full of ammunition, and everything. I can still see them pounding on, swigging from that keg, mud flying in every direction!" He threw his head back and roared with laughter.

And John Mosby laughed too—a chuckle at first, then an outright burst.

They rode on past White House—McClellan's main base—and Talleysville, and on to the Chickahominy, where it had been necessary to build a bridge to effect the arduous crossing of the swollen stream.

"Do you remember," Jeb recalled as they found some remnants of the burned bridge, "saying that with all of that captured Yankee champagne flowing, it seemed the troopers were under the command of Comus?"

Mosby nodded. It was like yesterday. Those tired, champagne-swigging troopers had come on one hell of a ride with Jeb. They'd disrupted McClellan's rear and made him look foolish. The information they'd garnered about the weak Yankee left flank would enable Lee to attack there. "You made every cavalryman in the Confederacy proud," he replied.

"*We* did, John. It was your idea."

They spent the night and rode on into Richmond in the morning, completing the circle as it had been made in '62. How patient Jeb had been throughout, how sensitive to his raw pain—yet exuberant in a manner that didn't offend. And when they trotted back into the capital, he had become a man who could cope again. . . .

And now Jeb Stuart was suffering, pained in a manner that no average person could understand. For the average person had no way of comprehending a Jeb Stuart, a man whose honor on the field of battle was the most vital element of his life—a religion holier than holy.

Mosby tossed the stick into the debris and turned away. He would gladly fight Jeb's duel for him, but that wouldn't be possible. It wouldn't be part of the code.

THREE of the other four Richmond papers commented on the *Examiner* article the next day. The *Whig*, which was closer to Pollard's philosophy than the others, ran a front-page story that though not nearly so harsh on Stuart, was more critical of Davis. Gettysburg was big news again. The whole city was abuzz, enjoying the opportunity to get excited about anything in the midsummer heat. A slightly drunken former cavalryman threw a rock through the front window of the *Examiner* building, and four mothers of young soldiers who had lost their lives at Gettysburg picketed in front of the War Department building with signs that demanded Stuart's head.

Bessica Adams Southwick, one of the city's wealthiest women and leading socialites, arranged a short-notice luncheon with seven of Richmond's most influential ladies to pledge support to the handsome cavalry general.

It was the third anniversary of the third and fatal day at Gettysburg.

In the office of the chief of cavalry at the south end of the War Department building by Capitol Square, the topic had consumed everyone since the morning before. From deputy chief to the lowest clerk, all were ready to draw sabers and charge the *Examiner*. But Stuart had forbidden any activity on their parts, under threat of official admonishment. They were all surprised to see General-in-Chief Beauregard stride toward Jeb's inner office shortly before two o'clock. He nodded briefly to a couple of clerks, seeming preoccupied. It was the first time the Little Frenchman had ever come to the bureau alone.

Jeb Stuart jumped to his feet, but Beauregard quickly waved him back to his seat as he took the closest chair. "This won't take long, Jeb," he said briskly. "It has been decided after much consideration by President Davis himself, that a court of inquiry will be convened soon regarding your activities in the Gettysburg campaign."

Stuart blinked at his chief in disbelief.

"You know what a ruckus Pollard's article has started. And this is only the beginning. Already people from all over the Confederacy are demanding answers. This thing can snowball into a monster, Jeb. The court of inquiry will nip it in the bud. And then we can put all the ghosts of Gettysburg to rest in one box. You understand, don't you?"

Stuart felt as he had the morning before when he read the *Examiner;* his legs went weak, his cheeks suddenly burned. *A court of inquiry— how could they?* He cleared his throat, still staring into Beauregard's eyes. His voice was low, hurt. "No, I don't, General."

The short general-in-chief shrugged. "Hell, Jeb, the president can't afford to let this get out of hand. You know about his plans for a Mexican adventure next year, and maybe another one in the Caribbean. The next few years can be such a formative time for our country. This Gettysburg thing is just a molehill."

"But why me? Can't you just convene a court to look into Gettysburg, then whitewash it, and get the same results?"

"No, I told you—this whole thing is about you. We can't duck that issue."

"Are you letting Pollard dictate policy?"

"Of course not. You know how His Excellency ignores that bastard."

Jeb shook his head. "I don't like it at all. People always believe where there's smoke, there's fire. I think there's something you aren't telling me."

Beauregard spread his palms, smiling with confidence. "C'mon, Jeb, you know better than that. We'll set up a good court and breeze right through this thing. It'll all be over in just a few days."

"And what if they find against me?"

"I'm telling you, it will be a friendly court."

Jeb was insistent. "You didn't answer my question, sir."

General Beauregard didn't like being on the defensive. The smile faded from his face. "General Stuart, I'm informing you personally —as a gesture of friendship—that a court will convene soon. I suggest that you cooperate, sir, and accept whatever judgments that competent body might make." He rose stiffly from his chair. "Good day, sir."

★ ★ ★

S TUART and Mosby walked slowly across the grounds of Capitol Square twenty minutes later. It was too hot and sultry for such a stroll, but Stuart wanted total privacy for their discussion. "What else can I do, John?" he asked. "Do you think I can trust them?"

Mosby shook his head. "I don't know. I would think the president should certainly be trustworthy. Beauregard too. Still—"

"It sounds too easy."

"I suppose so. I've never been involved with a court of inquiry, but I imagine it can be a pretty tricky affair. It's not a court-martial, but it *can* recommend disciplinary action. From what Beauregard said, I doubt there will be any charges—just an examination of the facts."

"Or the lies." Jeb clenched his fists. "I'm not going to let them blame me one bit!"

"What choice have you got?"

"I'll fight it! Right to the hilt. I'm *not* going down in history as the man to blame for Gettysburg!"

Mosby knew the determined look in Jeb's face, and knew his Scottish ire. Without a doubt, James Ewell Brown Stuart would be general-in-chief someday when the graybeards were gone—*if* he didn't struggle against the tide. But such logical thinking wasn't a part of Jeb now; this thing was more than ever a point of honor. "Just be careful," he replied.

"I will . . . I want you to be my counsel."

Mosby jerked around to look at his friend. Be his counsel. He had given a great deal of hard thought to going back to his law career in the days preceding Spotsylvania. But the excitement of four years of war, of finding his skills both as an officer and as a hell of a free-lancing ranger, had made the law look pretty dim. The opportunity for a career in his own specialty in the Regular Army had won, hands down. He might even make it to general someday, if everything went well and he kept out of trouble . . . didn't fight the system, like maybe acting as counsel in the wrong court of inquiry. But he had no choice—Jeb wasn't the only one who would have to prove his inno-

cence . . . *John Singleton Mosby had instigated the whole damned thing!*
Nope, he had no choice.

"Well, John?" Jeb asked.

"They say a man who defends himself has a fool for a client."

"What do you mean by that?"

"Hell, Jeb, you'd have gone all the way to Pennsylvania with Lee if
it hadn't been for me. So it's my court as well as yours. Course, I'm
pretty rusty."

"That doesn't worry me a bit."

"I'll have to burn some midnight oil, but I suppose the Judge-
Advocate Department in Blues Hall will have transcripts of all the
previous proceedings."

Jeb stopped, stuck out his hand. A quick smile touched his lips.
"They don't know what they're in for."

Mosby smiled back as he shook hands, but he didn't feel that confident.

★   ★   ★

THE C.S. Army Intelligence Department was located in two small
rooms on the upper floor of the War Department building.
The large office held desks for Captain Sam Chapman, the former
divinity student who was Mosby's deputy, and Sergeant Reverdy Ogg,
the mournful looking department clerk and sometime special agent;
both men were former rangers who had ridden with Mosby on dozens
of behind-the-lines exploits during the war. Mosby's office had one
window, his always cluttered desk, a filing cabinet, and two straight-
backed chairs for visitors. In one corner stood the colors of his former
command—the 43rd Partisan Ranger Battalion. Another corner held
the colors of a Yankee regiment Mosby had raided. A bookcase behind
his desk stored many of Shakespeare's plays and some of Edgar Allan
Poe's works. He was particularly fond of the latter.

"Got a note from the secretary's office for you, suh," Sergeant Ogg
said from the doorway.

Mosby glanced up from the sheaf of court proceedings he had been
perusing as Ogg handed him a small envelope bearing the seal of the
secretary of War. Opening it, he found a note from Secretary John
Breckinridge. It read: "I'm having a small buffet at my house tonight

25

at seven. Sorry about the late notice, but I would like for you to attend."

Mosby glanced at his gold pocket watch. Four-fifteen. Why would the secretary invite him to a party three hours beforehand? Why would he invite him at all? He shrugged, scribbled, "I will be delighted," on the note, returned it to the envelope, and handed it back to the long-faced Ogg.

"Get this back to the secretary right away, and don't bother to read it—it's only a supper party."

Sergeant Ogg sniffed as he took the envelope. "Suh, you make me sound like a snoop."

"You are, and a good one." As the sergeant departed, Mosby stroked his short beard. He had been invited once before to Breckinridge's house—to a reception during the previous Christmas holidays. But that was because he was a department head, not because of any closeness to Breckinridge. They were a couple of rungs apart on the social ladder; more, because John Mosby wasn't even *on* the ladder.

The sudden invitation had to be blatantly related to Stuart.

THE narrow-fronted, three-story red brick house with white shutters at 707 East Franklin had been the wartime residence of Robert E. Lee's family for a period of time. Originally rented to Lee's son, Custis, who shared the large house with several other zestful young officers and called it "The Mess," its reputation simmered down to quiet propriety and even veneration when the crippled Mary Custis Lee and her daughters moved in. Although it was now occupied by Breckinridge, Mosby guessed that it would be known for a long time as the Lee house.

John Mosby arrived at 707 East Franklin wearing a plain dark suit and his best brocaded gray waistcoat at a quarter past seven, having walked the six blocks from his own house. Standing just outside the low wrought-iron fence, he gazed at the two white columns supporting the portico and wondered what emotions Robert E. Lee might have brought to this house on his abbreviated visits. Could that magnificent old gentleman have found a few hours of respite from his overpowering responsibilities on those stops? Had he stayed there with his son after Gettysburg? And if so, what demons might have troubled him?

Lyrical strains from Mendelssohn drifted through an open window.

The butler, a tall middle-aged man with jet-black skin and a broad smile, met him at the door. Inside the high-ceilinged parlor, he saw General Longstreet, the vivacious and striking Bessica Adams Southwick, the mayor, the popular artist, Edward Valentine, and a broad sprinkling of other senior officers, politicians, and socially prominent people. He guessed there were well over fifty people packed into the two adjoining front rooms. He also decided that his last-minute addition to a guest list with this many luminaries was all the more suspicious.

Everyone was talking about Stuart.

He nodded to several people he knew casually, turned as John Breckinridge spoke to him and extended his hand. "I'm so glad you could come, Colonel Mosby." The secretary of War was slender, forty-five, with a receding hairline and long pointed mustaches. "Let me get you some good Kentucky bourbon and turn you over to someone interesting."

He was soon deposited with a handful of guests that included Major General John A. Rawlins from Washington. Mosby had first encountered the Union general at the armistice at Spotsylvania, and again several months later in the Northern capital when he accepted an invitation to meet with General Grant. Rawlins was Grant's chief-of-staff.

John Rawlins was a thin, intense-looking man of thirty-five, with a bushy black beard. He was in Richmond overnight, having performed a special errand for Grant. His grip was strong as he shook hands with Mosby. He smiled, said, "I don't know why it is, Colonel Mosby, that I always feel as if I'm going to lose my watch when I meet you."

Mosby chuckled. "I never stole a watch in my life. Generals, yes, watches, no."

"I was just listening to the conversation about Jeb Stuart. Seems as if everyone is all stirred up over him. Aren't you a friend of his?"

"Yes, sir."

Rawlins sipped his drink. "Must be uncomfortable. I don't know too much about Gettysburg. We were just ending the Vicksburg siege at that time, you know. I do find the reports of the battle quite fascinating, however. I understand you were with General Stuart at that time. What's your opinion of all this, Colonel?"

"Sir," Mosby replied quietly, "that newspaper has a long record of typesetting errors."

It was Rawlins's turn to chuckle. "Good answer. You ought to go into politics when you get out of the spy business."

Mosby nodded, glad for the out because several people were listening for his comments. "Everyone in Richmond is in politics, sir. I—"

"How come your pal, Stuart, isn't here tonight, Mosby?" Lieutenant General James Longstreet asked rather loudly as he walked up. Longstreet was burly, with a beard as bushy as Jeb's. His expression was dark and he had obviously had too much to drink.

Turning, Mosby replied carefully, "I have no idea, sir."

Longstreet glanced at Rawlins, nodded his head. "Probably gone up to Washington to see if the Yankees'll take him back after his day in court. Now, isn't that funny?" He leaned into Rawlins's face. "How about that, General, wouldn't McClellan like to hire him to protect his rear?" He laughed loudly as Rawlins and Mosby kept their silence and tried not to show any embarrassment.

"All I can say," Longstreet went on, "is it's about damned time Stuart got his comeuppance. He shoulda' been tried right after Gettysburg, you know. Imagine trying to fight a major battle without cavalry!"

"If you'll excuse me, General, Colonel Mosby . . ." Rawlins said, nodding his head and moving away.

"Well, what do you have to say for your damned Stuart?" Longstreet said, glowering at Mosby.

Mosby drew in a deep breath. General Longstreet had fought valorously for Lee throughout much of the war and had early on acquired the sobriquet of Lee's "Old War Horse." Known affectionately as Old Pete, he had commanded I Corps at Gettysburg. He now commanded the Department of Virginia. Mosby had never seen him drunk before.

"Answer me, goddamnit!"

Mosby stepped back, glancing at the staring faces of everyone close enough to hear. What the hell had gotten into Longstreet's craw? In the several years that he had known Old Pete, he'd never heard so much as one unpleasant word from him. He replied softly, "I really don't want to discuss it now, General. I—"

"*Supper is served in the dining room!*" Lee's butler announced in a booming voice.

"Excuse me, sir," Mosby said, relieved at the excuse to break away. "I wouldn't want our host's sumptuous spread to get cold."

And sumptuous it was, Mosby thought as he stood in line remembering the hungry years when flour soared to $1,000 a barrel and bacon to $70 a pound—when it was available at all. Lee's portly cook, beaming under her white turban, was carving thick slices from the juicy, rare-cooked standing rib of beef. The equally portly housekeeper stood smiling from behind a table of assorted dishes that included a sugar-cured ham, candied yams, several rich casseroles, a variety of pies, and a huge devil's food cake that looked as if its chocolate icing was an inch thick. Lee's butler, grinning more widely than ever, hovered over everything, recommending larger portions and assisting the ladies.

As Mosby tried to decide about a cheese casserole, a woman's low voice interrupted his dilemma. "I'm told that Cook's soufflé is the best in Richmond. Mrs. Southwick, no less, told me she has been trying to steal that woman from Uncle John for ages."

He started, quickly recovered.

It was the tall young woman with the large dark eyes whom he had encountered on the sidewalk on his way to the city jail the day before. The same whimsical smile played around her mouth, as if she knew a private joke that involved him. Her lips were full, and there was the hint of a dimple on the right side. And she was nearly as tall as he was. Not going out socially, except to a couple of dinners at the Stuarts', he didn't know much about the extremely low décolletage that was in vogue in evening wear. Flora Stuart certainly didn't wear anything so revealing; she was always prim and proper. But this young woman, with the whitest of skin, was exposing an absolutely disconcerting amount of breast. He thanked her and concentrated on the soufflé, hoping the flush he felt in his cheeks didn't show.

"I'm Spring Blakely," she said easily, "the Kentucky niece of your leader."

He reached for a roll, managing, "I have all kinds of leaders."

"In this case, the Secretary of War."

He bobbed his head. "Your servant, ma'am. John Mosby."

"I know—my longtime hero."

"Really." That made him feel less intimidated. Without thinking, he pointed to a couple of straight-backed chairs. "Care to join me?"

"Yes, that's what I had in mind. I was a spy too."

What was she talking about? "I've never heard of a spy who just came right out and announced the fact to a stranger."

Her laugh was low, like her voice. "And I've never met John Mosby before. Is what the *Examiner* says about Jeb Stuart true? Is it also true what my uncle says, that all hell might break loose because of it?"

Mosby shrugged as he tried to balance the heavily laden plate on his knees. "Do lady spies from Kentucky always use profanity?"

"I can do better. Is it true about Jeb Stuart? Did he really lose Gettysburg?"

"No," he replied, filling his mouth with roast beef so he wouldn't have to expand on his answer.

"Can he prove it?"

"Yes. Where is your home in Kentucky?"

"Lexington. I taught school there and will do the same here. How can General Stuart prove he wasn't to blame?"

"Miss Blakely, I think that will have to wait until the proper time and place. Were you in Lexington throughout the war?"

"Oh, mercy, no. I traveled. Spy, you know."

He shook his head, chuckled. "Yes, of course. And you aren't married?"

"No. I was engaged, but my fiancé was killed early in the war. Shiloh." Her expression was collected, her tone matter-of-fact.

He nodded, unable to comment, turned his attention back to his plate. He simply could not talk casually about losing a loved one, and particularly not with a young woman who so much reminded him of Pauline. Would he ever be able to speak so unemotionally about his tragedy? Surely this young woman still felt the pain—what had it been, four years? He finally cleared his throat to break the awkward silence. "Sorry. Uh, tell me about your so-called spy activities."

She smiled indulgently. "I learned about troop movements whenever possible. In whatever way I could. Soldiers always like to talk to a receptive young lady, particularly young officers who have designs on her."

"And how many times did you entice these Yankee officers?"

"Who said I was getting information from Yankees?" The whimsical smile was on her lips again.

He blinked. Surely she wasn't a *Union* spy . . . surely she was pulling his leg. No niece of John Breckinridge, *General* Breckinridge, could be a Yankee. But those crazy Kentuckians—there had been hundreds of families split open by sons serving on different sides. Union state with *slaves,* and sons fighting for the Confederacy.

"I wasn't famous like Rose Greenhow, or anyone like that. But I gathered all kinds of information and passed it on. Even my uncle doesn't know. I'll tell you about it someday, Colonel. I even have a commendation from a Yankee general. Would you like to see it sometime?"

He nearly choked on a bite of cake. "Not particularly."

"How do you feel about slavery? Do you have slaves?"

This was the most abrupt young woman he'd ever met! "I have two servants," he replied. "Servants" usually meant house slaves, since the word "slave" wasn't used. "My man, Aaron, who was with me all during the war—and his wife, Winnie, who keeps the house and cooks."

Her gaze was direct, without a trace of humor. "And you feel no guilt about it?"

He frowned. "Let's just say that I am a Virginian, Miss Blakely. And I have other, more pressing matters to worry about at the present. If it will ease your mind, I only whip my servants on Tuesdays and Fridays."

She laughed, showing lovely teeth. "I knew you were a regular Simon Legree when I saw you on the street yesterday. I—"

"Oh, forgive me, Colonel Mosby, but I must speak to you a moment about this terrible vilification of dear General Stuart." Bessica Adams Southwick stood in front of them holding a demitasse of coffee. Her gown of plum silk was cut at least as low as that of Spring Blakely; her smile was as dazzling as the huge diamond earrings she wore. "Tell me, sir, is there any truth to the rumor that General Stuart is fighting a duel with that horrid Pollard tomorrow at dawn?"

Mosby smiled as he shook his head. "No, Mrs. Southwick, I'm afraid there's no such luck. The man refused Jeb's kind offer."

Bessica Adams Southwick's very wealthy husband had died commanding his North Carolina regiment at Vicksburg. She had been in Richmond since early in the war, and had once spent $25,000 for a party *before* the days of skyrocketing prices. Honey-blonde and slender at thirty-five, she had turned down many offers of remarriage, enjoying her full independence as a rich widow in the city she liked to call "the Paris of America." "Yes," she said, "everyone knows Pollard is nothing but a coward who hides behind his printing press. Well, tell poor Jeb I'm doing everything I can for him."

As she moved on, Spring Blakely asked, "Is she the most beautiful lady in Richmond?"

Mosby grinned. It was the first normal female trait this perplexing young woman from Kentucky had shown. Maybe it was because she looked so much like Pauline, but he thought she was far prettier than Bessica Adams Southwick. "Possibly," he replied. "But that's one kind of intelligence I don't keep on file."

A short while later as the guests were settling into a game of charades, the butler asked Mosby to follow and led him upstairs to a private study. There, the handsome John Breckinridge stood before a low fire, sipping from a brandy glass. He turned, asked, "Do you like a good Napoleon, Colonel Mosby?"

"Yes, sir," Mosby replied quietly. The thin mystery about his invitation was about to be solved.

As Breckinridge poured, he said, "There is a rumor that you are going to serve as counsel for Jeb on his court of inquiry."

It was perfectly silent as Mosby took the glass and tasted the brandy. It certainly hadn't taken long for the news to get upstairs. Had someone at the judge-advocate's office picked up on his borrowing the files from two courts of inquiry? He nodded. "Yes, sir, I agreed this afternoon."

Breckinridge nodded, returned to the fire. Shaking the ashes from his havana, he spoke in his deep Kentucky drawl. "How much has Jeb told you about this matter? Do you know the court is just a formality, that it will be handled judiciously with no harm falling anywhere?"

"Yes, sir, he mentioned that."

"Good. Now, we're both lawyers, Mosby. You understand that the members who will be selected for the court, along with the assigned judge-advocate, will handle the whole matter, don't you? Informal, fact-finding—that's the procedure. There will be testimony from a handful of involved witnesses, and then a simple finding will be made, and we'll get on with running our army."

Mosby sipped the Napoleon.

"In other words, there is no need for a counsel, or to prepare any kind of a defense that would entail adversarial witnesses."

Mosby said nothing.

"You do understand that, don't you?" Breckinridge persisted.

Mosby could feel his ire rising. He drew in a deep breath, expelled it, spoke carefully. "I think, sir, that Jeb has every right to prepare a defense. Anything can happen in a court . . . a hostile witness can tip it over. Besides, it's up to him, not me."

"But you are his best friend," Breckinridge said, smiling through a cloud of cigar smoke. "It's your responsibility to convince him . . . in the best interests of the army and your country. There are factors that you are not aware of, huge issues involving our future. And as a lawyer, you know your duty lies in what is best for your client. We know he's hurt and not seeing clearly at this point. And we understand. But this court *must* be handled in the manner I have just described. Do you grasp what I am saying in its *exact* content, Colonel?"

Mosby looked into Breckinridge's dark eyes. The man knew how to use power; major general with important commands, vice-president of the United States before he was out of his thirties, almost president. The threat was there, open. He sipped the brandy, controlling himself. "I understand you clearly, sir. But I still have to do as Jeb wishes."

The secretary moved close. "Damn it, man, pound some sense in his head! He'll throw away a brilliant career if he fights this."

Mosby didn't budge. "A man's career shouldn't be threatened because he wants his rights, General. You mentioned the fact that we're both lawyers, so you should know better than to make such a statement."

"That wasn't official. I was only thinking about Jeb . . . and maybe you."

"Are you threatening me also?"

"I just want to point out the hazards—"

"Save your breath, General!"

Breckinridge held Mosby's angry gaze. "Then your position is against the War Department. Is that correct, Colonel Mosby?"

Mosby shook his head, regaining his control. "Sir, I respectfully submit that I am *not* against the War Department or any other part of our great government. A heroic general, with whom I served for nearly three years, has requested my services to help clear his name. I have no other choice but to do so to the best of my ability."

The secretary's eyes were cold. "Then, Colonel, we don't have much more to talk about, do we?"

Mosby nodded, turned to leave. Until this moment he hadn't actually realized just what Jeb and he faced. A powerful cabinet officer going this far to pressure him; a senior general getting uncharacteristically drunk. What the hell was going on?

Minutes later, as Mosby stepped outside the house between the twin white columns, he heard Spring Blakely's low voice behind him. "Leaving so early, Colonel Mosby? I was hoping we might be on the same team for charades."

He shook his head. "I've already been in my charade."

She looked at him quizzically. "Then can I beguile you into going for a walk with me? It's a nice night." She smiled. "Can I start beguiling you now?"

"I don't think your uncle would approve."

"I don't consult my uncle on such matters."

Mosby was still angry and he really didn't want to bother. He had too many important things on his mind to get involved in more silly talk with a crazy Kentuckian. Still, part of him was glad.

She took his arm with a gay smile. "How about a stroll along the moonlit river bank? Doesn't that sound romantic?"

It was the first time he had noticed her delicate perfume.

★　★　★

LIEUTENANT General James Longstreet was a bulky, private man of both power and tragedy. Once warm and fun-loving, he was now a grim bear of a man who had alienated himself from all of his old friends. His unruly hair had receded, leaving a high forehead over light eyes that seldom showed any expression—perhaps a habit of his poker playing years, but more than likely a result of guarding his emotions for so long. His brown beard was thick and long, his speech so slow he gave strangers the impression that he was dull-witted. He had graduated from West Point in 1842 and had been a close friend of Ulysses S. Grant; in fact, he had served as best man at Grant's wedding when they were young officers. At forty-five, Pete Longstreet knew deep sadness—he had lost three of his children to the fever in just one week the winter before Gettysburg and had never gotten over it. But that wasn't what troubled him now.

He was waiting at the general-in-chief's office when Beauregard arrived at eight o'clock the next morning. They exchanged greetings and went into the Little Frenchman's private office, where Longstreet took a chair. "What brings you by so early, Pete?" Beauregard asked from behind his large desk.

"Oh, I just wanted to say hello. I didn't see you at Breckenridge's soirée last night."

"No, I had another engagement." He waited; Longstreet wasn't here to talk about supper parties.

Longstreet cleared his throat; he never had been very good at talking around things. "Uh, I wanted to ask about this Stuart thing, General. I heard a rumor that he's going to get a court of inquiry."

Beauregard shook his head. "Can't keep a goddamn thing secret around this town. I don't know how in the hell we ever won a war."

"Then it's true?"

The general-in-chief nodded. "Unless his Excellency does an about-face. It comes straight from him, you know."

"It's a mistake."

Beauregard looked into his visitor's cold eyes. "I tried to tell him, but you know how he is. He wrote the damned book on everything and threw it away. A court of inquiry can be an unwieldy thing, it can—"

"Stuart should be court-martialed."

Beauregard frowned. "Why do you say that?"

"Don't even waste the time and money on an inquiry. Try him, kick him out of the Army, and settle all the Gettysburg rumors once and for all."

"Christ, Pete, you sound awful vehement. Jeb steal your favorite horse or something?"

"No, but I lost a lot of valiant boys there. And the man responsible should pay."

"You're positive Gettysburg was Stuart's fault?"

"None other. Court-martial him now, General."

Beauregard shook his head. "It's out of my hands, Pete."

Longstreet gripped the edge of the desk, spoke intensely. "Then damn it, General, make me president of that court of inquiry. I'll see to it!"

"The president has someone else in mind."

Longstreet's eyes narrowed. "Who?"

"Bragg."

"Huh." Longstreet pursed his lips. Braxton Bragg was everyone's favorite bastard—he might stick it to Stuart.

"And another thing, Pete. I don't think you ought to air your views with anyone else."

35

"Why not? It's the damned truth!"

"Because that goddamned Pollard would love to quote what you just said. I'm going to put that in the form of an order, Pete. Do not discuss the Stuart problem in public with anyone, anyone at all. Unless I miss my guess, you'll get your chance to talk in the court."

James Longstreet clenched his teeth. A lieutenant general didn't need direct orders. That was an insult by itself! He nodded his head slowly. "Very well, General, I'll keep my mouth shut. But you make damned sure I get a chance to say my piece when the time comes."

"You can count on it."

Longstreet saluted and left the office, angry, half sick to his stomach. They didn't understand, didn't know how much this goddamned peacock deserved to be ridden out of the Confederacy on a rail, with tar and feathers instead of a general's uniform.

★ ★ ★

JEB departed on the three-and-a-half hour train trip down to Martinsville in southwestern Virginia at 7:15. There, he rented a horse and rode out into Patrick County to his family home, Laurel Hill. Nearing the old place just after noon, he stopped on the dirt road that ran through the rail fence where the Stuart property began.

It was his favorite spot; whenever times were difficult, no matter where he was, he would imagine himself sitting on a fine horse at this very place, and he would immediately feel good. He looked out to where the white main buildings of Laurel Hill stood out prominently against the backdrop of green-black mountains, and drew in a deep breath.

The home of the Stuarts.

Elizabeth Stuart, who had brought a brood of eleven children into the world here, was a Letcher on one side, closely related to the wartime governor of Virginia, as well as the governor of Kentucky. It had been her place—really more farm than plantation, but good families didn't own *farms!*

He smiled when he thought of his days as a cadet at West Point and how he had often lied to his Yankee friends about his huge plantation that took up all of Patrick County. "We had so many slaves, it took a half dozen mean-looking overseers to whip them!" he would tell a shocked listener.

He was Elizabeth's youngest son, and her favorite.

He had brought his young bride here on their first leave from Kansas.

And it was here that he recovered from that horrible wound he received at Yellow Tavern.

It was at Laurel Hill that he had waited for Virginia to secede, following his resignation as a new captain in the U.S. Cavalry. How he had chafed at the bit! And finally his commission had come through: lieutenant colonel, *infantry!* Great day in the morning, those idiots at the War Department in Richmond hadn't even *known* what a real cavalryman was! But it had given him his first chance to fight with Stonewall, and that was a memory he'd never lose.

He looked again at the white buildings in the distance. The oak trees had always been tall, as if they had been there forever, watching imperiously as the Stuart saga unfolded beneath their august branches.

His papa.

His free-spirited father, Archibald Stuart, came back from the War of 1812 to be a country lawyer and politician while siring his large family—the fifth generation of Stuarts in Virginia. Old Arch, as his son fondly liked to remember him, served in the Virginia Assembly and in the Congress of the United States, but he was best known for his zest for life. A charming raconteur with a fine singing voice, Old Arch loved a good time as much as any man in Virginia. And he was quite a rounder, enjoying both spirits and the pretty faces that were always drawn to him.

It was because of Old Arch's drinking that Elizabeth had extracted Jeb's oath, when he was twelve years old, never to touch alcohol. And he had broken the oath only once—when the doctor insisted at the time of the Yellow Tavern wound.

He could see Old Arch now, riding into the yard on his handsome horse and shouting with gusto, "Come here, boy! Kiss your old daddy!" And with a hand like a ham, he would swing his youngest son up into the saddle and roar with laughter.

When the stories came back to Patrick County that Jeb Stuart liked to dance and have fun with the ladies, everyone just winked and said, "Takes after his daddy!"

Jeb laughed aloud, remembering more, the singing.

His papa.

Archibald had died ten years earlier, leaving the management of Laurel Hill, with its slaves and the many grandchildren who often visited, to Elizabeth. But then, hadn't she always run the place?

Jeb smiled, urging the black gelding forward. What a holy terror Old Arch would have been during the war.

Now, if only Flora had simmered down—

Two minutes later, amid the barking of a dozen hounds, he swung down from the gelding to the boisterous greeting of his son, Jimmy. Throwing him high in the air and kissing the six-year-old, he asked, "How's my big, bold trooper?"

"Fine, Daddy. Wait'll you see the new pony grandma got me!"

Jimmy had originally been named Philip St. George Cooke Stuart, in honor of his maternal grandfather. But when Flora's father made the decision to remain in the Union Army after the war began, Jeb had angrily changed it. "No son of mine will be named for a turncoat Virginian!" he had declared in a fit of emotion.

Jeb had relented after the war and made his peace with General Cooke, but the boy would always be known as Jimmy, junior.

Jeb's mother came running out of the house with his two-year-old daughter, Virginia, in her arms. She brushed back a wild wisp of white hair as he hugged them. "Oh, darling, darling, what are they doing to you up there in Richmond?"

"I'll tell you about it inside, Mama," he replied, kissing her and taking little Virginia in his arms. He sighed, looking at the large, rambling house set amid the tall oaks. He had taken leave in April to help paint it for his mother. "You know, honey," he said to his daughter, "that's the only house I've ever belonged to." He kissed her soft cheek. "But you don't care, do you?"

Virginia giggled, tugged at his flaming beard.

He kissed her again, said, "Now let's go in and see if your mama has relented any."

★　★　★

FLORA Stuart *hadn't* relented any; in fact she was totally miserable. She had come out to Laurel Hill in early June—ostensibly to get away from the stifling Richmond heat, but actually because of a squabble with Jeb that had gotten completely out of hand. To make the matter utterly unbearable, she had broken her right hip in a bad riding fall two days after her arrival, and had been immobilized on a board in a first floor bedroom ever since.

She had met Jeb when he was a stimulating second lieutenant in Kansas the summer of 1855. The daughter of Colonel Cooke of the 2nd Dragoons, she had recently graduated from a private school in Detroit. Quite plain looking with dark hair and eyes, she had been nevertheless vivacious enough to be the most piquant young woman on the post. Their mutual love of horses brought them together, and they fell in love while Jeb spouted poetry to her from the saddle on long evening rides.

The quarrel that brought her to this board in the Blue Ridge foothills was over the never-ending problem of Jeb and the ladies. She had put up with his romantic nonsense during the war because she understood it; he had been the most famous cavalryman in the world, an honest-to-God knight who never drank or used tobacco or profanity—dashing, brave and chivalrous, the epitome of honor. She had even been *proud* that the females flocked to her husband as if he were Sir Galahad; what woman wouldn't be? And she believed him when he told her it was all harmless—the dancing and the parties, even the kissing; the inevitable gossip that he dismissed as idle twaddle. She had understood the gifts from them, such as the golden spurs and the French sword, the tintypes and the silly love notes.

But when the perfumed letter arrived on June the first from a gushing old acquaintance at Brandy Station, she finally slammed her foot down and became furious. *"The war is over!"* she shouted to him in their kitchen. "I've had enough of this *harmless* nonsense, as you call it. There's no longer any room in our life for simpering girls hanging flowers over your horse's neck, or writing poetry to you, Jeb Stuart!"

"Aw, c'mon, Honey Pot," he replied with his engaging grin. "You know how meaningless it is. And as a public figure, there isn't anything I can do about it. You know that."

That had made her all the more irate. "I know that excuse, chapter and verse, Jeb Stuart. The fact is, you *love* it, and I don't think you'll ever stop reveling in it!"

He shrugged. "What do you want me to do?"

"For one thing, you can stop perpetuating this 'Knight of the Golden Spurs' nonsense. King Arthur's long dead, you know!"

He actually laughed! "What do you want me to do, run an ad in the *Dispatch* announcing that the Knight is dead?"

"I don't care what you do!" she blazed. "I'm taking the children to your mother's!"

She was packed and halfway to Danville before he knew it.

He had been gallivanting off on some inspection trip to Texas from the day after her departure until just before Pollard's article was printed. He hadn't even stopped to see her on his way to Richmond! Now he stood there in the doorway to her prison room, grinning as if he hadn't done a single damn thing!

"Hello," he said. "Thought I oughta come down and share problems with you, Honey Pot. Is there room for me to crawl on that board?"

She didn't smile. "Hardly."

He took her hand, kissed it, leaned down to kiss the cheek she turned. "You look nice."

She knew how terrible she looked, and now he just rode in without telling anyone! Always thinking of himself! Damn him! The next thing, he'd ask her something cheerful like how did she feel—

"How you feeling, Honey Pot? Lot of pain on that thing?"

"I'm not dancing a jig."

Elizabeth followed him into the room as Jeb took the straight-back chair beside the bed and lifted Virginia to his knee. Touching his daughter's lips to still her chatter, he said, "I guess you've read about what's going on in Richmond. It all started with that scoundrel, Pollard, and his scurrilous editorial. But now it's gotten much bigger." He told them about Davis and the court of inquiry.

Flora listened to him partly in resentment and partly in fear. She had always known something like this could happen—he was so headstrong and he had so many detractors. So many were jealous of him. And she knew what it must be doing to his enormous pride. Normally she would find the words of comfort to ease his pain, but not now. She had been down on this board in the most excruciating pain for nearly a month now, and he hadn't come to her for *one single minute!* Of course, she hadn't answered his letters, but why should she? What was she supposed to do now—wash the bitterness out of her mouth, take his handsome head in her arms, and sing away his miseries? Hardly!

She just lay there, tight-lipped as he went on.

When he finished, Elizabeth said, "I don't see why you have to fight

it. What makes you think they won't do as they say? I can't imagine
Mr. Davis going back on his word."

"It's politics, Mama. Believe me, if I don't fight it, they'll hang all
the blame on me." Jeb got to his feet, paced back and forth several
steps, frowned. "Flora, you remember Dick Garnett. Commanded the
Stonewall Brigade after Jackson moved up. Well, he did something
Jackson didn't like, and Stonewall court-martialed him for alleged
cowardice . . . There wasn't a braver general in the army, but Old
Jack put the taint on him. He had to die going up that hill in Pickett's
Charge to exonerate himself."

Jeb paused. "And even now there are those who wonder about him.
You can't hardly get rid of a taint. They hang Gettysburg on me, and
I'm done . . . forever."

Elizabeth shook her head. "But what if Beauregard *is* telling the
truth? Your whole career could be ruined for nothing."

Jeb reached for little Jimmy's hand and drew him close. "Not for
nothing, Mama. For my children and grandchildren, and Flora, and
you . . . and for whatever place history might be kind enough to find
for me."

He paused again, shook his head emphatically. "And mostly because
I'm *innocent!*"

3

T HE train bearing Salmon Brown to Oberlin arrived at 4:42. He stepped down to the platform, amid the many abolitionists coming in for the meeting, and looked around. He was worn out from the long ride from Pennsylvania, and felt as if he were wearing a coat of cinders. Except for all the people, the place looked the same. The last time he had been in the town was shortly after the war, when, still wearing his tattered uniform, he had come back to look for an answer. But after staying with an old friend of his father for several days, he had decided the visit was a waste of time.

Not only had he found no answer, but he had doubted he was even an abolitionist. In fact, he had yet to find the place that held the answer he was seeking. And he had been looking for a long time, ever since the end of 1859, when they executed his martyred father for leading the infamous raid on Harpers Ferry. When the guilt had splashed over him.

Now he was back, hoping he could find a reaffirmation, some kind of thread in the Cause that would give him a path, a meaning. An absolution.

It was the Fourth of July and the normally sleepy little college and farming town was jammed—not so much because it was Independence Day, but because of the great meeting that would take place that night at the fairgrounds. Salmon Brown had never seen so many people in Oberlin, not even when the town had been an abolition center well before the war. He had literally to push his way across the main street. Buggies, wagons, and nearly every other kind of conveyance lined the sidewalks, their horses standing stolidly in the hot sun. People of all ages were everywhere, dressed in their holiday finery, keyed up for the double celebration, teeming through the packed streets.

Red, white, and blue saturated everything: the women and girls wore red dresses, blue skirts, white blouses with bright red ribbons, pretty hats with all three colors; the men wore the same combinations, many with red and white stripes on straw boaters worn at rakish angles. Children ran about waving small American flags. In fact, flags and flag bunting were everywhere, draped from rooftops, from flagpoles, in windows, strung across the street in banners. Red and white carnations abounded.

Marching music burst forth from a bandstand where army musicians in blue uniforms made their contribution. The swinging arm of the bass player flashed the yellow stripes of a sergeant, the brilliant sunlight glinted off two tall, swaying tubas.

The visitors were from everywhere in America, and that included Canada and even the Confederacy. For the abolition movement was surging as never before, if for no better reason than to give the citizens of the United States a way of letting off steam from the frustration of having fought a horrible war for naught. Anti-slavery sentiment, with its revivalist fervor, was the great Cause, the return of meaning. Those four million slaves that Lincoln had freed were just a few hundred miles south, waiting once more to be saved.

Salmon had just reached the far side of the street when a familiar air stopped everything. The sound of his father's name quickly echoed through the street as the voices of the crowd rose as one:

> *John Brown's body lies a-moldering in the grave,*
> *John Brown's body lies a-moldering in the grave,*
> *John Brown's body lies a-moldering in the grave,*
> *His soul is marching on!*
>
> *Glory, Hally, Hallelujah!*
> *Glory, Hally, Hallelujah!*
> *Glory, Hally, Hallelujah!*
> *His soul is marching on!*

Salmon stood frozen as the song rocked through the three other stanzas. It was the anthem of postwar abolition, and there wasn't a child of five who didn't try to sing the words—from a cotton field in

East Texas to the streets of London. But Salmon hated it, flinched inwardly every time he heard it. He had even quit going to abolition meetings altogether because of it.

The anthem started over again, louder.

A pretty young woman leaned into his face, bobbing her head, smiling, waving her finger like a baton as she sang. He just turned away. She caught his sleeve. "Why doesn't a handsome man like you sing?"

He shook his head, felt hot.

She stood on her tiptoes, kissed him quickly on the mouth, and laughed.

"Glory, Hally, Hallelujah!"

He stared at her, saw her face blur into that of the prostitute that haunted his dreams, the one who taunted him and kept him away from young ladies. The harlot had the same red hair as always, the heavy rouge on her lips and cheeks. "Well, Salmon," she said in her mocking voice, "what are you going to do this time—hold my hand and kiss me, push against my pelvis with your limp noodle? But that's all right, Salmon, I get the same money whether you get it up or not." She leered, then roared with laughter.

"Are you all right, mister?" The face blurred back into that of the pretty girl. "You're really sweating."

He pushed her aside, headed for the nearby saloon sign.

Two beers later, he lifted his glass and stared into the long mirror behind the mahogany bar. An old face with a long beard was indistinct, laughing, singing, "John Brown's body lies a-moldering in the grave." The Old Man. They didn't know about the Old Man. They thought he was holy. They didn't know how he liked to kill. The license of the zealot, he once called it, when they were out in Kansas. When all the brothers were alive.

"I came in from Detroit, myself," the man standing next to him said. "How about you, mister?"

"Pennsylvania," he replied, clearing his throat, moving away.

He looked back into the mirror. The hazy face with the beard was still there, lips moving, mad. . . .

It was the crazy part he resented. Everyone said the Old Man was insane, and that was the defense at his trial. Of course it hadn't worked, and the Old Man was hanged. Killing had nothing to do with madness, it was part of nature. And it was for the Cause. A cause always justified killing. After all, God had issued a commandment about killing, but He endorsed holy wars, didn't He?

Salmon put the empty glass on the bar. Best he forget all this nonsense and walk on out to the edge of town where his father's friend lived.

★　★　★

SEVEN hours later, Salmon Brown stood just ten feet from the center of the stage that held the featured speaker. The huge, enthralled audience had just risen from its seats, jostling and shouting its enthusiasm as the famous abolitionist from Boston, the Reverend Thomas Wentworth Higginson, reached the climax of his three-hour-long address. Salmon had been spellbound for at least half of the lengthy harangue, hanging on the minister's words as if they had sprung from a fresh, untapped spring. It was the first sermon to reach him in all the years of his remorse.

He had met the famous abolitionist years before at the old Brown family farm near North Elba. Reverend Higginson had come there to offer solace to his mother just prior to the Old Man's trip to the gallows. But that was when his guilt had been new and overwhelming, and he had barely spoken to the minister. Now the man was a glowing messiah! He made the Cause once more sound noble, dynamic, battle worthy. . . .

"What I want to leave with you tonight, my dear friends, is the sense of *power* you hold in your hands! I speak not only of an exemplary sense of right and wrong, of a Cause more *just* than any in history . . . but, my warriors, I speak of a way to put a blade of light in that Cause, a mighty *sword* that will drive into the hearts of the enslavers! Use that power! America is with you! The *world* is with you! And Almighty *God* is with you! This is no new war that I speak of . . . *No! The old one has never stopped!*"

Reverend Thomas Wentworth Higginson threw his hands high as pandemonium broke loose through the more than two thousand shouting abolitionists assembled around the grandstand. The flickering light of the flambeau mixing with the glow of the bright full moon lit the cheering faces as the minister continued to hold his arms widespread. While the wild applause continued, a bugler, dressed in a blue army uniform, ran out to Higginson's side. Raising his shiny horn, he blew first *Boots and Saddles,* and then *Cavalry Charge!*

The crowd roared.

Salmon Brown cheered just as loudly as anyone around him. He continued to shout and throw his fist high in the air as the bugler blew the *Charge* again. How that bugle stirred him! It reminded him of the highlight of his war, the attack on Cold Harbor when, in spite of murderous fire, he'd thrown himself over the enemy parapet. He could still see the face of that first young Reb no more than a yard away. Wide-eyed, scared. Couldn't have been more than seventeen. But it didn't matter, he shot the boy right between the eyes and felt good about it. He must have killed a dozen Rebs before the bullet slammed into his shoulder, knocking him down and taking him out of that bloody, glorious fight. Out of the war.

And not one single exciting thing had happened to him since.

Not until tonight.

What was so special about Higginson? Had the minister touched the coiled spring that had once made him live? The man made his heart pound, made him want to grab a rifle and head straight south!

Had his devotion to the Cause finally been rekindled? Once it had burned fiercely—when he was much younger, when the Old Man took him and his brothers out to Kansas to fight their own holy war. During the killings at Pottawatomie.

God, how good he felt! He had to do *something* for the Cause! Was Higginson really the key? He had to talk to him! He pushed his way through the crowd toward the steps to the stage as the great man departed in a final burst of cheering.

★   ★   ★

THOMAS Wentworth Higginson was often referred to as a manifest aristocrat. In fact, his ancestors during the revolution sometimes referred to Queen Elizabeth as "Cousin Betsy Tudor." Tall and slender at the age of forty-three, with dark good looks and a short beard, he was both an aesthete and a militant who left little undone when there was an occasion for heroism or notoriety. He had commanded the first Negro regiment in the war. And he had been one of the "Secret Six" who had backed John Brown on his journey to martyrdom. Now, told that the Old Man's son wanted to see him, he smiled as if struck by an inspiration. "Yes, by all means, send him in at once," he replied.

He met Salmon at the door, pumped his hand warmly. "Come in, my good fellow, come in. My, how the years have flown. How is your dear mother?"

Salmon took the straight-back chair in the musty storage room beneath the stands and stumbled through answers to the amenities. Higginson poured some lukewarm coffee, then turned the full force of his handsome smile on Salmon as he spoke glowingly of the Cause. "Do you know there are over fourteen hundred groups at this time? My audience tonight had representatives from over *seventy* of them, right here along Lake Erie. With God's help, there will be two thousand in another year. Now, my good fellow, what can I do for you?"

Salmon wasn't ready for such a direct question. It was all so vague and exciting, as if he had downed a pint of whiskey but his head was as clear as a bell. There was something about this great man, something that made him think of a dark-bearded Moses, or Abraham. Such strength! His heart was pounding; he clasped his hands to still the tremor. Should he fall to his knees, kiss the great man's hand? Would the great man listen, help him? . . .

He took a deep breath, blew it out, began softly, "Sir, there are things I must tell you, that is, if you will listen . . . things that I have never been able to . . . tell anyone before." He stopped, looked away from the minister's dark eyes, inhaled again.

Higginson leaned forward, nodding. "Go on," he said gently.

Salmon's voice was a whisper. "I'm to blame for Harpers Ferry."

"In what way?"

"I didn't go."

"And if you had?"

"It would have been different, I know it. Or I'd be dead with the others."

"Why do you think that?"

"Because I'm good at killing . . . I like it." Salmon's gray eyes were wide, troubled as they bore into Higginson's. "You know how the Old Man was; he found no sin in anything connected with the Cause. I think it all started for me back when I was eighteen and went to Kansas with my brothers and him in the Free State struggle . . . those killings on Pottawatomie Creek, where those five men were shot and cut up—well, we did it. My brother, Oliver, and I—he was killed at Harpers Ferry, you know—we used broadswords on them, hacked them up good. Just like chunks of raw beef, like you throw in the pot to roast. That was when I first knew the Old Man was right—it was war and not murder. . . ."

Salmon went into more of the violent Kansas experience, telling about the battle at Osowatamie when his brother Frederick was killed. And of the activities of the following years, when he once killed a woman who threatened to give them away.

Higginson interrupted. "How did you feel about killing this woman, my son?"

Salmon shrugged. "No different than the others. She was an enemy."

Higginson stroked his beard, nodded.

Salmon's confession reached the Harpers Ferry Raid. As he touched the core of his torment, his voice became soft. "I really wanted to go on the raid, but something held me back . . . I knew he would *dally*, he always did. I just knew they would all die, and I didn't want to . . . I was just a coward, a rotten, craven coward afraid of death, afraid of the rope. Sir, *I killed them!*"

The words that had poisoned him for years tumbled out nonstop. "If I'd been there, it might have been different. I was strong, a good shot, a good fighter. My brothers wouldn't be dead. I doubt I could've saved the Old Man—no, I don't think, you see, no matter what, he would have dallied. . . ."

His eyes brimmed as the torrent of words continued to come, describing agonies, real and imagined, self-hate. "In the war, I volunteered for one dangerous mission after another. All I wanted to do was go out and *kill!* I was afraid of nothing, laughed in death's face. I *wanted* to die, but God charmed me so I could suffer, Reverend. That's right. Once—and they took my sergeant's stripes because I didn't have permission—I went behind Rebel lines on a killing spree the likes of which you've never seen. Must've gotten over thirty of them all by myself. And none of it helped one bit, sir. My brothers' faces never quit haunting my dreams. And the Old Man was always there, shaking his finger at me."

The tears flowed freely down his cheeks as he grasped the minister's hand and told him about his inability to pray, and how he had finally stopped trying. And of his impotency. "There is this red-headed whore

I dream about all the time, Reverend. I went to her in Philadelphia two years ago, and I couldn't . . . I couldn't do it with her, and she taunts me in my dreams. It's as if God is punishing me in every way. I'm not even fit for a whore."

Reverend Higginson encouraged Salmon Brown's long catharsis with a sure, professional hand, gradually draining the toxin from him. And as he did so, he also shaped the idea that had struck him when he had first heard the magic name at his dressing room door. When Salmon finally ran down, he said in a gentle voice, "Well done, my son. The Lord has heard you and He understands. He forgives you all. . . ." He continued to speak soothingly, closing the open wound that was Salmon's bare soul, reinforcing, salving. And as he did so, he welded his bond to the new disciple.

Then gradually, the Reverend Higginson eased more into the Cause, slowly stroking Salmon's lost dedication and reinforcing it. Another hour passed, and with it the last ragged edges of doubt.

Salmon Brown was ready, wide open for the Call.

Higginson said, "You have always been a true abolitionist, my son. And now your soul is crying for you to do something important . . . perhaps even more important than what your father did. God has tested you, and cleansed you for a holy mission." The minister's eyes shone as he leaned close and lowered his voice. "I have something vital to tell you, but first I must swear you to utmost secrecy."

Salmon blinked as he tried to follow his messiah. It was all so much at once. He would do anything! Yes, he would take an oath of secrecy. He raised his right hand and did so.

"Only a few people are privy to what I'm about to divulge," Higginson said in his broad Boston accent. "There is a very special group being organized within the Cause—an action cell with the code name of Amistad. Do you remember the *Amistad?*"

Salmon nodded. Yes, the Spanish ship on which the slave revolt led by the noted Cinque took place in 1839. It was the most famous case of Negro insurrection involving international law ever recorded by the U.S. Supreme Court.

"Amistad," Higginson went on, "will be composed of a few dedicated people whose goal it will be to incite revolt among the Negro population of the Confederacy. Bloodshed and headlines will be immediate objectives. Strike fear into the white Southerner, show the Negro how vulnerable his master can be. There is already an underground movement known as Abraham down there. Amistad will *ignite* it! And when the Confederacy is struggling with its bowels, the Federal Army can once more cross the Potomac and restore the Union. And all men will be free." The clergyman's eyes were bright. "But in the meantime, *we want the Negro to rise and burn his way to freedom!*"

Higginson paused. "That's the overall mission, Salmon. As far as execution goes, we have a training site in Maryland where a handful of recruits are already undergoing intensive training in the skills of anarchy and special fighting. When this first team is ready, they will be sent right into the very capital of the Confederacy itself. I have selected a number of potential targets, but nothing specific yet. One plan is to plant a member of Amistad in Richmond society, underground, to coordinate an assassination of a number of major Southern leaders.

Salmon watched wide-eyed as Higginson leaned close, intense, his voice nearly a whisper. "But Amistad lacks the right leader . . . a man strong enough to take up the sword and lead its soldiers straight to hell, if necessary, a leader who can kill without a blink, but control with an iron grip. I think you're that man.

"Salmon—Captain Brown, if you will—if you could lend your magnetic name and the power of your father to this great mission, the word would spread through the negro Confederacy like *wildfire!*"

★ ★ ★

STARING at the ceiling didn't do a bit of good. The single ray of moonlight that shone into the little bedroom struck a white porcelain washbasin and illuminated the small mirror over the dresser. Salmon Brown had tried counting every sheep in Pennsylvania and Ohio, but he simply could not keep even one eye closed. Every nerve in his body seemed to be awake and busy; his mind was as clear as the moonlight, reliving word after word of his marvelous salvation.

"The Lord has heard you and He understands."

"You have always been a true abolitionist . . . your soul is crying out to do something important . . . more important even than what your father did."

He wanted to wake up the house and tell everyone. His messiah had told him about how the Lord worked in such roundabout ways, His wonders to perform. He, Salmon, was alive and finally ready to take up the torch and the saber. He, Salmon, had visited his soul in hell for all these years in order to be cleansed and worthy of the mighty responsibility that had been draped over his shoulders this night.

"Surely, the Lord has brought you here at this very time to be anointed, to be filled with His power, and shown the way!"

Salmon swung his bare legs out of bed, wiggled to let his sweaty nightshirt shake out. He walked to the window, stood there staring down at the back yard where everything seemed unnaturally vivid. Shadows as dark as purple-black ink; the moonlight pale, cold as ice on a blue lake in winter.

A dog barked at the neighboring house, briefly, as if startled in his nighttime reveries. Doing his duty; probably old, Salmon thought. Doing his duty.

Salmon inhaled deeply. He had a duty to perform, the most vital duty of any man in the world, Reverend Higginson had said. His skin tingled. *"Amistad lacks the right leader, Salmon—Captain Brown—"*

Was this all part of a grand plan, as the reverend had said? Or was it some crazy dream that would send him reeling back to the pits of his own private hell when the sun returned normal light to the world in the morning?

He would know then, wouldn't he?

Yes, his duty. . . .

Captain Brown.

Salmon Brown awoke fresh and excited shortly after sunrise. The memory of the previous night was just as vivid as it had been when he finally drifted off to sleep. The great man, Higginson, and his burning dark eyes—his savior. And Amistad, his new mission.

He stretched, grinning into the bright morning sun. He was *whole*. Forgiven, needed, *alive* again! The Cause. The Reverend Higginson had given him a *mission*—he was going back to war under God's proud banner for liberty, and with his own independent command! What a great challenge! He could almost feel the minister right there in the bedroom with him.

He felt strong, sure of himself for the first time in years. Captain Brown, that's what they had called the Old Man; now that's what he would be. Captain Brown.

He splashed water over his face. He had just been reborn.

S ALMON Brown was said by those who knew the family in the fifties to be the second most handsome son of the fiery old abolitionist. He was just under six feet in his stocking feet, skinny like his father, with much the same chestnut hair color, but less angular features. His gray eyes were more of his mother, and he wore a short beard that he trimmed obsessively every day. He was twenty-nine.

The overnight change was remarkable; it was indeed as if he had been reborn. He stood erect, confident, as if he were back in uniform, standing in front of his squad on Saturday parade. He pictured captain's bars on his shoulder boards, and tried to listen carefully as Higginson gave him a briefing during a long walk.

"We will go into details after you're settled in at the farm," the minister said. "When I decide what our specific target is, I'll be down to plan the strike personally."

Finally it was time to head for Maryland. As the conductor cried, "All aboard!" he looked once more into his messiah's eyes and felt a wave of emotion coming. But he managed to stifle it. Tears were a thing of the past.

And Higginson was a human being.

"There will be changes, perhaps daily, Salmon," the minister said. "Just stay flexible." They shook hands and said goodbye.

The train ride to the capital took all day and part of the night. After a few hours sleep, Salmon climbed down from a trolley on the outskirts of Washington City to where a team of horses stood quietly in harness before a wagon. A slender black man nodded a greeting from the seat. His name was Crispus and he was from Liberty, the farm seven miles north where Amistad was in training. He had also been the acting commander of the group until Salmon's arrival. Salmon introduced himself as Mr. Smith, an alias his father had used on occasion, and threw his bag in back as he climbed aboard.

"Your real name Crispus?" he asked quietly as they pulled away.

"No," the driver replied with only a trace of a Negro accent. "All of us have selected names of historical meaning. Crispus Attucks was the first Negro killed in the American Revolution."

Salmon nodded. How well he knew! It was part of the lore the Old Man had driven into their heads as children.

Crispus went on, "I am a crack shot and served as a scout in Higginson's regiment during the war. I have gone to college, and I am a journalist. I wrote an abolition column for a Toronto newspaper before the war. In fact, I will be the most *noted* colored journalist on the American continent when this revolution is finished!"

"That will be quite an accomplishment," Salmon replied, glancing sideways. Crispus was slender, light-skinned, and constantly scowling. The top of his right ear was missing.

The Maryland countryside was lush from all of the recent rain. Salmon studied the rolling hills and heavy foliage of the trees as they continued north. Haying season was over, and the wheat wasn't yet mature. Though the area was nearly as rich as the farming country around Gettysburg, it wasn't as well developed. Finally, Crispus turned the team into a long lane that was closely guarded by thick bushes. At its end stood a boxy two-story house with a chimney on each end. It was made of fieldstone and dated back to before the Revolution. To its rear stood a large wooden barn and some small outbuildings. Black and white Holstein cows grazed in an adjacent field, and a number of horses in another. Several tall oak trees guarded the house. A large black dog barked halfheartedly for a moment, then returned to his nap.

The farmer and his wife were stout and in their fifties, Bertha and Horatio Friar. Humorless and businesslike abolitionists, they suited Salmon just fine. The recruits were quartered in the barn, which also served as their classroom. They were there waiting for him, taking a break in their casual training program that Salmon would change in short order.

They sat around the open area below the hay mow, eyeing him warily, waiting to make their first judgments. One of the Negroes, a big man with a slouch hat pulled low over his eyes, stared at the dirt floor. Salmon knew from Higginson's description he would be Nat Turner, a lumbering former slave who could work wonders with dynamite. And of course, the white man was Beecher Lovejoy, so named for the famous abolitionist editor.

Higginson had recruited carefully. In addition, there were two other Negroes, Cinque and Denmark Vesey. The youngest member of Amistad was twenty-four, the oldest thirty-six. The Negroes had all served in the minister's regiment during the war and were top marksmen; two besides Nat Turner were good with dynamite. Denmark Vesey had been a sharpshooter who specialized in killing Confederate officers; he claimed one general. The white man also had a violent war record, having been a scout who bragged about never letting a prisoner live. As Crispus said, each had adopted a name famous in abolition circles. And all were supposedly fully committed to the Cause.

Salmon stifled the nervousness that hit him—after all, wasn't he the one with the special calling? And in all that time in which he'd worn sergeant's stripes, hadn't he led plenty of ruffians? Not any coloreds, but what was the difference—privates were privates. And that's all these men were to him. There would be no closeness, none of the familiarity that marked the Old Man's campaigns. He was the commander and they were the soldiers.

He cleared his throat. "All right, I am Captain Brown. Colonel Higginson has selected me leader of Amistad. You all know about my father and that I was with him in Kansas. That's where I first learned how to kill. The war furthered my education along that line considerably—just as it did yours. Only now our mission has an even greater purpose. By the time Amistad's goal is realized, the white South will be in flames, and the black man will be free forever."

He paused, eyed each of them, stopped at the frowning Crispus. "I'm sure there is much to be learned and relearned if we are to operate as an effective team. Starting tomorrow, training begins at first light and ends at dark. And as of this moment, what I say goes."

Crispus pulled a long straw from his mouth and said, "I don't think we need all of this playing around, this training, Captain Brown. All we need is a target. I'm ready to go and so are the others."

There were several supportive nods of heads.

Salmon eyed them, scowled. "But Amistad isn't." He dismissed them.

The training schedule, as laid out by Higginson, consisted of familiarization in various areas: communications, including the telegraph and Morse code; tending of wounds; the use of dynamite and larger weapons up to light artillery; hand-to-hand combat; the silent kill with the knife or garrote; the use of several types of small arms typically found in the South, including various handguns, rifles, and carbines. The recruit most proficient in each phase was in charge of that instruction.

Although Liberty was a large farm, precaution had to be taken in regard to noise. The firing range was right in its center, in a gulley to muffle the sound of shooting. Salmon spent the rest of the day familiarizing himself with the equipment that had been accumulated over the past few weeks. After some deliberation, he selected a six-shot, single action Whitney caliber .36 as his personal revolver. He liked its cool heft as he held it in each hand. It was just the right size to have range and yet be able to stop a man in his tracks. He touched his cheek with its muzzle, smiled. Before Amistad was finished it would kill one hell of a lot of people.

★   ★   ★

H E WAS busy firing the long-barreled Whitney at shortly after ten o'clock the following morning when Bertha Friar drove up in the wagon. Beside her on the seat was what appeared to be a youth wearing a wide-brimmed planter's straw hat. He was about to berate the woman for bringing a stranger into contact with them when she spoke up. "Got another recruit for you, Captain Brown."

The youth jumped lightly down, handed over a note. It read:

My dear Mr. Smith:

In regard to the plan involving the invasion of Richmond society, the bearer of this note will be our underground member. We will discuss her full role later. She is Verita, a young woman of many talents who will be a most resourceful addition to Amistad. I would like for you to begin her military training at once. Good luck!

—T. W. H.

Young woman? Salmon glared into the blank expression under the broad brim. "Take off that damned hat," he ordered.

Her black hair with its tight, natural curls was cut unstylishly short. Her eyes, normally a luminous hazel, were now muddied to a flinty brown in her anger at his peremptory tone. She jerked the hat from her head and stood with her hands on her hips, her chin thrust forward proudly. "I am Verita," she said in a low, husky voice with an accent he couldn't place. "So named for Sojourner Truth, the great abolitionist. Back at the house I have another note from Reverend Higginson that gives you my personal history."

He knew he was staring, but couldn't help himself. She was strikingly beautiful with satiny ivory skin over high cheekbones, full and expressive lips framing the whitest of teeth. Her stance was impudent, giving her an air of strength. And he could see a touch of something foreign, something exotic . . . and even the men's clothes couldn't suppress the suggestion of shapeliness. She was tall—

"But I'll save you the time, sir. I'm an octaroon, which means that one-eighth of my blood is colored. I was born in New Orleans twenty-four years ago. My parents were a lovely quadroon lady and a white planter. Twelve years ago, my father gave us our freedom and the money to begin a good life in Boston. My mother married a good man with money, and I received an excellent education, including college at Oberlin and in Paris." Verita paused. "All of my loved ones are dead, *Capitaine* Brown-Smith, but my love isn't. I am wildly in love with a cause known as *Abraham,* and no one—not even the exalted son of John Brown—will keep me from pursuing that affair."

"Why didn't the reverend say you were a woman when I was with him a couple of days ago?" Salmon asked darkly.

Her voice was biting. "I hadn't made my decision yet when he left Boston. Besides, *Capitaine,* I can do just about anything a man can do. I can ride any horse, shoot that damned pistol dangling in your hand, and hike all day and night. I have various skills none of your men have, I'm an actress, and I don't have to tell you men find me desirable."

"This isn't a New York theater, lady!" He drew the Whitney pistol level, aimed at her stomach. "Now, you just haul your ass up on that wagon and head on back to Boston before something happens to you." He turned to Mrs. Friar on the wagon. "Have your husband drive her into town."

The heavy farm woman had been silent throughout the argument. "Can't," she said with a shrug. "My husband got a telegraph from Reverend Higginson this morning saying she was to stay, no matter what. And you know who the boss is, Captain."

"Damn!" Salmon slammed the pistol into its holster. For the first time, Higginson had lost his holy allure. What was the minister trying to do? For two bits, he'd tell him what he could do with the whole damned thing! He looked around to see all five of the recruits had gathered nearby, watching, listening. He hadn't been here two days yet, and already his authority was in jeopardy. He would swear Crispus was smiling. "All right," he said harshly. "You heard it. This is Verita. Unless I can talk Higginson into changing his mind, we're stuck with her."

Verita masked her anger, looking from one to another. There was no welcome whatsoever in their eyes—just suspicion, contempt, and in one pair, lust. They said nothing, simply turned with their weapons and went back to what they had been doing.

"Crispus!" Salmon ordered. "You take charge of this woman. Get her a weapon and see if she knows how to shoot."

Crispus scowled at Salmon, started to protest, then shrugged and motioned for her to follow him.

She went with him to a shed where he handed her one of the latest Spencer carbines. His tone was openly contemptuous as he said, "You get seven shots without reloading. Let's see if you can hit the target with *any* of them." He led her to a shooting position of sandbags and pointed toward a white cloth target mounted against a dirt embankment farther down the ravine. "This is the shortest range—a hundred yards. 'Course, we can move up to fifty or twenty-five if you think that's too far."

Verita calmly ignored him as she brought the carbine up to her shoulder to get the feel of it. It was slightly lighter than most rifles, and shorter barreled because it was designed for use by cavalry.

"You can lie on your belly to shoot." His tone was condescending.

The sight picture was good. Verita drew in a deep breath as she exhaled, squeezed off the first round, then a second. The Spencer felt good, much like the Sharps her step-father had given her for her seventeenth birthday. Breathe, squeeze; breathe, squeeze. In moments the other five rounds had been fired. She smiled innocently at Crispus as he said, "Not too bad. Now you watch as I reload it for you."

"Can't we go down and see what I hit?"

Crispus snorted. "If you insist, but it—"

"I'd like to see."

Five of the rounds were in some part of the bull's-eye; one had strayed, but only an inch away. Crispus pushed back his slouch hat and let out a low whistle as he stared at the target. He started to say something, but stopped and shook his head as Salmon walked up and gaped at the target.

"I'll try to do better when I'm more familiar with the Spencer," Verita said casually. "You see, the trigger pull is a bit stiffer than I'm used to. Now, if you could get me a Sharps—"

Salmon had already stalked away.

The moon had been up for nearly a half hour when Verita finished her bath in Mrs. Friar's old iron tub and went out to the front veranda for some fresh air before turning in. Leaning against a post, she sighed and listened to a cricket's serenade. It was difficult to correlate this gentle peacefulness, this *freedom*, with all that was wrong in the world. And particularly what was wrong in the Confederacy, where on this very night some four million people did not have the simple liberty she had. She could walk down off this veranda and just keep going in any direction for as far as she *wanted* to go. Yet down there, just a few miles away, there were women and children who had never been off a farm this big. Many had never enjoyed a leisurely bath in a real bathtub, never savored the flavor of the written word, or laughed or cried at a single play.

She sighed again, thinking of Thomas More's *Utopia*, that ideal island in the New World. It had been a satire, all right; the closest thing to Utopia most of those colored people had across the Potomac was not being hungry, and not having their families torn apart, and a church to go to . . . and maybe for some, love. But they weren't people, they were property—*contraband* they had been called by the Union during the war. Chattel!

And now she was finally about to do something *real* about it, something that could be measured far better than the rhetoric of the speaker's podium, or the innumerable editorials that had been written in the abolition press in the past century. She was a *revolutionary*. She thought of how her personal flame had been ignited . . . Karl Marx. She had gone to one of the German's lectures in a park in Paris one warm summer night. Popular among students at the Sorbonne, he personified their favorite pastime: plotting the next revolution. His subject had been "The Conduct of Revolution and its Devastating Effect on the Capitalist Leader." At first she had listened casually, but as Marx heated up his oratory she became suddenly caught up in it—like one being saved at a revival. And from the moment she had stood and wildly cheered the end of his moving speech, her course had been clearly charted. But that had been over two years earlier, when it looked as if the North would win the war and Lincoln's Emancipation Proclamation would solve the problem of the American negro— the great lost dream.

Back in the United States a few months later, she joined the entourage of Sojourner Truth, the famous female abolitionist. Nine months with the charismatic ex-slave had been illuminating, but it was too passive for one who had heard the siren song of the revolutionary. Abraham was flickering and whispering down there in the Confederacy, waiting to be fanned into a leaping blaze—a raging inferno of such brilliant magnitude that all other struggles in history would be dimmed. Even the principle of Marx's theme on that revival night applied, with minor change: Revolution and its Devastating Effect on the *Southern* Leader. It was the unwritten code of Amistad.

"Well, I declare. If it isn't our pretty little sharpshooter." Crispus slipped out of a nearby shadow, moving close to her, smelling of alcohol. His hand caught her chin. "I hear you're a high-yellow colored girl, honey. So you needn't bother with any more of those airs of yours."

Verita pulled back, but he caught her wrist, groped for her breast. "Now, little high-yellow girl, why don't you and me just go on out there and find us a nice grassy spot in the moonlight, and—"

"Take your hands off me," she said coldly.

He laughed, thrusting his face into hers, trying to kiss her. "I'll make you *really* glad you came here, girl."

"Get away or I'll kill you."

He groped again for her mouth. "C'mon, baby, I—" He felt a sudden sharp prick just below the navel.

Her voice was flat. "That is a razor-sharp Puñal stiletto sticking in your stomach. If you don't release me at once, I'll bury it to the hilt."

Crispus' eyes widened, darted down, caught the glint of moonlight off the slender blade. Slowly he released her wrist and edged back. Reaching inside his belt, he found a moistness, knew it was blood. He glowered at her. "I should kill you for that," he ground out.

"*No!*" Salmon Brown said sharply, stepping from another dark shadow. "Go on back to the barn and get some sleep. Now!"

Crispus nodded, his face harsh. "So that's how it is, eh? You and the fancy high yellow, huh, Captain Brown? She's too good for a lowly nigger, isn't she?"

"Go to the barn!"

Crispus glared back for a moment, then abruptly swung away. Salmon watched his retreating figure briefly before turning angrily to Verita. "You satisfied? You've only been here one day, and already Amistad is getting torn apart."

"Do they all get drunk every night?" she flared. "Is that what this glorious Amistad is—a saloon with guns? How many other rapists do you command, *Captain* Brown?"

His angular face hardened, knotting at the corners of his jaw. "Lady, you make one mistake, you cause one more problem like this, you even breathe wrong—and I guarantee you I'll run you back to Boston on the end of my damned gun barrel. Do you understand me?"

Verita just glared back.

Salmon spun on his heel, heading for the barn. The inside was lit by a lantern on a table where Cinque and Denmark Vesey were playing cards. Crispus sat glowering in a chair a few feet away, a bottle in his hand. Salmon got the other two men up, then casually lit a cigar before facing them. "I think it's time we laid down a couple of new rules," he said coldly. "Number one, there will be no more drinking during the training week—at all." He looked directly at Crispus, then back to the others. "Number two, this woman Verita has been forced on us against my wishes, but she stays until *I* send her packing. And she is hands off to *everyone*. Is that understood? You all know that Amistad can be just as good as you want to make it, but we have to pull together. If anyone here doesn't think he can do that, or doesn't like my way of doing things, he can get out in the goddamn morning—*early!*" He looked at each of them, meeting the angry silence of Crispus directly, then nodded and strode out into the moonlight.

He walked past the house, letting his anger continue to seethe. Looking up at the lighted window in Verita's bedroom on the second floor, he saw her shadow momentarily and felt a tug of arousal, a surge of excitement that frightened him. *Why had this woman come here—to torment him?*

★　★　★

CRISPUS sat off in a corner of the barn writing on a small table by the light of a short, thick candle. He glared at the page, balled it up and threw it to the floor. Goddamn Brown, the bastard had him so upset he couldn't even write! He dipped the pen again and started over. The man called Cinque walked up. "You a-writin' another one of them secret letters, boy?"

Crispus covered the page with his arm. "Get outta' here, Cinque," he growled. "I told you before, my writing is private."

Cinque laughed as he moved away. "Heh! You'd think you was a-writin' to the president, the way you acts."

Crispus laughed inwardly. If only they knew. This would be his *twentieth* letter to the president of the United States! He, Crispus Attucks, was taunting the president of the United States, toying with him as if he were a puppet on a string—*and getting away with it!* He was practically telling him everything Amistad was going to do, and *no one* was smart enough to catch him at it. He could tell the big man within a whisker of every move, probably even hand-deliver the letters, and they wouldn't be bright enough to figure it out. Stupid goddamn whites!

He laughed again, felt the surge of elation as he wrote, "Dear Mr. President." *Nothing,* not even laying with a woman gave him this much excitement! That's what separated him from these common people in Amistad—he *dared!* That and his brains. He carefully wrote the first sentence and read it back silently. *God, there was nothing like it!*

★   ★   ★

THOMAS Wentworth Higginson arrived at mid-morning the next day. As soon as Salmon came in from the training area, they walked down to the pasture behind the big barn. "Salmon," he said, "I want to apologize for not telling you about Verita. But when I was in Oberlin, I was certain she wasn't going to join Amistad. Now, the importance of her role is second only to yours. With her joining us, I can go ahead with my best plan—the assassination attack in the New Richmond Theater. She is absolutely crucial to it, and the machinery is already in gear to have her go underground, posing as an actress in order to coordinate the attack on the Confederate leaders from the inside."

Higginson pulled a long shoot of grass and stuck it in his mouth as they walked a few steps in silence. Finally Salmon shook his head. "She'll be nothing but trouble, Reverend. I'm sure we can do it without her."

"Captain, there are other reasons why this young woman will be so valuable to us, but her secondary mission is possibly the most important. At the time of the attack, in which she will be a prominent figure, she will announce that she is of *Negro blood*, thereby demonstrating to all the colored women in the South that they, too, can play an active role in the coming revolution. Her name will become a powerful rallying call. That kind of inspiration can be invaluable."

Salmon shook his head. "I still don't like it, sir. She's too pretty, too, uh—she has already caused a flare-up with the men." He recapped the incident with Crispus.

"She can handle herself, and you can handle the men. I don't think there will be any more trouble. I would explain all of this to them, but *you* are their captain, and I deal only with you to preserve the chain of command. All right?"

Salmon sighed. "Yes, sir. Since you give me no choice."

Higginson smiled. "Good. Now let's go back to the house so we can go over a floor plan I have of the New Richmond Theater."

★   ★   ★

"ALL right, Verita, it's your turn," Salmon shouted from beside the large oak tree. Eight yards away, the mock-up of a restaurant room with a table of dummy customers stood in partial shade.

"Yes, *sir!*" Verita replied from the side of the nearby arms shed. She drew the 1860 Colt Army revolver, held it up to her face to check the cylinders, and cocked the hammer. Pulling the hat brim low over her eyes, she dashed to the corner of the mock-up, halted, looked around, and then slipped through the doorway where she pinned herself against the wall. But just as she brought the revolver to bear on the dummy diners, Crispus attacked her from the other side, knocking the heavy Colt out of her hands.

She whirled, slashing upward with the heel of her right hand and catching him a glancing blow on the shoulder. She followed with a knee that stopped just short of driving into his groin. With a roar, Crispus grabbed her arm, throwing her to the ground. But she rolled aside just before he dove on her, reached for the hilt of her dagger, and stabbed it into the ground right beside his head.

The look he gave her as they got to their feet was through cold eyes. "You come any closer, girl, and I'm gonna make you eat that toad-sticker. Mark my word!"

She simply ignored him as she wiped the blade and returned the Piñal to its thin sheath on her hip.

"Pretty good," Salmon Brown said from the oak, writing a note on his tablet. "I like the way you took the time to make sure of your target before firing. And I think you'll be able to handle any normal-sized opponent who tries to stop you." He nodded. "Quite good."

It was late in the afternoon on the third day.

Two days later, on a ride-and-shoot exercise at the moving-target range, Salmon was handling the ropes that jerked the man-shaped targets up and down. With all of the men standing around him, he let out a loud whistle. In moments the pounding of a horse's hooves beat toward them, and a second later, Verita came riding around the corner of an outcrop of bushes at a dead gallop on a rangy roan. The big revolver was held high in her right hand.

"*Kill!*" she shouted.

Salmon jerked the ropes, pulling four targets dressed as Confederate policemen and soldiers to an upright position. They were at different elevations and spread out among trees, some ten yards apart.

Instantly the roar of Verita's Colt filled the air. Salmon counted the shots and checked his pocket watch as she thundered past. All six had been fired within nine seconds! "Let's see what she hit!" Nat Turner hollered, running forward.

They went from one target to the other, shaking their heads. She had hit every single one of them in either the chest or the stomach. Four of her rounds had hit within the twelve-inch circle that marked the center of the torso. Only Denmark Vesey had fired better, and he had been a top marksman for years.

When they turned, Verita was sitting a few yards away on the panting roan, one leg cocked over the saddle pommel. "Did I kill any slavers?" she asked, expressionless.

"Ma'am," Cinque said with a friendly tone of admiration, "you done wiped out de whole government!"

Once more, Salmon Brown wrote a note on his tablet: "fired second best on the moving-target range. In every exercise except those requiring brute strength, this woman proves herself as able as the other members."

He looked up, caught her eye and nodded his grudging approval.

But she was still upsetting to him. The red-haired whore hadn't bothered him since his cleansing by Higginson in Oberlin. But now this disconcerting young woman was beginning to crowd his thoughts . . . and keep him awake at night.

And that was all wrong!

4

MAJOR General John Rawlins boarded the horse-drawn trolley just down the hill from the Capitol, across from the Botanical Gardens. Since the car was quite crowded, he hung onto a strap and looked out the open window toward the canal and the string of boarding houses that faced Pennsylvania Avenue. Or at least he tried to see out the window, since the huge feather of a woman's hat kept bobbing into his view.

The young woman wearing the hat saw him moving his head in order to see around it. With pert smile, she said, "Sorry, General. It isn't a very good trolley hat, is it?"

He shook his head, returned her smile. "No, 'fraid not." Her eyes returned to his, lingered. She was quite lovely, nice teeth. The invitation was there, but the gold wedding band on her finger dissuaded him from following it up.

His attention drifted outside once more as the car stopped at 4½ Street. The American Colonization Society building stared back at him, reminding him that he had to speak at their convention in two days. Christ, he'd be glad when Grant got back and did his own politicking. Subconsciously, he tugged at his heavy black beard and lapsed into thought about Washington City on this July the 9th. . . .

It was extremely hot and muggy. Clouds that would grow into giant thunderheads were building up in Maryland and across the river in Virginia. Today's *Star* was predicting a high temperature of 102 degrees Fahrenheit and recommended that no one go out in the afternoon without an umbrella.

He smiled to himself. The residents of Washington City seldom worried about the weather—it rained or snowed, or it didn't. It was hot or cold, or in between, and only parades and outside parties were greatly affected by the variations. For the capital of the United States was still trying to pretend that everything had gone back to normal after the armistice, that nothing could ever dampen or chill its exuberance.

The social whirl was unceasing, with strong and beautiful women spending fortunes on appearance and status. In vogue were jaunty plumed hats with short coquettish veils and three-cornered, gaily flowered summer bonnets from William's exclusive shop farther up Pennsylvania Avenue. The discreet showing of a bit of leg, with dainty gaiter boots and white hose was popular among the younger set. And of course, status was most positively marked by superbly liveried gigs, coaches, surreys, and other types of carriages wherever the swarming competitors went.

After four years of absence, the Democrats were back in style.

But life wasn't the same; Washington was the capital of only half of America. Eleven of its former states now constituted a foreign country, and it had nearly been more because Kentucky and Maryland had teetered on the brink of joining the Confederacy. One couldn't even cross the Long Bridge or the Chain Bridge without going through both U.S. and Confederate Customs, because Virginia—wonderful green and rolling Virginia—was in a foreign country. Charming old Alexandria and Falls Church were alien towns.

And not a solitary person could get used to the idea that it would always be that way.

But perhaps the most disconcerting reminder was Arlington. Sitting high on its bluff with its massive white columns serving as powerful sentries, the Lee-Custis mansion—more popularly known as Arlington House—watched over the river below and the foreign capital beyond like a great white castle of medieval times . . . serene, commanding, perhaps judging the folly that unfolded daily under its gaze. It could be seen from nearly any vantage point in Washington, an embarrassing reminder of wartime failure—for behind those tall white pillars, Robert E. Lee calmly went about his affairs each day. General Robert E. Lee, the famed gray knight in his great white castle, had reclaimed his lands and now presided as lord over his domain.

But for the most troubled souls in these times, the symbolism of Arlington meant nothing, had never entered their thinking. They were the unemployed, the hungry and disillusioned. Many of them were Negroes, the veterans and others who had been freed by the war and were far from their roots. They knew they didn't want to cross those bridges and go back—yet for most, loved ones remained shackled in the South.

The trolley car slowed to a halt at Rawlins's stop. He touched his brim in an abbreviated salute, smiled at the pretty lady with the obtrusive hat, murmured "Ma'am." She returned his smile with the invitation still in her eyes.

Still too bad she was wearing that wedding band.

Stepping down into the middle of Pennsylvania Avenue, he picked his way through the slow-moving traffic on broken cobblestones, avoiding the mud and soon reaching the brick walk promenade on the north side of the broad street. It was nearly noon and already hundreds of government workers jammed the streets on their lunch time. Many stared at the two stars on his shoulder boards, though most were used to army generals—there had been so many of them during the war.

A convenient oyster bar with a bright red awning caught his attention. He turned in, nodded to the waiter at the counter. "Give me a half dozen on the half shell."

"Yes, sir," the young man replied. "Say, ain't I seen your picture somewhere? Ain't you head of the army or something?"

"Not quite," Rawlins replied with a smile.

It wasn't much of a lunch, but he had to be in the White House at 12:30. And he had to be on time—that was one thing President McClellan carried over from his army days, promptness. He had been to the president's office only once before, and that had also been during his boss's absence. Now Grant was in Chicago, and as his chief-of-staff, he had to fill in. It really was no difficulty for him, since he'd been privy to everything Ulysses S. Grant had done since the early days of the war. And they were usually of one mind—except when it came to alcohol. Ulys Grant had that drinking reputation from the old army, and John Rawlins kept him away from alcohol as a father would shield his young daughter from a rapist.

Not even an innocent glass of wine at a banquet would escape his hawkish eye. "Goddamnit, Ulys!" he would say. "You know better. You know the whole world thinks you're a sot. No!" And Grant would invariably shrug and listen to him. "Grant's abstainer," they sometimes called him around headquarters in the old days—but not to his face.

Rawlins dabbed at his lips with a napkin, wiping juice from the edges of his thick black beard. He wondered what McClellan wanted. He didn't have much use for the former general, the "Young Napoleon" who had commanded the Army of the Potomac, in fact, the whole army during the first part of the war. And it was a stand-off; McClellan didn't like what he called the "Illinois gang" either. He knew of Grant's open support for Lincoln in the '64 election, and of his closeness to Congressman Elihu B. Washburne, who had a direct line to Springfield, where the former president was still the center of Republican power.

Rawlins coughed, a succession of rasping noises that brought tears to his eyes and glances from those around him. The ever-present red handkerchief came away from his mouth with a trace of blood when he stopped; he had begun using a red one over a year earlier because the telltale blood somehow didn't look as ominous that way. Always, he tried not to look at it, but there was no way he could stop—that sign was his fateful yardstick of life. And always he said the same thing to himself or aloud, *"Sonofabitch!"*

A few minutes later, he glanced at the statue of Jefferson as he walked up the rounded drive to the White House. The thought of Thomas Jefferson always gave him comfort, but made him wonder what that great statesman could be thinking of the mess his heirs had made of his great republic. Returning the salutes of the two smartly turned-out army sentries at the front entrance, he hurried on upstairs to the president's office.

"Please have a seat, General Rawlins," the secretary, McClellan's senior aide from his last command, said. "His Excellency will be tied up for a few more minutes with the Speaker of the House."

Taking a chair, Rawlins snorted to himself. *His Excellency;* he'd never heard that affected title used in Lincoln's White House. The President was sometimes known affectionately as the Tycoon, but that was a private nickname of warmth among his intimates—and sometimes of derision among his enemies.

In fact, the President's house under Lincoln had been vastly different.

A giant had ruled, and now a pygmy tried to fill his shoes.

He thought back to when it all changed, and as he did so a cloud passed over the White House, casting its shadow over the building.

A terrible dark shadow had enveloped the whole nation then—as the
Union was disemboweled by an unknowing electorate. . . .

It was in the chilling gloom of the sodden morning of November
9th, 1864. He had gone up to the telegraph room in the War Department to get the latest election results. It was shortly before four
A.M. and the eerie stillness was broken only by the sharp clacking of
the telegraph machines. He nodded to Major Eckert, the chief telego-
rapher, and spoke respectfully to Gideon Welles, the secretary of the
Navy, who was seated at one of the machines trying to decipher the
incoming signals in stern silence.

He was about to see if there was any coffee when he noticed the
long legs propped up on a desk in the corner. In a shadow, President
Abraham Lincoln sat with his great head sagging on his chest. He was
staring straight ahead at the slowly moving thumbs of his crossed
hands, barely blinking, seemingly removed from the harsh reality of
the words issuing forth from the noisy machines.

He quietly asked the major for the latest tabulation.

It was bad: the president had lost New York, Pennsylvania, New
Jersey, Ohio, Indiana, and Massachusetts. Even if he held on to the
rest of New England and the West, he couldn't make it.

Slowly, the president untangled his legs and pulled himself to his
feet. His words were soft, barely reflecting the pain that nearly made
them choke in his throat, "Well, gentlemen, I guess I've gone and lost
the Union. I wonder if Washington and Jefferson will ever be able to
forgive me." He cleared his throat. "Well, no sense in letting any more
boys lose their lives now . . . General Rawlins, will you please get word
to General Grant that a cease-fire is in effect as of this moment? And
Mr. Welles, will you please notify Mr. Davis in Richmond?"

Rawlins would never forget the raw grief in his tired gray eyes or
how his voice had broken at those last agonizing words. Even now,
the thought of it clawed at his heart. . . .

"General Rawlins, His Excellency will see you now."

The president's office was a large square room on the south end
of the mansion, dominated by a huge oak table in the center that
served the president's cabinet meetings. Against the south wall stood
a tall desk, its pigeonholes crammed with some of the huge load of
letters that flooded in daily from disgruntled veterans, as well as the
normal communications the head-of-state received. Two haircloth so-
fas and three chairs attended this desk. Framed maps hung on the
walls, and over the mantle in the place of honor hung a huge painting

of the president on his favorite dark bay, leading a column of victorious troops in a parade down Pennsylvania Avenue—a work McClellan had commissioned shortly after the election. At the lower end of the room, framed against a bright window, the seventeenth president of the United States stood with his right hand inside his coat, brooding, Napoleon-like.

Stocky, with thick auburn hair, a full mustache and a tiny goatee just below his lip, the thirty-nine-year-old George B. McClellan was still the boy wonder. He had graduated from West Point at nineteen, received three brevets in the Mexican War before he was old enough to vote, and had been the toast of Washington when Lincoln gave him command of his armies when the general was thirty-four. "What's Grant doing out in Illinois," McClellan asked as Rawlins saluted, "plotting with the Republicans?"

Rawlins shook his head. "No, sir. He's attending the reunion of his old Illinois regiment—the one he commanded when he first came on active duty in Sixty-one."

"Yes, well, I suppose that's as good an excuse as any." McClellan scowled as he handed a letter to Rawlins. "Read this, General."

The letter was on plain paper, with no date; it was postmarked "Boston" five days earlier. Unsigned, it read:

> John Brown's body is arising from the ground, and when it does, the sword of abolition will strike you down and reignite the war of justice that will forever free the negro and reunite the Union! The days of peaceful pleading are over—the new Army is reaching for its guns. LIBERTY TO ALL!!!

Rawlins shrugged, handed the note back to McClellan. "We've received a couple along this line, Mr. President. I wouldn't worry about it."

"That's my *nineteenth!* They all read somewhat different and come from other places, but the theme is the same. Abolition wants to start the war all over again, and get *me* in the process. It's anarchy. Those bastards are crazy!"

Rawlins was staunchly anti-slavery, but his abolition enthusiasm had dimmed to a bare flicker during the war. He simply couldn't get all shiny-eyed over preaching and shouting anymore. As far as the slavery went, he was pragmatic about it—the Confederacy had won and was a sovereign nation; eventually internal and external forces would bring about change in her approach to slavery. But it would not happen at once, and no *war* could shove it down her throat. Christ, it had just taken the worst conflict in history to prove that! "Like I said, sir, it doesn't mean anything."

"General Rawlins, I want you to concentrate on this personally. I want to know if these abolition bastards are really going militant, who's behind it, how far it has gone, and how it can be stopped. Do you understand?"

"Yes, sir."

McClellan frowned, sticking his hand back inside his coat. "There will be *no* return to war. I will use my *broadest* powers to trample any such movement. Do you understand that, General?"

John Rawlins resented the president's overbearing use of that question. "Yes, sir. Am I to break away from my other duties?"

"As soon as Grant gets back." The president scowled out the window, nodded. "In fact, you are on detached service as of this moment as my special representative. My intelligence agents are on it, but you are an astute lawyer I'm told—in spite of being a Republican—and there are doors open to you that no agent can penetrate. I understand you are a friend of Ambassador Benjamin—is that correct?"

"Let's say we know each other on a favorable basis."

"Good. I want to cooperate fully with the Confederate government in this matter. Not only do I want to know what they know, I want them to understand that I'm doing everything possible to stamp out trouble from this end. Talk to Benjamin as a starter. Spend whatever time you feel is necessary in Richmond. Make your presence known." McClellan nodded, stared out the window, mused, "Yes, it'll look good to have someone as important as Grant's chief-of-staff in charge, so to speak."

"Very well, sir." Rawlins brought his heels together to salute.

"Oh, and another thing, General." The president's eyes glittered. "You were down in their capital a week ago—how is this thing over Jeb Stuart shaping up?"

Rawlins nodded to himself. Twice during the war, Jeb Stuart had led his cavalry nearly unmolested around McClellan's huge army. And each time the Young Napoleon had been mightily embarrassed. How he must relish the thought of Stuart being in trouble. "All I know is what I read in the papers, Mr. President," he replied. "A court of inquiry will be convened one of these days to look into his Gettysburg actions."

"I hope they hang the bastard!"

Rawlins looked coolly into the president's gaze. "Is there anything else, sir?" When McClellan shook his head, he saluted and departed. He detested being the man's personal agent. And one thing was certain—if a head had to fall over this damned problem, it wouldn't be the Young Napoleon's!

★ ★ ★

R AWLINS placed the memorandum of his visit to McClellan's office on Grant's large desk. A glance at the wall clock told him he had a few minutes to burn before heading for his important appointment at Washburne's house. Brushing past the general's flag with three white stars embroidered on its field of red, he gazed out the window past the famous Indian Rock to the west end of the White House.

He couldn't shake off the feeling of uneasiness that had persisted since his earlier visit to the president's office.

A return to war?

Of course there had been such talk ever since the cease-fire, talk of forcing the government to return to a state of war and to reinvade Virginia. It would probably be another decade or two before such an idea lost its interest.

But an outright act that might make it unavoidable?

He remembered the night when he heard that Rebels had fired upon Fort Sumter, the first outright act that had triggered the great War Between the States, or whatever one wanted to call it. April 12, 1861.

It was months before he could join the colors and commence a journey that would be quite spectacular for a country lawyer. When his poor consumptive wife died, he took advantage of his friend Brigadier General Ulys Grant's open offer of a staff job, and became his adjutant general. He sure as hell wasn't a soldier, but he was smart and a good administrator—and a brash devil's advocate for Grant. He started off as a captain, and by the time of the armistice he was a general—another one of those goddamned political generals . . . almost.

Certainly, he never had a command, nor fired a shot in anger . . .

except that night when his unruly temper got the best of him and he emptied his revolver into a tree. . . .

And now what was he? A president he detested was making him a special agent, his own private messenger boy. Was he forever to be a bishop, an arranger? Would his guiding hand help thwart whatever it was that might be threatening the ship of state?

Where was he going in what was left of his life? Would John Rawlins *truly* leave a mark of value before the goddamned consumption drew a veil of death over his ashen face? *Goddamned consumption—goddamned specter of death!* Why should he even care? He probably wouldn't live long enough to see the end of this charade, anyway.

But it didn't matter, he always played the game to the last card, didn't he?

It was just too damned bad the deck was stacked. He grunted with satisfaction to himself—he liked that term. In fact, that gravestone they would soon erect over his fresh plot of dirt should read: *Here lies John Rawlins, a discard, the victim of a stacked deck.*

He turned his thoughts to something far more pleasant—his upcoming appointment. How wonderful it would be to see the great man.

Minutes later, Rawlins hurried down the steps of the War Department and strode briskly up 16½ Street on the west side of Lafayette Park to I Street, on his way to Washburne's house. He whistled as he walked, thinking of other days when he had visited the White House in Grant's absence. Back in the days of the giant.

Rounding the corner of 17th and K streets, he spotted the tall, narrow-fronted house a couple of hundred yards away, and stepped up his pace. Now, being a bishop was suddenly exciting, for how else could a country lawyer from Galena rub shoulders with the gods?

He was soon inside the red brick house, shaking hands with Elihu B. Washburne—the testy, bearded congressman whom McClellan often disparaged as the "whip of the Illinois gang." He and Washburne had been friends back in Galena when Grant was broke and clerking in his father's store there. Elihu Washburne had not only become Grant's sponsor during the war, but was an old and trusted friend of the other great man who was presently his house guest.

"Good afternoon, my friend," Rawlins said. "How is he?"

Washburne shrugged as he led the way down a high hall to the dining room. "He never looks good, you know that. But he's all right. Busy."

"Is he here alone—I mean other than his bodyguard?"

"Yes, but his son is joining him this afternoon from Harvard."

Rawlins couldn't help but feel a sudden quickening as he entered the dining room. There, in somber profile against the outside light was the tall familiar figure, his knees drawn up and held by his hands in one of those strange, informal positions of his—for all the world, lost on a window seat. He turned at the sound of their footsteps, untangling his long legs and getting to his feet. His dark hair was tousled, but his beard was short and neat, as if it had just been trimmed. His mournful eyes lit up as he broke into a grin and stuck out his hand. "Hello there, John Rawlins. How are you?"

Rawlins never noticed his big ears or the warts. No one who understood the greatness of this man did. He shook the huge hand, replying quietly, "Just fine, Mr. President."

The smile continued. "You keeping the army straight for General Grant?"

"Trying to, sir, but we've got lots of help."

Abraham Lincoln chuckled. "Yes, I know all about that. When you've got a former general living over there in the president's house, or a meddling country lawyer from Illinois sticking his nose in, you have *more* than enough help. How's Grant? He invited me to that regimental reunion, but I couldn't make it."

"Tougher than ever. He got your cigars, by the way."

The oversized dining room was the nerve center of Washburne's house. Though Rawlins had been in the place many times, he had never spent a minute in the parlor or in any kind of study or library. In fact, there was one whole tier of bookshelves in the room, and always there were papers and writing materials on the table—a round massive piece of oak that could be expanded by many leaves. The room was bright and airy, with two tall windows flanking the broad one with the windowseat. Only the corniced high ceiling was of a darker hue, and that was because its fading mural of cherubim cavorting with tiny American flags had not been repainted in its fifty years of existence. From the oak sideboard Elihu Washburne said, "I've got some fresh coffee for you teetotalers, if you want it."

He brought the tray to the table as his guests took chairs. Rawlins stole a glance at Lincoln, noting the addition of several gray hairs in the thatch on top of his head as well as in the beard—in fact, the whiskers on his chin were suddenly quite white. And the great hollows that held his sad eyes were as dark as ever under their shaggy brows. "What brings you to Washington, Mr. President?" he asked.

"Oh, I was kinda' bored out there in Springfield. I'm not used to being a rich lawyer—or a rich anything, for that matter. And I needed some material from the Archives for my manuscript, so it was a good excuse to come in and feel the pulse of this asylum they call a capital." He shook his head. "I reckon I'll never get it out of my blood."

"Huh!" Washburne interjected. "Speaking of getting rich, he's got every publisher from New York to Timbuktu running around with an open wallet for that damned book."

Rawlins sipped his black coffee, wondering how much this frank, but often mysterious man would reveal of the intrigues that had beleagured him during his incredible but distressing term of office. What a lamentable bunch of bastards the poor man had inherited and acquired during his four years! Would he be candid about his cabinet full of self-seekers? Would he be straightforward about McClellan's reluctance to fight? And about the other mediocre generals he had had in the early part of the war? Abraham Lincoln was a strange mix of honesty, humility, and downright hard-rock toughness. But as head of the Republican Party, he had responsibilities that some would feel overrode the integrity of a book. They would want him to tell all about McClellan, for one thing.

"Anything new with the Confederate Army?" Lincoln asked, toying with his spoon.

Rawlins smiled slyly. "I hear they're all studying Spanish."

Lincoln chuckled. Davis's aggrandizing aspirations toward Latin America weren't a very well-kept secret. "Do you really think they'll make a move toward Mexico if he gets reelected?"

"No doubt about it. The South needs about everything there is except cotton, rice and tobacco—and there are still untold mineral riches in those Mexican hills."

"And it would be an excellent place to ship those free Negroes, don't forget that," Washburne said.

No one said anything for a few moments. There had been a dozen schemes in the North to find a home for the Negroes, and a number in the South. Many freed slaves in the South had been given the opportunity to return to Africa by the American Colonization Society, but fewer than three hundred of them had gone.

"Always it's the same," Lincoln said softly. "Free 'em or keep 'em

—someone always wants to send them somewhere or put a fence around them. You know, I kept a country mile between me and those abolitionists . . . fact is, I'm not so sure the Emancipation Proclamation wasn't all pure politics when you get right down to it. But you know, while I've been sitting out there in Illinois trying my double damnedest to figure out how I could have done things better—and the Lord knows I wonder about it every single waking hour—I've just about decided that maybe I should have been more forceful about freeing the slaves. . . .

"You know," he added wistfully, "it's kind of hard to be set up as a great emancipator, to have the gall to go out there and make all of those promises, and then to have to sneak off in the middle of the night with your tail between your legs." The gray eyes clouded up. "You have no idea how hard it was to ride out those last few months as a president who had not only broken his promise to those poor people, but had also lost one-third of the Union in the process. I—"

Lincoln pushed back from the table, got to his feet, forced the emotion down as he walked back to the windowseat. "I've never told anyone this, gentlemen, but I thought somewhat of leaving the country, of going maybe to Europe for a while . . . but my responsibilities were too heavy . . . my wife's illness and all. And then. . . ." He turned away, stared out the window, his voice dropping to almost a whisper. "And then, I thought about doing away with myself, taking a pistol to my head and ending all of the misery."

Rawlins and Washburne flicked a glance at each other in the heavy silence. Neither could imagine what it would be like to not have this great man somewhere—anywhere within reach of the telegraph or a letter. Rawlins immediately shook off the idea, noticing the sudden increase of light behind Lincoln as if the sun had just broken away from a cloud. The tall man's dark silhouette seemed for a moment encased in a special brilliance, and then he broke the spell, walking back toward them. He had re-covered the wound, found a smile. "And then I realized that since I messed everything up, I'd better hang around and see if I couldn't try to patch it up." He shrugged. "I don't know *how*, but I ought to try."

Rawlins got to his feet. He couldn't imagine continuing to sit when Lincoln stood before him. "Sir," he said quietly, warding off a violent urge to cough, "you know the country is still in your hands. The people are just beginning to realize how much they sold themselves down the river when they voted McClellan in in Sixty-four. They've temporarily lost their moral root—which is one reason there is such a swift rise in abolition. Then add the hard times—no war contracts for the factories, a million ex-soldiers looking for a job . . . they need you again."

Washburne clapped his hands from the table. "That's pretty good for a dumb general, John. Fact is, that's what I've been trying to drum into his stubborn old head."

Lincoln poured himself some more coffee, said nothing.

"Are you going to run again, Mr. President?" Rawlins asked. The question was presumptuous, but he had never been known for excessive tact.

Lincoln sipped from his cup. "No, I don't think it would be the thing." A fleeting look of pain crossed his face. "I don't think Mrs. Lincoln would be up to it . . . even if the people did want me."

Rawlins nodded. It was common knowledge that Mary Todd Lincoln was hanging to the last threads of sanity. He watched as Lincoln walked back to the window. He wanted to reach out and take his arm, embrace him, tell him that he had already given as much as any ten men could possibly give. How he had lasted four years under that strain was incomprehensible . . . to work all of those hours every day with a body that wasn't always well, to carry the management of the government and the war on those gaunt shoulders—and then share his few hours of privacy with a mad woman—must have been a gargantuan accomplishment. And until he entered his grave, he would be saddled with the guilt of having disrupted the Union.

"I was kind of thinking about someone else," Lincoln said. "Like maybe General Grant. In spite of the way the war ended, he is still a big hero, and I think we could sell him if he never got out of bed. Even Washburne agrees on that." He turned from the window. "Do you think he would run, John? He says, 'No.' "

Rawlins shook his head emphatically. "Not as long as there's a bare chance that you would, sir. He's too loyal."

"Well, then I think we all ought to start pointing him in that direction." Lincoln smiled. "You know, there's a funny thing about being president. Once a man starts getting it in his head, the strangest things start happening. His mouth keeps on denying that he ever wants any part of it, but that head of his starts getting more and more familiar with Pennsylvania Avenue."

Rawlins nodded. The idea wasn't new—Missouri had nominated Grant in '64, and there had been a lot of talk. The idea was staggering when he thought of what his own role might be. He decided to change subjects. "Speaking of Pennsylvania Avenue, I just saw McClellan this afternoon. He has given me a special job." He told them about the meeting.

Lincoln listened attentively. When Rawlins finished, he asked, "What about this Abraham movement I've heard about in the Confederacy—is there anything to it?" He smiled wistfully. "Kind of different having a rebellion named after me."

"Same as the abolition movement—all talk, far as I know."

Lincoln stared into his coffee cup for a moment, then looked up with what Washburne called his infamous storytelling expression. "You know," he said, "one day back in Springfield, I got into a fit of musing in my room and stood resting my elbows on the bureau. Looking into the glass, it struck me what an ugly man I was. The fact grew on me and I made up my mind that I must be the ugliest man in the world. It so maddened me that I resolved, should I ever see an uglier, I would shoot him on sight. Not long after this, a lawyer named Andy came to town and the first time I saw him I said to myself: 'There's the man.' I went home, took down my gun, and prowled around the streets waiting for him. He soon came along. 'Halt, Andy,' said I, pointing the gun at him. 'Say your prayers, for I am going to shoot you.' 'Why, Mr. Lincoln, what's the matter?' he asked. 'What have I done?' 'Well, I made an oath that if I ever saw an uglier man than I am, I'd shoot him on the spot. You are uglier, surely; so make ready to die.' 'Mr. Lincoln, do you really think that I am uglier than you?' 'Yes.' 'Well, Mr. Lincoln,' said Andy deliberately and looking me squarely in the face, 'if I am any uglier, fire away!' "

Lincoln smiled as he often did when he used one of his stories to make a point. "All Andy and I did was talk about 'ugly.' Seems to me as long as they keep talking and don't take down their guns, there isn't much harm."

"And if they've already taken down their guns?"

Lincoln shrugged, tugged his beard. "Then who knows—someone might have a problem over there across the Potomac."

Another presumptuous question shot into Rawlins's head. "Mr. President," he said softly, "where would you stand if something happened to start the war again? Far as I know, that is a purely speculative question, but what if there were something—an incident, or an uprising of some sort—that started it all over again . . . where would you stand?"

Lincoln looked him in the eye, fooled with his beard again. At length he replied, "I've asked myself that question a dozen times, General, and I still don't know. One voice says to finish the job—bring those Rebels back into the Union and free the slaves once and for all." He sighed tiredly. "And then a second voice says hasn't there been enough blood spilled already, and besides, what good would it do? . . . So I truly don't know."

Rawlins could hear his own breathing as he waited.

"But," Lincoln continued quietly, "I suppose I could overcome that second voice if the occasion arose. A wrong doesn't become a right just because it stops."

Rawlins nodded, looking again into the great gray eyes that were now dark, brooding. This was all hypothesis, but the possibilities were staggering. . . .

"You know, General," Lincoln said with a sudden lift in his voice. "You might look into this Abraham thing if you get down to Richmond . . . See if there might be a way some sympathetic people up here could support them."

Washburne nodded briskly. "That could be a sure way back into the White House, Mr. President—whether it be you *or* General Grant."

"Absolutely!" Rawlins said. "If a recognized movement of Southern negroes were to ask for open support, the whole United States would be behind us in demanding their freedom."

Lincoln pursed his lips. "Yes, General, see what we might be able to do."

"Sir," the butler announced from the doorway. "Mr. Robert Lincoln is here."

Lincoln's eyes lit up as he stuck his hand out to Rawlins. "Thank you for coming, John. Give my regards to your boss when he gets back, and start getting his mind fixed on the White House, like I said." A moment later he was embracing his eldest son.

As Washburne led Rawlins out, the general stopped in the doorway to look back. Framed once more in the bright sunlight, the tall man stood holding his son by the shoulders at arm's length. He was smiling warmly, speaking in a low tone. Rawlins wanted to reach out one more time and touch him . . . and suddenly he wondered how different it all might have been had Lincoln been reelected in '64. . . .

★ ★ ★

THE thunderheads in Maryland and Virginia had built to full maturity by the time John Rawlins crossed Lafayette Square to 748 Jackson Place that night. He glanced up briefly to watch the lightning, silent and busy as its darting fingers poked in and out among their giant canyons. It would be a wet one tonight, he told himself. He hummed in tune with the spirited music from the Marine band playing a concert on the White House lawn. He should have brought a raincoat.

The house to which the general was headed was the embassy of the Confederate States of America, but everyone still called it the Decatur House. The three-story mansion had housed many important people in its time—Henry Clay and Martin Van Buren, to name a couple—but its builder and first resident had been the celebrated Commodore Stephen Decatur, hero of Tripoli. Decatur, who had died in the house from wounds received in a duel with another naval officer, had originated the toast that had been corrupted to: "Our country, right or wrong"—a phrase, Rawlins thought wryly, that could easily be applied to the Confederacy at times.

And Judah P. Benjamin, the only Jew to hold high office in the Confederacy, was its current resident.

Ambassador Benjamin, referred to by many as the "Brains of the Confederacy," was a stocky, urbane man with a short dark beard and large expressive black eyes. A wealthy lawyer and former U.S. senator from New Orleans, he had held three cabinet posts under Jefferson Davis, including secretary of State. But now he felt he could best serve his country in the vital United States ambassadorship. Strangely, he had lived in the Decatur House before the war during his tenure in the Senate. It was then that the only major setback of his life had occurred—his wife had become involved in the scandalous affair that not only rocked Washington, but had sent her off to Paris in the middle of the night.

Rawlins had met Benjamin at a buffet shortly after the ambassador's arrival in the city and they had become close enough friends for Benjamin to see the general on such short notice, in spite of the fact that he was hosting a dinner party that included both the French and British ambassadors.

Rawlins knew that the Confederate intelligence apparatus flowed through the Embassy—or at least parts of it. With such a long open border between the countries, the whole boundary was porous. "Have you heard of any new developments?" he asked.

Benjamin had a habit of tugging at his right ear lobe when he exercised his memory or had to make a decision. He did so now. "No, I don't recall hearing anything along that line. You know how they are when they get up on that soapbox and start screaming hellfire and brimstone—you can't call any of it pacific. We do know the movement seems to be getting stronger and stronger, like a swarm of flies heading for the honey pot. Before you know it, John, your whole country may be carrying a torch and singing 'John Brown's Body.' "

Rawlins shook his head. "I don't think it'll ever get that big. It's just something the disgruntled public can grasp. We both know about the multitudes of frustrated ex-soldiers, many of them running around with one arm or one leg wondering just what the hell they fought for. And then there are the throngs of people who lost loved ones, Judah . . . most of them don't really know anything about states' rights or some of the other reasons for the war. They think it was only a struggle over slavery. And they know it still exists."

"Yes, and abolition is the standard to which they can pour out their discontent." Benjamin scowled. "We *understand* it, John, but what they don't want to realize is that slavery is *our* goddamned business. We know it is a dying custom, and the time will come when it is abolished completely. And maybe sooner than anyone thinks. As you know, there is a man named Lee right over there across the river at Arlington. Everyone knows he's going to be president of the Confederacy one of these days . . . and he hasn't had a slave on that huge plantation since *Fifty-nine!*"

Rawlins shook his head. "But that's a maybe. You know how fast something can flare up. We don't want any more Harpers Ferrys or Kansas-type shootouts, do we?"

Benjamin moved to a cabinet by the open window, where his hand went absently to a candlestick of Sheffield plate. He turned back to Rawlins. "Nobody wants any of that. What do you want me to do, John?"

"Just have your people keep an ear to the ground, the ones who are close to it, and let me know if you hear anything. All right?"

"Of course. I'll get word to Mosby right away."

"He must be a busy man—didn't I read in the *Post* that he is going to be involved with Stuart's court of inquiry?"

"Yes, I think he'll have his hands full."

They shook hands. "Thanks for breaking away," Rawlins said, suddenly realizing the absurdity of what had just been arranged: McClellan, the general who spent half the war trying to take Richmond, now had the C.S.A. Military Intelligence Department working for him.

★   ★   ★

T HE next morning, one hundred miles south in Richmond, John Mosby finished reading for the third time the proceedings of the court of inquiry of Major General Mansfield Lovell regarding the fall of New Orleans. Four times he had been through the court of Major General Earl Van Dorn regarding his actions at Corinth four times. Although neither proceeding had any direct relationship with the nature of Jeb Stuart's upcoming court, Mosby was becoming mentally comfortable with the procedure, and that was the primary purpose behind studying them. Personally, he found Van Dorn more interesting, probably because he knew the dashing general had later been shot to death by a jealous doctor whose wife the general had allegedly seduced. Mosby had also studied some Federal cases.

Stuart's court was becoming an overriding specter. More than a week had passed since it had been unofficially announced, but no orders had been cut. Richmond was rife with rumors about its possible members and what its proceedings would entail. Each newspaper ran something on Gettysburg every day. Mosby wished they would get on with it so he could get back to his own work. The morning courier from Washington had brought him a message from Ambassador Benjamin concerning the Northern abolition movement, and he needed to establish closer contact with his agents in the field.

He picked up the copy of the court of Captain T. E. Hall, a Federal quartermaster officer—

"There's a Miss Blakely here to see you, Colonel."

Mosby looked up to where Sergeant Ogg stood grinning in the doorway. What a pleasant surprise! He had thought about her often in the past several days, even considered going by her uncle's house, but he didn't think Breckinridge would be too pleased to see him. He was in the outer office in a moment, greeting her warmly. She wore a light blue frock with the new looped-up skirt and a flowered little jockey hat over her waterfall hairstyle.

The tiny dimple on the right side of her mouth showed as she smiled brightly. "I had to see my uncle," she said, "and since you are in the same building, I thought I'd say 'hello.' So hello, Colonel Mosby."

He showed her into his office and closed the door to Ogg's eager eyes and ears. "Have they talked you out of it yet?" she asked as she glanced at his war mementos.

"Out of what?"

"You know, being one of the bad boys in that silly court of inquiry."

He wondered if her figure was so curvaceous because she wore a corset. "No court of inquiry has ever been silly, Miss Blakely, I assure you."

She turned quickly from a photograph of his top-ranking rangers that had been taken just after the cease-fire. "It would be silly if it caused you undue trouble, wouldn't it? I mean, honor among knights is fine, but the round table is a thing of the past."

She was just as impertinent as she'd been at the dinner party. He kept the edge out of his voice. "Did the secretary of War send his niece to ridicule me?"

"Certainly not! It's common gossip that the noble Jeb Stuart and John Mosby, the dashing knight and his barrister lackey, are sailing into turbulent waters. And I just wanted to see if the fast current was intimidating you, that's all, Colonel."

He pointed to a chair. "Would you like to sit down and tell me why you really came, Miss Spring Blakely?"

"No, much as I'd like to stay for some spy talk, I have another appointment. I really came by to ask you to a dance. You may have heard that Bessica Adams Southwick is having a dance in honor of Jeb this Saturday night. Her way of showing that the women of Richmond support him, she says. Personally, I think she has other motives, but anyway, Colonel Mosby, if you could be my escort, I would be most pleased. I realize this is quite forward of me, but when one is a spinster of twenty-five, one gets that way." She blew out a breath, smiled. "There, I got it all out."

He had heard of the dance, in fact, told Jeb it was a bad idea and suggested that he have the Southwick woman cancel it. But not Jeb —he insisted it was a manifestation of support that he couldn't refuse. And Jeb had never missed a dance in his life. He shook his head. "I can't," he said quietly. "I've made plans to visit my mother out by Lynchburg this weekend."

"Oh, I see. Yes, another time." She nodded, found another smile. "Just remember, at twenty-five, an unmarried woman tends to have her frantic moments."

He, too, found a smile. "I'll try to keep it in mind." He walked her to the door, wishing she didn't have to go.

★   ★   ★

JUBILO nodded his head in greeting to the two elders of his church as he walked up the steps to the front porch of his store in Rocketts.

"How's you today, Reverend Jubilo?" the taller one asked. The man was also an officer in his company of secret guards—the hand-picked military unit he was training for Abraham.

"Just fine, just fine." Jubilo lowered his voice. "I just came from the warehouse. Them new packages from up North just arrived by steamer."

The tall man grinned widely, exposing his proud gold caps. "Does you think they'll make a big bang, Reverend?"

Jubilo nodded again. "I purely do. 'Specially if you light a match to them."

The other elder grinned. "I got me some big matches, Reverend."

Jubilo smiled. "Good. Keep 'em dry." He went inside.

His wife smiled from behind the counter. "They's a man waiting to see you in the back office."

Jubilo nodded. At forty-two, he was a huge man, weighing over two hundred and fifty pounds and standing well over six feet. Erect, commanding. He had learned the word stentorian and liked to think of his deep voice in that manner when he preached or issued commands. He was deep black, with eyes that could wither or reach out in compassion. A sharp knife scar ran along his right cheek. He looked like some fabled African king.

He had been butler to a plantation owner who, just before dying, freed him during the first year of the war. Adopting the single name Jubilo, he was one of the first to enlist in the 1st South Carolina Volunteers in 1863—a regiment commanded by Colonel Thomas

Wentworth Higginson. Bright and literate, with a dynamic leadership strain, he had quickly been promoted to sergeant, and shortly thereafter to first sergeant.

He liked the Union Army, and gave serious thought to reenlisting in the regulars when the war was over. But other avenues tugged at him. He wanted to be with his family, he wanted power and wealth, and he wanted to be a preacher. And then there was the growing whisper among the South's colored: *Abraham.* Instinctively, he knew it was his vehicle. Later it became his true cause.

On his way back to South Carolina to get his wife and children after the armistice, he stopped off in Richmond. It took just one day for him to decide that Rocketts was the place for him. All he needed was the capital to get started.

And he had it.

He had found the gold in October, 1864, just a few weeks before the Union election. He had gone into a shelled-out house to look for food when he saw the body of an old white man lying on an upstairs bed. Still clutched in the dead man's arms was a small, rusty strongbox. The box contained three hundred and thirty-nine gold U.S. dollars! Two weeks later, after having heard that McClellan was favored to defeat Lincoln in the election, he took advantage of the fifty-to-one exchange rate and cashed his gold dollars in for nearly $17,000 in Confederate paper money. Although this sum was devalued after the war when the government stabilized its currency, he was still left with $8,500—probably as much money as any Negro in Virginia had in cash.

And now, less than a year and a half since war's end, Jubilo was the most powerful black man in the Old Dominion state.

Halfway through the storeroom, the shaggy brown dog met him with a vigorously wagging tail. "What do we got going on, Dog?" Jubilo asked with a pat on the head.

In a chair in the cluttered office, seated by the old roll-top desk, his visitor waited. The man called himself Thompson and he was a Negro from Boston. He brought word from Higginson. Handing Jubilo an expensive cigar, he told him about Amistad.

When he finished, Jubilo slowly lit the cigar, blew out the smoke. "I don't know if I like the idea," he said quietly.

The visitor put the cigar case back in his breast pocket. "The Reverend," he said earnestly, "has it all worked out from a political standpoint. Fact is, he has a name that will make your blood tingle, Jubilo. . . .

Salmon Brown will be Amistad's leader—Old John Brown's son. You know what it will mean when the people hear *that* name!"

Jubilo shrugged. "Harpers Ferry didn't do too good."

"It stirred a country."

"Yup, but it also got lots of people killed. And this isn't Harpers Ferry. Times have changed."

"The Reverend wants to know if you have any ideas about targets or other uses for Amistad."

Jubilo blew out a big cloud of blue smoke. He didn't like the idea at all—this Amistad. Bunch of strangers coming in to blow things up. Salmon Brown. It even gave him a sense of foreboding, like he'd had the day he was wounded, and like he'd had recently with Mosby. But he couldn't just tell Higginson not to send these people in. His former colonel meant too much to him. "I'll think on it," he said.

"Amistad will be ready in about three weeks."

"I'll think on it right carefully."

When the man from Boston was gone, Jubilo leaned down beside the old roll-top desk and scratched the shaggy dog's ear. "You know, my friend," he said thoughtfully, "there's a phrase in the Bible that says, 'You shall not plow with an ox and an ass together.'"

★ ★ ★

THE following night John Mosby met with Israel Jones at the government stables on the north side of Capitol Square. He had arranged a job for the informer as a groom there. Jones was waiting in the appointed harness room when Mosby walked in at exactly nine-thirty. "What do you have for me?" the colonel asked briskly.

Israel Jones cleared his throat, looking nervously over Mosby's shoulder. "I, uh, Cunnel, suh—there was a meeting last night. Yes, suh, and there was a man from Atlanta there, and he told about the folks they have organized down there."

Mosby nodded. "His name?"

"Howard, they called him. But I don't think it was his real name."

"What was the name of his group in Atlanta?"

"He just called it Georjuh Abraham, suh."

"Did he mention how many people were in this Georgia Abraham group, Israel?"

"Nigh onto a hundred, suh."

"Did he mention any other names?"

"I didn't catch any, Cunnel, suh."

Mosby finished jotting down the last note. "You've done well for the first time, Israel. Now, I want you to pay particular attention for something special from now on. You know what abolition is—well, I want you to learn anything you can about any connection Jubilo might have with Northern abolitionists. Also, anything new or exciting that they might be doing up in Yankeeland. You understand what I mean?"

Israel's eyes grew wide. "Yessuh, but I don't like getting too close to Jubilo. I heard from one of his old soldiers he can be powerful mean."

"Just listen, Israel. Anything about abolition. All right?"

Jones found a smile. "Yessuh, Cunnel, suh."

★ ★ ★

I T WAS an abrupt change from the poverty in Rocketts to the gaiety and resplendent attire of the so-called Cotton Aristocracy assembled in Bessica Adams Southwick's yellow brick mansion at 920 East Clay that Saturday night. Of course all of the guests were not truly from the Cotton Aristocracy, but most were in one way or another related to it. Bessica Adams Southwick had arranged the ball on relatively short notice to show Jefferson Davis that Richmond society was solidly behind Jeb Stuart.

That was one reason; another was that the handsome Stuart was again the most talked about man in the South, and the catch of the season. A dozen Richmond hostesses would have broken a leg to get him as a guest of honor. Bessica would have broken a leg to get him in another way.

Although the president and his lady had declined, along with John Breckinridge and two other cabinet members, nearly fifty of Richmond's finest had turned out in their best fashions. A fortune in fine gowns and jewelry filled the ballroom, and to see the buoyant

87

faces of the guests, one would have thought a victory was being celebrated.

Bessica smiled gaily as Jeb whirled her round and round to the music of the lively little band that always played at her dance parties. He was so light on his feet, and everyone was watching! She loved it!

When the waltz ended, Jeb applauded loudly. "Oh, Bessica, you surely know how to throw a party," he laughed, wiping his brow and heaving a big breath.

She took his arm. "I have a surprise for you, darling." She signaled to the band, and a short fanfare followed.

Jeb looked at her quizzically, then turned back to the band at the sound of a banjo chord. "Look!" he cried out. "You've brought Old Sam!" He clapped his hands loudly as Sam Sweeney, the superb banjo player who had accompanied him everywhere through the war, strode to the center of the floor.

Sweeney tossed a salute to Jeb and held up his hands for quiet. "Ladies and gentlemen," he said when he had their full attention, "I don't 'spose there's anyone here knows how much this general means to me. And I don't 'spose there's another musician alive who's been as spoilt as I was in Jeb's cavalry. I played for him when he was happy and I played for him when the death of one of his men like to broke his heart. I've seen my music make the tears run down his cheeks like little rivers, and I've seen it make him dance 'til dawn, but the most joy I ever saw it give him was when I played his theme song."

Sweeney paused, grinned, then broke into "Jine the Cavalry."

Instantly, Jeb's strong voice joined in: "If you want to smell hell . . . if you want to have fun . . . if you want to catch the devil . . . *Jine the Cavalreeee!*" By the third chorus, everyone in the ballroom was swaying or stamping to the beat and singing. Jeb roared with laughter when it was finally over.

The dark-haired and slender Sweeney went on with more of the general's favorites: "Listen to the Mockingbird," "The Dew is on the Blossom," "The Bugle Sang Truce, For the Night Cloud had Lowered," and "Sweet Evelina."

When at last it ended, Jeb bounded forward and pumped the banjo player's hand. "You old sonofagun! Where you been hiding out? Lord, it's good to see you!"

Bessica let them carry on for a couple of minutes before she pulled Jeb away. "I need some fresh air," she said, linking her arm through his again and leading him toward the French doors that opened to the terrace.

"Do you know that Old Sam almost died on me once? It was during that smallpox thing back before Christmas of Sixty-three."

She sighed as they stepped into the bright moonlight on the garden side of the house. How like an overgrown bear cub this zestful Jeb Stuart was—he never seemed to run out of energy or exuberance, a fun-loving boy in a stimulating man's body. How he loved to play. And he made it so contagious! What an exciting lover he'd make. . . .

"I can't tell you how much that meant to me," he said softly, taking her hand and staring off into the night. Sam and his wonderful banjo . . . he could see a hundred campfires with hearty male voices booming out the old songs. His superb men. Faces danced before him, the ones who had been close and would never sing again. Pelham, Farley, Gordon . . . the soldiers, heroes all, his boys. They had all Jined the Cavalry and ridden the great adventure with him.

"I have to fight back the tears every time I think of the fun and sorrow when Sweeney played that banjo of his." He nodded his head. "You can't believe how much his music had a way with my boys. I know he soothed my savage breast many a time when it hurt." He smiled wistfully, moving close and looking directly into her eyes.

"It's all part of it, Bessica . . . those brave young lads and their fine horses, the sudden roar of battle, the clash of flashing sabers, the thrilling bugle calls . . . and then suddenly, as if the Lord had commanded silence . . . the final fading rebel yell, the last report of a carbine, the smoke and dust settling in the reddening sun."

He paused, sighing. "And then the sound of a banjo being plunked, softly—you could barely hear it, but it was coming closer . . . 'Listen to the mockingbird, listen to the mockingbird.' And it was sure as anything God's blessing, that music."

She saw a tear sliding down his cheek and instinctively reached up to brush his lips with hers. He was so gentle, so utterly sincere in his sorrow, so vulnerable—

"Thank you," he said softly, clearing his throat, wiping his eye. "You'd think I was just a baby, acting like this. But when I think of all those boys who'll never come back, that music just kinda' gets me, that's all."

"I understand, Jeb," she said softly. "There's a song that was my husband's favorite, and every time I hear it I cry." Her face was still close to his. She brushed the moistness from his cheek.

He kissed her, gently at first, then more fervidly, holding her tightly in his big arms, finding her ready tongue. She felt his arousal and his power, pressed tightly against him, returned his sudden passion.

Suddenly he drew back, searching her wide blue eyes. "I don't suppose I should have done that," he said quietly.

"I'm glad you did."

"I am too, Bessica." He lifted her chin and kissed her again, quickly, and then released her. "Now, I guess we'd better get back inside before someone starts thinking the beautiful Mrs. Southwick is out here fooling around with a married man." He laughed, taking her hand as he headed for the French doors.

She had to smile—the noble knight had returned.

SPECIAL ORDERS,　)　　　　　　　　　ADJT. AND
　　No. 52　　　　)　　　INSP. GENERAL'S OFFICE
　　　　　　　　　　　　　　　Richmond, Va., July 16, 1866

*　　　*　　　*　　　*　　　*　　　*　　　*

XVI. By direction of the President, upon the application of the General-in-Chief, a Court of Inquiry, to consist of Gen. Braxton Bragg, Maj. Gen. John Bell Hood, and Brig. Gen. George E. Pickett, will assemble at Richmond, Va., on the 6th day of August next, or as soon thereafter as practicable, to examine into the facts and circumstances attending the march to and battle of Gettysburg in June and July, 1863, and the conduct of then Maj. Gen. J. E. B. Stuart regarding the actions of his command. Col. M. R. Axline, assistant adjutant-general, is appointed judge-advocate and recorder of the court. The Court of Inquiry appointed in Special Orders, No. 131, Adjutant and Inspector General's Office, January 27, 1866, paragraph XIX, is hereby revoked.

*　　　*　　　*　　　*　　　*　　　*　　　*

By command of the Secretary of War:

HORATIO L. HUNTER
Assistant Adjutant General

SPECIAL ORDERS,)   ADJT. AND
      No. 54   )   INSP. GENERAL'S OFFICE
                                        Richmond, Va., July 17, 1866

 *   *   *   *   *   *   *   *

XXII. The Court of Inquiry directed in paragraph XVI, Special
Orders, No. 52, current series, will sit without regard to hours.
Lieut. Col. John S. Mosby, intelligence officer, will serve as counsel and adviser to Brig. Gen. J. E. B. Stuart during the conduct
of the court.

 *   *   *   *   *   *   *

By command of the Secretary of War:

                              HORATIO L. HUNTER
                              Assistant Adjutant General

G ENERAL Braxton Bragg had come to Richmond to confer with Beauregard and tend to some business matters. He was a close friend of Jefferson Davis, having spent the last part of the war as the president's top military advisor following his nearly ignominious defeat at Chattanooga in November of 1863. Therefore his visit to the Davis Mansion on the morning of July 19 was both a social call and a duty.

"Braxton, I'm handing you an uncomfortable assignment." Davis slowly turned a floor model globe of the world, a habit he had acquired in the last year. Absently, he let his finger trace a line to Mexico. "As you well know, our country is like an infant with a gray beard and premature wrinkles. It had little time in the womb, then rushed into adulthood via a grueling soldierhood instead of a childhood. There is so much to be accomplished in the next few years that it staggers me to think on it. . . .

"You know of course that my reelection is vital. Only I can be the rudder for this course our country must follow. And now this damned Gettysburg thing has risen from its grave to haunt us. I know you've talked to Beauregard, but I want you to hear it directly from me."

"Yes, Your Excellency." At fifty, Braxton Bragg was graying rapidly. The physical problems he had struggled against for the past two years, plus the strain of his personal disappointments, had not been good for his health in general or his disposition. If anything, the most difficult senior officer in the C.S. Army had grown even more querulous since going to Charleston to command the Department of the Southeast.

Braxton Bragg's contentiousness had not been confined to the C.S. Army by any means. During his many years in the Union Army, he had gained a reputation as the most fractious officer in the service. In fact, a popular story followed him around: "It seems that Braxton Bragg, as a captain, once served at a post where he was not only an artillery battery commander, but he was also the post supply officer. One day as battery commander, he requisitioned a particular item. But as post supply officer, he turned the requisition down . . . proving, of course, that not only could he not get along with anyone else in the Army—*he couldn't get along with himself!*"

"I want this Gettysburg story tidied up and put away. Do I make myself clear, Braxton?" Davis said.

Bragg nodded emphatically. He had never cared for the flamboyant young Stuart, anyway—too much of an upstart. "There has never been any doubt in my mind that Gettysburg would have been a victory if Stuart had been there, instead of off on that stupid jaunt."

The president looked up from his globe. "He's going to fight it, you know."

"That's what Beauregard told me. Got Mosby as counsel, I hear."

"Yes, and I'm sorry about that. Mosby's a bright young man, and if some of my plans work out in the next four years, I'll have strong need for his extensive intelligence talents."

Bragg wanted to ask: Mexico, Cuba, or Central America? He knew the president was considering various colonization possibilities, and any or all might involve the use of military force. "But Stuart's the one being tried," he said.

"He's not being *tried*, Braxton. This is a court of inquiry."

Bragg scowled. "From the way Beauregard laid it out, it amounts to about the same thing."

"Just be more discreet."

"I see you loaded the court up with Pickett and Hood. Can you trust them?"

"They're loyal officers, Braxton."

Bragg nodded. "Is it coincidental that they were both Longstreet's boys? You looking ahead to something I don't know about, Excellency?"

A fleeting smile touched the president's lips. "Let's just say I don't want any surprises."

★ ★ ★

I T SEEMED to John Mosby that he was spending more time in the basement of the War Department building studying Gettysburg papers than he was contributing to his primary job. But one never knew what one might unearth. As the word *spy* caught his eye, he was suddenly alert. The letter he was scanning was to General James Longstreet's favorite staff officer:

Headquarters, Army of Northern Virginia
July 1, 1863

To Lt. Col. G. M. Sorrel
   A.A.G. First Corps

Colonel: General Lee requests that you express his appreciation to the spy Harrison, who brought the timely information about the disposition of the Army of the Potomac on June 29th. While the general was at first dubious about the validity of Harrison's report, he used it to make the opportune consolidation of his forces that is now taking place. If a great victory results here in Pennsylvania, it will be in no small measure due to Harrison's contribution. Please convey the general's thanks.

   I am, Colonel, very respectfully, your obt servt

W. H. Taylor
A.A.G.

Mosby reread the letter. General Lee, who didn't much like spies and euphemistically referred to them as scouts, had pulled his whole army together at Gettysburg on the word of *one?* How? Why? In what way was the spy involved with Longsteet's First Corps?

He read the letter again, feeling a growing sense of excitement . . . *If Lee had sound information about the location and disposition of the Union Army as early as June 29 there was no validity whatsoever to the charge that Stuart's absence caused the following defeat!*

He had to find out!

And not through Longstreet, not after the general's antagonistic remarks when he was drunk at Breckinridge's dinner party.

After making a few notes, he hurried back to the intelligence office, where he found Sergeant Ogg and explained his new find. "I want you to locate this spy, Harrison," he said. "I have a feeling he can be mighty important to us."

"Where do you want me to start, Colonel?"

"Get a wire off to Sorrel. I believe he's in business down in Atlanta now. If need be, go down and see him, but I want this spy here for the court."

★　★　★

A T HIS headquarters in Petersburg, the commander of the Department of Virginia, Lieutenant General James Longstreet, stared at the special orders Beauregard had just sent him "for information." The words swam around, but soon became overly clear and glared back at him. . . . *"to examine into the facts and circumstances attending the march to and battle of Gettysburg—"*

He reached for the half cup of coffee on his desk and drained it without realizing it was cold. It was official. And he had no control over it whatsoever, that was what was bad. He had known the night he got drunk at Breckinridge's party in Richmond that it would be like this— *futile.* Tugging at his bushy beard, he turned to the tintype of his children on the credenza behind his desk. Now and then when he was troubled he spoke to them, but never aloud. Maybe I should go see the general, he said. Up at Arlington. He knows. He has always known.

Sam Hood and good old George Pickett, they knew how it was.

And Stuart knew. He should. Now he was finally going to get what was coming to him. Stuart should have his buttons ripped off, his precious saber broken, and be drummed out of the service. If the cavalryman had been under First Corps at the time of Gettysburg, by God, he would have been court-martialed a long time ago!

The damned peacock—Lee's fair-haired boy.

Braxton Bragg was president of the court. That would take care of the peacock, for damned sure.

He'd read in the Richmond *Enquirer* where Braxton Bragg was visiting in Richmond. Wouldn't hurt to go see the old bastard. . . .

★　★　★

H E LEFT an hour later on the 11:07 train, arriving just before noon and hurrying to the Exchange Hotel, where General Bragg was staying. He caught the irascible North Carolinian eating lunch alone in the dining room. "Hello, Braxton," he said cordially as he approached the table. "Mind if I join you for a minute?"

Bragg wiped his mouth, nodded without the hint of a smile. He and Longstreet had had their differences when Old Pete's corps supported him at Chickamauga in '63, but they buried them during Longstreet's convalescence following his serious wound in the Wilderness campaign. "No, of course not. Sit down, General."

After the waiter brought him some tea, Longstreet said, "Beauregard sent me a copy of the Stuart court orders. I'm glad to see you're going to run the thing."

Bragg belched, excused himself. "His Excellency wants an unimpeachable hand at the helm."

How could he use that word? Longstreet asked himself. He remembered back to the time following the Mexican War when one of Bragg's angry soldiers almost impeached *him*—he exploded a twelve-pound shell under his commander's cot in an attempt to blow him all the way to hell. The cot certainly went to hell, but Bragg didn't get a scratch. "I prefer the term 'iron hand,'" Longstreet said. "A forceful president who won't let anything stray away from the *truth.*"

"Stuart may try some flim-flam, you know," he added.

"I talked to that colonel who'll be the judge-advocate today. Axline, his name is. Sweats a lot, but he's a shrewd bugger. Gave me the impression that he thinks this court will make a general out of him."

Longstreet smiled. "Sounds like just the kind of bastard we need, Braxton."

Bragg looked sharply at his visitor. "You sound as if you're already braiding Stuart's noose, General."

Longstreet shrugged, spread his palms. "Well, I am deeply interested. You know how involved I was in Gettysburg. If Lee would have listened to me, Stuart would have finished the war as a private in the rear ranks."

Bragg frowned. "Did you officially recommend a court-martial?"

"No, you know how the general was. It was a bad time."

"Yes, a bad time. And you had your own detractors at the time, if I recall."

"But sometimes it takes time for justice to come around, doesn't it, Braxton?"

"Uh, huh."

"This time, he can't get away, can he?"

Again, Bragg looked closely at the general across from him. "Why the personal vendetta, General? One would think Stuart had shot you in the balls or something."

Longstreet drew himself up. "The Gettysburg dead demand justice," he said righteously.

Bragg just nodded, returned to his fish.

After a pause, Longstreet said, "Stuart may come after me out of pure vindictiveness, you know. You'll handle that, won't you?"

"Of course. No one will pull any shenanigans in *my* court."

"A court of inquiry can get out of hand."

Bragg threw his napkin down and banged his fist on the table. "Goddamnit, Longstreet, who the hell do you think you're lecturing? I'm going to run that sonofabitch, and I'm not going to let *anyone* tell me how to do it. Now, I don't know what the hell you're so worried about, but I'd just as soon get on with my lunch without any more interruptions!"

Longstreet got slowly to his feet, his face beet red. It took all his will power to keep his temper under control. Ignoring the faces that turned to stare, he said quietly. "Thank you, General."

★　★　★

O N THE 27th, Jeb sauntered into Mosby's office and put a sheaf of papers on his desk. "Here are all my notes, John. Is there anything more I can do? Seems like you're doing all the work."

"No, we're in pretty good shape. A couple of witnesses said they'd have trouble getting to the court, but they'll be there."

"I can get more, you know."

"Too many will make it look as if we doth protest too much. No, our plan is sound—we build our case directly to the situation in the Blue Ridge when you received your orders to depart from the main army. Those orders are indisputable proof that you were authorized by Lee himself to take the action you chose. *They are really our case.* In the meantime, we parry whatever they throw at us." Mosby went to the window, looked out. "I'm sure Axline will try to portray you as irresponsible."

"He'd better watch himself."

Mosby turned, frowned. "Now, Jeb, you've got to get it through that head of yours that this might get dirty. You can't be jumping on the judge-advocate or any of the witnesses who may be unfavorable to you. Sitting there at that table, you'll have no rank or pride to exert. You'll just have to damn well behave."

Jeb frowned, nodded.

"First, I think they're going to come after you for Brandy Station, trying to establish irresponsibility. But we'll refute that. As we head north toward the situation in the Blue Ridge, they'll hammer away at that same theme. Then we hit them with the orders. I'll use Longstreet on the stand for that, although he sounded as if he was really against you the night of Breckinridge's party."

"I don't think Old Pete has anything against me."

"We'll see. That's also when I'll bring in the spy, Harrison."

"Have you found him yet?"

"Harrison? No, Ogg's still working on that. Sorrel didn't know much about him, thought he was an actor. But we should locate him in plenty of time."

"What if we don't?"

"Let's not borrow any trouble; we may have enough as it is."

Jeb pursed his lips. "How do you *really* feel about this, John?"

"Confident, but wary. Again, those orders authorizing your move through Hooker's army are irrefutable. They are hard legal documents that can't be ignored. For the court to disregard them would be an act of criminal misconduct. When we get to them, it should be all over."

"I hope it's as simple as that."

Mosby shrugged. "The court will have done its job, and we can put this stupid thing to bed and get back to normal."

"Good. Then why are you wary?"

"I just have the feeling some blood may get spilled along the way."

"I don't want that, you know."

"If they go for *your* blood, it's simply a matter of survival. There's little honor in a court of anything, you know. Just rules that can be friendly or unfriendly." Mosby came back to his chair. "You know, Jeb, we keep referring to you, but don't forget who talked you into going on that trip to start with."

Jeb shook his head, smiled. "Nobody ever talked me into anything, John Mosby. You know that."

"All right, now if you'll get out of here, General, I have an awful lot of work to do. By the way, how's Flora?"

Jeb shook his head again as he turned to leave. "Still mad, I guess. She won't answer my letters."

"Well, she's probably in a lot of pain."

"Right. But she's still Flora *Cooke,* too. And the Cookes have never been short a ration of stubbornness."

Mosby arched an eyebrow. "And Bessica—you still using your head about her?"

Jeb Stuart touched the brim of his hat in a casual salute. "Like a choirboy."

★　★　★

A WEEK later in Washington City, the evening storm clouds were again building and rumbling. It was Friday, a popular night for the theater. While many wartime successes were enjoying a revival, new musicals and plays that used the postwar era as a theme were thriving. Effie German was starring in *Aladdin, or The Wonderful Lamp* at Grover's Theater, while at the Ford Theater, the popular John Wilkes Booth was leading the cast of the new hit, *Alexandria,* a satire on the dilemma of that Virginia town across the Potomac during the past cease-fire.

For lighter entertainment many people were listening or dancing to "O'Flannigan at the Fair" or "The Peep O'Day Boys" at the popular Canterbury Hall. Others were marveling at the animals and high-wire feats at Stone & Rosston's Circus of the World. Further singing and dancing for the more energetic was available at the Oxford Music Hall—where one could also watch gymnastics.

But at one old theater, closed since a fire shortly after the war, there was no dancing, only serious, and at times inspired, faces—and rhetoric such as the old building had never heard before. Wearing civilian clothes and sitting hunched down in the back row, Major General John Rawlins scratched his tender chin as he listened to William Lloyd Garrison, the sixty-year-old president of the American Anti-Slavery Society, wind down his fiery speech.

It had been nearly two years since the general had last shaved off his beard, but that morning he had decided to alter his appearance for a while. He flicked his hooded black eyes around, looking for more familiar faces. His mental list already included: Senator Sumner of Massachusetts; the crusty old Thaddeus Stevens; Salmon P. Chase and his striking daughter, Kate; former Secretary of State Seward from New York; the hawk-nosed Ralph Waldo Emerson; and several other prominent Washingtonians. The luminaries of abolition.

None of the information sources had picked up anything of value in the short period since President McClellan had given him his special assignment—neither the Pinkerton Agency, which still handled most of the Federal intelligence gathering, nor Judah Benjamin down in New Orleans.

Garrison's words broke through his thoughts: *"As long as one single child of God is born into the fetters of bondage, as long as one single young girl has to stand naked and ashamed on the auction block to be sold as soulless chattel. . . ."*

Garrison was the anchor speaker for the Society meeting. He had been preceded by Wendell Phillips, the Reverend Thomas W. Higginson, the famed Negro abolitionist, Frederick Douglass, Sojourner Truth, and other notables of the movement. All of the heavy artillery, Rawlins thought—and right on the doorstep of the Confederacy.

Essentially, there was nothing new in their speeches: the history of rebellion against Rome, Spartacus and the slaves, the Maroons in Jamaica, the Santo Domingo story—all tired abolition material that Rawlins had learned when he was involved with the cause before the war. And preached in the style of a revival. All of it was militant, but Higginson had been particularly aggressive, urgent; perhaps it was because of his military background. He might consider having Pinkerton put the minister under some kind of surveillance.

But there was really nothing to cause alarm. . . .

"As long as one abused girl can have her bare back slashed to the bloody quick by an overseer's vicious whip, we are to blame. . . ."

Somehow John Rawlins had failed to recognize the tall, dark-haired woman sitting behind one of the abolition notaries. But he had only met her once before—at the supper party at John Breckinridge's house a month earlier. And he couldn't see the dimple on the right side of her mouth when she smiled—which she was doing right now.

★ ★ ★

S PRING Blakely had come up by train from Richmond that morning, and was now completely caught up in the rousing enthusiasm and stirring revival spirit of the meeting. She had attended three other abolition meetings since the movement had resurfaced so strongly—one in Oberlin and two in Cincinnati. But none had been as loaded with leaders as this one. And to top it off, she was seated directly behind the vivacious Kate Chase Sprague—the strikingly beautiful young queen of Washington during the war. Her father, the former secretary of the Treasury under Lincoln and an avowed abolitionist who still had his eye set on the White House, sat applauding enthusiastically on her left.

It was so exciting! If only there were some way to show the people of the South how wrong it all was. She'd talked to her uncle until she was blue in the face, but he had all the stock Southern answers, his favorite of which was "It will all take time." Fiddleydee damn! Just pass a law, that's all it would take! One flourish of Jefferson Davis's pen on a piece of paper and all four, almost five, million slaves would be emancipated at once. Why did they have to be so *stubborn?*

She thought of John Mosby. Typical Southerner—had two slaves in his house; Aaron, whom he inherited, and Aaron's wife. And he thought nothing of it! How was she ever going to make him see how vital to the continuance of civilization this cause was. And she had to, because there was no doubt about it—somehow, someday, John Mosby was going to be her husband. If it took her forever. And there would certainly be no slaves in her house!

She drifted off into a fantasy where she was in Mosby's kitchen in her wedding gown; it was the middle of the night and she was carrying a candle as she went to the two slaves, who waited with light bags packed. She handed them a bag of gold coins and two train tickets to Washington City. She eased them out the back door, and just before they disappeared into the darkness, they turned with shining eyes and grateful smiles to thank her. They were free!

★ ★ ★

T HE bald and bony Garrison raised his voice to closing pitch as
Rawlins took out his watch. The meeting had lasted well over
three hours. He shook his head imperceptibly—these damned abolitionists were not only as long-winded as ever, but they had to have
exceptionally large bladders.

*"God has called us as his chosen to change this terrible wrong that exists on
our proud continent—to bring his children out of bondage and show them the
way of freedom. . . ."*

Suddenly pandemonium broke loose!

The skinny man with the reddish beard on his right jostled him as
he jumped to his feet, applauding and cheering wildly. When the
theater erupted with everyone singing "John Brown's Body" at the
top of his lungs, the man's clear baritone blasted into Rawlins's ear.
A glance showed him the naked fervor in the man's shining gray eyes.
If there were enough of these, Rawlins thought as he turned to go,
the movement couldn't be stopped.

The man's hand clutched forcefully at his sleeve. Turning, Rawlins
thought he recognized the man; there was something in the face, but
he couldn't place it. "Wasn't that marvelous?" the man shouted over
the din.

Rawlins nodded, trying to show enthusiasm. "Yes, exciting."

The man was about to say something else, but was interrupted when
a beautiful young woman with short black hair and striking hazel eyes
rushed up and grabbed him by the arms. "Oh, Salmon!" she exclaimed. "Isn't this the greatest meeting you've ever seen? I feel as if
I could go out and free every slave in the world this very instant!"

Rawlins seized the opportunity to slip away, headed for the door.
Just outside he stopped, reaching for his handkerchief as the coughing
spell hit him. When it ended, he wiped his mouth and glanced down
through the tears at the touch of fresh blood. *Sonofabitch!*

★ ★ ★

S INCE there could be no public connection whatsoever between Higginson and Amistad, no contact had been made with him at the theater. Therefore, while he remained and mingled after the meeting, Salmon and Verita drove back toward Liberty to await him there. The other five members of Amistad had been given an all-night pass to remain in Washington City and relieve some of the pressure Salmon's continuous dawn-to-dark training had built up.

No one had quit, and Salmon had experienced no more open conflict with Crispus, although he continued to watch the man closely. The other members had pulled together and proved fully reliable. Salmon thought Amistad was ready for any mission within its capability.

Both Salmon and Verita were still excited as the horse trotted up Wisconsin Avenue toward Maryland. The ardor of the meeting hung over them like an aura, stimulating their conversation and providing an intimacy that was new to their relationship. In fact, the strain of their everyday encounters had diminished considerably in the past week as Verita continued to prove her high proficiency in weapons and the physical skills. And in the classroom work, she topped everyone. Of course, he hadn't told her how well she was doing; in fact had barely spoken to her since that first day.

Now this sudden closeness. Much as he enjoyed it, it worried him. Tonight, in a low-bodiced dress of rose-colored silk that revealed her full, creamy breasts, she was extremely fetching. Fact was, he had to tear his eyes away from their swell every time he looked at her. Only at the meeting had he been able to get his mind off her and forget his sinful desire. Hell, it was the first time he'd ever seen her in women's clothes!

But he had to stop this wicked thinking, this fanatasizing he'd been doing at night—the hazy picture he had of her naked, coming toward him with her arms out, her lips moving, telling him how much she wanted him. God, how it excited him! But he was truly afraid—even if she ever would have anything to do with him, how did he know he could do his part? He wasn't going through any more of those letdowns that left him burning with shame and frustration.

His dreams had been free of the taunting red-headed whore since that night in Oberlin, and he certainly didn't want her coming back.

The night was bright, starlit, as they headed north out of Chevy Chase. Suddenly Verita exclaimed, "I think Frederick Douglass is one of the most exciting men I've ever met!"

Salmon nodded, but he didn't like the way she said it. The forty-nine-year-old mulatto was one of the most highly respected abolition leaders; he had escaped from slavery, bought his freedom, become a lecturer and newspaper editor for the Cause, and a recruiter for two Negro regiments during the war. But he didn't want her feeling like that about the man . . . he was still *colored.*

"He's terribly stimulating, you know. And handsome. I'll have to get to know him better."

"Uh, yes. Interesting man, for someone older—I mean he was a friend of my father, you know. Like me, he backed out just before Harpers Ferry. Yes, he's all right." His voice sounded flat, unconvincing.

Verita leaned close, smiling coyly. "What's wrong with older men?" she asked. "They are *experienced,* especially in making love."

Salmon almost choked. How could she say such a coarse thing? He tapped the reins sharply on the horse's rump as he pictured her kissing that old *Negro,* lying down with him!

She persisted. "Is something wrong with older men?"

Salmon cleared his suddenly dry throat, tried to fight down the anger, the shock. "It's just . . . that you're so young and—"

"And *what,* Salmon Brown? Do you think I learned to make love from *boys?*"

Inwardly, he shuddered. He stared straight ahead, his ears as hot as stove lids. He had never heard such a coarse thing from a proper young woman in his life! He should tell her to shut up. He was her commander, he could just order her to close her filthy mouth!

"Don't fret, *mon cher,*" she laughed. "My interest in men is as restless as the wind. Only the Cause matters. And tonight the Cause is magnificent. Maybe it's because I'm about to contribute something important, but I've never been so full of it. I wish I could go down to Alexandria right now and blow up the whole town! Now that would be better than *ten* men, young *or* old, Captain Salmon Brown!"

He had been an eyelash from slapping her, now the idea of an attack dulled his ire. He nodded. "Yes, well, that would be good for us, a target . . . I agree."

She ran her tongue around her lips. "I wish Higginson would turn us loose. I want something right now! I want to blow Davis's head off." She leaned close to him, her eyes wide, excited. "Think of what that would do, Captain Salmon Brown. Think of the headlines in the Richmond papers. 'Yankee Agents Kill President!' 'Negro Uprisings Throughout the Nation!' 'Confederate Congress Declares War as Plantations Burn Across the Belly of the South!' Now that, sir, is what Amistad is all about!"

She was absolutely right! He nodded enthusiastically, forgetting his anger. "I agree completely. Remember what Garrison said tonight— all the Southern Negroes need is to be shown that the hand with the whip is openly vulnerable."

"Yes! And we need to chop that hand right off!"

★ ★ ★

BOTH Verita and Salmon were wide awake on the front porch of Liberty when Reverend Higginson rode up on a big rented sorrel two hours later. He gratefully took the cup of steaming coffee Verita handed him, and in moments was zealously telling them about some of the inside developments that had not been brought out at the meeting. "By Christmas we'll have another thirty thousand adherents, Douglass told us—triple that if something positive happens."

"Then why don't we *make* something positive happen, Colonel?" Verita asked directly.

A broad grin spread over Higginson's face. "Amistad will do just that," he said, pulling a copy of the Richmond *Examiner* from his coat pocket. Tapping it against his left palm, he went on, "The whole city of Richmond is abuzz over Jeb Stuart. Seems there's going to be a military court of inquiry over his dereliction at Gettysburg. It'll be an open affair with many of the high-ranking Rebel officers there, maybe even the top civilian leaders, since it's a political matter too . . . a perfect target, and with far more attention from the world press."

Verita and Salmon looked sharply at each other.

"When is it, sir?" Salmon asked quickly.

"It starts in three days, perfect for our theater timetable."

"What exactly is a court of inquiry?" Verita asked, her eyes bright.

"It's sort of a tribunal to determine further action on a matter—a courtroom investigation, so to speak."

"Do you think Davis might be there?"

"Very possibly," Higginson replied. "And it will fit in very well with our Richmond plan. You will still go underground, young lady. Pose as the French actress and do everything the same as you would have for the other attack. Since the lady who will be your hostess is deeply involved with Jeb Stuart, you will be *inside,* and perhaps privy to vital information. It's perfect!"

Verita smiled. "I'm ready to leave right now!"

"Not so fast, young lady. You have another mission. And, Salmon, listen closely. Verita's hostess is a close friend of Judah Benjamin, the Confederate ambassador to the United States . . . and the highest ranking Jew in the South. I just found out he will be in Richmond to observe what's becoming known as the Stuart Court. Now, there are a handful of rich Jews in the South who are contributing money to Abraham. Silent abolitionists. It is essential to the future of the Cause that their identities remain a secret. We need to know if Ambassador Benjamin knows anything about them, and if he does, learn who they are so we can protect them. While the attack on the court is being set up, Verita, you are to use your considerable charms to get this information. Do you think you can do that?"

"He's a man, isn't he?"

"Good. Everything is set for you to go to Richmond Sunday."

Salmon frowned. "What has this ambassador part got to do with Amistad?" He didn't like it a damned bit. Not just the idea of her being out of his direct control, but playing *whore* with this Benjamin. It almost made him sick to think of it.

Higginson's voice was soothing. "The money from those men is what, in most part, is financing Amistad. It's all for the Cause, Salmon."

"I still don't like it."

Verita said, "I think it will be exciting. Besides, maybe I can recruit the good man to our side."

Salmon snorted. "Recruit him and then kill all of his friends—now, that's *purely* insane!" He shook his head. "All right, what about the rest of Amistad, Reverend?"

"You will move everyone to Richmond within twenty-four hours."

6

VERITA had felt a strange uneasiness, an eerieness of sorts, since the train pulled into the outskirts of Richmond. It seemed that for most of her adult life that city had held a special fascination—the focus of iniquity, the dark and threatening center of oppression and all that was evil, the very core of cruel enslavement. Gomorah. Always the goal of Union armies shouting, "On to Richmond!" Always, mystically, unconquerable. But now, as the train eased down Broad Street toward the Richmond, Fredericksburg & Potomac Railroad Depot, the capital of the Confederacy looked like a dozen other American cities she had seen. Though the people in the streets were her sworn enemies, they looked no different from residents of Buffalo or Cincinnati. The women were wearing the latest styles out of *Godey's Lady's Book,* and a man she saw in front of a store window could have just left a tailor shop on Savile Row in London.

It had recently rained and touches of steam rose here and there from a stone or metal surface. Puddles on the cobblestones blinked back the blue brightness of the clearing sky, and a pretty young woman dressed in an old-fashioned hoop skirt daintily lifted its hem as she started across Seventh Street. A large yellow mongrel with a wagging tail trotted along beside a young man on a high-wheeled bicycle, and a church bell pealed in the distance.

Not more than a half dozen blocks away, a huge building dominated everything. Seated on the brow of the bluff that was Shockoe, and stark against the dark clouds that remained to the southeast, stood the white-columned replica of Thomas Jefferson's esteemed Maison Carée of Nîmes—the proud Roman style Capitol of the Confederacy. And suddenly she thought of Edgar Allan Poe, who had spent so many years in Richmond. A stanza from *The City in the Sea* came to her: "While from a proud tower in the town, Death looks gigantically down."

She nodded to herself—Death was looking majestically down, all right. But it was from the hazel eyes of a young woman sitting in a railroad car . . . a young woman with a great mission to free her people, and to kill anyone who might stand in her way.

Her guise had been carefully contrived—she was now Marie Jolie: Parisienne; the twenty-four-year-old daughter of a French colonial officer and a wealthy planter's daughter from the island of Ceylon off the tip of India; a promising actress. Somehow, in such a short time, Higginson had arranged for her to take over the role of the French ambassador's wife in the new comedy, "Lincoln Splits Rails Again." The abolitionist had a connection with Edwin Booth, the famous actor who had come down from New York to direct and star in the play.

Rather than affecting a strong French accent, she had decided to speak her natural Creole with a bit of New England mixed in. It would be impossible to pinpoint. The language itself was no problem—in addition to her native New Orleans French, she had lived in Paris for nearly a year during the war. And she had been exposed to the Parisian *théâtre* through a short love affair with a young actor and a longer affair with an older director. Polished and confident, she was ready for her first demanding role.

Shortly after the engine wheezed to a halt, Verita adjusted her bustled tan silk dress and stepped into the sunlight of the Confederate States of America. A tall negro coachman in full livery stepped forward at once, holding up a sign that read "Mademoiselle Jolie." She took a deep breath and said, "I am Miss Jolie."

The coachman grinned widely. "Miz Southwick say she is sorry, ma'am, but she couldn't come to meet you. I'll take you to our fine house most quickly, ma'am." He bowed pleasantly, took her bag, and led her to an elegant barouche with two handsome mahogony bays in harness.

Soon they were driving past the greenery of Capitol Square in a roundabout way to the yellow mansion on East Clay Street. "That big statue there, ma'am, is General George on his horse," the coachman chuckled, pointing to a magnificent monument. "But General George, he's gonna have to move over 'cause everybody say that General Lee, he's gonna have the biggest statue in all of America. Yes, ma'am!"

Verita stared at the imposing statue of Washington, then felt herself drawn back to the adjacent Capitol building. Even though its grounds were overflowing with people strolling or just lounging around its neatly trimmed acres on this Sunday afternoon, it gave off an alien, hateful aura. It symbolized the very heart of what she wanted to devastate.

★　★　★

"*C'EST DU JOLI!*" It was Bessica Adams Southwick's favorite expression, meaning, "That's a fine thing!" She liked to say it with enthusiasm, and sometimes with different emphasis, even contemptuous at times. It seemed the perfect phrase when Marie Jolie came to her outstretched hands on the portico of her home a few minutes later. "Oh, I am so happy to see you, my dear. Ever since I opened dear Cousin Harriet's telegram from Boston, I've felt as if you were a new part of my life. Do come in—oh, I hope you can stay for a long time!"

It was just the warm, informal welcome Verita needed to dispel her last minute jitters about the challenging role she had undertaken. She smiled, responding quietly as Bessica drew her inside the lovely house and bombarded her with enthusiastic chatter.

"When Cousin Harriet said a real live Parisienne would be coming down to join an acting troupe, and could I put her up, well, I just can't tell you how *excited* I was. Fresh from the New York stage—I can't *wait* to hear all about it! And you must be full of news from the Left Bank. I haven't been in Paris in *years! C'est du joli!* I want to learn more French while you're here, my dear. Oh, my, how *lovely* you are. I won't even dare go out in public with you."

Moving inside the Southern aristocracy was absurdly easy, Verita thought contemptuously, as Bessica led her down an upstairs hallway to a luxurious corner bedroom suite done in bright lemon and lime. A uniformed maid was already unpacking her bag. A small trunk that had been shipped from New York City had arrived the day before, and the dresses it had held were hanging in a huge closet. The bath was spacious.

"You will want to freshen up after that horrid train ride," Bessica said. "And then we'll have lunch. After that, I will personally conduct you on a tour of our gracious city—the Paris of the Confederacy. And tonight we are having a most charming man to dinner. He is Judah P. Benjamin, the Ambassador to the United States, and one of the most powerful men in the Confederacy. He is a man of exquisite taste, and an old friend, Marie . . . just returned from New Orleans where he has extensive business holdings. I know you'll just *love* him."

Benjamin at dinner that night? It couldn't have been easier.

★   ★   ★

SALMON Brown, with forged papers identifying him as Byron Smith, had arrived in Richmond the day before and had checked into the popular Spottswood Hotel on the corner of Main and Eighth streets. The Spottswood, with its paneled bar and fine restaurant, had a rich wartime tradition, having served for a period as Jefferson Davis's White House. Byron Smith was the buyer for the American Importing Company, Ltd., a London company doing a nebulous business in tobacco and firearms. His base was in the Washington City office, an actual address manned by a receptionist. Higginson had set it up well—even having a London connection arranged in case of an inquiry.

Late on this Sunday morning as he drove past old Libby Prison, where the Union officers had been detained, he thought about Verita and wondered if she had arrived all right. Damn it, he straight-away missed her. And he didn't like the idea of her being mixed up in that high-society plot Higginson had dreamed up.

And he didn't like being Byron Smith either. The whole Confederacy should know that Salmon Brown was here!

He flicked the reins against the little black mare's rump, urging her into a trot down the hill to Rocketts. In another minute he turned up Royal Street and spotted the one-time schoolhouse that was Jubilo's church. He was surprised that it was no better painted than the rest of the dilapidated buildings on the street. Finding room at a nearby hitching rail, he left the rented rig and headed for the front door of his destination. He was taking a chance by coming down here, but when the time came, he wanted the people to know that Salmon Brown had walked in their midst. Their Saviour. Taking a deep breath, he removed his hat and entered.

The rough wooden pews were filled to overflowing, and as if to greet him on cue, the congregation burst into a swaying, soul-stirring hymn:

> *Oh, Lord, We's gwine come,*
> *Oh, Lord, when de day is done,*
> *Dear Lord, We's gwine come,*
> *Gwine come, when de work is done.*

Such was the fervor of the singing that only a few heads turned as Salmon slipped behind those standing in the rear and found a place against the wall. Spontaneously, he began nodding his head up and down to the rhythm as he studied the huge man leading the singing from the simple wooden pulpit up front. Ramrod straight in a black robe with a scarlet collar, he had a handsome face of shining ebony marred only by a thin knife scar on his right cheek. His deep bass boomed out above the others as the intensity of the hymn increased even more.

The final notes were followed by several "Amens" and shouts of "Praise the Lord Jesus." As the congregation took its seats, the eyes of the man in the pulpit seemed to flick back at Salmon, wash over him, and then dismiss him as meaningless. He brought his hands up for quiet. "Before we do anything else here today, my brethren," he said loudly, frowning ominously, "we must give guidance to the sinful."

"Yeeessss, Reverend Jubilo," the congregation chanted.

"There is only one way, and that is the way of Jesus and his Holy Father in Heaven."

"Amen, Reverend Jubilo," was the response.

Jubilo frowned sternly. "I call Jason Simpson and Mattie Kelly before the brethren!"

There was a loud stir, punctuated by many moans, as heads turned and centered on a couple in the middle of the seventh row on the right. "Oh, no, dear Lord!" the woman cried out, dropping her face into her hands. The man beside her tried to look firm, but he slumped as the congregation began to chant, "Sinners repent, sinners repent." And in moments the church was filled with the rhythmic clapping of

hands. White turbaned heads swayed as the intensity grew. And finally, the wide-eyed man led the white-aproned woman out of the
pew and up the aisle. She still held her hands up to her face, trying
to stem the streaming tears. Reaching the pulpit, she dropped to her
knees and began to pray loudly. The man stood beside her, blinking,
trying to stare straight ahead.

"Sister Kelly and Brother Simpson," Jubilo said in a manner that
reminded Salmon of a stern judge about to hand down the death
penalty. "You have brought yet another child into the world in your
sinful ways, and you continue to live together without the blessing of
the good Lord in marriage. You have been warned before. Now you
must be gone from this church, cast out as wicked sinners, damned
to hell!"

"No!" the woman shrieked. "He won't marry me!"

"You must be gone from my church for as long as you refuse to
have the Lord Jesus bless you as man and wife."

The distraught woman clutched at Jubilo's robe, but he ignored
her, breaking into a new hymn. In moments the congregation was
swaying to a mournful lament about sin. Salmon toyed with his neatly
trimmed beard, watching impassively, thinking about the naked power
a man like Jubilo had in such a situation.

★　★　★

"I SAID to myself, 'That white man astanding back there can only
be a policeman, an army man, or the man who was coming.'
And after a second look, I just knew it was John Brown come back
from the grave. You look just like his pictures."

Salmon nodded at Jubilo. They were in his little office in the back
corner of the church. "I suppose I should have come at another time,
but I wanted to see your church and hear you preach. I'll describe it
all to Reverend Higginson in my next letter. A fine service indeed."

"Yessuh, Captain Brown, the cunnel had the best church calls in
the army," Jubilo laughed. "We just fell them niggers out and marched
'em right into the service, wherever it might be."

Salmon recalled some of his Sundays in the army when he was
deeply troubled. He had truly tried, even different denominations,
but his guilt had been too intense to take even to the Lord. Once,

when he was a sergeant, his captain had threatened to take away his stripes if he didn't make church call.

Jubilo laughed again. "I guess I should have stayed in the old army."

"Yes, there were good times with the bad, and that's a fact. But I understand you have your own army now—that you are your own colonel."

The preacher smiled as he shook his head. "I don't know where you heard that, Captain Brown. There are just some people who come to me and talk about all the colored folks being free, that's all."

Now it was Salmon's turn to grin. "Come now, Reverend Jubilo, Colonel Higginson told me you have control over all of Abraham in this part of the country."

Jubilo ignored the comment. "Tell me about Amistad."

Salmon eagerly gave him a quick synopsis about the group and what its potential mission in Richmond was. He then went into its long-range goals of organizing other teams or cells throughout the Confederacy. "—Once we have proven ourselves here." His eyes glowed as he went on, "But we'll need your help. When my father went to Harpers Ferry, he thought the coloreds would flock to him and the insurrection would spread through the South like wildfire. A massive rising. But there was no organization within the negro community at that time. No one even knew he was coming, or seemed to care. Even Frederick Douglass pulled away.

"But things are different now with Abraham. You have communication. You have goals. If you join us on this mission, Reverend Jubilo, every negro in the South will know that we are united. Amistad and Abraham will be one, and the glorious revolution can begin." Salmon paused, went on, "Colonel Higginson wants your support in this, sir. Can we count on it?"

Jubilo sighed, pursed his lips. He wiped the sweat off his forehead with a huge white handkerchief, then sighed again. Finally he said, "I want to say 'yes' to you and the cunnel, Captain Brown. Truly, I do. But I've got heavy troubles with it."

"In what way?" Salmon asked. How could this negro possibly have any doubts about anything so inspired?

Jubilo frowned, trying to find the right words. His voice was low, quiet. "You see, it ain't quite like you Northern folks see it. You think you can just blow the roof off and the house will be clean—but it don't work that way. Fact is, these white folks down here just fought a whole terrible war to keep things the way they want them . . . and they ain't gonna have nothing shoved down their throat. You get their hackles up high enough and everyone will be shooting at each other 'til kingdom come."

Salmon shook his head. "Colonel Higginson says they can't afford another war. It wouldn't last a year."

Trouble was, Jubilo thought, the colonel wasn't dealing in *what* made people fight—only how. And this man with fire in his eyes, this son of the great martyr, what did he know about how long it would take? The trouble with blowing something up was it often just opened the powder keg. "That may be so, and it may not. For a long time now, you Yankees haven't done too well in figuring out just what a Southerner will do." Jubilo smiled. "Thank you for coming, Captain Brown. I'll think on your request most seriously. Please give my regards to Reverend Higginson."

Walking back to his rented rig, Salmon Brown clenched his fists. How could that stupid colored man act like that? What did he want to do, sit on his ass until kingdom come? That was the trouble with them—give them too much power and they lose their heads! Just who did this damned Jubilo think he was, anyway? Was he going to be another vacillating Douglass? Didn't he appreciate the opportunity to serve with the son of John Brown?

Climbing into the buggy, he felt sudden elation. He had thought for some time that his father's spirit might be involved, might be watching over him in some supernatural manner. Now, for the first time, he felt as if it were right there with him . . . inside.

★   ★   ★

B ACK at Jubilo's church, the preacher was just hanging up his robe when his wife came to the office doorway. "Who was that white man?" she asked.

"He's the man from Reverend Higginson."

"Son of old John Brown?"

"None other."

"I don't like him," she said softly.

Jubilo took her hand. "He's just a dedicated man with a mission, that's all."

"He frightens me, Jubilo."

Jubilo looked into his wife's troubled eyes. "He has picked up a big broken cross to bear, woman. We have our multitudes of troubles, but none of them may be equal to the personal Lucifers that may be plaguing him."

"I don't want you to have anything to do with him."

"I'll be careful."

"I mean it, Jubilo. When he walked past me, I felt a cold shiver."

Jubilo smiled indulgently. "I'll keep a coat handy when he comes, and a close eye on him. Now, I have to go on down to my warehouse."

Five minutes later he tapped three times sharply on the side door of the old tobacco warehouse that stood between the Powhatan building and a part of the Port Mayo wharf next to the river. A low voice asked, "Who goes der?"

"Cunnel Jubilo."

The door swung quickly open. Just inside a man wearing a black military uniform with red piping stood at attention, saluting. "Stand easy, soldier," Jubilo said as he entered and returned the salute. Before he had gone three steps, a burly man wearing the red and yellow stripes of a sergeant major hurried up and clicked his heels together in an exaggerated manner. "Suh!" he said as he saluted and fell in on Jubilo's left.

"How are things?" Jubilo asked, taking in at a glance the half-dozen squads drilling on the damp dirt floor.

"Middling, suh." The sergeant major nodded toward a squad that was being rebuked by a skinny corporal. "The recruits still don't know one foot from the other."

Jubilo nodded, moved on to his small office. The warehouse was perfect for his needs. A fire had broken out in the old structure during the war, and there hadn't been time to fix it up. It had long been abandoned. The good part of its location was that seldom did anyone ever come near it on weekends or at night, when his guards regiment had its drills.

He put on the black frock coat with the brass buttons and red shoulder boards embroidered with the eagles of a Union colonel. The slouch hat bore a red and gold badge he had designed to be the regimental insignia ... the crest of the 1st Abraham Guards Regiment.

★　★　★

"**S** UH, they's a pretty lady to see you."

Mosby looked up at Aaron, his general manservant, from the desk in his small study. Closing the English translation of Octave Fuillet's *Romance of a Poor Man*, he asked, "What lady?"

"Name's Miss Blakely, suh. Mighty pretty, even if she is wearing pants."

Spring Blakely sat primly on the edge of a Queen Anne chair in the parlor. She was indeed wearing pants, a flaring type of tan breeches tucked into boots that reached to her knees. Mosby didn't even notice her mannish shirt and bright yellow scarf, just the trousers. It was only the second or third time he had seen a lady wearing them in public, and on a Sunday at that!

She smiled brightly. "My saddlebags are filled to overflowing with delectable food, *mon* colonel. And my eager horse wishes to be ridden to a pretty, flower-sprinkled glen, where we might sit in the sunlight and converse about the world. May I entice you away from your abode for such an adventure?"

He liked it. The narrow-brimmed, flat-topped hat that was rakishly cocked over her right eye added just the right touch of femininity to offset the rest of her ensemble. He laughed. "Are you sure I won't be accused of picnicking with my brother?"

She raised an eyebrow in mock disdain. "I haven't ridden sidesaddle since I got my first pony twenty years ago. That's about as silly as saying a lady shouldn't invite a handsome man out for a picnic."

Mosby bowed deeply. "Your servant, ma'am. I'll have Aaron saddle my horse at once."

They rode leisurely down the James River toward Petersburg. At times when they met other riders, he dropped behind. And when he did so, his eyes were drawn to her shapely buttocks bouncing in the saddle. God, he told himself, if she were an example of what a woman was supposed to look like in pants, dresses were most assuredly on their way out!

Her smile flashed in the sunlight as she chattered on about life in Kentucky. How fresh and animated she was; what white teeth, and those dark mischievous eyes—the sun made them look a lighter brown, with dark flecks. Once when they rode side-by-side, their knees touched, and their eyes quickly met. Just that tiny touch aroused him.

She said, "A brilliant man once remarked, 'The most beautiful horses in the world needed a bit of heaven to graze upon, so God invented Kentucky.' " She laughed and he liked it.

"No, that was Virginia," he chuckled.

"No, if it had been Virginia," she retorted, "the man would have said mules."

They both laughed and she urged her chestnut gelding into a trot.

He was glad she was carrying the conversation—he didn't even know *how* to make small talk, or be witty with a woman. She was the first woman he had been alone with since Pauline's death. Not being a hand-kisser, he hadn't even *touched* one in that period. And now she was edging into his life. He had run into her twice on the street since the day she came to his office, and he had thought about her frequently, but he didn't know how to approach her. And there was the added fact that she was Breckinridge's niece.

She turned, tossed him another of those one-dimpled smiles. "Going too fast for you?" she asked.

He shook his head, smiled. She was fun. And what buttocks.

Again, he felt the arousal.

And then his conscience intervened. It was still too soon. Just a year? And how much of him was left? Would he ever be whole enough for another woman? Some of him had died, surely. Pauline had been so much of his life; he had tried fiercely to blot out the memory of her charred body, but it still clung to him . . . ravaged in the most devastating of deaths, so totally unjust, so Godless.

And now this sparkling young woman who reminded him of her so much. . . . No, it was too soon. He shouldn't even have come. He'd go through the motions, get it over with and—

"Are we going to ride all day, Colonel?"

"No, the lane I was looking for is just ahead."

"Remember, a flower-sprinkled glen, and private."

He led the way down a path, through tall trees to the river's edge. Close by was a secluded bank, partially shaded by a large willow tree, that opened to a good view of the James. They dismounted and spread a red-and-white checkered tablecloth on the short grass. The broad expanse of river, muddied somewhat from the recent rains, reflected back the joys of a peaceful Virginia Sunday. Multicolored sails on small rivercraft blinked against the rich green background of the other shore, while a young beau in a straw hat, wooing his sweetheart in a nearby rowboat, strummed on a guitar and sang soft words of love to her. Overhead in the bright sky, a pair of white gulls that had flown too far inland squawked in near harmony. The few clouds were soft, lazy.

Mosby twisted the cork from a bottle of red Bordeaux as Spring laid out a spread that included fried chicken, potato salad, sugared ham and beans, hard rolls and a thick strawberry jam. "There," she said, eyeing her handiwork. "Our first intimate meal together, Colonel. All that's missing are the candles and violins."

He found his humor, pointed to the rowboat. "We have yon troubador."

She nodded, squinting toward the young couple. "Oh, yes, the singing admiral. But, sire, methinks he doth have his intents firmly fixed on yon Desdemona."

They ate quietly for several minutes, sipping the wine. She spoke of plans for teaching in the upcoming school year. And he told her about his mother on the farm out by Lynchburg. He read the compassion in her eyes as he spoke of going there for seclusion at times. He knew she knew all about the tragedy; someone would have told her.

She poured more wine in his glass and their hands touched momentarily. As on the trail down, they looked briefly into each other's eyes, then looked away as if it had been an intrusion. And suddenly he felt as if he wanted to open up. He said, "I'm afraid I'm not a very good conversationalist. I don't even know how to go on a picnic with a lady, or be a single person . . . I was married ten years, you know."

Her hand closed over his. "I know," she said softly. "I really know how it is. And I can feel your sensitivity. It's all the more moving because I know how strong you are. I wish I could take you to my breast, hold you, and heal your wound. But I can't. I'm already so brazen it's a wonder you don't reject me outright."

"I couldn't do that."

"Would it help to talk about her?"

He got to his feet, looked away for a moment. "No. It would feel strange."

"As if you were betraying her?"

"Maybe."

She held out a chicken leg, cleared her throat. "All right, Colonel John Mosby, do you want me to talk about my anti-slavery sentiments? I can carry the conversation for an *hour* on that subject."

He shook his head, produced a smile. "No, how about that nonsense about you being a spy?"

She made a mock frown. "*Men!* All right, it was in Chattanooga in the fall of Sixty-three. I was spending some time with a cousin, teaching school there. And I just did some spying. As you know, when the war broke out many families in Kentucky had trouble making up their minds about being Union or Rebel. There were countless cases of one brother going one way, and another the opposite. I was engaged to a fine young man named Richard. He was from one of those families—he enlisted in the Union Army. . . . He was killed at Shiloh in Sixty-two." She paused, stared away for a moment. "I was, of course, devastated back in Louisville, but soon found solace in the anti-slavery movement."

It was Mosby's turn to take her hand and feel the compassion. "I'm sorry," he said quietly. "I forget that others lose loved ones. Forgive me."

"No, it's all right. When Grant came to command the Union forces in Chattanooga early that winter, my uncle was a corps commander in Bragg's army that was laying siege to the city. Well, I talked a young Union major from Kentucky into giving me a pass through the lines to visit him a couple times. Each time I looked around at troop locations and listened closely to what was being said—and when I returned to the city, I reported my observations. And then later, I did the same type of thing around Nashville. And I was never once suspected."

Mosby shook his head, a smile touching his lips. "Well, I'll be damned. You really *were* a spy!" He shook his head again. "Well, I'll be damned!"

She poured more wine. "But from what I hear, your exploits were far more exciting. Tell me about when you kidnapped the Yankee general."

He heaved a deep sigh. Now this sort of thing he could talk about. He launched into the tale, and then another and another. The time rushed by and suddenly when he looked at his watch it was after four. "We really have to go," he said. "I still have some work for the court."

Spring nodded. "Yes, you turn back into a lawyer tomorrow, don't you? Are you going to clear our romantic general? He is, you know. Every female in the South, from nine to ninety, will be pulling for him."

"No, I won't clear Jeb Stuart. The truth will clear Jeb Stuart."

"From what my uncle says, it won't be that simple."

"Then we'll just have to see, won't we? By the way, how do you feel about the court?"

"Why, I want you to win, of course."

"Want to be a spy again?"

"How?"

"If you hear anything at home, at your uncle's house, that might be in any way outside the pure search for truth in the court . . . let me know. Only anything you hear that might sound shady. Would you want to do that?"

"Certainly."

He took her hand. "Spring," he said softly, looking into her eyes, "thank you for being such a nice person. This afternoon has been very special."

"I know," she replied. She got to her knees and kissed him gently on the lips.

★　★　★

MOSBY had been home only an hour when he had another visitor.

"Please pardon my intrusion, Colonel Mosby, but I knew you would be pretty busy in the morning and I might not be able to find you." Major General John Rawlins was in civilian clothes, a tasteful gray suit. He held out his hand as he introduced himself. "We talked at Breckinridge's supper party about a month ago, if you recall. I had a beard then."

"Yes, by all means, General. Please come in." He took Rawlins's fedora.

"For the record, Colonel, I'm down here on special duty for President McClellan and the U.S. Army as a most interested observer at General Stuart's court of inquiry."

Mosby pointed to the same chair on which Spring Blakely had been seated earlier in the day. "My pleasure, sir. What may I do for you?"

"Off the record, I'm here for another purpose. Are you aware that I have a most cordial relationship with Ambassador Benjamin?"

"Yes, sir. He has mentioned it."

"And did he mention that I have a specific interest in any new developments in the abolition movement?"

"Yes, sir. I have my people who are monitoring the movement

paying close attention, but nothing of any particular interest has been detected. Just that the number of adherents keeps increasing."

Rawlins withdrew a sheet of paper from his breast pocket. It was a copy of a note McClellan had received three days earlier. Mosby read it quickly.

Dear Mr. President:

I've written you before and told you John Brown's body is arising from the ground and that the war of justice will free the poor slaves and reunite the Union. It has started, and within one month the first battle will be joined. On to Richmond!
—Crispus Attucks II

"Hmmm," Mosby said. "May I keep this?"

"Yes, of course. Normally, we wouldn't pay any attention to such a thing, but there have been a number of them—and this is the first to include a time frame. And I wonder about the last phrase."

Mosby smiled. "Could be just that slogan you Yankees used throughout the war." He couldn't resist the jibe.

"Yes, I thought so too. But if you reread those last two lines, it seems to fit together with the first battle—as if it's supposed to happen in Richmond." Rawlins shrugged. "I don't know, but that's the second reason why I'm here. President McClellan wants me to be right on top of any damned possibility that something could happen to make the U.S. look bad and create any strain between our two countries. I'll be checking in with General Beauregard in the morning, but I wanted this to be a personal thing between us, if possible. And totally discreet." He smiled, extending his hand. "All right, Colonel Mosby?"

"Yes, sir."

"I'm staying at the Spottswood Hotel. Please feel free to get in touch with me at any time. Good day, sir."

★　★　★

VERITA sipped from a glass of sherry. The music room was most delightful with its pale-blue brocaded drapes that reached nearly to its high ceiling, its richly carved cornices, the oil painting that was undoubtedly a genuine Romney, and the gold-framed mirror that dominated the mantle and made the room seem even larger. On one side a Loud & Bros. square piano, black-lacquered and ornately trimmed, stood proudly while the other side held a tall, noble Gesso harp.

Verita regarded Bessica with disguised contempt. In any other circumstances the lovely lady would be likable, but as a wealthy white woman with many slaves in her vast holdings, she personified precisely what Verita had sworn to crush. She was a typical example of pampered womanhood in the elite cotton aristocracy—shallow, excessively feminine, uncaring about anything outside her private, limited world of Southern culture and social life. Except for a few carefully chosen barbs about her competitors in the Richmond social whirl, she seemed quite naive, with a childlike enthusiasm about everything from her great wealth to which horse she favored in a local match race. And she was particularly enthusiastic about this General Jeb Stuart, the man whom the hubbub was all about.

In fact, the silly woman was obsessed with the man.

"If only he weren't so *noble*," Bessica was saying. "I'm a grown woman who understands the world. He doesn't have to marry me— I'll settle for just a little fling. Ah, Marie, he is the most *beautiful* man in the Confederacy, hands down! But nobody except that plain little wife of his has ever been able to corner him." She chuckled. "Why I'd buy a big river steamer with three orchestras if he'd just cruise up and down the James with me for one whole night!"

Verita smiled, changed the subject. "Tell me more about your Mr. Benjamin."

Bessica rolled her eyes. "Oh, Judah is wonderful. The word *suave* was invented for him. He is so bright, has such exquisite taste. If he weren't such an old friend, I'd become *his* lover again and tell that old Jeb Stuart to go jump!"

"You've been his lover before?"

"Oh, it doesn't count for much. It was sometime after his wife's return to Paris, a one-night escapade when he was lonely and I was feeling adventurous. I was in Washington shopping, and since he was an old friend . . . well, you know."

"You said he is still married?"

Bessica sipped her sherry. "Oh, dear me, yes—the poor soul. He'll never divorce her. She's been back in Paris with their daughter ever since that dreadful night when she ran away from him. And he just keeps sending her money as if everything is normal and she is merely away from home temporarily. I don't think he's seen her once in all these years."

Verita shook her head. "How strange." Strange indeed that she was already excited by this man of the world she was about to inveigle into her web, and she hadn't even met him yet.

Bessica went to the mantle, picked up an Oriental vase. "He had a friend auction off all of the rich furnishings he had purchased for the Decatur House. This is one of the items; that gilded chair you're sitting on is another. I went up to the capital to the auction to get them—"

"Mr. Benjamin is here, ma'am," the butler announced.

Bessica rushed to the hallway. "Judah!" she exclaimed, kissing his cheek.

"You look as lovely as ever, my dear," the ambassador said, handing her a box of chocolates from the French Quarter. He followed her into the music room where Verita turned coolly from where she stood by the piano in her revealing gown of lemon ice.

She could see his eyes open ever so slightly at his first glance and hold their interest as Bessica introduced them.

He bent low over her extended hand. "What a beautiful flower you are, Mademoiselle," he murmured in his flawless French.

"Thank you, sir," she replied quietly in English. "Now I know why Bessica speaks so enthusiastically of you." He had such large, expressive black eyes, and she could sense his strength just standing close. A truly powerful man. Men of power were always a challenge, always fascinating. His glowing eyes held her, excited her. She would have to be very careful with this compelling man, very careful.

"I have a wonderful new champagne, darling," Bessica said. "Let me pour you a glass."

"Thank you, my dear," Judah Benjamin said, continuing to look into Verita's cool expression. "I hear you are from Paris, via the New York stage, Mademoiselle Jolie."

Her smile was controlled. "Yes, sir, I'm here for a new play to be directed by Edwin Booth. And you, sir—on your way back to Washington?"

"Not directly. I plan to attend the court of inquiry of our famous General Stuart, which I'm sure Bessica has told you all about."

"The whole city is talking about nothing else," Bessica said, handing Judah his champagne. "I shan't be able to sleep a wink tonight in anticipation. Now be a dear and tell us about the glories of New

Orleans. Maybe they will take my fretful mind off what they're doing to poor Jeb."

Verita looked back into Benjamin's intense eyes, knowing he would most certainly come after her. His desire was already obvious, and it would be so simple to further entice him. The irony of it made her want to laugh. Here she was, an octaroon—a Negro in the South—as well as a dedicated revolutionary, about to begin an affair with a man who had often been referred to as the "Brains of the Confederacy." She felt the thrill, the mutual attraction. It was almost too easy—this morning she had been on the farm, and now she was at the very top of Richmond society . . . with two of Dixie's leading citizens right in the palm of her hand, to use or to crush at will.

And in the next instant, she wondered what it would be like to blow the life out of this proud and powerful man.

★   ★   ★

And so, after weeks of preparation, the Stuart Court is finally about to get under way. General Beauregard has his forces aligned and chomping at the bit—or should we say President Davis does, because we all know he is pulling the strings for his own devious game, and the Little Frenchman just bounces up and down like the puppet he is.

And what a court of inquiry it is! General Braxton Bragg, everybody's sweetheart, is the lovable president. If they're out to pin this Gettysburg thing solely on Stuart, you just couldn't have a more qualified hangman as president. Yet he is free of any personal interest because he wasn't within a frothy three-day-ride of the place in July of '63. But what about having Hood and Pickett on this military circus?

Major General John Bell Hood—whose friends call him Sam —was brought all the way in from Texas to participate. His proud division, part of Longstreet's First Corps, had a rough time of it at Gettysburg. And the general lost the use of his arm there. What memories has he got of that terrible battle? For what reason is he serving on this court?

And finally we get around to Dandy George, with his per-

fumed ringlets down to his shoulders, and his child bride. Brigadier General George Pickett, whose only claim to fame other than being last in his class at West Point was leading the most famous charge of the war. There isn't a soul in North America who doesn't know about "Pickett's Charge," but what has that to do with the Stuart court? Surely, Dandy George must have some preconceived nasty ideas about a cavalryman who went a-gallivanting.

Yes, Mr. President, you sho' nuff got yourself a dandy fact-finding body there. Were these the only generals available? We know Braxton Bragg would hang his little sister if you told him to, but what about Hood and Pickett?

Revenge?

The fact that Jeb should be hung from the nearest elm tree doesn't excuse the fact that our noble president has stacked this one.

Brigadier General George Pickett pounded the *Examiner* sharply into his palm as he strode angrily down Main Street toward the Spottswood Hotel. Pollard's editorial was bizarre, *grotesque!* That bastard had once called him a fop in print during the war, and he had threatened to shoot the newspaperman then. But that was before Gettysburg and all of the fame that followed. Newspapers all over the world had cheered the glory of his charge at Cemetery Ridge on that hot day in July of '63 as one of the bravest examples of raw courage in the history of warfare! There were those who said it surpassed the famous Charge of the Light Brigade, for God's sake!

He absently touched one of his long dark ringlets of hair, and in the same motion subconsciously stroked his handlebar mustache. The *bastard!* And to even mention his beloved Salli like that. When this court was over, by God, he and Pollard would get something settled once and for all . . . why the bastard hadn't even mentioned anything about Chapultapec, when he'd been first over that high wall with the flag . . . or that the Khedive of Egypt had offered him everything but a pyramid to go over to the Nile and command his army. Dandy George, indeed!

If old Pollard only knew it, George Pickett didn't want to serve on this damned court, anyway. Nosireebob. There were things that were better left alone and Gettysburg was one of them. Let sleeping dogs lie, by Glory!

★ ★ ★

S ITTING in the lobby of the Spottswood, Major General Sam Hood also had his mind on Pollard's editorial. Shifting his weight to relieve the discomfort in the stub of his right leg, he asked himself for the umpteenth time just why he was on this court. When he got the orders down in steamy San Antonio, he asked himself the same damned thing—and when he arrived in Richmond two days ago, he asked the Little Frenchman. But all Beauregard said was, "We wanted a general who is above reproach, and everyone agreed that it was you. Besides, no one has ever questioned your loyalty to His Excellency."

What a loaded answer that had been, bringing up loyalty.

But he should have wired his refusal to serve on the court when he first got the orders. He *wasn't* impartial about Gettysburg—he'd lost many of the finest soldiers the world had ever seen at its god-forsaken Little Round Top. Not to mention his arm. So, if this inquiry was to be a sham—like that damned Pollard said—then his own integrity was at stake. And he didn't like that one iota.

He nodded to a pretty young woman who smiled at him, then turned and approached him. "Aren't you General Hood?" she asked pleasantly. "No, please keep your seat," she insisted as he reached for his crutch and started to pull himself to his feet. "We played charades once when you were on leave here in Richmond during the war. You and me and Jeb Stuart and Hetty Cary. Do you remember, General Hood?"

He grinned. "Yes, I remember. You're—"

But the young woman had turned as someone called out to her. She smiled back over her shoulder. "Good luck in the court, General."

Seems as if *everybody* is involved in this court, Hood said to himself as he saw George Pickett coming through the front entrance. He smiled—a few years ago that girl would have stayed and continued talking to him if the *president* had hollered at her. That was when he caused many a fan to flutter and was considered the most prized catch

in the city by those swarming Richmond belles. When he had all of
his arms and legs. . . .

"Howdy, George."

★ ★ ★

" A TOAST, my boys, to the valiant old First Corps."
Longstreet held his glass of wine at eye level, grinned at
his former subordinates. "Never was there a finer collection of valor."

"Hear! Hear!" Sam Hood and George Pickett responded, raising
their glasses and sipping. They were dinner guests of Longstreet in
the elegant dining room of the Spottswood.

Lighting a cigar, Longstreet blew out a liberal cloud of smoke and
said quietly, "Seems a couple of centuries back to Gettysburg, doesn't
it?"

"At least," Hood replied, shifting his weight. He could seldom sit
in one position for any length of time. Having to be strapped in the
saddle during the last part of the war had been terribly uncomfortable,
but at least he'd been able to keep on fighting instead of sitting on
some front porch and telling war stories to little boys. His right leg
had been sawed off just behind the lines at the Battle of Chickamauga
in September of '63.

His right hand strayed to his useless left arm—invariably a sub-
conscious gesture when the subject of Gettysburg popped up. He was
tall, blond with very light eyebrows and pale blue, melancholy eyes—
the sad eyes of a bloodhound, it was often said. He had raised hell
with Jeb Stuart more than once when they were cadets at West Point,
and as a fierce fighter, he had commanded the famous Texas Brigade
early in the war. Handsome, with a full beard, he still led a zestful
life in spite of his severe infirmities. It was he who had nearly replaced
General Joe Johnston at Atlanta in the critical command decision that
had been the root of the South's victory in the war.

"A couple of centuries ago, and only moments ago," he said. How
vividly he remembered the savagery of the battle for the Devil's Den
and Little Round Top. How could he ever forget? He didn't think
Longstreet would even want to discuss it. Fact was, he still didn't feel
comfortable with Old Pete.

George Pickett absently twisted one of his long auburn curls, stared into his dessert. "You know how it is with me, Pete—the most vivid event of my life. I still don't believe it happened." Tough and amiable, Pickett was still a dandy at age forty-one. He was also a lawyer, but he had never done anything but soldier. Three times fate had knighted him with fame: first as a young lieutenant in the attack on lofty Chapultapec Castle in Mexico City when he grabbed the colors and led the assault on the walls; then as Union Army captain before the war when he had bristled at an overwhelming British force up in Puget Sound in a silly little fracas known as the Pig War; and finally at Gettysburg. His voice was low as he added, "I just can't help feeling, though, that this whole thing is better left alone." He shrugged. " 'Course, I suppose His Excellency knows what he's doing."

"Of course he does," Longstreet replied. "If the people of this great country are going to trust him with another four years, he has to be honest with them and give Stuart his due."

Hood just stared at his plate.

"You know," Longstreet went on, "you and George were picked to serve with Bragg specifically because of your roles at Gettysburg, because of your inside knowledge."

Hood struck a match to light his cigar, nodded uncomfortably.

"Bragg *has* talked to you boys, hasn't he?" Longstreet asked.

"Yes," Hood replied quietly, "we've been informed of what the president wants."

"Clear as day," Pickett said, nodding emphatically.

Longstreet blew out another cloud of smoke and lifted his glass. "Then I trust the court will come to an expeditious finding, and we can all get back to the business of training for Mexico. I can't wait to get back down there, you know." He laughed. "I've been studying Spanish so I can teach them how to play poker. I may even win me a hacienda this time." Sobering, he added, "You boys *are* going to make sure this court doesn't get out of hand, aren't you?"

Hood glanced at Pickett before replying, "It's a court of inquiry, Pete. You know what that means. We'll just have to listen to what's presented."

Longstreet nodded his head vigorously. "Well, of course. I just meant, well you know—we wouldn't want this thing to turn into a three-ring circus where the proud old First Corps was made to look bad, would we?"

Both of the court members knew exactly what Longstreet meant.

Pickett nodded, grinned. He had always been Old Pete's favorite, had been promoted over older and more senior brigadiers to division commander. "Don't worry, my friend, Bragg won't let anything get out of hand—and if he does, by God, I'll step in and grab it!"

★   ★   ★

JEB Stuart had bought the old Samuel Cooper house at Third and Grace just after the war. The elegant old place had both quality and charm, as well as the historical status appropriate for a man with his position and ambitions. It was also more than adequate for the children, and he would never feel remiss in leaving his family there in the event of an assignment that would cause him to be away. He had dropped Flora and the children wherever it was convenient during the war, and he'd sworn it would never happen again. But tonight, on the eve of perhaps his greatest test, the big house was overly empty. The two servants were out for the evening, but it was the absence of his family that made it so vacant. Flora still hadn't written to him, though he'd twice sent candy since his fruitless visit to see her at Laurel Hill.

He had gone to the early service at St. Paul's and sung in the choir, which always gave him great pleasure. And he'd been invited by Bessica Adams Southwick to meet her new house guest from Paris, but this wasn't the night for it, he'd told her.

He wandered into little Virginia's room, picked up a rag doll that he had given to her the previous Christmas. Holding it next to his cheek, he recalled how she had done the same under the tree that happy morning—looking up at him with a pleased curiosity, uncommitted to the new gift but aware that it would be meaningful to her. He wondered why she hadn't taken it to Laurel Hill—could Flora have made her leave it behind from spite? No—

Good Lord, he missed them tonight!

He made his way downstairs, went to the study, and pulled out a piece of paper that had a single gray star in the upper left corner. The pen scratched as he began:

My Dearest Flora,
    Several people asked about you at church tonight, and also many said they were praying for you not to suffer and to recover

quickly. I wish I were at your side tonight and holding your dear hand while I sang one of your favorite songs. I am very lonely tonight, my darling, because you aren't with me. Some of it is this impending court, too. It starts in the morning, you know. John Mosby and I are both certain that it will be over in short order all in my favor, but you never know. Still, you should not worry a single iota, my darling. Good night, my love. Kiss our babies for me.

  Your Knight of the Golden Spur,

Jeb

 Stuart licked the envelope and tossed it on the desk. He should try to read, he told himself. But he knew it wouldn't work—every other line, he'd be thinking about the court. He sighed, went to the wall where some photographs from the war hung in frames. His gaze centered on one of himself and General James Gordon. His throat tightened as he thought of old Gordon—what a fine cavalryman, first-class brigade commander. Killed in a valiant action east of Richmond the day after Yellow Tavern. In '64.

 Yellow Tavern, the battle that came within an eyelash—no, a miracle—of doing him in. Subconsciously he reached to his side where the scar from the wound was a constant reminder of mortality. But then no cavalryman worth his salt was supposed to live forever, was he? Yellow Tavern . . .

 It was one of those sunny May days that are too bright because of all the smoke and dust particles for the sun to reflect on—all the minute bits of the air of battle. Yellow Tavern was six miles north of the outskirts of Richmond, a run-down old inn from another age that held no military value but was one of those places where two opposing forces tend to meet and make history.

 Grant's Yankee cavalry was making a drive on Richmond, and his own Rebel cavalry was in position on that day to block them—highly outnumbered by the bluecoats, but never ready to be outfought. He had ridden to the center of the fight where the flamboyant Custer's 5th Michigan troopers were being repulsed by a 1st Virginia Cavalry counterattack shortly after four P.M. A handful of private soldiers in Company K of the Maryland riders was surprised to see him, whistling nonchalantly as he came up to their immediate rear. The Yankee troopers broke off contact on the other side of a rail fence. Noise and smoke jammed the air.

130

"Bully for Old K!" he shouted. *"Give it to 'em, boys!"* He emptied his huge, silver-chased pistol at the fleeing bluecoats. His big gray horse shied and started to rear, but he held him in tow. "Steady, men, steady!" he called out. He didn't even notice the forty-five-year-old dismounted trooper who turned and ran back toward the fence with his .44 cavalry pistol raised. The Michigan soldier was only twelve yards away when he fired.

He would never forget how he grunted when the big bullet crashed into his side, nearly unseating him. Reaching in surprise to where he felt he'd been kicked, he let his head drop momentarily and his plumed hat fell off. Sharp pain struck him. *No!* he shouted to himself, *not yet!* His horse shied, he was falling . . . No!

"General, you hit?"

"Yes." *He couldn't fall out of the saddle in front of his men!* The courier was reaching for him, face terrified. "Go ask General Fitz Lee and the doctor to come here," he managed. The company commander and some troopers reached him, steadying him in the saddle. He tried to grab the captain's hand. "I am shot. Save your men! No, leave me—see to your men." They were lifting him down. No, he had a battle to fight—had to block the Yankees off, no escape. Get Fitz, he would know what to do. His side was sticky, his yellow sash dark, blood dark. Why were those troopers running toward him?

He pushed back against the tree trunk, shouting, *"Go back! Go back! Do your duty! I'd rather die than be whipped!"* They lifted him into the ambulance and with a lurch, it began to roll. . . .

In Richmond they said he wouldn't survive, but he proved them wrong.

He looked back at the picture of himself and Gordon. Why—on this night over two years later in old Sam Cooper's house—was it all so vivid again? Did it have something to do with tomorrow, with the court? He shook his head and again touched his side.

Tomorrow . . .

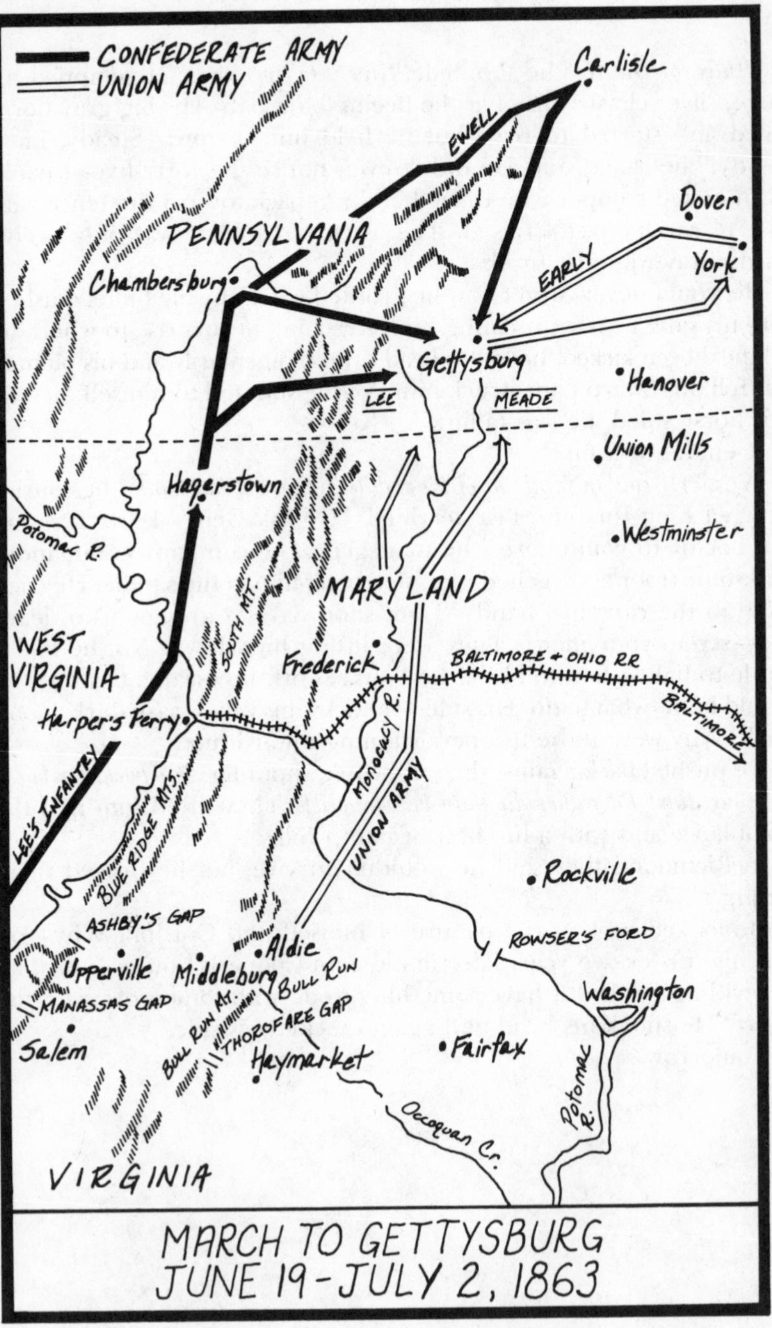

MARCH TO GETTYSBURG
JUNE 19 - JULY 2, 1863

7

To those whose God is honor,
disgrace alone is sin.
—Mary Chestnut's *Civil War*

S INCE the real purpose of the court of inquiry was to give the
voters a brief and final glimpse of Gettysburg, Jefferson Davis
wanted the proceedings open to the public, and particularly to the
press. It had been suggested that various buildings could be readied
for the court, but the president wanted the setting to have just the
right touch of stature. He therefore decided that the Stuart Court,
as it was being called everywhere, would be held in the main courtroom of the State Court House.

The building stood amid some partially grown oak trees on the
southeast corner of Capitol Square, just down the hill from the tall
Capitol building. The main courtroom was a large, high-ceilinged
chamber with tall windows that allowed plenty of light and a certain
amount of fresh air when opened as they were at the present. Oil
lamps hung on the recently white-painted wall between the windows.
The Virginia Supreme Court had sat on many cases in this room;
however this was the first time any military proceedings had been
held there.

The bench behind which the three members of the court would sit
was of darkly stained oak set on a dais above the oiled hardwood main
floor. At the right end the national flag hung limply on its staff, while
on the left stood the light blue standard with the great seal of the
Confederacy. Behind the bench hung a Confederate battle flag with
its stars and bars set in vivid red, white and blue. Below the bench,

the recorder's clerk had his small table complete with a ream of paper and a full supply of writing tools. He was a skinny little sergeant with a bald head and a huge red mustache that bounced up and down as he chewed a large cud of tobacco.

Twelve feet away and close to the front row of spectators, the table that served Brigadier General Jeb Stuart and Lieutenant Colonel John Mosby faced the bench from the left—the same side as the open windows. Colonel M. R. Axline and his assistant, Captain Marwell, sat at the judge-advocate's table to the right front.

The rest of the courtroom was noisily filling with eager spectators. The first four rows to the right were allocated to top government officials and senior military officers. A space was reserved for the president on the aisle in the front row. Next to that, Secretary of War John Breckinridge and his attractive niece Spring Blakely sat behind Axline. General Beauregard was among others in the balance of the front row. The second row included Judah P. Benjamin and Major General John Rawlins, who was nurturing the stubble of his rapidly returning beard. The first four benches behind Stuart overflowed with members of the press, including Edward A. Pollard of the *Examiner* and reporters from many out-of-town papers, for the Stuart Court was big news not only all over the South, but in the big cities of the North as well.

The remaining benches through the seventh row were reserved for non-official spectators with enough pull to get the highly coveted special passes. Leading Richmondites such as Bessica Adams Southwick, a former governor, and an ex-mayor, were crowded into these benches. The final seven rows held those people who had been in the front of the line that had formed well before daybreak: the general spectators. Several former cavalrymen were among this group. And along the walls, a half dozen soldiers from the provost guard stood quietly at parade rest in their dress uniforms, the glistening bayonets of their rifles firmly announcing that no nonsense would be brooked from the onlookers.

Excitement buzzed through the courtroom and a sense of anticipation permeated the already warm and muggy air. The Stuart Court was the biggest event of the year, hands down!

At the judge-advocate's table, Colonel M. R. Axline wiped his always sweaty brow with a large red handkerchief—his trademark. A portly lawyer from Austin, Texas, who was the assistant adjutant general of the C. S. Army, he liked to think of himself as a thickset man who exuded power. At forty years of age, Axline wore his disappearing blond hair heavy on the sides of his face in the manner of the Union general, Burnside. He spoke with an East Texas twang and affected a country boy's innocence at times, but he had a quick mind and a razor-edged memory. As the judge-advocate and recorder of the court, he was not only responsible for the physical conduct of the procedure, but would serve in much the same capacity as a prosecutor in a civilian case. He and Mosby had been involved in several administrative matters, but had never met socially. Privately, he considered both Stuart and Mosby privileged prima donnas.

At 9:14 a provost sergeant commanded that the courtroom be silent.

Moments later, the three members of the court entered from the right and stood at their chairs behind the bench. The tall General Braxton Bragg, wearing a short gray beard and his normal scowl, was in the center as president; to his right, Major General John Bell Hood placed his crutch on the floor and looked curiously with his mournful bloodhound eyes at Jeb Stuart; and on the other side, Brigadier General George Pickett simply stared ahead impassively. All wore the gray undress uniform with yellow sleeve braid and the wreath-enclosed three stars of a general officer on the collar.

General Bragg looked coldly about the room, then cleared his throat. "This is a military court of inquiry," he announced loudly. "It is not a court-martial, therefore there is no formal prosecution nor defense. Witnesses will testify in no specific order, but in a semblance of chronological order as the events involved in this inquiry are examined. It will be the responsibility of the judge-advocate to cast a critical eye on these events. . . .

"I must stress that you spectators are here only by special consideration. If your behavior in any way should be detrimental to the conduct of this proceeding, I will gladly have you removed individually or *en masse*." Bragg paused, still glaring about the room. Raising a Colt .44 Navy revolver by its long barrel, he tapped its butt on the top of the bench loudly. "Convene the court, Colonel Axline," he ordered.

The judge-advocate read the order constituting the court, and then asked Stuart if he had any objections to the members named therein.

"No, sir, I do not," Jeb replied briskly.

Axline then approached the bench and swore in the three generals, after which Bragg gave him the oath. Axline returned to his table where he stated, "Inasmuch as the judge-advocate is also the recorder, Sergeant Ross will serve as my clerk assistant." Loudly he added, "This court of inquiry is now open!"

Axline pulled out his large red handkerchief and wiped his brow before continuing. His voice was clear, metallic. "In this case, no charges have been brought against General Stuart. Nevertheless, he would now like to make a statement." He nodded to Jeb.

For the first time since all of this began, Jeb felt a peculiar uneasiness. Could he stop it? No, of course not, the wheels had begun to turn. He looked up at Bragg, at Hood, and then Pickett. Could he really trust his career to these men . . . his life? If they found against him, they could recommend punishment, even a court-martial. They were waiting. Silently. He had no options, only to meet everything squarely in the face. All that mattered, everything that had brought him from his first steps on the Plain at West Point until the present, was at stake.

His uniform was subdued at Mosby's insistence—low boots, no sash or sword, the same gray undress as worn by the generals he faced. He was one of them.

He glanced at Mosby, who nodded his encouragement.

Rising to his feet, he again looked slowly from one member of the court to another as Axline swore him in.

Moments later, he began quietly, "Gentlemen, before we proceed I wish to draw your attention to these facts . . . I have been a soldier since I entered West Point at the age of seventeen, and after serving honorably on the Indian frontier with certain distinction, I became an officer in the Confederate Army at the beginning of the rebellion. I believe the records will bear out the fact that I have served honorably since that time. In that period, no man in *any* army could find reason to call me a coward.

"I have accumulated nothing of the world's wealth, having devoted my whole time and energies to the service of the country I love so dearly. Therefore, my reputation is all that belongs to me. Without it, life to me would be as valueless as the fallen leaf of autumn."

He paused, flicked a direct look into the eyes of each of his judges. "As a personal favor to me, I ask that the investigation on which you are about to enter be thorough and complete. I invoke the fullest scrutiny on your part into my conduct. It is the only way in which I can secure exoneration from allegations damaging to any soldier's reputation . . . I am guilty of none of them." He nodded slowly, then turned to rake the audience with a sweeping gaze before taking his seat.

Bessica Southwick Adams dabbed at her suddenly moist eyes.

Axline moved surprisingly fast for a man of his size as he went from the trial-counsel's table to the witness chair. He held a sheaf of papers before him. "At this time," he said clearly, "I will state the situation that led to this inquiry. The war in the east at this time had progressed through a number of campaigns that surged back and forth through Virginia. Union strategy had decided early on that if Richmond fell, the Confederacy would fall. Therefore, during the preceding two years of war, the mission of the Union Army of the Potomac had been to take the Confederate capital. One Union general after another had tried and failed, primarily due to ineptitude on their parts and brilliance on the part of General Robert E. Lee and his valiant subordinates in the heroic Army of Northern Virginia. In early May of Eighteen-sixty-three, during the Battle of Chancellorsville, Lee was perhaps at his finest as a tactician when he defeated General Fighting Joe Hooker in the Wilderness, while outnumbered two to one.

"But Virginia itself was tired. Its crops and forage had been constantly depleted by one army or the other. The land, frankly, needed a rest.

"And it was well known that the people of the North were sick of losing battle after battle and son after son. Their will to continue was faltering.

"Therefore, with General Lee's victorious army refreshed and re-fitted in early June, the decision was made to strike north into Pennsylvania—to Harrisburg, if possible—taking the war deep into Union territory. If such a campaign could be successful, it was assumed that the people of the North would demand an end to the fruitless struggle, and Lincoln would be forced to come to the peace table and grant the Confederacy's demands."

Axline stepped closer to the bench and untied a large, rolled-up map of northern Virginia, Maryland, and southeastern Pennsylvania that hung there on an easel. Pointing to its bottom, he said, "Lee moved his large army north through Virginia on the west side of the Blue Ridge Mountains in early June. Meanwhile, General Joe Hooker—trying to determine what Lee's plans were—began to move his massive Union Army of the Potomac north on a parallel course east of the Blue Ridge."

"But before Lee could get his entire army into Pennsylvania, General Stuart decided to take the major part of his cavalry corps and ride around behind Hooker, leaving Lee without his *eyes* on the flank."

Colonel Axline paused, turned to the audience. "Cavalry is known as the eyes and ears of an army because of its mobility, and is usually used as a sceening force to fix the location of the enemy. I—"

"We don't need a lesson in tactics, Colonel," General Bragg said caustically.

Axline nodded vigorously. "Yes, sir, I just thought—"

"Proceed with your opening statement, Colonel."

"Yes, sir." Axline wiped the sweat off the back of his neck.

"With Hooker still groping for Lee, but unaware of his plan, Stuart proceeded on an extended course far to the east of Lee's army—eventually, after some minor skirmishes, winding up in Carlisle, Pennsylvania. There, Stuart heard that a major battle was already in progress at a small town called Gettysburg, thirty miles to the southeast.

"The meeting of the two armies at Gettysburg was actually an accident. General George Meade had just replaced Hooker in command of the Union Army and had only a portion of his troops there initially. After the first day of fierce fighting on July first, Lee lost his numerical advantage. By the time Stuart finally reached Gettysburg late on July second, the Yankees controlled the dominating terrain of the Round Tops and Cemetery Ridge. By the following day the die was cast—in spite of the heroic charge led by our famous General Pickett," Axline nodded to the general behind the bench, "Lee was forced to withdraw back to Virginia and abandon his great plan."

Colonel Axline scowled. "Although no formal charges were ever made, there were opinions both in the military and in the government that General Stuart . . . in his usual headstrong and independent manner . . . took actions detrimental to the conduct of Lee's march —taking away his flank intelligence in regard to the shadowing Army of the Potomac. These opinions hold that *had* General Stuart maintained his position between the two armies, the Battle of Gettysburg would not have taken place, or if it had, the battle would have been an impressive Confederate victory, and the war would have drawn to a successful close at least a year earlier. In effect, this opinion places the blame for the outcome of the battle squarely on General Stuart's head.

"The army has chosen to convene this court of inquiry to examine all facts involved in Stuart's actions, and subsequently determine what action should be taken."

Mosby sensed the stiffness in Jeb, saw the hard set to his jaw. "Easy," he whispered. "This is just the beginning."

"Do you have an opening statement, General Stuart?" Bragg asked from the bench.

John Mosby drew in a deep breath and got to his feet. The impact of what he was about to undertake hadn't really hit him until this moment. Using his wits in behind-the-lines adventures during the war was *nothing* compared to this. He looked at the faces of those generals behind the bench and realized that he had to outwit a determined government machine while the world watched. And he hadn't been heard in a courtroom in over five years. He tried to quell the butterflies that plagued his stomach.

Somehow, his voice was clear. "Gentlemen, as General Stuart so movingly stated, he welcomes this opportunity to dispel all criticism in regard to his actions in this campaign. Not only was General Stuart *not* derelict in any manner in respect to Gettysburg, he was brilliantly heroic in his dangerous thrust in the enemy rear . . . To even hint that this magnificent feat of arms should be the cause of what happened at Gettysburg is an outrage. Gentlemen, I submit that General Stuart's actions involving Gettysburg were not only sound and heroic, but fully *authorized* by competent orders. In addition to his being legally empowered to enter into these actions, he had the courage to make them heroic. I suggest that this court, in the end, recognize his accomplishment for its worth."

There was no warmth in the eyes of two of the general officers facing him. Bragg just blinked back frostily, while Pickett seemed to be staring through him, displeased. Only Sam Hood seemed neutral.

★　★　★

SAM Hood adjusted the sling that held his useless arm as memories of the beginning of that invasion flooded back . . . It was Friday, the 8th of June—a sunny, dusty day for his men to take a hike to see a bunch of prima-donna cavalrymen hold a parade. But General Fitz Lee, one of Stuart's brigade commanders and a nephew of Marse

Robert, had invited him to come along and see the review Jeb was staging for the Old Man—a repeat of the big show he had put on earlier in the week. So he had come, bringing thousands of his Texans along. He could still hear the friendly jibes as they drew up beside the assembled cavalrymen . . . "Hey, Zeke, you ever seen a dead man with spurs on? I hear tell they're so scarce the reward's done been upped to *ten* dollars if you find one!"

And, "Ain't them long toad-stickers pretty?" "You mean them there sabers?" "They're *swords*—you s'pose they ever accidentally cut off anything *personal* with 'em?"

Even Jeb was catching it, and from the Old Man. Decked out in his fancy dress uniform and wearing a fresh black ostrich plume the size of a small tree, Stuart was astride a big prancing horse that was sporting a huge wreath of bright flowers—reportedly a gift from some of his lady friends. And the Old Man said with a benevolent smile, "Best you take care, General, for that is the way General Pope's horse was adorned when he went to the Battle of Manassas, and you know what happened to *him.*"

Hood chuckled to himself when he thought of that Yankee general's asinine pomposity—telling reporters that "his headquarters was in the saddle," which prompted the Confederate Army to jeer, "His headquarters is where his hindquarters oughta be!"

The parade had been impressive. After a fast inspection by the Old Man and Jeb, the cavalry corps had passed in review in a column of squadrons—at a walk because General Lee wanted no effort wasted on parade; his horses had too much ahead of them on the long march to Pennsylvania, a march that would begin the next morning.

Sam Hood looked down at Stuart. It was a long way from that day at Brandy Station to this court. He pursed his lips and wondered how many of his proud Texans had died because of this man's thirst for glory. Particularly after what happened early the next morning. . . .

★ ★ ★

"—so help you God."

"I do," said the witness to complete his oath. He was five-feet-nine inches tall, slender, with a narrow aesthetic face set off by a drooping black mustache and goatee. His large dark eyes were expressive, but quick to harden. He was used to authority and wore it easily. He was twenty-eight.

"Please state your name, former rank, and duty assignment, sir," Axline said from in front of the witness chair.

"Walter Herron Taylor, lieutenant colonel. I was orginally aide-de-camp to General Robert E. Lee, but during the last two years of the war I was his A.A.G.—assistant adjutant general."

Axline, mindful of the press, asked, "And what are the primary duties of an A.A.G., Colonel Taylor?"

"Primarily management of administration that directly involves the commander, issuance of his orders, communication, reports—things like that. Sort of a secretary, you might say."

"These reports, Colonel Taylor, they do include those from all subordinate commanders in regard to battles, don't they?"

"Yes, of course."

"Are you familiar with the Battle of Brandy Station that took place on June the ninth, Eighteen-sixty-three?"

Taylor had returned to the banking business in Norfolk following the armistice and was preparing to run for the Virginia Senate in the upcoming election. He was quite sure of himself. "No, Colonel, I am not *familiar* with that battle, only with its facts."

"Very well, will you tell the court what you recall of these facts?"

"Yes, sir. Before dawn that morning, the Confederate Cavalry Corps under General Stuart was surprised in an attack by Union cavalry crossing the Rappahannock at Beverly's Ford and Kelly's Ford in the Brandy Station area. The fight that followed was called the biggest cavalry battle of the war."

Axline nodded emphatically. "You said surprised—isn't it a fact that General Stuart was caught flat-footed because of improper attention to Yankee movements, and his own amusements at a late-hour ball the previous night?"

"I object, sir!" Mosby said sharply. "Those are presumptions."

General Bragg reacted instantly. "This is not a court-martial, Colonel Mosby. You cannot object to anything, only cross-examine. You should know that!" The last phrase had the tone of an angry school teacher reprimanding a wayward student.

"Pardon me, sir. I forgot." Mosby hadn't forgotten a thing. He just wanted to break into the flow. "However I don't see where such presumptions on General Stuart's off-duty activities are important."

"They are part of the general dereliction involved in this whole case," Axline said quickly.

"I didn't know General Stuart had been charged with dereliction," Mosby retorted. Shaking his finger at the judge-advocate, he added, "The special orders you just read state that this court is to look into the facts and circumstances involved, not to make false accusations!"

Thump! Bragg's pistol butt slammed into the bench top. "Colonel Mosby, I'll not hesitate to remove you from this courtroom!" he thundered. "I just told you that you could cross-examine. We all know what the orders say. I won't warn you again."

Mosby nodded. "Yes, sir." He had known Bragg would be biased, but not this hostile. He leaned over to Stuart, whose jaw was set. "I was just testing the water, Jeb," he whispered. "And it looks as if Bragg is really flowing against us."

Stuart nodded. "What does Brandy Station have to do with the march?"

"They're just starting a pattern to indicate dereliction. Might as well get used to it."

Axline had returned to the witness chair. "Now, Colonel Taylor, let's resume your account of the morning of June ninth. Wasn't General Stuart caught flat-footed?"

"If you would describe being totally surprised by the enemy in that fashion, I would say so."

"What effect did that battle have on General Lee's plans to march north?"

"It was a bad beginning for us. The general needed fresh cavalry to screen for the main body as we moved north on the west side of the Blue Ridge Mountains. He knew Hooker would guess what we were up to—at least as far as moving north. But he didn't want the Yankees to know anything else."

"And by Stuart being caught with his britches down at Brandy Station, his cavalry was battered and crippled—is that right?"

Taylor nodded. "In essence, yes. General Stuart lost over five hundred men, and we don't have any figures on what effect it had on his mounts. You know a cavalry soldier had to supply his own horse at that time."

"Yes, and weren't some of Stuart's key people killed at that battle —his chief scout, Farley, for one. And one of his top brigade commanders—General Lee's own son, Rooney—was badly wounded."

"Yes."

"It has been said, Colonel Taylor, that this battle in which the Yankees achieved such great surprise and success against the hitherto vastly superior Confederate cavalry gave the Union cavalry the confidence to become a major factor in the remainder of the war, in fact Brandy Station *made* the Yankee cavalry. Do you agree?"

"I'm afraid more qualified military historians will have to make such a determination."

"Wasn't General Stuart humiliated by that battle?"

Taylor showed his displeasure. "I can make no statement to that effect, but the newspapers were critical."

"Sir," Mosby said to Bragg. "You can't allow that last comment. I think we all know how unreliable newspaper editorials can be."

Bragg frowned, nodded. "You're right, Colonel Mosby. Colonel Taylor, please refrain from further comments along that line."

Mosby turned to where the journalists were seated, found Pollard, and gave him a level look.

Axline went on, "Colonel Taylor, do you recall General Lee's remarks when he heard about the Battle of Brandy Station?"

"No, sir. Not exactly. He was disappointed and deeply concerned about the serious wound his son had suffered. But I don't recall a specific comment."

"In summary, Colonel Taylor, would you say that the Battle of Brandy Station had a deleterious effect on the Pennsylvania campaign of the summer of Eighteen-sixty-three?"

"Of course."

The judge-advocate nodded. "Thank you, Colonel Taylor. I have no further questions at this time. But you are subject to recall."

"Now, Colonel Mosby, you may question the witness," General Bragg said.

Mosby got to his feet. "Thank you, Colonel Taylor, for such a fair appraisal. Now I would like to ask you this—did the Union cavalry play any major role in the march north to Pennsylvania?"

"What do you mean?"

"Was Union cavalry close on General Lee's flank during that march, close enough for contact in any meaningful way as the army crossed into Maryland and Pennsylvania?"

"General Stuart had contact with them."

"No, I mean after General Stuart broke away through Hooker's Army?"

"No, I would say not."

Mosby turned to the bench. "Then I surmise that the statement 'the battle of Brandy Station *made* the Yankee cavalry' is a fallacy . . . that the battle of Brandy Station was at least as harmful to the Yankee cavalry as it was to ours." He looked at Taylor. "Do you agree, Colonel?"

"I would tend to agree."

"Then, Colonel Taylor, do you not also agree that Brandy Station was just as deleterious to the enemy as it was to us?"

Taylor scowled. "They had the superior numbers. Any losses were bound to hurt us more."

Mosby looked back at the bench. "I believe this entire testimony leads to nothing but supposition, gentlemen. Since the witness wasn't even there, I have no further questions."

As Lee's former adjutant-general walked away from the stand, Jeb leaned over to Mosby. "Couldn't you have challenged him harder?"

"No, I don't want to badger him. He has really been quite impartial, and I have a hunch we're going to see him again."

"The court calls Colonel Elijah White to the witness stand," Axline said in his clear voice.

Lieutenant Colonel Elijah White had commanded the 35th Battalion of Virginia Cavalry, a sometimes irresponsible but hard-fighting unit that had been in and out of favor with Jeb during the war. White, now a civilian businessman in Leesburg, was just under six feet, slender to the point of looking gaunt, with blue eyes and a neatly trimmed blond mustache. His mouth was set in a grim line and he stared blankly ahead, as if he didn't want to meet anyone's gaze. Elijah White was thirty-four years old. As Axline swore him in, Stuart leaned close to Mosby. "He has held a grudge against me since we went into Maryland in Sixty-two when he was a captain. He was insubordinate and I had to take him to General Lee."

"Jeb, you've got to get used to the fact that they're not going to call your best friends," Mosby whispered back.

The judge-advocate began his questioning. "Were you at Brandy Station in June of Eighteen-sixty-three as part of the cavalry corps under the command of General Stuart?"

"Yes, sir, I sure was."

"Would you please tell the court what transpired early on the morning of June ninth?"

Elijah White's voice came out forcefully, as if he had been storing up the words for a long time and they were breaking their bonds. "My Thirty-fifth Battalion was attached to General Grumble Jones's brigade that morning, and it was a good thing, because if it hadn't been for us, General Stuart might not have had *any* cavalry left by sundown that night—maybe even by noon. That Yankee cavalry splashed over those fords and crashed into our sleepy boys like an ax, shouting blue murder.

"We didn't have any idea they were gonna hit us. But how could we? All Stuart had had us doing for days was parading and showing off for the high mucky-muck generals and the local ladies. All old Hooker had to do was climb up in one of his balloons and even he could see we were all bunched up like the biggest horse show in history."

The former battalion commander paused, flicked a scowl at Stuart and then out to the crowd before continuing. "Hardly anybody in the whole command had shook the sleep out of his eyes when those bluebellies galloped in. They almost overran the artillery in the first minutes. I tell you it was a close shave, and that's a fact. Somehow old Grumble got his brigade moving—I'll never forget how he looked, bless his soul. All he had on was his britches and shirt—no boots, no hat—shouting and swearing, and waving his big pistol on his bareback horse.

"But we stopped the first thrust of Yankee cavalry coming from Beverly's Ford, where they crossed the Rappahannock about four miles northeast of Brandy Station. It seemed for a while as if Hooker had sent his whole army across that damned river. The fighting was fierce, I'll tell you. And then all at once, I was ordered out of the line and back up to Fleetwood Hill, where Stuart's headquarters had been located. Seems as though the rest of Hooker's boys were threatening that place. And it commanded everything from its height.

"We barely got there in time. As we galloped up the hill in a column of fours, my battalion was split right in half—two squadrons, in fact, stayed with a recoiling regiment, while I re-formed the other two and dashed around the hill to attack a battery of three guns. And then it was back up the hill, where my boys were a major factor in retaking it."

Colonel Axline broke in. "Yes, your report was quite comprehensive in its battle description." The judge-advocate turned to General Bragg. "I have a copy of Colonel White's official report available, should anyone wish to peruse it, sir."

The president of the court looked at each of the other members with a raised eyebrow, then shook his head. "That won't be necessary.

However, I would like to ask the colonel a question. . . . Sir, in your opinion, was the surprise attack by the Federal cavalry that morning made possible by circumstances resulting from *poor judgment* by General Stuart?"

White nodded. "Yes, sir, it was. No doubt about it."

"Please expand on that."

Mosby frowned. Bragg had actually put words in the witness's mouth. He watched White's expression harden again as the former cavalry officer replied, "If we hadn't been showing off and parading all week, maybe Stuart might of been trying to find out what the Bluebellies were up to. That's one thing. The other is, he should of had pickets posted on the *other* side of the river at those two fords. No Yankee general could have moved eleven thousand men into an attack position without *somebody* finding out. The whole damned thing was frivolous, that's for sure, General."

Jeb's hands gripped the edge of the table as he glared at his former subordinate. The moment of silence that followed held even the spectators. Axline broke it. "Then, Colonel White, you are certain that the Battle of Brandy Station would never have occurred if General Stuart had exercised proper prudence. Is that correct?"

"Absolutely."

"Would you agree, sir, that the loss of over five hundred men and officers, including General Rooney Lee, was a distinct blow to the cavalry command as it prepared to head for Pennsylvania?"

"Yes, sir."

"Thank you, Colonel White." Axline turned to Mosby. "You may question the witness, sir."

Mosby rose behind his table. "Colonel White, did you ever have differences with General Stuart of such a nature that he took you to see General Lee?"

White's face hardened in the witness box. "I *demanded* to see General Lee. Stuart ordered me back to Virginia—"

"Because that wild bunch of his tried to tear up Frederick!" Jeb barked, springing to his feet.

Bragg's pistol hit the bench. "General Stuart, if you want to conduct your own inquiry, go ahead. If you want your counsel to handle it, sit down and keep your silence!"

Jeb continued to glare at the witness as he took his chair. "Sorry, sir."

"Colonel White," Mosby said, "let me redirect my question. Isn't it true that you and General Stuart had differences back in the fall of Sixty-two?"

"Yes, sir, we did."

"Did you ever reconcile those differences?"

"I served under him."

"Did you ever grow to like him?"

"I didn't have to *like* him. Him and his peacock ways."

Mosby pounced, moving close to the witness box. "*Peacock ways!* Colonel White, isn't it true that you *hate* General Stuart?"

White struggled to regain his composure. "Let's just say I'll never be in love with him. But that has nothing to do with my testimony, Mosby. I—"

"I have no more questions."

General Pickett spoke from the bench, "Colonel White, *I* have a question—in your opinion, could the embarrassment of being caught short at Brandy Station have influenced General Stuart to do something rash later on to make up for it?"

"Sir," White replied. "General Stuart *never* needed an excuse for doing something rash. In answer to your question—without a doubt!"

Mosby stared at George Pickett and felt as if he'd been kicked below the belt. The general had just shown his colors by asking such a terribly improper question. *Two judges out of three openly against Jeb.* God! He looked at the stolid look on Hood's face. Was it three?

As White left the stand, Jeb leaned close and asked, "How many witnesses is Axline going to call regarding Brandy Station?"

Mosby looked at his tablet. "Enough to take up the whole day, I'd guess. I'd also hazard he plans to swamp them with enough negative testimony from anyone who ever had a grudge against you to make Brandy look like the biggest defeat in history. But just relax, I have the stopper." He patted his papers.

Jeb just shook his head.

★　★　★

THE small warehouse was located at Ludlum Wharf, off Water Street on the river by Rocketts. It was easily large enough to hold the arms, ammunition, and explosives that would be arriving shortly from Alexandria. Salmon Brown flicked a glance of approval to Crispus. The ever-prickly Negro from Toronto nodded in agreement. With a small office for any needed privacy, the place could accommodate storage, meetings, and even lodging—if it became necessary for anyone to hide out.

Salmon extracted a United States twenty dollar bill from his large leather wallet. "We'll take it for six months as a starter," he said to the portly real estate agent. "I'll give you a check drawn on the account of the American Importing Company, Limited, later today. About the boat, whom did you say I should see?"

"Mr. Blum, sir. The last place down on the water."

Salmon liked the idea and the drama of an escape by water, and he wanted to cover every contingency. Crispus claimed a working knowledge of sailing, so a small boat that would carry a dozen people, complete with oars and a sail, would suffice.

When the real estate agent departed, Salmon asked Crispus about the others.

"Beecher Lovejoy came down Saturday and moved into that white boarding house on Canal Street. Us coloreds are all here in Rocketts. Nat Turner and Denmark Vesey are enjoying their roles as Texas freedmen come east to find jobs. Cinque was the last to arrive—he came in this morning with his story about being from Georgia. In my case, I'm not telling anybody anything until they press me . . . Mr. Smith. There's so many itinerant coloreds milling around this town from other places that I could be here a year before anyone got really curious. I could *own* the place."

Salmon nodded. There were times when he could hardly stand this uppity nigger, and by God that was just what he was! There were Negroes and coloreds, and there were *niggers,* and there just wasn't any other way to describe them. "And you all have a place to stay?"

"Yes, I can reach them all in a few minutes." Crispus handed over a scrap of paper. "This is my address. A pretty widow woman runs a small boarding house. But always send a colored boy if you need me. A white man like you would be too obvious—though I guess half of Rocketts knows you went to Jubilo's church yesterday. That wasn't too smart, Mr. Smith."

Salmon frowned. The bastard really *was* an uppity nigger. But he didn't want to struggle with him now. "Maybe not," he murmured. "Let's go see about that boat."

★　★　★

F OLLOWING a three o'clock recess, Colonel Axline interviewed three more witnesses to further bolster his charge of dereliction at Brandy Station. As the final officer left the stand, Mosby stood behind his table and said, "If Colonel Axline has finished his case against the Battle of Brandy Station, perhaps we can get on with the march to Gettysburg." He looked pointedly at the judge-advocate and paused. "Are you finished with Brandy Station, sir?"

Axline refused to be baited. "I believe the court is satisfied that General Stuart's actions leading to that engagement were at least slipshod, and at any other time, probably worthy of punitive action. And as General Pickett most perceptively pointed out, the embarrassment caused by this napping could certainly have led General Stuart into later rash action to make up for it."

Mosby spoke quietly. "Then you have nothing further to offer about Brandy Station, sir?"

"Nothing further."

Mosby picked up a sheet of paper and strode to the bench. Laying it before General Bragg, he said, "This is a true copy of a letter from General Lee to General Stuart following that engagement. In it, General Lee refers to Brandy Station as Fleetwood Hill."

Bragg glanced at the paper and handed it back to Mosby, who read:

To Maj. Gen. J. E. B. Stuart, *Commanding Cavalry:*
General:

I have received and read, with much pleasure, your report of the recent engagement at Fleetwood.

The dispositions made by you to meet the strong attack of the enemy appear to have been judicious and well-planned. The troops were well and skillfully managed, and, with few exceptions, conducted themselves with marked gallantry.

The result of this action calls for our grateful thanks to Almighty God, and is honorable alike to the officers and men engaged.

Very respectfully, your obedient servant,
R. E. Lee,
General.

Mosby walked quickly to Axline's table and gave him the sheet of paper. Turning back to the bench, he said, "I believe that should resolve the matter."

★　★　★

M OSBY looked up from his desk at the knock on the outer office door. He glanced at the clock on the wall—it was ten minutes after eight; he had been in his office over three hours since the recess of the court. The knock was more persistent the second time. "All right, all right," he said, opening it to find Spring Blakely standing outside twirling a silk parasol that matched her pale blue dress.

Affecting a jaunty pose, she asked, "Could a lady make an appointment with the barrister?"

Mosby smiled. "How did you get past the sentry? This is the War Department, you know."

"And my uncle's the boss, remember?"

"Uh huh. C'mon in. I was just thinking about you. In fact, you were disturbing my work."

"Good. And since I know you are so busy, I've decided to throw all custom aside and openly pursue you. Will that bother you, John Mosby?"

He chuckled, taking her hand. "It seems that half the Army of the Potomac pursued me at one time or another—why not a former Yankee spy? C'mon back and have a seat."

"Not until you kiss me."

She came lightly into his arms, standing nearly as tall in her heels. Their kiss was sweet, lingering, more promising than passionate. When it ended she looked deeply into his eyes and found them free of pain, soft and unguarded. She kissed the tip of his nose and hugged him tightly for a moment before stepping back. "I liked that, John Mosby," she said softly.

He nodded. "Me, too." He held one of the straight-backed chairs for her, forced his mind back to clarity. "I'm trying to catch up on some of the everyday work."

"I gathered. You were very good today, you know."

"Been a long time."

"But I sensed your patience. Bragg is an ass!"

He smiled. "You have just joined a consensus that includes all of the old pre-war Union officers and a large number of Confederates."

"So is Axline."

"That's his job."

"I know, but he enjoys it too much. John, I have been spying inside the enemy camp as you asked."

"Good! What have you got for me?"

She got to her feet, moved to the 43rd Battalion flag in the corner. "Longstreet came by for coffee last night and mentioned something that might be important. . . . Did you know anything about a spy coming to him just a few days before Gettysburg?"

"Yes, a man named Harrison. We're trying to locate him."

She frowned. "Oh, drat. And I thought I had something big for you. I was going to tell you all about Old Pete taking this spy to General Lee and all."

"It was a good try, but it's in the official records."

"Let me finish. Last night, General Longstreet said the information this Harrison provided was more accurate than any cavalry could have provided. Isn't that meaningful?"

Mosby stared at her for a moment. "Pete said that, *specifically?*"

"I heard him as I came up to pay my respects."

Mosby banged a fist into his palm. "God, if we could only get him to say that on the witness stand! It blows away any premise that Lee was caught flat-footed because Stuart was away. Wait'll Jeb hears this!"

She came back into his arms, delighted that she had pleased him. Her lips brushed his. "How long do you have to work tonight?" she murmured.

"Just long enough to blow out this lamp. Then I'll walk you home on my way over to Jeb's house."

Spring stuck out her lower lip in a mock pout. "See what kind of a reward I get."

★   ★   ★

IN THE New Richmond Theater on Broad Street, Verita was more than glad to call it quits for the day. The play Higginson had arranged for her to be in, *Lincoln Splits Rails Again,* was due to open in two nights and it had taken all of her considerable cheek and ingenuity to cover her inexperience and to adapt quickly. Fortunately her role as the French ambassador's wife called for her to be on stage only eight times. And since she was supposed to be French, everyone overlooked her minor bumbling. Also, the great tragedian Edwin

Booth, who had come down from New York for this change of pace, had been most kind.

It was twenty minutes before nine, and the cast had been in rehearsal since early afternoon. As Verita started to leave, the stage manager said, "Oh, Mademoiselle Jolie, I nearly forgot—a note came for you." He handed her a small envelope.

A wax government seal was on the flap. Opening it quickly, she read:

> My dear Mademoiselle,
> Your most charming hostess has granted me permission to provide supper for you tonight when you finish rehearsal. My carriage awaits in front.
> Yours with enchantment,
> Judah

Her weariness eroded instantly as the flash of excitement surged through her. She didn't think he would make his move so quickly. But then, it would be like him; a man of such power wouldn't wait. Those black eyes of his had probably burned in anticipation all day. She smiled to herself as she placed the note in her bag and made her way to the stage entrance.

The carriage was black enamel trimmed in gold, the horses handsome and pure white under a shiny black harness with brass accoutrements. The liveried driver was light-skinned, a huge man with the bearing of a servant who attended someone highly important. "Mademoiselle Jolie?" he asked in a deep, haughty voice. "I am from the house of Ambassador Judah P. Benjamin, and I am to take you there at once."

She wondered what such a pompous man might do in the coming revolution. But she merely nodded and murmured, *"Enchanté."*

★ ★ ★

JUDAH Benjamin had leased the Davenport house at 9 Main Street early in the war when he moved out of the Spottswood Hotel. A dignified old brick home of three stories, it had served as a billet for the transient congressmen from Louisiana and any friends from New Orleans who might be spending time in the capital in those days.

But early in '65 he had purchased the place, had it fully remodeled, and made it his permanent residence. A full staff of servants kept it ready for his frequent visits. It was a far cry from Bellechasse, the plantation mansion he had sold many years earlier in Louisiana, and much less elaborate than the Decatur House in Washington.

Now, in the high-ceilinged dining room, the beaming cook placed a chocolate cake in front of Judah. Atop the thick dark icing burned five large candles and five smaller ones. He thanked her, turned his warm smile to Verita on his right. "Oh, I forgot to mention—today is my birthday."

"How lovely!" Verita replied brightly.

"Yes, and now I must make a wish." He touched her hand. "It is the custom that one must do so secretly . . . but I openly wish, my dear, that our relationship may be one of warmth and beauty." He blew out the candles.

"I wish you had told me," she murmured, held by his intense gaze. "A present perhaps—"

His hand lingered over hers. "You are a dazzling gift, *cherie*. And now . . ." He reached for a decanter. "A marvelous old brandy from the cabinet of Napoleon."

They toasted each other.

"And where did the rich life of the suave ambassador begin?" she asked.

"It was on St. Croix in the Virgin Islands. Although my parents were humble merchants from London, my mother's ancestors were prominent Sephardic Jews from Spain who fled to Portugal at the time of the Inquisition.

"When I was two years old, my parents came to Wilmington, North Carolina, to begin a new life. Later, about the time of that terrible slave uprising in Eighteen-twenty-two, we moved to Charleston. . . ."

Verita knew the facts of the '22 uprising effort vividly. Denmark Vesey, a free Negro, had planned the Charleston insurrection that was to include the commandeering of a ship to take the insurgents to Santo Domingo—an independent Negro state. But word of the plan leaked out, and eventually thirty-five of the participants were hanged as an object lesson. Vesey was one of the first on the gallows, and at one time twenty-two black bodies were strung up side-by-side.

She stared through Judah. *Nothing would be right until the day when twenty-two WHITE bodies hung side-by-side in Charleston!*

Judah went on, "I attended Yale and then went down to New Orleans where I became a lawyer and finally entered politics: eight years in the United States Senate and then four in the cabinet of this country." He chuckled. "And there you have it, my dear, from womb to brandy." He raised his glass. "To the beginning of my new life."

She washed Charleston away, smiled, held up her glass. "To your new life. And where does it lead?"

"To the White House on Clay Street."

Verita blinked, genuinely surprised. "You mean you are going to be president?"

"I want to be the first Jewish president of a major country."

"Do you think you have a chance? I mean, doesn't the South resent Jews almost as much as Negroes?"

His dark eyes bored into hers, radiating his natural confidence. "I've been attorney general, secretary of War, and secretary of State in this government—and at times during the war, I was called 'the Brains of the Confederacy.' Certainly, these are logical qualifications."

"When is this going to happen?"

He cocked his head, raised an eyebrow. "I must be patient. Davis will win this time, and Lee will probably follow—if his health permits. Then it will be my turn."

She raised her glass again. "As I said, to your new life."

He went to her chair, drew her to her feet. She inhaled his subtle cologne, felt the strength in his thick body. She had known from that first moment in Bessica's music room that he would arouse her. He was the enemy, the *epitome* of the enemy, and she wanted him wildly, violently—she wanted to drain him, suck that proud power right out of him and smash him to the ground like a mass of jelly.

Those eyes, the touch: he would be a master in bed, so magnificent that any passionate lover would become his slave. Any but her, because already she hated him. Hatred was her weapon; and it would be unmatchable.

Her skin tingled, she touched his arm. She looked straight into his eyes without blinking as her lips met his. His tongue was firm, inquisitive, probing but gentle. Capable. His short black beard was wiry, more of his strength. Her fingers tightened on his arm. The urge, the want, was immediate; her pelvis moved closer, undulating ever so slightly. Under control, but for how long? She wanted to bite his lip, crush him to her! Rip his skin, envelop him and devour him, *destroy* him!

He ended the kiss, firmly pushed her back just enough to break the body contact. Quietly he said, "I knew it would be wonderful, my dear." Holding her chair, he added, "Now I believe we should try cook's cake. She makes the best devil's food in Richmond."

She exhaled slowly, fighting to purge the desire. *The bastard!* Maintaining full control. The master; toying, managing. Naturally—it was part of his prowess. *The dirty white Jew bastard!* She crossed her legs, steadied her hand as she picked up her brandy glass and found a casual smile. "Yes," she said quietly, "I think I would like something rich and dark."

"The coffee is right out of New Orleans . . . strong, if you want it straight."

"Yes, that will be fine."

"And then I must send you home. You must be weary."

She let the smile work at the corners of her mouth. He did play the game superbly. But she had to start working on her mission with him. "Yes, but I want to know more about how Jews regard slavery here in your country. I would think they would be staunchly against it because of their own persecution."

He sobered. "The Jews in the South, as everywhere, quietly go about their life. Most are respected, few are genuinely taken to the bosom of the populace. There is no persecution, only a lack of acceptance, so to speak. Holding a major office, I am an exception."

"But what about the slaves—don't the Jews commiserate with their sad plight?"

Judah looked at her quizzically. "What are you, a lovely French abolitionist?"

Verita smiled, controlled her vehemence, replied softly, "I believe all people should be free. How many slaves do you have?"

"I no longer own a plantation, and my servants here are freedmen."

"What will you do when the revolution comes—support the negroes, or grind them into the dust?"

Judah shook his head. "You French, always plotting a revolution."

"You didn't answer my question."

He looked into her eyes for a moment before replying, "Mademoiselle, I am a Southerner."

She decided not to push it any further.

★ ★ ★

B ENJAMIN'S pretentious driver stopped his carriage in front of
Bessica Adams Southwick's mansion on East Clay at shortly
after eleven. The three-storied house was dark except for the parlor
and a light burning in the entry. She thanked the driver, Charles, as
he helped her out of the vehicle. But as he drove away and she started
up the walkway, a voice called out to her from the shadows across the
street where a one-horse shay was parked.

It was Salmon.

She glanced around quickly to see if anyone was watching, and then
hurried across the street. He held out his hand from the dark interior.
"Get in, I have to talk to you." His tone was peremptory.

"Why are you following me?"

"What were you doing at that man's house all evening?"

"He asked me to dinner. Why?"

"I just don't like you getting too involved with him, that's all."

"Really, Salmon, you sound peevish. You know perfectly well that
I have to work my way into his confidence to get the information
Higginson wants. What do you expect me to do—just come out and
ask him, 'Look, Mr. Ambassador, do you know about the Jews who
are financing a Negro revolution?' "

"I just don't like it one damned bit."

"You don't have to like it."

Salmon grabbed her wrist, leaned into her face. "I'm not blind—I
know what he wants! That goddamned old man, I don't want him
touching you!"

She jerked away from his grip, her eyes blazing. "He isn't old and
never will be! He has a special charm and vigor that stems from an
intellect you wouldn't understand. Now stop acting like a jealous *child!*"

It was the closest he had ever come to hitting her. "*I* am the leader
of Amistad, and you will do as I command. Do you *understand?*"

Her voice was brittle. "You forget, *mon cher,* that no one rules me,
and *no one* tells me what men I will have in my life."

Silence followed until suddenly she laughed. The whole thing was
ludicrous. She laughed again. "Do you think you are in love with me,
Salmon Brown?"

He had trouble answering. "Of course not. I just won't have our
mission endangered by, by your involvements, that's all."

"What do I have to do to prove my burning loyalty, Captain Brown,
go to bed with you?"

The question hit him like the lash of a whip. God, there wasn't anything he wanted more. Since that night of the anti-slavery meeting in Washington, he had been smothered by desire for her. He hated himself for it. But why did she have to *talk* about it? No lady talked about such things. "No," he managed gruffly. "Of course not. Just don't forget where we're going—straight toward our goal. No deviations, no entanglements that could threaten our plan."

"Then why are you here?"

"To bring you up to date." He pushed away the tightness in his stomach as he told her about the rest of the Amistad members and the warehouse.

When he finished, she gripped his arm. "I'm so glad. Oh, Salmon, let's not fight. We have a glorious mission, and that's all that's important. And, in case our Mr. Benjamin troubles you, he is going to get one of my first bullets!"

He looked into her shining eyes, glanced down at her hand on his arm. "Yes, well—" He cleared his throat. "I just don't want you getting so involved with him that you lose sight of our major mission." He managed a "good night" as she jumped down from the shay, then stared at his arm where she had gripped it. Her touch lingered. And the anger returned, the taste of bile when he thought of her naked in the dark, hairy old Jew's arms.

★ ★

8

★ ★

DAY 2

"MAJOR von Borcke," John Mosby began as he approached the witness stand, "I want first of all to thank you for coming down from Washington to appear at this court, and also for your considerable services to the cavalry of the Confederacy during the recent war. Now, I would like for you to tell us, as informally as possible, about the skirmishes and other battles that occurred in the Blue Ridge Mountains with General Stuart's command following the Battle of Brandy Station in June of Eighteen-sixty-three."

Heros von Borcke was a blond giant of six feet four inches, weighing around two hundred and forty pounds. It was said during the war that he weighed thirty pounds more when his massive cavalry sword was strapped to his side. Von Borcke had served on the staff of the Prince of Prussia before taking ship to the great adventure of the American Civil War. Robust, lover of a good time, and a consummate cavalryman, he was destined to serve with the Knight of the Golden Spurs, as certainly as if it had been ordained at some great international round table. Riding what was reported to be the largest horse in the Confederacy, he became Stuart's chief-of-staff.

He was now thirty-one and spoke with a thick accent.

"Well, gentlemen," he said with a broad grin to the generals of the court, "I must say for sure this whole thing is a mistake because General Stuart would never do anything that wasn't best for his army—I know, I rode at his side for a whole year. In battle he was a *meister*. I will never forget the day I met him. . . ."

"It was at the Battle of Seven Pines, and I had this letter of, how do you say it? . . . *introduction* from your Secretary of War Randolph. The battle was so big, with so many brigades jammed onto the field, that cavalry couldn't be used effectively. So General Stuart's command was in reserve.

"But the general wasn't—he was everywhere, in the thickest of the fray, helping here, encouraging there. Once, *Herr* Generals, a North Carolina brigade in the center began to give way and General Stuart was, how do you say it—Johnny on the spot! I saw—"

"Major von Borcke!" General Bragg said sharply. "We are not here to discuss the Battle of Seven Pines. If you will, sir, please stick to the matter before us."

At the Stuart table, Mosby chuckled to himself. Heros von Borcke had always been one of his favorite, most entertaining people. But it was hard to contain him. Mosby said, "Will you please tell us, Major, of the activities in the Blue Ridge Mountains?"

At his side, Jeb Stuart smiled encouragement to his old friend.

"*Jawohl, mein* Colonel . . . but to be more *genau,* it was in the Bull Run Mountain. You see, General Hooker had moved his huge Army of the Potomac away from Fredericksburg and placed it between the Blue Ridge and Washington in a good blocking position near Manassas—in case General Lee might try to attack the Union capital from the west."

Von Borcke gestured excessively in normal speech; now his huge hands moved about in wide circles trying to show direction and movement. "But Hooker, he was going crazy trying to figure out where General Lee was—so he sent his cavalry to find out. It was Stuart's mission to hold the mountain passes and provide a screen to keep them from doing so. But as the last of Longstreet's Corps crossed the Blue Ridge, the Yankee cavalry got more persistent.

"And *Herr* Generals, you must realize this was not the same cavalry we had trampled like toy soldiers for so long. They had good long-range carbines and knew how to shoot from the ground. And they had some new commanders who were pretty good."

The Prussian pointed to the map. "So on June seventeenth, they attacked fiercely. Our brigades were spread out west of the long Bull Run Mountain from Aldie, through Middleburg, to Upperville, higher up to the west in the Blue Ridge. A wild battle occurred at Aldie, where a full Union division crashed into Fitz Lee's regiments."

Von Borcke looked out at the crowded benches, first smiling, then frowning like a schoolmaster about to make an important point. "You see, most military organization is triangular, meaning that a corps has three divisions, a division three brigades, and a brigade three or more regiments. And of course, artillery was separate, and at this time the average regiment had between three and four hundred men—"

"*Major von Borcke!*" General Bragg's voice cracked like a bull whip. "This is not a military academy, sir! We are not here to educate the masses. If you wish to continue, do so in an orderly manner to the officers of the court. Do I make myself clear?"

Heros von Borcke smiled, unperturbed by the scowling general. "*Jawohl, Herr General.*" He pronounced the rank with the German hard *G*. Mosby and Stuart grinned and shook their heads as the audience broke into laughter. Even Pickett and Hood smiled discreetly.

Bragg pounded the bench with his revolver. "There will be order!" he shouted. When quiet returned, he fixed his stern gaze on the Prussian. "I'll brook no levity, sir. Continue in earnest or I will dismiss you from this court."

Von Borcke nodded soberly. "When the Yankees attacked, it was a vicious fight. But our lads did admirably, as usual. Late that afternoon, I rode into Middleburg with General Stuart. We were met with a huge welcome. . . .

"It was a hot, clear day with the sun still bearing down like a great fire. Jeb, on his big horse, Highfly, laughed as he saw the ladies running out to meet us. 'Looks like this town might be fun, Von,' he said to me.

"I joined in his good humor, quieting my mount so he wouldn't hurt any of those eager *frauleins*. There must have been ten of them initially, but as shouts of '*Jeb!*' echoed up the main street, they came pouring out of stores and other streets until it seemed there must be a good forty of them swarming around us like happy locusts. They pulled at our boots and swords, at the saddles and our horses' tails. Several of them handed up bouquets of bright flowers, jabbering all the while like a bunch of magpies . . . 'I love you, Jeb!' 'Are we having a dance tonight, Jeb?' 'Will you dance with me, Hero?' 'Have you seen my Charlie?' "

Mosby groaned inwardly. *The well-meaning von Borcke was playing right into Axline's hands!* Earlier, when they had discussed his testimony, the Prussian had been more serious, but now, unaware of Axline's tack, he was unguardedly becoming a negative witness. He started to break in, but it was too late—

"You see, Herr Generals, Jeb had this theory: it wasn't all fun and sweet kisses for us when we weren't fighting. He knew the true power of your South lay in its *women* . . . they pushed, flattered, demanded, cajoled, and reached to the core of their iron grit for the war effort —sometimes throwing away a man who wouldn't fight as readily as a fisherman might toss back a minnow. And if they wanted to make a fuss over him and his cavalrymen, it fueled their flames, he liked to say.

"But soon, about four o'clock, the fun was over. With a loud clatter and only one warning shot from our pickets posted outside of the town, the lead elements of a Union cavalry regiment came galloping down the street. There wasn't a moment to spare! It was every man for himself. I jumped into the saddle, but Jeb's horse was too far away and he had to make a run for it.

"*Mein Gott,* it was close. It was a good thing that General Robertson's brigade was just outside of town or we would have been finished. Those Yankees fired their pistols and shouted at the top of their lungs; dust was everywhere. I swung around to find Jeb just in time to see him dive over a stone fence in a very undignified manner among Robertson's pickets. Ha!"

Mosby closed his eyes and groaned inwardly again.

"That made Jeb mad! At seven that evening, he sent Robertson to take the town back. And it was a damn good fight those bluebellies put up, but shortly after dark we chased the last of them out of town. And in an *augenblick*—the blink of an eye—Jeb and I were back with those lovely ladies. But the fun was gone—they were too busy caring for the wounded."

Von Borcke shifted his weight in the witness chair, smiled at Jeb, and went into a detailed account of the next two days' battle in which Jeb blocked all of the mountain passes and held off Hooker's cavalry corps and a full infantry division. At the end, he told of his own misfortune . . . "I felt a severe blow—as though somebody had struck me with his fist on my neck. Fiery sparks glittered before my eyes, and a tremendous weight seemed to be dragging me from my horse. Blood streamed from my mouth, my left arm was useless—"

Heros von Borcke twisted in the witness chair, faced the generals.

"Sirs, that bad wound in the neck took me out of the most glorious war the world will ever know. I missed General Stuart's ride through Hooker's army and I didn't get to Gettysburg, but I know one thing for damn sure—the greatest cavalryman in history never let those damn Yankees get through those mountains to find Lee!"

Seeing that the Prussian was finished, Mosby said to Bragg, "No further questions, sir."

The president of the court nodded to the judge-advocate.

Colonel M. R. Axline stood abruptly at his table. "Thank you, Major von Borcke, for your contribution. I, too, would like to express gratitude for your heroic contribution to the Confederate cause . . . however . . ." The portly Texan let the word dangle as he wiped perspiration from his forehead with the red bandanna. "However, you mentioned being caught napping *again,* fooling around with the ladies in Middleburg. You said that General Stuart had to run and dive over Robertson's stone fence to save himself. What *possible* military worth can be found in dallying with females when a huge enemy force is fighting all over the area?"

Von Borcke frowned, glanced at Stuart. "There was no battle going on at that time. And I told you the general's theory about the women and—"

"Do you honestly believe playing *ring-around-the-rosy* on that day was sound military judgment, Major?" Axline was incredulous.

The Prussian's scowl deepened as he twirled his right mustache. "I do not see that it did any harm."

"Why was there only one warning shot from the pickets?" Axline barked, striding to the witness stand.

"I guess the Union cavalry arrived so suddenly that they were surprised. That can happen with cavalry, you know."

"Were they fooling around with the girls, *too?* Who was soldiering at Middleburg on that June afternoon, Major—*anyone?*"

Von Borcke drew himself up angrily. "Herr Colonel, I resent your accusation! I have never been derelict in *any* assignment in *any* army where I have served!"

Axline's tone was sarcastic as he directed his words to the court. "Of course not, sir. You were only following the lead of your commanding general. Oh, by the way, did he have his banjo and fiddles playing 'Boots and Saddles' when the Yankees galloped into town? . . . If there are no further questions from the court, you are excused, sir."

The court had no questions. The red-faced von Borcke stepped down from the witness stand as a buzz went through the audience.

Stuart leaned angrily into Mosby's ear. "Axline makes everything sound so dirty, so cheap. I should have the bastard's fat, sweaty head on my saber. I don't know how much more of this I can take."

"You'll have to take whatever they dish out because we're going to walk out of here with a smile on our face when it's over."

Stuart turned to watch the broad shoulders of Heros von Borcke leave the courtroom. "Poor Von," he said. "He tried so hard to help. I'm buying him the finest meal the Spottswood has on its menu tonight. I only wish it were possible to throw a dance for him, with Sweeney and all of the old boys. Fitz Lee and some others are joining us—would you like to come along?"

Mosby nodded. It would be pleasant to rehash some of the old days. "Perhaps for a few minutes, but I have a pile of work." He looked at his notes. Axline would now run through a series of witnesses from the different regiments in an attempt to fix more irresponsible conduct on Jeb. But he was only building up to General Longstreet's appearance that afternoon.

★　★　★

JUBILO leaned back in the chair in front of his old roll-top desk and reread the letter from Higginson, this time aloud to his brown, shaggy dog.

Dear Sergeant Jubilo,

I trust that by now you have become acquainted with my friend, Mr. Smith, and perhaps with his associates from the famous slave ship. I can't tell you how much I am counting on you to support their effort, or how very important it is to our Cause. And to me personally. I remember how much I was able to rely on you during our glorious days in the past war. Now that trust is even more important. Thank you, my friend.

Yours in God and freedom,

Your colonel, T. W. H.

Jubilo shook his huge head, touched the knife scar on his cheek. "You know, Dog"—it was the only name he had ever given the big mongrel—"I just don't rightly know how I can step out of the way of this thing. Deep down, a voice keeps nagging at me, telling me it's all wrong . . . but then another voice keeps a-pecking away at me and asking, 'You gonna wait forever, big man?'

"It's like I told Old John Brown's boy—these white folks down here ain't gonna have anything shoved down their throat. They just won a big, terrible war rather than be told what to do. And only the good Lord knows just how bad they will make it if we rises before we are ready. The Lord only knows, Dog."

The big man wiped the sweat from the back of his neck, got out of the chair and walked to the room's open window. The stench from a nearby pile of rotting garbage attacked his nose. Was it a sign? he asked himself. Or was it just a reminder of what the Negroes of the Confederacy had in life? The rotting remnants. How long would his people be the refuse of such a society if they waited for change?

The rest of the world was changing; slavery was becoming an abomination in nearly all civilized countries. Would, as the abolitionists said, the world powers eventually bring enough pressure to bear on the C.S.A. that its leaders would abolish the crime?

When? In his lifetime? In his son's? Maybe not even in his grandson's life.

And the freedmen, when would they have equality? Ever?

The colonel, the Reverend Higginson, he knew. Higginson had trusted him in the war, and now he was calling on that trust.

He ran the big wet handkerchief over his face, closed his eyes in prayer: Oh, Lord Jesus, help me to make the right decision. Thou hast given me gifts to learn and to lead, to preach thy word and inflict thy will. . . . Should I do as your other leader says, your white servant? Oh, Lord Jesus, there is no turning back. If I tells them to take up the sword, our holy Abraham will be baptized in blood that will never stop flowing. Help me, oh Lord. . . .

Jubilo concentrated with all his will, his eyes shut tightly, all else detached, pleading for a sign, anything, waiting.

Tell me, oh Lord, give me a word. . . .

His hands were fists, the nails biting into his palms.

Help me, oh Lord. . . .

A tiny river of sweat ran down his back.

But his only reply was the silence of the room, broken by a deep breath from Dog as he rolled over.

He wiped his face again, went back to his desk, and looked at his ledger. There was so much more at stake than those people up north could understand. And the wild ones of the South were no different. Shoot and burn! They didn't know you couldn't just turn a mob loose in the streets. That was why he had his guards regiment—so he could control the movement in Richmond. Long as those hot bloods were organized and commanded, he could keep them from going berserk. They were *soldiers,* not crazed animals. Nosuhreebob, Cunnel Higginson, there has to be sanity and control. When the smoke fades, someone's gotta keep the ledger books. . . .

Oh, he could do it, he could recruit enough ex-soldiers to form dozens of guards regiments like his own. He could be the boss man for everything, the whole Negro South. And that's what he wanted. But not now, not like this, with other people pulling the strings . . . uh uh! *No, suh, Cunnel!*

A clerk stuck his head through the door. "They's a white man to see you, Reverend."

Jubilo pushed his other thoughts away, relieved that he had made a sensible decision. "He give you a name? No? Bring him back."

The tall man in a gray suit with a short black beard was Major General John Rawlins, who stuck out his hand as he introduced himself. "I'm down here as an observer to the Stuart court of inquiry, which I'm sure you are aware of, Reverend Jubilo. But unofficially, I'm here for another purpose." He held out an identity card. "A much more *vital* purpose."

Jubilo nodded, watching his visitor's black eyes and deciding at once that he could trust this Yankee general. He also remembered hearing or reading about Rawlins from time to time. He was about the most important man Jubilo had ever met, he guessed. More important than Colonel Higginson, even.

"May I ask that this visit be kept a complete secret? The reason will be obvious when I explain my purpose."

"Yes, suh. Please have a seat, General."

"I'll get right to the point, sir. Unofficially, I represent certain parties who are interested in freedom for the Southern slaves. These are powerful men with strong political connections outside of the abolition movement who believe in enforcing the Emancipation Proclamation's conditions. They know about the movement known as Abraham, and wish to find out how they can be of help. Now I know you can't admit a connection to Abraham to a total stranger, and a white man at that, but I know you are the movement's major leader in this part of the

Confederacy. And I assure you that information is safe with me, because I could be shot for even talking to you about this matter."

Jubilo continued to listen impassively.

"There are various kinds of support possible—from equipment to educational needs, such as books, to outright money. But my people want to make sure it will reach the right hands, and that it will all be used to the best advantage. Are you with me up to this point, Reverend?"

Jubilo nodded. "The people in this movement would be mighty pleased to get such support, and that's a fact, General. That is, if there *is* such a movement."

"I understand your need for secrecy and caution, so there is no hurry. What we need to find out is how we can provide this support—who might be able to coordinate it, and who would be responsible to see that it is used properly." Rawlins paused. "If that man is you, we have to know your intentions and how you plan to carry them out. Then we can set up a channel."

"Can you tell me the names of any of these people, General?"

Rawlins looked deeply into the big man's dark eyes and found what he was seeking. He spoke quietly. "I'll give you just one—the man who *personally* asked me to see you . . . Abraham Lincoln."

Jubilo knew his eyes were wide, and that his mouth dropped open. He just nodded, unable to think of anything to say. Finally, he replied, "Yes, suh, General, that's a mighty strong name."

"When do you think we can talk further?"

"What hotel are you staying in, General?"

"The Spottswood."

"I'll send word if I hear of anything."

Rawlins nodded, shook hands. "I'll be waiting."

As the Yankee officer departed, Jubilo couldn't restrain a broad grin. "You hear that, Dog? *Mr. Lincoln, himself!*"

★　★　★

SPECTATORS were streaming back into the courtroom as Mosby craned around to watch Spring Blakely precede her uncle, John Breckinridge, into their seats. She caught his eye as she sat down, held up the note he had sent her, and nodded her head with a broad smile. He nodded that he understood—she would join him for dinner that evening.

"I wonder what Old Pete will have to say," Jeb said from his elbow.

"He won't do you any favors."

"Speaking of favors, here comes your lawyer friend."

Mosby looked up as Colonel Axline approached their table. "Uh, Colonel Mosby, there's a problem with my agenda. General Longstreet is ill and won't be able to appear today. Do you have a witness you would like to use?"

Mosby frowned, had a sinking feeling. *Goddamnit!* Was Longstreet really sick? He had been all prepared to bring this court toward a logical end with Longstreet. He was the key to the orders. The surprise witness, the Yankee general, could be brought in on a day's notice. The only missing element was the spy, Harrison. Still—

"I said, do you have a witness, Mosby?"

Mosby shook off his disappointment. "Yes . . . me."

Axline's eyebrows went up. "You?"

"Yes, it's sequentially time for someone who knows exactly what happened at that stage of the march to Pennsylvania to present the facts."

"Isn't that irregular—I mean, you are counsel for the—"

Mosby smiled. "Counsel for the *defense*? Colonel, I dearly wish you would admit that in open court."

Axline didn't even smile.

"Besides, this is a court of inquiry, and anyone can provide testimony—right, Colonel?"

As Axline moved back to his table, Jeb asked, "Isn't it dangerous for you to take the stand? I mean, you won't let *me* on the stand."

"It's better than having him parade some more antagonistic witnesses there to get us deeper in the hole."

Five minutes later, Mosby took the witness stand and was reminded that he was under oath. He began his statement pleasantly: "For those of you who are wondering how our heroic Major von Borcke fared after the nearly fatal wound that damaged his windpipe and lodged in his lung, he had a miraculous recovery that included evading the Yankees in a close call." Mosby smiled. "As we all know, he recovered full use of his voice."

He cleared his throat, spoke in a calm, clear voice, "Shortly after the Bull Run Mountain battles that he spoke of, the Union cavalry pulled away, leaving the vital passes in General Stuart's hands. On

June twenty-first, Lee's main army continued to move northward up the Shenandoah Valley, nearly seventy thousand strong. While east of the mountains, Hooker acted tentatively, waiting for word of Lee's intentions—leery that he might wheel and drive for Washington. His Army of the Potomac numbered well over a hundred thousand.

"General Ewell, recovered from his loss of a leg, already had his Second Corps across the Potomac into Maryland when he received word from General Lee to proceed into Pennsylvania. Ewell moved fast, and elements of Longstreet's First Corps crossed the Potomac behind him."

Mosby smiled. "Fact is, there is a story that a number of Maryland women will never forget that river crossing—it seems that a whole bunch of Old Pete's men scrambled out of the water with their trousers carried above their heads."

The titter in the audience quickly spread to a loud laugh, broken swiftly by the crack of General Bragg's revolver butt on the bench. "Colonel Mosby, are you trying to be a clown?" he demanded.

"No, sir. Forgive me . . . the next day, General Stuart received orders from Lee stating his fear that Hooker might 'steal a march and get across the Potomac before we are aware.' He then ordered Stuart to leave two brigades behind and move north to guard Ewell's flank, if that were the case. But Stuart had a problem in getting to Pennsylvania—roads ahead were clogged with troops, guns, and supply trains, and Hooker's huge army was east of the mountains.

"At this point, I had just returned to General Stuart's headquarters from a mission that had taken my command deep behind the Union lines . . . and I knew the disposition of Hooker's army. His corps were widely separated, allowing room for a swift enemy force to move through them. I went to Jeb with this plan: He could swing through an unguarded gap in the Bull Run and cut through Hooker's army on a lightning thrust to the east. The rewards for such a daring move were manifold—*it would serve to confuse the enemy as to Lee's real intent, provide a feint toward Washington, allow the possibility of disrupted Union communications, and most important—draw the Union cavalry off Hooker's west flank where it was looking for Lee's main army.*

"And while accomplishing all of this, Stuart could be taking the most direct route toward Ewell's force in Pennsylvania."

Mosby crossed his legs as he paused for a moment. "General Stuart liked the idea, but he had to be sure of Hooker's latest dispositions. I volunteered to scout back into the Union army for a second look, and left immediately. Finding Hooker's dispositions essentially the same with little or no movement, I hurried back to report to General Stuart."

Mosby looked first at Pickett, then held Hood's sad eyes for a couple of moments. "And that, gentlemen, is my side of it as it happened. I'm sure when General Longstreet is feeling better, we can examine this decision more closely. Are there any questions?"

General Bragg looked toward the judge-advocate's table. "Colonel Axline?"

The sweaty Texan rose from his chair and approached the witness stand. After a pause in which he made a show of studying Mosby's face, he said sharply, "Colonel Mosby, are you trying to say that *you* are to blame for General Stuart's unsound action?"

"No, I brought him the information I just described. And I know of *no* unsound action."

"Then you are trying to justify your *own* action."

"I'm not *trying* to justify anything, Colonel. I'm merely providing the truth and facts so the court can fully understand the situation at the time."

"In your *biased* opinion."

Mosby leaned forward, spoke bitingly, "Colonel Axline, if you have other facts on which to base that comment, you'd better produce them. Otherwise, I'm going to request that the court remove you for misconduct—and *then* I'll deal with you personally."

Bang! Bragg's pistol hit the bench again. "I want no more of this bickering between counsel. Mosby, no more threats. Axline, if you don't have any sound questions regarding the facts, sit down!"

"Yes, sir," the judge-advocate replied. Turning back to Mosby, he said, "When you rode into Hooker's army, was it possible that you were looking for a way for General Stuart to do something flamboyant to make up for his getting caught asleep at Brandy Station?"

"No, sir. That would be impossible because our entire cavalry was proud of the victory at Brandy Station."

Axline turned to the bench. "I have no more questions for this witness, gentlemen. But I strongly recommend that you view his statements in proportion to his close friendship with General Stuart *and* with regard to his own involvement."

★　★　★

I T WAS just over four years earlier that the Brockenbrough mansion at 12th and Clay became the White House of the Confederacy—better known as the Davis Mansion. Large and stately with three floors, it was noted mostly for its Carrara marble mantlepieces that bore the figures of Hebe and Diana. A committee of noted Richmond ladies had outdone themselves in making sure it was furnished to suit a Southern president before they proclaimed it ready for the Davis family to move in. And Varina Howell Davis had done nothing to diminish that effect in the ensuing years. Her personal touches included a profusion of tropical plants in the dining and drawing rooms, as well as a thick cream colored carpet in the reception room—a fright to the generals with muddy boots who came in a long line to see the president during the war.

For Davis had never been one to delegate authority. Coupled with his intense belief in himself as a gifted military strategist, he had simply been unable to keep his fingers out of daily operations. Nor could he keep out of the Stuart court on this hot August night.

"General Beauregard," he said abruptly from behind his desk—he never would find any warmth for this man who had so opposed him early in the war—"I don't like the way this court is proceeding. I told Bragg that I wanted it short and clean, get it over with and file it away, so we can get on with more important things."

"But Your Excellency," the general-in-chief protested, "it simply can't be rushed. You might say the whole world is watching. It's being carried in dozens of papers from New Orleans to Berlin."

"Speaking of Berlin, that damned von Borcke nearly made a travesty of the proceedings from what I was told. I've a good notion to have the Prussian ambassador speak to him."

"Your Excellency," Beauregard said patiently. "You must try to realize how popular Jeb Stuart is—not only with those who served under him, but among the people. Did you hear about the demonstration in front of the courthouse today? Over thirty women with placards supporting him paraded up and down in the hot sun during the entire day's proceedings. This whole court may have been a mistake."

Davis glowered at his general-in-chief. "I don't make mistakes, sir. And this silly sign-carrying by a few giddy women is all the more reason to get this over with and, if necessary, hang Stuart out to dry." He jerked to his feet, paced a few steps. Pointing to the evening extra of the *Examiner* that lay on his desk, he snarled, "People like that ass, Pollard, are warping it all out of shape."

Beauregard had seen the newspaper with its headline: JEB AND HIS PRUSSIAN PLAYMATE FROLIC WITH THE LADIES WHILE DAVIS WAITS. He, too, would like to hang Pollard by the thumbs, but he had to be realistic. "Do you want the court closed to the press and public?" he asked.

"No, that would defeat the whole purpose."

"Then, Your Excellency, what do you propose?"

"Talk to Mosby."

"That would be a mistake. I've already tried once, and it merely made him angry. If he wouldn't listen to the secretary of War or me, he won't even listen to God." The general's point wasn't missed by Davis.

"Then, damn it, have Bragg tighten the screws."

"I'll speak to him. And what did you hear from Pickett—that General Hood seems uncooperative?"

"Yes, Your Excellency, he seems to feel that he shouldn't be on the court at all."

"Damn it! He isn't being paid to have feelings. This is an assigned duty and, by God, he'll follow orders! And what about Pickett—is he steadfast?"

"He says so, but I think something is bothering him. He mentioned opening Pandora's box. I think it may have something to do with The Charge."

Davis slammed his fist on the desk. *"What the hell kind of a court have we got?* I thought everyone agreed that Pickett and Hood would be perfect."

Beauregard glared back at the president. "If you recall, Your Excellency, you are the one who picked them."

"But you concurred!" Davis got up from his desk, went to his world globe and stared at it. "Well, by God, I want this jellyfish court of ours straightened out. Do you understand?" He turned to the Little Frenchman. "And, General . . . this is an *army* court of inquiry."

Beauregard nodded as he saluted. He knew his neck would get into it sooner or later.

> *For the moon never beams without bringing me dreams*
> *Of the beautiful Annabel Lee;*
> *And the stars never rise but I feel the bright eyes*

Of the beautiful Annabel Lee;
And so, all the night-tide, I lie down by the side
Of my darling—my darling—my life and my bride,
In her sepulchre there by the sea,
In her tomb by the sounding sea.

Spring Blakely smiled as she finished reciting the poem.

"To Richmond's own Edgar Allan Poe." In the slightly worn but still elegant dining room of the Exchange Hotel at Fourteenth and Franklin, John Mosby smiled over his glass of white wine. "You really must visit his former home, you know."

Spring raised her glass. "To my hero's hero. I shall do so on the morrow, sire. How long have you been a worshiper?"

"I began collecting Poe just before the war, but became serious about him in the last year. I have probably eighty percent of his works, evenly split between the poetry and the prose. I have a bookstore in New York trying to collect the balance for me."

The fine lamb dinner and the talk about Poe were only part of the reason for his exhilaration. The beautiful lady across the candles from him was the key. No longer did he worry about what to do when he was with her. Their blossoming relationship was so relaxed, so stimulating, that he had no concept of time.

The waiter appeared with the chocolate mousse and two large brandy snifters. Deftly, the man flicked a match to the cognac Mosby had ordered and a bluish flame flicked around the inside of the glasses.

"Don't destroy all of that precious alcohol!" she scolded.

"I didn't know you cared that much for it."

"Oh, yes, I'm a regular sot." She blew out the flame in her snifter, held it by the stem. "You don't expect a girl who comes from the heart of good bourbon country to be a teetotaler, do you?"

He chuckled, returned to Poe as they sipped. "He was immensely versatile, you know, with a wide variety of styles to suit his range of purposes. An astounding ability to assimilate and, of course, he was perhaps the greatest innovator of our time."

Spring had not missed the presence of the Poe works on Mosby's office shelves, and had refreshed herself on the author by reading everything by him in her uncle's library in the past few weeks. "Don't you think he saw himself in many roles?" she asked. "As Coleridge, often as Byron, as the epitome of the quixotic Southern gentleman-scholar—an egotist who liked to glamorize his past and his perhaps contrived romanticism?"

Mosby's eyes widened. How could she have such a grasp of the man? He nodded. "Yes, on all counts, but each point must be broken down because of the complexity."

"And what about his fixation on morbidity?"

"Now that, my dear, is a subject that could require weeks to discuss." He laughed.

"John," she said quietly. "I want to ask you something very personal, very private. May I?"

"Of course."

"Did your interest in Poe grow because of the death of your wife?" She reached for his hand, felt it tense.

His eyes clouded briefly, shutting her out. But he soon answered. "Yes, now that you mention it."

She sighed, hesitated, then took the risky step that could ruin it all. Her voice was just above a whisper. "Is it possible that you have been feeding on his fixation with the death of beautiful women . . . nourishing your grief?"

It struck deeply. How dare she intrude that far? Edgar Allan Poe had written with such beauty, such acute understanding, of the very shreds of his grotesque pain—it was almost as if he had known. All of the author's tragic and hauntingly beautiful women *were* his Pauline. His beautiful, blessed Pauline. He nodded. "Possibly," he replied stiffly. She had no right.

Her hand tightened over his. "I'm sorry, my dear. But I'm afraid I've fallen impossibly in love with you, and I must do any and everything I can think of to eliminate the barrier that is clinging there between us."

He knew the anger was childish, a backlash. He wanted to reject the naked accusation outright. But in retrospect . . . how he had bled over those poems, read them over and over, memorized them, suffered, and twisted the blade that tore his heart, reveling in the pain and the self-pity. Yes, maybe he had wrapped himself in the balm and fed on it, but was that a crime? He should tell her right here and now that it was none of her business.

But her dark eyes had lost all of their bravado, they were wide, brimming. He saw the fear, the awareness that she had gone too far, and he knew she was holding her breath. He found a short smile. "Yes, perhaps I have been a little irrational about my Poe. But maybe it was the way for me. Maybe it still is. Maybe I can put it in perspective now."

He saw the tear slip out of the corner of her right eye and run down her cheek. Taking her hand in both of his, he added softly, "Thanks, Spring."

Her smile was wet, bright. She cleared her throat. "Oh, that's all right. Tomorrow night we'll discuss why you like Shakespeare."

★　　★　　★

O N THE way back from walking Spring home, Mosby's thoughts turned from the warmth she gave him to the court. Longstreet might be well enough to testify the next day . . . *might*, the sergeant who was recording the proceedings had told him earlier in the evening. There was something about Longstreet that bothered him—the uncharacteristic outburst about Jeb that night at Breckinridge's, the possible involvement with a spy no one could locate.

The word conspiracy smacked at him, but he couldn't bring himself to believe that this particular general could be so involved. No, such an idea was too far afield. It was probably just that Old Pete was the hinge to the wrap-up, and he didn't want anything to go wrong at this late moment.

In short, it was like he had told Jeb: "Anything can happen in a courtroom."

Turning into the front of his house, he nodded. That was it, he was worried about that "anything."

9

DAY 3

E VERYONE in the courtroom was in an expectant mood when
Bragg reopened the proceedings at ten o'clock. He nodded
toward Colonel Axline. "Bring on your first witness, Judge-Advocate."

"I call Lieutenant General James Longstreet," Axline announced
in his clear twang.

Mosby watched George Pickett's fond smile as the former First
Corps commander moved his bulk to the witness box and took the
oath. He had looked into the relationship between these two general
officers and found that Pickett had been treated like a favored son
by Old Pete. He shook his head—if this were a court-martial, he'd
have challenged Pickett off the court so fast. . . .

Axline smiled as the general tried to make himself comfortable in
the witness chair. "And now, sir, will you please tell us your part in
the unfolding drama of General Jeb Stuart prior to Gettysburg?"

Longstreet began in his slow, deep drawl. "When the Army of
Northern Virginia was moving north toward Pennsylvania during the
latter part of June, I was the closest senior commander to the Bull
Run Mountain, or mountains—whichever you care to call that hill
mass. As such, and since General Lee had such strong faith in me, I
had supervisory command over General Stuart while he was fighting
in those passes with the Union cavalry.

"Shortly before I moved into Maryland, General Stuart and I went
to see General Lee about the disposition of the cavalry corps. Stuart
wanted to slice through Hooker's army, in between the main body

175

and Washington, then go north to find Ewell. He would leave one or two of his brigades behind to guard the rear of our army and to continue screening for the enemy.

"Soon after that, General Lee sent a letter through me to Stuart giving him permission to leave two brigades to guard the Blue Ridge and to take the other three into Maryland, meaning for him to rejoin the main army as soon as he got across the Potomac."

Longstreet withdrew a small notebook from his jacket pocket and glanced at it. "That was on the twenty-second of June. I sent the letter on to General Stuart, and informed General Lee that I had done so, since the order was subject to my approval. I added something to the effect that he should guard my flank as well as possible."

Longstreet nodded up at Pickett. "You remember, George, we discussed it that night." He turned back to Axline. "That's about it from my end. Everybody knows what happened—Jeb took off in his usual hell-bent-for-leather way, right into the rear of Hooker's army, and by the time he got done fighting his own private war and looking for some more of that glory he liked to accumulate, two days of fighting at Gettysburg had taken their toll.

"If he had just followed orders and stayed close, we'd have known exactly what was going on to the east of the Blue Ridge throughout the march into Pennsylvania. Then, as I had been suggesting to General Lee all along, we could have picked a good defensive position and soundly thrashed the Army of the Potomac. As many people have said, the war could easily have been over a year earlier."

The former First Corps commander nodded again, as if that was all that had to be said.

★　★　★

AND behind the bench, John Bell Hood's hand crept to his left elbow and slowly rubbed it. His eyes were masked, as he tried to listen to Longstreet's testimony objectively. He knew he would experience some prejudice when Old Pete went on the stand . . . the old memories would ensure that . . . the hot late afternoon sun beating down on the flat ground below the Round Tops at Gettysburg . . . the feeling—no, the instinctive knowledge—that his proud men would suffer tragically if they tried to go up that slope. He could see Old Pete's face now as they discussed it . . . the set to his jaw in that glaring, dogged sunlight . . . he looked more stolid then, dogged, like the sun.

The cover-up was beginning. He glanced past Bragg to where George Pickett was listening to his old boss as if God were speaking from the Mount. There sure as hell wasn't any objectivity there! Cover-up . . . oh, it was all so easy. A hanging judge and a puppet. And what kind of wood was Sam Hood whittled from? The kind that rotted, that's what—because he was just going to sit there on his dead ass and play the old regular army game . . . and let them get away with it!

★ ★ ★

"GENERAL Longstreet," Axline asked, "is there any doubt in your mind that General Stuart understood the intent of General Lee's orders, or of yours?"

"No, sir. None."

"Then do you feel that he was insubordinate?"

Longstreet had the look of a reproving school teacher as he settled his gaze on Jeb. "I think perhaps he was a victim of his own whim more than insubordinate. He was willful—filled with great and noble intentions—but willful. And self-seeking."

Axline paused for several moments to get the effect he wanted for his clinching question, then asked in a tone all could hear, "Would you say, General, that Gettysburg was lost because of his actions on that march north?"

The courtroom was utterly silent as everyone strained for Longstreet's vital answer.

"There is no doubt in my mind," he replied in a clear voice.

The courtroom buzzed with a loud sudden reaction, and for the first time that day, General Bragg had a reason to pound his revolver butt on the top of the bench.

Flushed, Jeb stared at the witness box. "I don't believe it," he said through clenched teeth. "He's always been my friend. I can't remember how many times I've gone to him for advice. . . . I can't believe it."

As soon as the noise settled down, Bragg nodded to Mosby. "Do you have any questions, Colonel?"

Mosby sprang to his feet. "Yes, sir, I most certainly do! General Longstreet, do you recall the specific wording of General Lee's written orders to General Stuart?"

The general frowned in an intimidating manner. "I do not."

"Do you recall your own endorsement to General Stuart on that letter of the twenty-second?"

"Not exactly. I know the gist of it."

Mosby lifted a page from the table, strode to the center of the bench and handed it to General Bragg. "Sir, this is an official copy of that endorsement. May I read it to the court?"

Bragg frowned, nodded.

Mosby began:

> "General Lee has enclosed this letter for you, to be forwarded to you provided you can be spared from my front, and provided I think you can cross the Potomac without disclosing our plans. He speaks of your leaving via Hopewell Gap in the Bull Run Mountains and passing by the rear of the enemy. If you can get through by that route I think you will be less likely to indicate what our plans are than if you should cross by passing to our rear. . . .

"I will omit the next few lines because they are not pertinent. It is signed 'James Longstreet, Lieutenant General' . . . But there is a vital addition—

> N.B. I think your passage of the Potomac by our rear at the present moment will, in a measure, disclose our plans. *You had better therefore not leave us unless you can take the proposed route in the rear of the enemy.*"

Mosby handed the handwritten page to Longstreet for his scowling perusal, returned to his table and picked up another page. "This is General Longstreet's reply to Lee: 'Yours of four o'clock this afternoon is received. I have forwarded your letter to General Stuart with the suggestion that he pass by the enemy's rear if he thinks he might get through.'"

He handed the page to Longstreet. Softly, he said, "Sir, I respectfully submit that because of the lapse of time, and the many battles in which you so heroically led your commands—to say nothing of your grievous wound—that you simply forgot what transpired on that day."

Longstreet fixed him with a cold gaze, cleared his throat, started to say something, stopped. He glanced back at the two pages, nodded.

"Nevertheless, General, you did give General Stuart *permission* to take three brigades of his command through the Bull Run and Hooker's army, if he felt it the best thing to do. Fact is, you *recommended* it."

Longstreet shook his head. "How do we know these aren't bogus?"

"The handwriting from which these were copied matches that of your other orders of the time."

"Well, I suppose it's possible."

Again, the courtroom was still.

Following a long pause, Mosby moved close to the witness box, leaned in. "General, do you recall a spy or scout by the name of Harrison?"

"What name?"

"*Harrison*—a man who may have come to you with vital information a few days before the battle."

Longstreet cleared his throat again. "I used many scouts—you know that, Mosby."

Mosby looked straight into the general's blue eyes. "Sir, I asked you if you recall a spy or scout named *Harrison*."

Longstreet pursed his lips, nodded. "Yes, as a matter of fact, I do. Secretary of War Seddon sent him to me early in Sixty-three, and I did see him while we were heading north that June. But I don't remember the details."

Mosby nodded, turned to the front row, gazed for a moment directly at John Breckinridge. *Just three nights earlier Harrison had been discussed at Breckinridge's table—and Longstreet had recalled specifically how the spy's information was as valuable as any cavalry report.* How blatant was this conspiracy? "Do you recall this Harrison's first name, General?"

"I do not."

"May I ask what this spy thing is all about, Colonel Mosby?" Brigadier General George Pickett asked angrily from the bench.

"Yes, sir. I'm trying to locate a witness who may have information pertinent to this court."

"Then I suggest you go to the adjutant general and stop this undue harassment of General Longstreet. In fact, Colonel Mosby, you had better remember that you are talking not only to one of the greatest leaders of the Confederate Army, but a senior *general!*"

Mosby nodded slightly, looking Pickett directly in the eye. Then he turned and looked this time at General Pierre Gustave Toutant Beauregard for a fleeting second. "Yes, sir," he said quietly. He had made his points. "That will be all, General Longstreet."

As soon as the former First Corps commander departed the bench area, General Bragg called the two counsels forward. "Gentlemen," he said, stroking his forehead with his right hand. "Seems my old sick headache is making another visit. I'm getting the white jagged lines that announce its arrival. Within a quarter hour, it will be splitting beyond reason. I'm, uh, afraid we will have to have a recess until tomorrow."

Axline was overly solicitous. "Should I call a physician, sir? I'm sure there is one in the audience."

"No," Bragg replied, reaching for his revolver. "All I can do is go to bed. It will be less severe tomorrow. We'll continue then." He pounded the desk. "This court of inquiry is recessed until tomorrow morning at ten o'clock!"

As Bragg hurried toward the chambers, General Hood nodded his head. "I saw this a dozen times in Georgia. He'll be for duty tomorrow, as he says, boys. But don't plan on him being his usual merry self."

★   ★   ★

G OING back to the table, Mosby pounded his fist. "Of all the *goddamned* times for that son-of-a-bitch to get a *goddamned* headache, it has to be *now!* Everything I've planned is coming together like clockwork. Longstreet couldn't have been a better witness for us. The setting was perfect for me to bring in our Yankee general and start the closing argument."

Jeb shook his head. "I still don't believe Old Pete said what he did. What's wrong with Bragg—have he and Longstreet been drinking the same bad whiskey?"

Mosby shook his head. "No, it's his old affliction, he says. Goddamnit!"

"Pardon me, gentlemen. Can you spare a moment for a lady?" They looked up into Bessica Adams Southwick's warm smile.

Jeb found a smile. "Of course, pretty lady."

"First of all, Colonel Mosby, I want to congratulate you on a most brilliant probing of General Longstreet. Why do you think he would want to be so duplicitous?"

Mosby shook his head. "I don't know, ma'am. I referred to it as forgetfulness."

"Huh! I don't think anyone listening believed that. What's going on, John Mosby—is the whole world against our poor Jeb?"

The power of the Southern woman—should he tell her? No, every woman in Richmond had already guessed that some great conspiracy was out to get Jeb; the flames needed no further fuel at this time.

She touched Jeb's sleeve. "Jeb, you poor darling. I hope this is over soon and you are vindicated to high Heaven. I'm glad about old Bragg calling a recess, there's just so much to do. My darling house guest is probably beside herself, what with the play opening tonight and all." She smiled, not taking her eyes off him. "Our supper party will be just wonderful. You all do have your theater tickets, don't you?"

They both nodded. Mosby excused himself; he had a date at the stables, and he had to simmer down.

★ ★ ★

I SRAEL Jones leaned on his pitchfork in the harness room. "I ain't got no particular news, Cunnel, suh, but they's some strange goings on in Rocketts."

"Like what?" Mosby asked.

"Well, the word's a-stirring that something mighty big for Abraham is coming along. And it all started last Sunday when this white man come to Jubilo's church."

"What white man?"

"I don't know, but he come right in the middle of Jubilo's service. Just stood there in the back, watching away like he was some kinda' visitor from the Lord or something."

"What did he look like, Israel?"

"Kinda skinny, short beard, sharp nose."

"Anything else?"

Israel fidgeted nervously, looked at the floor. "There's been some talk that he was Old John Brown done rised from the dead . . . come back to lead the People to the Day of Jubilee. That's what they's saying, Colonel, sir."

Mosby chewed on a piece of straw. "Have you seen him since, Israel?"

"No, sir."

"Maybe he was just curious."

"No, sir, I hung around outside after the service. And he sure 'nuff stayed and talked to Jubilo. Didn't come out for nigh onto a half hour. And Jubilo, he saw him to the door."

Mosby nodded; could be a dozen reasons why a white man would visit Jubilo's church and talk to the man. But on Sunday? During the services? Could have been just a passing preacher, or a Yankee wanting to see a good old rolicking negro church service. Maybe some kind of writer. "How old was he?"

"I never know 'bout white folks. Maybe thirty, forty."

"Okay. Now tell me about this word about Abraham that's stirring."

Israel shrugged. "Ain't got nothing hard, just that I heard Jubilo met with his closest old soldiers last night. And one of them is supposed to have said that something exciting is gonna happen. That's all I know, Cunnel, suh."

Mosby nodded. That, too, could be anything—a man like Jubilo would use a hundred gimcracks to keep things stirred up. Still, he couldn't discount anything. Not with Rawlins's warning. And the name, John Brown. He thought of the note to President McClellan and the threat that John Brown's body was rising from the grave . . . most assuredly it was pure coincidence, but nothing could be overlooked in this business. "Very well, Israel. Thank you. Now I want you to try as hard as you can to find out some more. See where this John Brown thing got started; see if anyone has seen this white man from the church since Sunday. And find out what Jubilo's up to. All right?"

"Yes, suh, Cunnel, suh."

"And Israel, maybe you could get a little closer to Jubilo . . . perhaps offer to get into a more active role in Abraham. There could be a nice bonus in it for you. Maybe as much as fifty dollars."

Israel Jones had never even seen that much money before. But trying to sneak something close to Jubilo? His eyes widened. "I'll think on it, Cunnel, suh."

★ ★ ★

THE air was heavy, hot, and uncomfortable, but the gay and expectant crowd that worked its way into the New Richmond Theater that evening didn't mind. Handkerchiefs and fans would take care of part of the body moisture; an ample dose of perfume or cologne would cover most of its offense. But no one would really worry about that, for it was party night in Richmond—opening night of a grand new play starring and directed by the magnificent Edwin Booth. That and the title were enough to bring out people who hadn't been to an entertainment all summer.

Lincoln Splits Rails Again was in itself a celebration for Richmondites. Its posters, plastered all over town, had in many cases been torn down as souvenirs. The title had just that right note of humor and derision to get a rise out of nearly anyone who read it—for in no other city in the South had that man been hated more during the war than in the capital. The fact that the title was a misnomer, that the play was really a farce about President McClellan, didn't matter—the eager playgoers were going to get a double barrel of enjoyment.

The town's dressmakers had been busy in the preceding weeks, as had the dry goods stores that stocked silks, satins, and crinoline. And new hats were as common as the fireflies that would greet the theatergoers when they returned to the outside air at play's end. The last ticket had been sold nearly two weeks earlier, and the only ones available at the last minute were going on the street in front of the theater for six times their original cost.

The New Richmond Theater was the name for the old Marshall Theater that had burned and been rebuilt in 1862. Over four stories high, with an ornate interior, it was the finest theater in the city. Spring Blakely smiled happily over her shoulder to John Mosby as an usher led them over the red carpet of the second floor hallway to Bessica Southwick's large box. They were the last of the party to arrive— already present were Jeb Stuart and Judah Benjamin, who flanked Bessica, and General John Rawlins. Bessica's butler, in white gloves, served champagne from a magnum in an ice bucket.

The greetings had just been completed when the orchestra struck up a bright rendition of "Yankee Doodle." A loud round of laughter echoed through the gay audience, something that would not have happened a couple of years earlier; then the orchestra would have been attacked for playing that song. John Rawlins offered Spring his front seat, but she declined, taking a crushed velvet chair beside Mosby.

Since the lower box was situated so close to the proscenium, they were practically seated on the stage.

"President Davis and his party are sitting in the box right above us," Bessica said to Spring. "But I promised Jeb I wouldn't go up and give him a piece of my mind!" She laughed. "Wait'll he hears who is down here!"

"Yes," Jeb chuckled, leaning toward Judah. "He might have a new ambassador to Washington by morning."

"Hardly," Benjamin replied.

The roar of the crowd drowned them out as the orchestra swung into "Oh Susannah."

★　★　★

WHEN the song came to an end, Jefferson Davis turned to John Breckinridge, who was seated just behind. "That's quite a party Mrs. Southwick has collected below us, isn't it?"

The Secretary of War and his wife were two of the president's eight guests. Breckinridge replied, "I'm sorry, Your Excellency, I don't know much about it."

"You know your niece is one of them—with Colonel Mosby, of course. I understand she's quite taken with him."

Breckinridge glanced at his wife, shrugged. "Yes, to some extent, Your Excellency."

Davis frowned. "That's breaking bread with the enemy, you know. I don't think it looks too good for her to be involved with Stuart, at least until this court is over."

The secretary of War shrugged. "She has a mind of her own, but I'll speak to her."

"And while you're at it, I don't particularly like the idea of McClellan's general playing ring-around-the-rosy with them either."

Breckinridge shook his head. "I really don't think I can tell him what to do socially, Your Excellency . . . uh, anymore than you can tell Mr. Benjamin." Breckinridge was another who was not intimidated by Davis. He had held too many high offices.

Davis gave him one of his cold looks, but turned back to the stage without saying anything more.

B ACKSTAGE, Verita sat before a mirror in the tiny dressing
room a lesser performer was allotted in the New Richmond.
On the table stood a dozen yellow roses, a gift from Judah Benjamin.
The acrid smell from the kerosene lamp had already made the room
stuffy, so she was pleased to hear the curtain call. "You are here merely
as a small portion of the major part you are playing in a magnificent
cause," she told herself firmly. "There is no reason whatsoever to be
nervous over a simpering little part in a play."

She stood, erect and beautiful in the soft gold silk gown that she
would wear in the first act. The gown was perfect for her, comple-
menting her coloring—particularly her luminous hazel eyes—to the
finest advantage. She ran her hands down over her hips, smiled at
herself. She was in complete control and would remain that way the
rest of the evening.

In the right wing, Edwin Booth stood with his hand inside the front
of his uniform jacket, frowning down at the floor, Napoleonlike, silent.
He was, of course, playing the role of McClellan in the farce. He
finally glanced up, saw her. "Well, hello, Mademoiselle Jolie," he said
with a quick smile. "You are the prettiest ambassador's wife in all of
Dixie tonight."

She smiled, asked, "Does it help to pray before a performance?"

"I wasn't praying, merely gathering myself."

"Places everyone!" the prompter shouted.

A minute later, the heavy curtain rose on a play that would long
be remembered in the city of Richmond.

★   ★   ★

T HE music of Ludwig van Beethoven, played by a string quartet
from the Richmond Symphony, drifted lightly through the
yellow mansion at 920 East Clay. The night was still hot and quite
sticky, and the millions of fireflies were indeed doing their best to

illuminate the outside air, but the theatergoers and members of the cast who were nibbling away on Bessica Southwick's late supper were enjoying themselves. The play had been a smashing success with a rousing *fourteen* curtain calls, and now the champagne was flowing. No hostess in the capital could even approach the feat of Bessica Adams Southwick on this night: not only did she have Jeb and Mosby, but the star of Richmond—Edwin Booth himself.

Booth, eyes flashing, was the center of a group in a corner of the large dining room. Another collected around Jeb nearby, while yet a third had as its core the lovely newcomer from Paris. "You know, Judah," Rawlins said, from where they stood off to the side. "I'm kind of glad McClellan finally took Richmond." He chuckled. "But it has been one hell of a long campaign. Do you suppose I ought to include a synopsis of the play in my report?"

Judah smiled. "He'd probably put you on the rack, and then call up his army again."

Rawlins sobered. "Speaking of that, I received a dispatch this evening with a note from Grant. The frequency and urgency of those warning notes to McClellan has increased. The latest stated, 'On to Richmond! The Battle of Gettysburg will pale compared to the slaver's Armageddon! Raise your legions!' Another said, 'The blood of the Rebel leaders will run like a mountain torrent through the streets of Richmond'—*in August*."

Benjamin sighed. "Surely, Little Mac must know by now that someone totally insane is behind this. Or a comedian. Why does he let it bother him?"

Rawlins withdrew a paper from his coat. "Here is an excerpt from an article in the Toronto *Star* from last Sunday. I intend to give it to Mosby later on."

Judah read the copied passage: "A former journalist from this city, a negro who must remain unidentified for obvious reasons, has in a recent letter stated, 'At last a revolutionary hand has gripped the sword of justice and liberty. Before another September reaches the oppression of the Confederacy, this sword will sever the head of the dragon that enslaves millions.' The Negro man further stated that he was a finger on that revolutionary hand."

Mosby caught the last as he walked up. "Something I should know about?" he asked.

Judah handed him the newspaper account.

Mosby read, frowned. "Do you have any record of Negro journalists in Toronto in recent years, General? That shouldn't be too hard to check out. I can send a telegraph to our Canadian consulate there."

Rawlins nodded. "That's what we're doing, and checking present whereabouts. I'll pass on whatever we learn as soon as I get it."

"What do you think about this, Colonel Mosby?" Judah asked.

"I don't know. Seems as though too many things are piling up to ignore the possibility that it may be real. I'll have my people concentrate on all contingencies."

★ ★ ★

"SLAVERY is an abomination. I personally think France will assert herself on the matter within the next few years." As clever as Verita was at her role, it was impossible to resist a response when an anti-slaver spoke her mind. And the lovely Spring Blakely had just done so. "It will take the form of protest, then official restraint on trade."

"Do the people of Paris care—I mean the everyday people?" Spring asked. Chance had provided them a minute of privacy near the corner of the buffet table.

"Of course, *cherie*," Verita purred. "Paris is the *home* of revolution, remember? And I have been involved with that brilliant Karl Marx and his movement."

Spring's eyes widened. "You're a communist?"

"Yes, of sorts. I like their thinking."

Spring smiled. "Oh, I think that's fascinating. Now, tell me about New York—is there much interest in abolition there?"

Verita nodded, wanted to laugh. "Yes, there is very strong interest in New York—not like in Ohio or Boston, but heated. I believe the movement will sweep the North in the next year. It is becoming like a beneficial fever, the way it is spreading."

"Good! I'm certainly glad to hear that. You seem very knowledgeable for a visitor to this country, Miss Jolie."

"It's because I care, and I read."

Spring was delighted. "Oh, we must have lunch together soon. The Stuart court is filling my days, but maybe next week?"

Verita nodded. The niece of the Secretary of War—of course. "I think that would be lovely," she replied.

"And another thing—would you consider speaking to a small group of people sometime soon? They are abolitionists, Southerners all, so you know we have to be pretty discreet."

"Yes, that might be possible. But what about Bessica? Naturally I haven't discussed my anti-slavery sentiments with her."

Spring patted her arm. "I'll arrange it."

"What about your Colonel Mosby—how does he feel about your dedication to the Cause?"

Spring shook her head. "I haven't been able to screw up my courage enough to discuss it with him. I'm trying to think of some easy way to do it."

"He's a slaver, isn't he?"

Spring's expression lost its enthusiasm; she shrugged. "Yes, he has two servants, but they have been with him a long time and are just like family."

Verita couldn't stop herself. "Isn't that what they all say?"

★　　★　　★

"I WOULD like to take this play on to Atlanta, Charleston, and New Orleans following a good long run here in Richmond," Edwin Booth said. "And then—on to Washington—it should be a *smashing* hit there."

"You'll need a vidette of cavalry to guard you," Jeb laughed. "Little Mac'll blow up the theater."

"I'd like to see his expression when he reads the Richmond papers tomorrow," a sharply handsome young man said as he strolled up with Bessica on his arm. He laughed. "It may accomplish something we Rebs never could—blow the roof off the White House!"

Everyone in the group laughed.

Edwin Booth bowed to the newcomer with his best Hamlet flourish. "Ladies and gentlemen, General Stuart, allow me to present my mother's favorite son. An actor who presumes on my reputation and talent, but is nevertheless becoming quite a star . . . my younger brother, John Wilkes Booth."

The new arrival bowed even more deeply. "The introduction humbles me beyond words, fair sibling." He shook hands with everyone.

"And how goeth the noble defense of the most popular hero in the south, General?"

"Fact is, I'd rather be attacking a staunchly fortified position," Stuart replied. "I know for sure I'd win there."

The younger Booth's eyes danced. "Yes, I believe all politicians should get the rack. You know, I was in on a plot to kidnap Lincoln early in the war. Just think, if it had been successful, there might never have been a Gettysburg."

Jeb laughed. "And I might still be some obscure colonel."

Bessica took his arm. "No, my dear, you would *never* have been obscure."

Again everyone laughed.

★ ★ ★

THE tray of desserts was seductive to anyone with a sweet tooth, and no one was more plagued by that malady than John Rawlins. It held whipped cream cake, orange marmalade cake, sour cream chocolate, blueberry torte, cheesecake, an assortment of French pastries, and some others that were total strangers to him. As the butler held it before him, he asked, "May I have one of each?"

"Try the Lady Baltimore cake. I had some this afternoon and it is delightful."

Rawlins looked up into the eyes of Marie Jolie. "Thank you, *Mademoiselle*, I mean *merci*. That's about one-fifth of my French vocabulary." He selected the Lady Baltimore.

She smiled. Dazzling, he thought. All evening he had tried to remember where he had seen her before, or whom she looked like. One didn't see many like her, even in a lifetime.

"Then I won't exhaust your whole repertoire at once," she replied.

The smile, those teeth. He had seen this beautiful young woman up close somewhere recently, and she had been happy, excited. "You look familiar to me, Mademoiselle. Have you ever spent any time in Washington?"

"Yes, *mon général*, I have." She dropped her eyes. "But I have no pleasant memories from it."

"I'm sorry. I didn't mean to intrude. You were absolutely delightful on stage tonight."

"Thank you, sir." She smiled softly. "Bessica tells me you are here for the trial."

He swallowed some cake. "The court of inquiry—there is supposed to be a big difference."

"Bessica says it isn't even a fair trial—that her Jeb is being crucified."

"Let's just say I've seen fairer examinations," he said dryly. "My friend Judah seems quite taken with you, and I can readily see why."

She curtsied slightly, looked directly into his dark eyes. "I'm highly flattered, but I hope it's only a passing fancy. I must be free to pursue whatever might interest me."

"And what might interest you?"

"A song, a breeze . . . a man. Who knows?"

"Do these new interests arise suddenly?"

"Sometimes."

He held her gaze, reading her implication perfectly. The air was charged. "Yes, freedom for new friendships is an important element," he murmured.

"You are married, General Rawlins?"

"No." They were over two feet apart, but it seemed as if they were touching.

"Good." She broke the look, glanced away. "I see the people are beginning to leave. I should be with Bessica. *Au revoir.*"

He nodded, watched her remarkable figure as she moved away.

Stopping near the piano, she turned back and gave him another long look.

Interesting! was the only word he could muster.

★ ★ ★

VERITA slipped outside to cool off on a back porch. The possibilities of her great idea were truly exciting . . . Major General John Rawlins! Judah had told her Rawlins was deputy or something to General Grant, and privy to President McClellan! What a remarkable opportunity his presence offered. If she could work out something with him, be seen in public with him, present an involvement of some kind . . . it could have overwhelming possibilities.

She dabbed at her brow with a tiny kerchief.

If she could somehow work it so it *looked* as if he was part of Amistad, the hotheads of the South would go straight out of control . . . a Yankee general, tied directly to McClellan, close friend and chief assistant to the hated Ulysses S. Grant, a part of the grotesque attack on beloved Confederate leaders . . . using a guise of friendship, but plotting with those horrible killers.

She laughed. The press would jump on it and blame the whole Amistad attack on McClellan! And those berserk hotheads would declare war in minutes! *It was perfect!*

★ ★ ★

AFTER dropping Spring Blakely off at her uncle's home, John Mosby had the hack drive him to the War Department. Lighting a lamp in his darkened office, he looked at the pile of paperwork that his executive officer, Sam Chapman, had left for him. On top was a note from Sergeant Ogg:

Sir:

I'm still having trouble locating our favorite spy. He may be in Raleigh. Apparently he is not an actor as most think. I'm staying on it.

Mosby stared at the note, reread it. Who was this suddenly spectral Harrison? What was it about him that would make Longstreet lie? Maybe he was nothing, just one of those inconsequential cogs that sometimes give out in a piece of machinery and cause the whole engine to break down. But it didn't matter now; it was too late for him to appear in the court anyway.

He switched his tired mind to the Abraham problem, and remembered what Rawlins had said at the party. Reaching for a pen, he dipped it and began a note to Chapman: "Send word to the consulate in Toronto. Request names and present whereabouts of all negro journalists who may have worked or lived in Toronto. Also description, if possible."

He got to his feet, yawned. When was he ever going to clear up his mind so he could sort out his feelings about Spring?

★ ★ ★

"I LIKE your friend, John Rawlins," Verita said from the over-stuffed chair in Judah's library. "He's quite handsome, you know. I imagine he is very fierce looking when his beard is full. It's so black!" She wanted to taunt Judah, make him jealous, keep the upper hand. It was the only way to beat him, the confident bastard! She had been stimulated in her *tête-à-tête* with Rawlins and thoroughly aroused by Judah in the carriage on the way to his house.

"Yes," Judah replied, smiling coolly. "I would imagine women find him quite attractive."

"And my famous director's brother, John Wilkes. How appealing he is. And exceptionally handsome! There's something special about him, something *intense*, exciting, even dangerous. I wonder what it would be like to do a love scene with him?"

Judah came to her, took her hand, and drew her out of the chair. "But my dear, I want you to do a love scene with *me* tonight, not some panting actor." His eyes were bright, compelling.

He kissed her, slowly, like the first time, exploring again, drawing her close. His tongue came outside, softly running around her lips; gently, insistently, finding her neck, her lobe, venturing into her ear, briefly but long enough, then back to her neck, and down to her shoulder, the first swell of her breast. He inhaled her fragrance, went back to her mouth. His hand slowly stroked down from her waist to the curve of her buttocks.

She arched up to him, undulating, gripping him tightly, biting his lip, drawing in his tongue. Running a foot up his leg, she hooked it behind his knee, drew him even tighter. She would devour him! God, how she would devour him!

He picked her up as if she were a little girl, and carried her to the stairs. His bedroom was the middle one, the largest. The fire was burning low, the bed turned down. He put her there. "Shall I undress you?" he asked quietly.

"No," she replied. "I want to take every stitch off in front of you." She'd make him lick his damned lips!

She went to the oil lamp on the nightstand, turned it up, and unhooked the top of her dress. Moving in front of him, she continued with the fasteners. He was on the bed, removing his shoes, watching. She kicked off her shoes, hummed a naughty melody she had learned in Paris. She stepped out of the dress and the outer petticoats, until only the full slip remained. Running her tongue around her lips, she held a bare arm high, stroked it with a caressing hand, ran her fingers down through her tousled hair, over her lips, pausing there to caress, and then down her throat to her breasts, where she stopped to stroke each one before both hands glided down and paused at her pelvis— then moved over the inside of her soft thighs.

Deftly, she was out of the last garment and naked before him. She laughed, moved close to him, undulating her pelvis and caressing her breasts in front of his face. She twirled and danced away, stood with her back to him, gyrating, swinging her hips, turning her head back, mouth open, eyes closed, messing her hair.

She was in control!

His hand touched her, surprised her. When had he gotten undressed? He turned her to him, his strong hands moving to the bottom of her buttocks, lifting her, drawing her to him. And then carefully he lowered her to the deep carpet, and slowly, powerfully, entered her.

She hadn't wanted to cry out, but never before had she wanted to *conquer* like this. His mouth found her breast, bit gently, found the other. She cried out again, unable to help herself. And again. *Oh, God, as surely as she breathed, she would kill him for this!*

DAY 4

THE line of thunderstorms that finally passed through eastern Virginia sometime after midnight was the frontal attack of a deep mass of low-hanging rain clouds that extended from the coast to the Blue Ridge. At Laurel Hill, in Patrick County near Martinsville, it was a sodden morning. In the rambling white house among the tall oaks, Flora Stuart was still flat on her back on the board in the first floor bedroom. For over two months now she had been married to that bed, and the sores merely added to the misery of her discomfort and unhappiness.

The foreman—her mother-in-law insisted on calling him the over-seer—had just returned from town with the Richmond papers, from both the previous afternoon and this morning. Elizabeth Stuart adjusted her spectacles and tilted her head back as she read from the *Whig,* the other anti-administration paper in Richmond:

> **The Stuart court continues to be more appropriately the Stuart circus. It seems that clowns are the order of the day. In the case of General "Old Pete" Longstreet, it was a burly, forgetful clown who held center ring. He couldn't clearly recall his own orders or actions at the time of what we are now calling The Stuart Ride. And when Jeb's counsel, Lieutenant Colonel John S. Mosby, asked Lee's Old War Horse about a spy named Harrison, the forgetful clown went blank. No wonder Gettysburg was such a massive blunder. One would have thought that**

Commander-in-Chief Jefferson Davis was on hand waving the signal flags and sending the smoke signals himself.

Flora stared blankly at the spot on the ceiling. That spot was the single most familiar element of her life—she stared at it in pain, in anger, and as she tried to hypnotize herself into elusive sleep. And she played her private games with it. It was a small brown waterspot, a series of thin brown circles—in all, no bigger than a silver dollar. It was her enemy and her friend. She talked to it when she was alone, and she cried to it—more often lately.

"That isn't derogatory toward Jeb at all," Elizabeth said.

"No," Flora replied. "What does Pollard have to say?" This was the highlight of her day, hearing the newspaper accounts and trying to picture the happenings on the inside of the old State Court House. And later each day when she was alone, she played a game to while away the tedious and painful hours: she pretended she was attending the court, and painstakingly imagined all of her activities, from selecting the clothes and jewelry she would wear, the innovations in her hairdo, to observing the participants and spectators and dreaming up amusing or entertaining situations for them. She played the game constantly, stretching it out until all hours. She particularly liked making bad things happen to Braxton Bragg—once she spent a whole hour having him look furiously around his quarters for his false teeth, only to find they had fallen into the chamber pot under his bed.

Elizabeth read from the *Examiner:*

There are now two hit plays in town, and both are farces. The one at the New Richmond Theater makes a fool out of McClellan; the one at the State Court House makes a fool out of Davis & Company. Old Pete Longstreet can't remember his lines, and Stuart's white knight, Mosby, hints at some dastardly spy. Ah, melodrama! All of the actors are fooling around with orders and non-orders and even the sleepiest observer is sure that Stuart and his cavaliers are about to ride off into the sunrise and capture Washington. But back to the playhouse—Stuart's newest admirer, the beautiful Bessica Adams Southwick—

Elizabeth caught herself, cleared her throat. "The rest of this is just nonsense," she went on lamely.

Flora closed her eyes tightly. "Read it to me!"

"Well, it just tells about her having some people to her house for supper after the theater—you know, opening night. One person was the great Edwin Booth. Isn't that interesting?"

Flora glared into her mother-in-law's eyes. "Read it to me, or hand it over. You know I'll see it anyway."

Elizabeth cleared her throat, returned to the editorial:

—Southwick, who not only took him to opening night, but brought the noted Edwin Booth home to her supper party later. Rumor has it that Booth will play Davis in the finale at the Court House, where Mrs. Southwick will sell flowers for the neck of Stuart's horse. And the farce continues.

Elizabeth smiled, patted Flora's arm. "You know how it goes, my dear, these terrible newspapermen—and particularly that evil Pollard—will print *anything*. And you remember how it is with those wealthy Richmond women—they'd pay a king's ransom to get Jeb at a party right now!"

"He doesn't *have* to go!"

"Now, honey, you know Jeb."

"Yes, I do! And that's just why I'm lying here like such a wretch. If he'd just quit turning so many pretty heads, and *enjoying* it so damned much, I would still be in Richmond."

"Sometimes a woman just knows her man is being faithful."

The tears burst, running down Flora's cheeks. "And sometimes she knows it's otherwise. I never told you this, Mama, but twice during the war I got a letter from girls who said they had slept with him. A girl in Charlottesville and one in Winchester. And there were other stories . . ."

Elizabeth held her daughter-in-law's hand. "Some females'll do anything to get a man like Jeb. I had the same thing with his father— how that man loved a good rollicking party! I remember one time when this young lady in Danville said she had gotten in the family way with him—pretty thing, with the blondest hair. I thought I'd die of mortification! Archibald just laughed, said she was nothing but a darned old sockdollinger of a man trap. Turned out she wasn't even with child."

"But you still don't *know*."

"I didn't *want* to know, and it sure doesn't make any difference now. Old Arch couldn't be in any hotter hell than he's in anyway."

Flora blinked away the tears, stared at her brown waterspot on the ceiling. "Have you ever seen Bessica Adams Southwick?"

"Can't say as I have."

"You wouldn't be so casual if you had—she's positively beautiful and so *rich!* I heard tell she could buy Richmond, if she were a mind to. No, Mama, I'm telling you for sure that if Bessica Adams Southwick wants my man, he'll be sorely tempted."

"Why don't you write to him tonight, honey? Tell him how much you love him and wish you could be there to support him in this terrible thing. That'll help him with his resolve."

The waterspot was sharply distinct. "No, I can't. If all he has to do is go to plays with beautiful women, that court can't be too bad . . . *Damn him!*"

★ ★ ★

J EB Stuart didn't know what made him so restless at daybreak that morning, but there was no sense trying to stay in bed. He dressed hurriedly, quickly drank a strong cup of coffee, and saddled his horse Virginia. With a glance at the threatening sky, he stuck his rolled-up old slicker behind the saddle and rode out of the carriage house.

Riding down Third toward the river, he nodded to the few people who were up and about, but mostly he was lost in his own thoughts. There was a sad, gloomy mood cloaking him for some reason—probably the weather, he told himself. Or because he still hadn't heard from Flora in all these weeks. Poor thing, lying there in all that pain and misery . . . That was it—*guilt!* He'd been sorely tempted to accept Bessica's open invitation to spend the night, even kicked himself when he got home for not at least visiting her bed. But how could he, with his poor wife—

He'd dreamed about that provocative blond woman and been aroused just before dawn. But he couldn't let it happen, not yet. Not ever, if he had any moral strength.

He touched the brim of his hat in greeting to an attractive young woman hurrying along Franklin. What could she be doing up so early . . . scampering on home from an all-night assignation? Maybe she was a lady of the night—one couldn't tell by looking anymore. But here he was, making hasty judgments. The poor girl could have spent the whole night at the bedside of her sick mother, and he was casting aspersions just because of his own conscience.

He turned west at Cary, rode by Mosby's house, wondered if his friend was really serious about that pretty Blakely woman. God, he hoped so. John Mosby had suffered long enough. . . .

Virginia moved leisurely down Laurel Street, glad to be out and shaking off the boredom of the stable. He knew she would dearly love a rousing gallop. "Maybe later, old girl," he said, patting her neck.

They were soon at the end of Laurel and moving down the sloping drive into Hollywood Cemetery. Jeb glanced around, thinking about the cloudy day when his cavalrymen had had their postwar ceremony here. He rode on up President's Hill to the east and looked first at the black wrought-iron tomb of James Monroe and then at the tall white monument of John Tyler. He still couldn't get used to the fact that these noble Virginians were ex-presidents of a *foreign* nation. Monroe's remains had been moved down in '58 by a New York regiment. Someday, in a trading of sentiment, would the bodies of these two leaders be dug up and moved to Washington?

He sighed. There were still so many things that took getting used to in this sister country situation.

Riding back around on a narrow lane, he approached the center of the large cemetery and dismounted before a statue of a charging cavalryman. As chief of the new C.S. Army Cavalry Bureau, he had originated the subscription among his veterans to pay for "a commemorative statue to honor all dead cavalrymen in the War of the Rebellion." More than enough money had been raised immediately, and this central plot had been donated for what was officially named by President Davis "The Cavalry Memorial."

Three men were buried there: Major General James B. Gordon, the fiery North Carolinian who had been called the "Murat of the Army of Northern Virginia," and had been mortally wounded fighting the rear of the Union cavalry following the battle of Yellow Tavern; Major John Pelham, the handsome young commander of Stuart's Horse Artillery after whom Jeb's daughter, Virginia, had been given her middle name; and Private William Teagarden, a hero at Cold Harbor from the 1st Virginia who was buried in the middle and represented all troopers everywhere.

Jeb removed his slouch hat, dropped to one knee and prayed for several minutes, but instead of lifting, his despondency only darkened. He thought of the blond, blue-eyed Pelham dashing about with his guns, whirling a pretty girl around the floor at a dance—*he* had been the epitome of the modern knight! Jeb's throat tightened, his eyes clouded; it never failed when he came here—the memory of Pelham dying with the shout of battle on his lips, a shell fragment in his skull. . . .

The scene at Yellow Tavern came back to him: the too bright day, the roar of battle, the smoke and dust . . . he had the big LeMat pistol roaring in his hand. "Bully for old K!" he was shouting. "Give it to 'em, boys!" He held the horse from rearing, shot a Yankee trooper. "Steady, men, steady!" And then the blow to his side, as if he'd been struck by a sledgehammer. The pain, trying to stay in the saddle . . . No! Sliding, the hot sun, everything red, loud—

"Morning, General, sir."

He turned. A short man in a floppy hat and a dark suit that didn't quite fit stood a few feet away. He looked very young, held his right hand up to his brow in a rigid salute. "Good morning," Jeb replied softly, returning the salute.

"Corporal Tommy Perkins, sir. South Carolina. I was a sharp-shooter in Hampton's Legion."

Jeb smiled, stuck out his hand. "Nice to see you, Corporal. Been here before?"

"No, sir. Been my dream to see it. I gave seven dollars and thirty-one cents—every penny I had—when they come around asking for the money. Never thought I'd see Old Jeb, hisself, here though."

Jeb's eyes suddenly clouded again. He wondered how many of them had given every cent they owned. He cleared his throat. "Just visiting, son?"

"Yessir—'til they get done with that darn fool court and everyone knows you're okay, General." He looked down, moved the toe of his boot in a small circle. "What they're doin's not right. I was along to Gettysburg. I remember almost falling out my gosh-durned saddle. I don't think I slept more'n forty winks for three days there. No, sir, ain't right."

Jeb cleared his throat again. "Where are you staying?"

Perkins grinned. "Oh, there's a whole passel of us, sir. We have us a tent outside at the fairgrounds. Just like the old days, General, sir!"

Jeb shook his head. They often didn't have even a tent in the old days. He put his foot in the stirrup. "You boys need anything, you let me know. You hear?"

Corporal Perkins rendered another stiff salute. "You just get this nonsense over, General. We're just fine, and that's a fact."

Jeb smiled, swung into the saddle, returned the salute. It would take more than dark clouds to make this day dreary now.

★　★　★

"ALL right, you can come in now. Single file and no pushing. Those of you what have been here before know the rules. The rest of you just take it nice and easy." The provost sergeant opened the huge front door to the State Court House. "You all know that if you don't behave, Old General Bragg, he'll throw you right out on your ear."

Salmon Brown was ninth in line; he had been there since sunset the previous evening and had slept little. But he had brought some sandwiches and purchased coffee from a vendor twice since sunup, so aside from being a little stiff, he didn't feel too much the worse for wear. Many nights without a bed in the army had been worse. He was directed to the last bench on the north side of the spectator area.

He wanted to take his suit coat off, but decided against it. If everyone else did, then he would; but not until. In no way did he want to draw any attention. Already, the man seated beside him—one of Stuart's former cavalrymen—had asked too damned many questions.

The man wiped his brow with a stained handkerchief. "Like I said, Smith, it gets pretty damned hot in here."

Salmon nodded, looking around the huge room. He wanted to burn every single detail of this room into his memory so he could draw an accurate floor plan when he returned to the hotel. He wanted every detail, so there could be no possible slip-up from a physical standpoint. He stared at the door on the north side of the bench. It was the other exit, leading to the rest of the building. They should have no use for it. He glanced around. The door in front was large enough, and the guards would be dead anyway. Horses outside, ready. Yes, that was the way to go.

The possibility of anyone other than the sentries being armed was slim—except for General Bragg having the famous pistol that had gotten so much attention in the newspapers. It would—

The cavalryman beside him nudged his elbow as some of the journalists strolled in and headed up front for their seats. "There's Pollard. He's the one what started this whole damn thing. We oughta get some tar and feathers, and run him out of town."

In moments the spectators with reserved seats began to stream down the aisle. Salmon noticed a gaily smiling Bessica Adams Southwick with another lady. Just behind them walked Spring Blakely, followed by the secretary of War.

"And there's that Jew ambassador," the cavalryman said, pointing to Judah Benjamin. "He used to be Secretary of War, you know. Can you imagine that?"

Salmon nodded, noting that the tall man with the short black beard who was with Benjamin must be the Union general, Rawlins. He looked somehow familiar; there was something about his eyes . . . But Benjamin was the one who held his attention. The one who was lusting after Verita. He glared at the back of his head—right where he planned to fire his first bullet!

"All rise! This court of inquiry is about to open!" the provost sergeant shouted as the three members of the court strode into the room.

★ ★ ★

J OHN Mosby glanced through his papers one last time as the court convened. Again he felt butterflies and tried to calm them. This should be the last day of the court, and he would need all of his skills to pull it off the way he'd planned. The orders—thank God, the legal world was built on facts, and he had them on his side. Surely these generals whose careers had been anchored on honor and legality could not ignore them.

Major Henry McClellan was his last link in that critical chain of orders.

Henry B. McClellan—fair, cleanshaven, and slightly round-faced —had been Stuart's adjutant for the last half of the war and was now a schoolteacher in Fredericksburg. Coming from an old New England family, he was raised in Philadelphia, but moved to Virginia following graduation from Williams College when he was eighteen. There, he was soon caught up in the Rebel cause. He was now twenty-six and the first cousin of the president of the United States.

As soon as McClellan was sworn in, Mosby approached the witness stand. "Sir, you have heard the contents of General Lee's letter to General Stuart on June twenty-second. And General Longstreet's endorsement. Would you now please tell us about the letter orders that Lee sent Stuart on the twenty-third."

The former adjutant turned in his chair and nodded a greeting to the court. "Yes, sir. The night of the twenty-third was miserable with an unceasing downpour. Our headquarters was at Rector's Cross Roads, west of the Bull Run. There was an old house there, but General Stuart had his oil-cloths and blanket spread under a tree out in back. I remonstrated with him about exposing himself needlessly, but his reply was, 'No! My men are out in this rain, and I won't fare any better than they do.'

"However, he directed me to sleep on the front porch of the house so I would be readily available to light my candle and read any dispatches that might come in. Sometime after midnight, a courier rode in from Lee's headquarters bearing a dispatch that was marked 'Confidential.' General Stuart always opened these personally, and under ordinary circumstances I wouldn't have ventured to break the seal. But with the rain and all, I didn't want to disturb him. So, with some hesitation, I opened it and read it. It was a lengthy directive from General Lee, containing instructions on which Stuart was to act.

"I immediately went out to where the general lay under the dripping tree and aroused him. With a mild reproof for my having opened such a document, he read the letter, then returned it to me and went back to sleep. The letter discussed the plan of passing around the enemy's rear."

Mosby approached the bench. "General Bragg, this is a certified copy of General Lee's letter, which I would like to have the witness read aloud."

Bragg nodded. "Proceed."

Mosby said, "Major McClellan, please read the pertinent parts."

McClellan glanced quickly over the letter. He began:

June twenty-third, Eighteen sixty-three, five P.M. Major General J. E. B. Stuart, Commanding Cavalry General:

Your notes of nine and ten-thirty A.M. have just been received . . . If General Hooker's army remains inactive you can leave two brigades to watch him, and withdraw the three others, but should he not appear to be moving northward I think you had better withdraw this side of the mountains tomorrow night, cross at Shepherdstown the next day, and move over to Fredericktown. You will, however, be able to judge whether you can pass around their army without hindrance, doing them all the damage you can, and cross the river east of the mountains. In either case,

after crossing the river you must move on and feel the right of
Ewell's troops, collecting information, provisions, etc.

McClellan looked up. "The rest is pertinent to the disposition of
the brigades to be left behind, and the movement of the corps of
Longstreet and Hill. It's signed 'I am very respectfully and truly yours,
R. E. Lee, General.' "

"Thank you, Major McClellan," Mosby said. "Now, General Bragg,
with your permission, I would like to summarize the situation at this
time. Of course the court can grasp it, but I think it is imperative that
the press and the audience be familiar with it."

Surprisingly, Bragg agreed. "Keep it brief."

Mosby went to the map, using his finger as a pointer. "At this time,
Lee's main army is continuing its march northward up the valley to
the west of the Blue Ridge. The river he refers to in his letter is, of
course, the Potomac. Ewell's Second Corps, which Lee refers to, is
hurrying on to Pennsylvania, with Early's division on his right. The
Union Army under Hooker is preparing also to cross the Potomac in
search of Lee, but continues to stay between Lee and Washington."

Mosby returned to the bench, spoke quietly. "What followed a week
later is one of the fiercest battles in the history of warfare, a conflict
that will be studied as long as there is war . . . but, it was *not* lost when
a cavalry commander *followed orders* written on the twenty-third of
June. . . ."

Mosby milked the pause.

"Gentlemen of the court, you have heard the testimony of Major
Henry McClellan. General Stuart's movement east was valid. One
sentence in Lee's order says it all—'You will be able to judge whether
you can pass around their army . . . and cross the river *east* of the
mountains.' *East of the mountains!*"

He paused again.

"Based on this evidence, I move that this court of inquiry find
General Stuart *innocent* of all allegations and blame in regard to the
Battle of Gettysburg."

A red-faced Axline was on his feet instantly. "Sir! I am hardly
finished with these orders. There is further testimony!"

The courtroom was suddenly filled with the angry voices of the
spectators, and once more Bragg's Navy Colt was banged on the bench
top. *"Order!"* he shouted. *"Order!"*

The hubbub slowly subsided.

"Request denied," General Bragg announced firmly. "This court is far from satisfied at this point."

Mosby's fingers dug into his palms as he fought his sudden anger. *"Sir! The orders are clear!"*

"Not to this court, they're not!" Bragg snapped back.

Mosby stood staring at the general, not believing what he had just heard. His legs felt suddenly weak. He found his voice, controlled it. "Sir, these orders are valid. I—"

"You're out of order, Colonel!"

"But you can't ignore—"

Bragg's pistol crashed on the bench. "General Stuart," he thundered, "either you control your counsel, or I will have him forcibly removed from this court!"

Mosby tore his eyes away from Bragg's, walked woodenly to the table and sat down. "I don't believe it," he said hoarsely to Jeb.

Before Jeb could reply, Axline said loudly, "The court calls Colonel Marshall to the stand."

A man in a dark brown suit came forward and was sworn.

"Please state your name, rank, and position at headquarters of the Army of Northern Virginia."

"Charles Marshall, Colonel. During the Pennsylvania campaign I was aide-de-camp to General Robert E. Lee and wrote most of his orders."

"Colonel Marshall, did you write the letter orders from General Lee to General Stuart on the twenty-second and twenty-third of June, Eighteen Sixty-three—the ones that have been introduced as evidence in this court of inquiry?"

"Yes, sir, I did."

Colonel Axline handed copies of the letters to the witness. "Are these orders in your handwriting, sir?"

Marshall glanced briefly at the exhibits, nodded. "They are."

He was a thin man, skeletal in the face, with a scraggly brown mustache. Steel-rimmed eyeglasses in the shape of small hen's eggs sat on his prominent nose. Descended from an eminent Fauquier County family—his great-grandfather commanded the Third Virginia Regiment in the Revolutionary War, and his great-uncle was the famous Supreme Court Chief Justice, John Marshall—he was a lawyer who joined Lee's personal staff in March of 1862. He spoke with an easy confidence that could be due to his being to the manner born and to his years of intimacy with Robert Lee.

"Colonel Marshall, would you say that you are quite familiar with most aspects of the Gettysburg campaign?"

Marshall's look was steady, his voice calm. "Colonel, there is only one man as familiar with that campaign as myself, and that is General Robert E. Lee."

Axline shrugged, smiled at the court and the spectators. "How do you qualify that statement?" he asked.

Marshall cleared his throat. "I have in my possession a copy of the official report of the Pennsylvania campaign—the same as that forwarded by General Lee to the Secretary of War. That report was prepared by me after much coordination with General Lee. I had the official reports of the corps, division, and brigade commanders, those of the artillery and cavalry commanders, and the medical staff.

"I conversed with the authors of these reports and was able to get explanations regarding what was doubtful. I was able to reject that which was conflicting or contradictory. I had General Lee's private correspondence with the officers of his army, with the President and the departments, his orders—general and special, public and confidential. And most of all, I had the advantage of his own plans and purposes from General Lee *himself*."

Charles Marshall turned, with what Mosby took as a touch of hauteur, to meet the gaze of each general sitting behind the bench. There was utter silence in the courtroom, as if this pronouncement had come down from the Mount.

Axline broke it. "Please tell the court, Colonel Marshall, the truth about the issuance of these orders."

The skinny man recrossed his legs, cleared his throat again. "There has been much discussion about these letter orders to General Stuart from General Lee, and their endorsement by General Longstreet. Naturally, I wrote the Lee letters, and I retained copies. . . . The first one, of the twenty-second, clearly directed Stuart to place himself on the right of General Ewell after crossing the river. However, General Longstreet's endorsement *was* inconsistent, in that it would permit Stuart to ride east through the Union Army, thereby placing the enemy *between* Stuart and Ewell.

"Therefore, General Lee instructed me to write the letter of the twenty-third. I remember saying to the general that it could hardly be necessary to repeat the order, since General Stuart had had the matter *fully explained to himself verbally*, and my letter had been most full and explicit.

"But General Lee said he felt anxious about the matter and desired to guard against the possibility of error, and desired me to repeat it, which I did. And of course we well know that General Stuart took his three brigades east into Hooker's army. The question is—did he have true authorization to do so. *He did not.*"

Mosby tried to listen closely, but he was still angry at the whole absurd criminality of the matter.

"There is no doubt about the intent of the order," Colonel Marshall went on. "Much to-do has been made about the phrase, 'cross the river *east* of the mountains.' This did not give General Stuart license to go all the way to the coast. There were several places between Hooker and the mountains where he could cross and still maintain the contact General Lee desired."

Marshall glanced coldly at Jeb. "The fact remains that there was no way he could get to Ewell's right once he let Hooker get between them. And there is no doubt in my mind that General Stuart knew *full well* what was in General Lee's mind, *regardless* of General Longstreet's endorsement."

Axline nodded triumphantly. "Sir, would you please repeat your last sentence?"

"There is no doubt in my mind that General Stuart knew full well what was in General Lee's mind, regardless of General Longstreet's endorsement."

Axline continued to nod his head vigorously. "And, Colonel Marshall, do you feel that General Stuart's actions in taking himself and his three brigades out of contact to the east of Hooker was a primary factor in the outcome of the battle at Gettysburg?"

Marshall didn't hesitate. "There isn't one single doubt about it."

Again the courtroom buzzed with noise, and again General Bragg's pistol pounded the bench. Axline waited until it was quiet before saying, "Thank you, Colonel Marshall."

"Do you have questions for this witness, Colonel Mosby?" Bragg asked.

Mosby inhaled, collected himself. He had to keep fighting. "I certainly do, sir." He stood at his table, spoke loudly, "I can't help but think, Colonel Marshall, of an old phrase that goes something like— 'he doth protest too much.' Certainly, due to your rarefied position with General Lee, you are most familiar and knowledgeable about the subject at hand . . . but why have you gone to such length to qualify yourself . . . unless you feel you have something to defend?"

Marshall visibly stiffened in the witness chair. His eyes narrowed, fixed coldly on Mosby. "Sir, I came here to present the truth of this matter. To do so, I felt it logical to present my credentials. As a one-time lawyer, you should know that."

A faint smile touched Mosby's lips, acknowledging the barb. "*Do you have something to defend, Colonel Marshall*—perhaps the fact that your writing of these letter orders lacked clarity?"

"I see no lack of clarity in them."

"Do you disagree that they gave General Stuart ambiguous directions?"

"Most certainly I disagree. General Stuart knew precisely what General Lee's intentions were."

"That's an assumption. How can you presume to know precisely what General Stuart knew? And furthermore, how did you know exactly what was in General Lee's mind? Were you present at the conference between Lee and Stuart?"

"No, but the general told me about it."

Mosby turned to the bench. "Gentlemen, as general officers, you have seen and written hundreds of orders. In many cases, you have had aides or adjutants write them for you. Often—whether busy, tired, or just distracted—you have given them a brief look to make sure the gist is right. And signed them.

"I submit that this is the case here. Colonel Marshall, in all good faith, tried to write General Lee's desires in the last letter, but they were simply not explicit enough if Lee was directing only one course for Stuart. And General Lee, perhaps, signed the letter after only scanning it. Whatever the reason, it was an *imperfect* order and General Stuart had license to follow his own best judgment. In fact, we must remember the phrase—'*You be the judge.*'

"And he was. Based on his intelligence about Hooker's army sitting mostly still, he saw that his most direct route to meet Ewell's right wing in Pennsylvania was through Hooker and straight north, doing all the damage he could!"

Mosby paused. "Nowhere, in either letter, was there an order to stick to the side of the main army. Nowhere, gentlemen." He turned back to the witness. "Thank you, Colonel Marshall. I know your intentions are most honorable and I admire your loyalty. That will be all."

Marshall didn't want to leave it at that. "You don't understand; you weren't there."

Mosby smiled tightly. "But, Colonel, I *was* there. I was with General Stuart. Remember?"

"But you were only a scout, a—"

"I have no more questions, Colonel Marshall."

The witness blinked, cleared his throat, got to his feet.

"I wish to remind the witness that he is subject to recall," Colonel Axline said.

★ ★ ★

W HEN the court recessed for the noon meal, Sam Hood went out a back door and lowered himself to a rock under a nearby shade tree. Leaning on his crutch as he watched a white steamer making its way up the river, he blew out a deep breath. It was so good to get out of that damned courtroom. He had just hauled out the paper bag that held his chicken sandwich and apple when a woman's voice interrupted his thoughts. A voice from out of the past.

"Hello, Sam," Bessica Southwick Adams said. "Mind if I sit for a minute with you?"

He reached for his crutch to get up. "I've been thinking about you, Bessica. Whenever I look out into the audience, I pick out the face of the prettiest lady there and just stare at it."

Bessica fluttered her fan. "And who, pray tell, is that, Sam?"

"You know. You've smiled back at me a hundred times."

"Just flirting, Sam."

"I know—you're in Jeb's camp. That's why all I've said is hello."

"Do you mean, Sam Hood, that this silly court means the end of our friendship?"

Hood shook his head. "No, of course not. But at this moment it seems important things like friendships don't mean much."

Bessica lowered herself to the grass at his feet, spread her wide skirt. "They do to me," she said softly.

He was disconcerted by her stylishly low bodice; the view reminded him of how buxom she was. Their short affair had occurred while he was in the capital recovering from his arm wound shortly after Gettysburg. She had been in mourning for nearly the entire required year following the death of her husband. It had been completely improper, exciting, lusty, and irresponsible—an interlude of passion with no attachments. And they had gotten away with it without her reputation suffering. A few whispers was all, but in wartime, there were always whispers.

They chatted for several minutes, catching up.

Finally, she got to her knees, touched his only knee. "We had a spicy, wonderful time, didn't we, Sam?"

He grinned. "You and your mourning clothes."

Her smile was shameless. "They came off easily, didn't they?"

He threw his head back and laughed for the first time since returning to Richmond. "And often."

She picked a daisy, sniffed it, smiled into his eyes. Her voice was low. "They still aren't fastened on, Sam."

He tugged at his beard for a couple of moments as he digested her invitation and thought of how very much he would like to go to bed with her again. "But, my dear, the rumor is that you are panting after Jeb every waking moment. Why me?"

"We were talking about the end of friendships. Weren't you and Jeb once friends?"

"To a point, yes. But what has that got to do with making love?"

"You can save him, Sam. Don't they have such a thing as a hung jury?"

He scowled, beginning to lose his temper. "That's in a civilian trial, Bessica. Which this is not." He sighed, finally asked, "Are you actually offering to make love to me to save Jeb's tail?"

Her eyes brimmed as she whispered, "Yes, Sam, I guess I am. . . . It wasn't a very good try, was it? I'm sorry, I do still feel something special for you, darling. Really. Will you accept my apology, Sam?" A tear slipped down her cheek.

He flung her arm away. Turning aside, he said, "Go away, Bessica."

She got to her knees, touched his shoulder. "Can you forgive me, Sam? I didn't mean to hurt you."

He stared into the distance. "Just go away, Bessica."

Moments later, as he watched her walk toward the Capitol, he smashed the sandwich in his good hand. *This goddamned court!* It was poison. Eating away at countless people—making people crazy. Making one of the most desirable women in the Confederacy throw herself at a goddamned *cripple!* He had no damned reason to be angry at her— so what if she wanted to prostitute herself to save the man she loved? That was a hell of a lot more honorable than what he was doing!

Sitting in there listening to all this claptrap hour after hour was grinding away on him to the point where he wanted to stand up behind that damned bench and shout, "This is all a goddamned *farce! I'm* a goddamned farce because I sit here like a bump on a goddamned log and don't have the goddamned guts to do anything about it!"

But he wouldn't. They'd retire him in a minute.

How did he ever get in between this rock and a hard place?

It was boring sitting down there in San Antonio, handling everyday routine—but it was *honest*. God, if they'd just wrap this stupid thing up, he'd take some leave and go on up to the quiet hills of Kentucky where he grew up. Be nice to sit back and do a little fishing maybe. Maybe even find a pretty young woman who wanted him for himself. . . .

Damn, he wished he could take Mosby aside and say, "Listen here —this is what *really* messed up Gettysburg. . . ."

Or he ought to give Old Braxton apoplexy by saying, "I'm sick of this lie—*I* want to take the stand!"

A judge becoming a witness?

Sam Hood's eyes narrowed as the revelation struck him. *He and Pickett were on the damned court so they couldn't testify!*

The bastards!

It was so damned obvious it was pitiful. Sam Hood would tell it straight, and George Pickett—who was still living with ghosts—would be an undependable witness. So put 'em on the damned court. Huh! Brilliant. The bastards.

★　　★　　★

MOSBY was still angry when the court reconvened, but he was well under control. He had spent the entire noon recess looking through the records to see if a court of inquiry's findings had ever been appealed, and had found no such action. Finally, he had shrugged and reminded himself that the final authority, the president, was in on the plot. To whom else could he appeal—God?

He had made up his mind. No matter what the cost, he was going to play this damned thing out to the last breath. Somehow, some way, there had to be an answer. . . .

"The court calls Brigadier General Thomas Taylor Munford to the stand," Axline announced in his clear East Texas twang.

Jeb's head jerked around to watch his former subordinate stride down the aisle. "Now, what's he doing testifying for Axline?" he asked Mosby.

His friend shrugged.

Munford was tall, with thick gray hair and a drooping dark mustache. At thirty-five, he was, as one staunch Episcopalian lady described him, "a handsome devil." At the end of the war he had resumed his life as a Virginia planter.

Following the administration of the oath, the judge-advocate addressed no one in particular as he said, "Rather than waste time, I would like to move ahead to Gettysburg and end this inquiry once and for all. . . By the afternoon of the second day of the battle, July second, the massive forces of these two armies had been brought into position. Their horns were already locked in bloody combat—" He nodded toward General Hood, "Or they were poised to fight the next day." He inclined his head toward George Pickett, "—with immense bravery.

"Already dead on the Union side was General Reynolds, the commander of Meade's left wing, and on the gray side innumerable heroes had paid the ultimate price. The name Gettysburg was already becoming a household word from Canada to Mexico, and would reach to the rest of the world in the near future.

"In the midst of the heavy fighting, when brave Southern troops were attacking heavily defended rocky hillsides, our errant knight in the black plume finally rode on the scene. Having finished his glory jaunt, he rode contritely to General Lee, hat and some captured wagons in hand, to see if his long-lost legion might be of help. He—"

"That is a confounded lie!" Stuart roared, jumping to his feet. *"I had nothing to be contrite about! I had completed a hazardous mission only to find that the battle was elsewhere. I—"*

The butt of Bragg's Navy Colt came once more crashing onto the bench top. "General Stuart, you are out of order!"

Jeb glared back. "I don't care! I've been sitting here for nearly a week now, listening to lies and cheap allegations, and I'm *sick* of it! Where was this fat lawyer during the war, sitting on his butt somewhere having tea and crumpets? By George, I want to hear nothing more than facts from him the rest of the way!"

"Sit down, General Stuart!" Bragg thundered. Turning to the judge-advocate, he snapped, "And I'll have no more insinuations from you, Colonel Axline. This is a court of inquiry conducted by gentlemen. Keep it that way, sir!"

Mosby tugged at the seething Stuart's sleeve. "C'mon, Jeb, take your
seat."

Jeb slid slowly into his chair. "I mean it, that sweaty Texan can have
it any way he wants it—pistols, swords, or fists."

Colonel Axline wiped his face with his big red handkerchief and
returned to his narrative. "Since the issue is now whether or not
General Lee's *intent* was clear, as Colonel Marshall stated earlier, we
must go to that day to prove it. . . .

"On July second, General Stuart reported to General Lee at his
command post outside of Gettysburg. Some of Stuart's staff and commanders were with him. One of them was General, then Colonel,
Thomas T. Munford. Sir, would you please describe the scene to me?"

"Yes, sir, I will," General Munford said quietly from the witness
box. He looked sadly at Stuart. "Sorry, Jeb, but I have to tell the
truth." He paused, collected himself. "It was a painful situation to
find General Lee upset with us after our momentous ride around the
Union army. When General Stuart dismounted and saluted, Lee raised
his arm as if to *strike* him. His face was red and angrier than I'd ever
seen it. He glared and said, 'General Stuart, where have you been?'

"Well, the tone was like a glove striking across Jeb's face. He blanched
and drew in a deep breath—actually wilted, if you can imagine—and
in a low voice gave the general a brief summary of our recent movements.

"But Lee's face was still red and his voice was tinged with vexation.
'I have not heard from you for days,' he said. "And you are the eyes
and ears of my army.' 'I have brought you one hundred and twenty-
five wagons and their teams, General,' Jeb said.

"And Lee said, 'Yes, General, but they are an impediment to me
now.' But then his manner changed abruptly to the kind old man we
all knew. It seemed like a wave of great tenderness swept over him,
like a father forgiving a prodigal son. He put his hand on General
Stuart's shoulder and said, 'Let me ask your help now. We will not
discuss this matter longer. Help me fight these people.'

"And Jeb nodded, barely able to speak, and asked what he could
do. It wasn't long before we rode back to our headquarters and then
went on a long reconnaissance. And that's the way it was."

Mosby glanced sideways at Jeb, saw the tear slip out of his eye and
run down his cheek until he caught it with his finger.

"Thank you, General Munford," Axline said, moving to the center
of the bench and addressing the court. "Gentlemen, I think this scene

the general has just described most feelingly makes the most important point of this entire proceeding. General Lee was *angry* at Stuart for his actions. Now we all know that this fine man, in all of his gentleness, could not be *angry* with a subordinate whom he regarded as a favored son, if that favored son had not been extremely derelict.

"And, gentlemen, we also see the penitent reaction of this favored, but prodigal son—that of contrition. For General Stuart *knew* he was wrong, and the wrath of his patron brought it home to him." Axline paused. "And there it is, gentlemen. Regardless of the ambiguity of orders or the manner in which they were interpreted, General Lee never meant for General Stuart to run off and leave him, and General Stuart *knew* it."

The courtroom was deathly quiet.

Mosby glanced back at the faces and saw them all silently riveted on Colonel Axline. It was the most damning testimony of the proceedings. He had to think of something at once, or it was all over. . . .

"I recommend that this court of inquiry be closed," the judge-advocate said quietly.

General Bragg nodded. "Now the court has definitely heard enough." He raised his Navy revolver. "This court is hereby—"

"*No!*" Mosby shot to his feet. "*I request a recess, General!*"

"I see no reason, Colonel Mosby."

Mosby's voice cut through the silence, "Sir, I *most* respectfully request a recess."

Bragg showed his displeasure, but said, "Very well, this court will adjourn for fifteen minutes."

★   ★   ★

THE chambers was an office with a desk, a table with several chairs, and bookcases full of law books that were used by judges in the normal civil cases that were heard in the State Court House. Hood sat at the table smoking a meerschaum, while Pickett thumbed through a book in the corner. Axline was seated at the other end of the table, while both Mosby and Stuart stood before the desk where Bragg sat with one leg draped over a corner.

"All right, gentlemen, now why can't this proceeding end right here?" Bragg asked.

"Because, sir, it hasn't been fully aired," Mosby replied.

Bragg swung his gaze to Stuart. "All right, Jeb, I'm appealing to your sense of propriety. His Excellency, himself, wants this proceeding to come to an end—now, as comfortably as possible for everyone involved. I would like to recess until tomorrow morning, at which time both counsel can summarize, and then the court will close to come to a determination. What do you say?"

Jeb Stuart looked into Bragg's unyielding expression, glanced at Mosby, returned his gaze to Bragg. Drawing himself up, he replied, "No, sir. For as long as Gettysburg is studied, and that might be for a very long time, there will be those who will whisper that it might have been different if only Stuart had not ridden off on a joy ride. I can't accept that."

Bragg's eyebrows shot up. "What did you say?"

"No. We aren't finished, General."

Bragg threw a glance at each of his other court members. "I don't believe this. What do you want to prove?"

Mosby spoke up. "Who is *really* to blame for Gettysburg."

Everyone stared at him. It was so quiet the sound of Pickett closing the book was like a small explosion.

Sam Hood just sucked on his meerschaum.

George Pickett broke the silence. "The blame has already been placed—with Stuart!"

Braxton Bragg's face was growing rapidly red. "It is not the purpose of this court to find blame for the battle. I will rule against such drawn-out testimony. In fact, I will not condone a goddamned bit of it!" He caught himself, took a deep breath. "And, General Stuart, if you persist with this course, you are a fool."

Jeb replied quietly, "If I don't, I'm not a man."

Bragg shook his finger. "This court is over."

Mosby stepped forward, stood rigidly before the president of the court. His voice was even, his eyes cold. "General Bragg, we must insist on a continuance until Monday morning. And if you won't permit it, I will have to do something extremely distasteful. Not General Stuart, but *I* will do it . . . I will go to Pollard and the other journalists and tell them about the conspiracy that has marked this entire sordid affair."

Bragg jerked to his feet, his face livid. "What damned conspiracy?"

"General, I was threatened by the Secretary of War and the general-in-chief back in the very beginning. And I can draw attention to a whole pattern of connivance and collusion."

Bragg stared at him, finally thundered, *"By God, sir, I will have you court-martialed!"*

Mosby snapped right back, "And then this whole goddamned mess will be aired in its entirety, General!"

Quietly, Sam Hood said, "I think he has a point there, Braxton. Why don't we give them until Monday?"

Mosby held his breath; his whole future was hanging right there in Braxton Bragg's furious eyes.

The North Carolinian drew in a deep breath, exhaled, cleared his throat, and finally replied. "All right. Until Monday. And then you get one goddamned day, and that's all. And Mosby, let me give you fair warning—don't you *ever* threaten me again. You hear?"

Mosby clicked his heels together. "Yes, *sir!*"

He sighed inwardly—now he had to figure out what to do.

★ ★ ★

M OSBY stared at the newspapers spread over his desk, but it was all a blur. He had decided coming to the office and voiding his mind of all thoughts involving the court would cleanse it for the job ahead . . . finding his way out of the pit. His bluff with Bragg had worked to gain time, but he was still empty-handed when it came down to concrete blame for the battle.

He tilted his head back and sighed, rubbed his short beard.

He'd get it, he *had* to.

He turned at the knock on the doorframe. It was a telegraph clerk. "Got a message for you, Colonel." The young man entered the office, handed over the receipt to be signed.

Mosby thanked him, opened the telegraph as he left. It read:

Subject negro journalist you requested information about no longer in Toronto. Name is James Grace. Former U.S. Army soldier. Vehement abolitionist. Last believed whereabouts Boston.

Mosby nodded, glad to switch his mind to the Rawlins conspiracy from the goddamned Stuart Court conspiracy. He reread the message and tossed it on his desk, put his feet up on the corner and closed his eyes. The wire was about what he expected. Now they had a name to work with. That was the way it was with intelligence—the dashing around behind the lines, the daring stuff, that was only a particle of it. The rest was slow and mechanical. In peacetime, it was *all* slow and mechanical. "Well, Mr. James Grace, I hope you're some kind of a fool, but we'll still have someone in Boston check into you."

He opened his eyes and shook his head. He had hoped for something of use from Israel Jones, but the man still had nothing of value to report. In fact, he was halfway convinced that General Rawlins's concern about those ridiculous letters to Little Mac was overwrought, that there was no connection to Abraham. Crazy people wrote letters every day. Yet Rawlins had no choice if his president was worried. Perhaps that was just an excuse for the general to be in the Southern capital. Any number of plots could be going on. . . . But there he was, playing intelligence officer again, seeing an enemy behind every blade of grass. He shook his head again.

If he had any real intelligence, he'd figure out what to do about the court. He'd talked mighty big when he stuck his jaw out and threatened Bragg. Damn fool.

What am I going to do, Jeb—where's the miracle?

Jeb.

This couldn't be the end of the line.

He got up from the desk, went around to the bright-colored flag of his old Forty-third Ranger Battalion. Touching it, he pushed back the years to the summer of 1861, shortly after Virginia had entered the war. . . .

He was a skinny twenty-seven-year-old private and Jeb Stuart was already a legend, a swashbuckling young lieutenant colonel commanding the 1st Virginia Cavalry. He'd never forget the first time he saw Jeb. . . . He was resting in the bright sun beside the road north of Winchester when this thickset man astride a remarkable bay horse rode up. Stuart was wearing a Yankee undress uniform with Confederate insignia. He leaned down from the saddle, slapped an officer on the back, and laughed loud enough to be heard on the other side of the enemy lines. Flowing brown mustaches, a flaming beard, and merry blue eyes. A yellow sash, bright sun reflecting off the hilt of his cavalry saber. Unmistakable confidence, strength. That was the most vibrant sign Stuart gave off—sheer, inexhaustible *strength*.

Mosby touched the bright-colored flag again. A lot had happened between the skinny private and the swashbuckling cavalry commander since that day, and now they needed more than Jeb's great strength.

A miracle?

He'd never seen one.

What the hell was he going to do?

★ ★ ★

A MASSIVE thunderstorm was dumping a heavy flood of rain on Richmond, but the warehouse at Ludlum Wharf, off Water Street in Rocketts, had only one leak. And that was at the back of the building. Near the front, Salmon Brown placed the large drawing he had made of the courthouse floor plan on a makeshift easel. The watching members of Amistad grew suddenly quiet, shifting their weight to get comfortable on the assorted boxes they were using as chairs.

Jubilo stood impassively behind them, an invited guest.

Using a hickory switch he had whittled down as a pointer, Salmon began his briefing: "All right, this is the way the courtroom is laid out. It's a large, solid room with windows on the—" He went into a detailed description and when he finished, he looked at each of them: Crispus, in the middle, frowning; Nat Turner, idly sucking on a long stem of field grass; Cinque and Denmark Vesey staring with narrowed eyes at the drawing. Beecher Lovejoy looked up from the pad where he was making notes. "How far is it from the front door to the bench?" he asked.

"About sixty-five feet, near as I could estimate it."

"You didn't pace it off?"

Salmon smiled. "Hardly."

Everyone but Crispus chuckled.

"Oughta be able to hit a gnat in the eye from that distance."

"Trouble is, gnat's eyes get smaller when it's real."

"Amen," Denmark Vesey said. He was the one who had killed a Rebel general with his heavy sharpshooter's rifle.

"Do you think we could set some charges the night before?" Cinque asked. He was one of the dynamiters.

"No. Too much chance of detection. And besides, we want the world to know that dedicated people *can* upset the apple cart. With us charging in there—black men and white—and killing those people, it's a personal thing." Salmon thought a moment. "Just as personal as my father and brothers going into Harpers Ferry . . . except this raid will overshadow even that." He glanced at the stolid Jubilo.

"Salmon's right," Crispus said. "We don't want to blow the place up—we want to kill them individually. I want to see Jefferson Davis splattered against one of those benches with his brains spilling out on the floor in his own pond of blood."

The others chimed in. "Uh, huh, and I hope there's enough Reb generals in there so's we can all have two or three!"

"I'd like one of them high mucky-muck politicians."

"Yessuh, and I hear one of them's got a pretty niece. Any reason why we can't splash her blood around too?"

"She's a Reb, ain't she?"

"We oughta kill several women. That'll make 'em quiver all the way to Texas!"

Salmon broke in. "I'll have a detailed plan of where people are supposed to be sitting, and we will have specific targets. Of course, a great deal depends upon when Davis is coming to Court and who will be with him."

"Speaking of women, where's our fancy Verita?" Crispus asked.

"She's proceeding with her undercover plan. If you read the papers, she's quite a hit in the play."

"She sure doesn't have any trouble *passing*," Crispus snorted. "A high-yellow New Orleans gal—fancy-pants nigger, that's all. How many of those white Rebs is she laying down for?"

Salmon felt a flash of anger, sensed his cheeks heating up. She was no—

"Uh, huh, how do we know we can depend on her if she don't come to our meetings, anyway?" It was Beecher Lovejoy, the white man, asking.

Salmon cleared his throat. "She'll be okay when it's time." His voice sounded strange. Why did those words tear at him so? *High-yellow, fancy-pants nigger!* He felt suddenly hot, sticky.

Jubilo stepped forward.

At first he didn't say anything, just fixed a stern gaze on them, then turned slowly to Salmon. Waited. Finally, he scowled darkly and said, "I don't think I want to be any part of this, Captain Brown."

The only noise was the rain on the roof as everyone stared at him.

"You see," he went on after a moment in his deep preacher's voice, "you all sound like the Devil's own. Can you tell me anywhere in the Bible where it says those going to the promised land have to kill *women* to get there? *Can you?*"

A vicious clap of thunder accented his anger.

His size, his voice, his eye, were all intimidating. Even the scar on his ebony cheek stood out in the light of the kerosene lamp. "You say you're champions of the downtrodden and enslaved Negro, his saviors in modern form? Well, let me tell you something. I don't care whether you are black or white, you sound just like crazy fanatics to me.

"Jesus Christ was a savior—did you ever hear of him talking about splashing the blood of women around? *Did you?* You coloreds, you think you can wear a Yankee uniform, and spend a little time in the North—and *then* come back down here and change everything by a mass killing? Hell, you don't even know what it's all about, this being a nigger in today's South."

"What difference does a few years make?" Crispus growled. "A colored man still has to take his hat off and stare at his feet when he talks to a white man. And I don't care *how* many of us are freedmen, there are still nearly *four million* slaves down here!"

The others murmured agreement.

Jubilo stabbed his forefinger at Crispus. "I'm telling you, you don't know *nothing!* Particularly you. Where you coming from? Chicago, I hear. Canada—ain't that where you wrote for a white newspaper? You don't know *nothing!* You think all those folks up North want us to be equal? Ha! boy, you got some learning to do.

"Do you know that while a colored regiment was storming Fort Wagner near Charleston Harbor in July of Sixty-three, draft rioters bludgeoned, burned, and *lynched* their way through the negro part of New York City? Do you know why we were called *contraband* during the war by the Yankee commanders?"

Jubilo moved closer to Crispus, glared down into his eyes. "Of course you don't know. It was a *legal* way to take the property of the Southern white man and put him to work for the Yankee army! But it backfired—wherever the Yankee army did this, the contraband laborer brought his wife and kids. And that presented a whole bushel basket of problems . . . it was all right to free the Negro to work for a pittance, but when they had to free and feed his *whole family*, that was a different mess of possum!

"Only people that wanted a flood of contraband coming up North was the abolitionists. And that's a fact. Still is." Jubilo looked at Salmon.

"Your father never bothered to find out that the Negroes in those countries around Harpers Ferry were treated good. That's why none of them turned out for him. And he never thought about feeding them if they *did*. Nossiree. You can't just cut the fetters off four million uneducated people, most of whom ain't done nothing more than raise some cotton or tobacco, and tell 'em to shift for *themselves*. They gotta have land, and some money to make it work—"

Crispus snapped, "They *take* it. That's what revolution is all about!"

"Revolution ain't for everybody!"

"No, it's for those who aren't afraid of their shadow! I hear you've got some kind of an army—are they all cowards too?"

Jubilo's voice was cold. "I have a small guards regiment so I can control the hotheads and people like you who would burn the world."

"You'd never get me!"

"That's *enough*, Crispus!" Salmon barked.

Jubilo nodded, again looked from one to the other, stopping at Salmon. "I'm sorry, Captain Brown. When you get these folks thinking logical-like, you come and see me. Meantime, I'm dealing myself out." He tugged the brim of his hat lower over his forehead and strode toward the door.

★   ★   ★

MOSBY yawned, pulled out his watch. 1:12 A.M. He got up and went to the one window, high up, that served the Adjutant General's official records repository. He craned his neck, rolled his head around to get rid of the stiffness in his neck. Still raining. The raindrops were the only sound in this dungeon. And still no answer. He'd been at it in these damned records for over five hours, and all he had was a stiff neck.

Balled-up sheets of paper with worthless ideas and pursuits down dead-ends lay all over the floor.

Why wouldn't it come out—the clear-cut lead to the villain, the one to blame for Gettysburg? He'd been working on the Ewell approach until he was certain that was the answer. Lieutenant General Richard S. Ewell, the bald-headed, one-legged pretender to Stonewall Jackson's throne the famed Second Corps. Ewell had been called back to

Gettysburg from his drive to Harrisburg and thrown into the battle by Lee with discretionary orders. Many said his inability to read between the lines as Stonewall always did kept him from decisive action. One senior officer openly charged him with indecision and lack of aggressiveness in not attacking the northern hills while they were unoccupied.

The problem was Lee's discretionary orders—if they wouldn't hold up for Jeb, they certainly wouldn't hold up for Ewell.

So now, after reading every single order, every scrap of correspondence relating to Ewell, he knew it wouldn't work. The villain of Gettysburg had to be clearly defined, etched so sharply against his crime that not even Braxton Bragg could deny the fact.

He went back to the table with its piles of orders, reports, and letters. The single oil lamp was his only companion. Five hours of pursuing Ewell for naught. Who was left? He rubbed his forehead, tried to pull out an answer. General A. P. Hill was out—his Third Corps had fought valiantly. And no division commander could be singled out.

Lee? Impossible!

Slowly John Mosby wrote on a blank sheet of paper the name Longstreet.

Who had acted irrationally at Breckinridge's party in the beginning? Who had lied about the spy? Why had he lied about the spy? Why, when he was on the stand, had he so vehemently accused Jeb of dereliction . . . a younger general for whom he'd always had a kind word? It was totally out of keeping . . . unless he was trying to hide something.

He had read Longstreet's report on Gettysburg three times. Nothing wrong. The general had disagreed with Lee about fighting an offensive battle at Gettysburg, but that wasn't villainous. . . .

Longstreet.

Maybe there would be something in his division commanders' reports.

Twenty-five minutes later, after going through all the files on Gettysburg, he had found the report of every single division commander in the Army of Northern Virginia, except for those of Hood, Pickett, and McLaws—*the three division commanders in Longstreet's corps!*

Why? He could understand why Hood hadn't written one because of the general's severe wound and subsequent hospitalization. But Pickett—why wasn't there an official report on the most famous charge of the war by its commander? And Lafayette McLaws; he hadn't been wounded, nor had his division been as badly decimated as Pickett's. What possible reason could he have for not writing a report?

Could those reports have been destroyed?

They would have been submitted to the next higher commander —Longstreet. Why would anyone want to destroy them—could there be something incriminating? God, a conspiracy even then?

Mosby's eyes narrowed; he was excited. Maybe something in the division's files. . . . He'd start with Pickett's—the dapper general had always been Old Pete's fair-haired boy. . . .

He spent another half hour reading the letters of all three headquarters and was just about finished when a letter from Hood's adjutant caught his eye:

July 4th, 1863

To the new Commanding General,

Hood's Division

General,

Before confusion hides the facts of this sad time, I wish to state that prior to the attack on July 2nd, 1863, General Hood twice appealed to General Longstreet to cancel the attack plan and let our division go around the enemy's unprotected left flank and wreak havoc in his rear. When General Longstreet refused to listen, General Hood sent me personally to plead with him. That effort was also in vain, and history will reveal its tragic result.

I remain, sir, your obedient servant,

W. H. Sellers,
A. A. G.

Mosby let out a low whistle, and tried to remain calm as he read the letter again. He thought he could feel goose bumps on his neck. He tore through other letters, finding nothing. But it didn't matter, the Sellers note was the leak he'd been seeking. *Pete Longstreet had done something so grievously wrong that an adjutant had felt compelled to record it!*

He wondered if he could find Sellers soon enough to get him in court Monday? What would Hood have to say about that? God, he couldn't say anything—he was a member of the court and couldn't testify! And Sellers was another junior staff officer. . . .

And then it dawned on him . . . two of Longstreet's division commanders from Gettysburg were on that court, insulated from testifying! And they were the only two left in the army, because Major General Lafayette McLaws had resigned to go into the insurance business in Savannah when the war ended. McLaws—surely he must have known about Hood's pleas prior to that July 2nd battle . . . surely.

He was the goddamned key!

Mosby slammed his fist on the table. *He had it!* He'd get a telegraph off to McLaws at once!

11

DAY 5

His Excellency's old crony waves his big Navy pistol around the courtroom as if it were a saber at Chickamauga—which was, by the way, Bragg's last victory in the dim past. While there is no doubt in this writer's mind that Jeb Stuart is guilty as sin of playing the glory role on the way to Gettysburg, and being without doubt to blame for that setback (Mr. Davis refuses to call it a defeat even to this day), it seems there are other dastardly deeds hiding under rocks. If we had an impartial court of inquiry into the *president's* activities from then until now in regard to that unfortunate campaign, we might better find the truth. But is it the truth our fact-finding court of inquiry really wants?

Mosby laid the *Examiner* back on his desk top and nodded his head. The editorial, while a typical Pollard swipe at the president, couldn't have been more timely. He doubted that the editor had any facts to base it on, but facts had never gotten in the way of his writing before. Believe it or not, he said to himself, that bastard may turn out to be our strongest ally.

He had told Jeb the big news about his discovery in regard to Longstreet, and telegrams had gone out at 3:00 A.M. to General McLaws in Savannah, and also to Harry Sellers, Hood's former adjutant, in Texas. There wouldn't be time for the latter to get to Richmond, but perhaps a statement would be of some value. Now, if only they could find that damned Harrison to destroy Longstreet's credibility. . . .

★ ★ ★

THE captain in the adjutant general's office looked up from his desk when Mosby walked in. "I was just about to go to lunch, Colonel. But I was going to leave a note at your office. I think I've found your man."

Mosby nodded, took the page of notes and glanced at it.

"As you can see, this man's name is *H. T.* Harrison. It seems that Secretary of War Seddon was his boss. He authorized a voucher from the army contingency fund to pay one hundred and fifty dollars to him on February twentieth of Sixty-three. The signed voucher says 'for services rendered as a scout within enemy lines.'

"Then here's a note directing that H. T. Harrison be paid seventy-five dollars on March seventh of that year in North Carolina. A separate receipt for that money is signed by H. T. Harrison that same day, and he gives his position as 'Scout for Lieutenant General *Longstreet!*' "

Mosby grabbed the receipt, exclaimed, "There it is!"

"And that's not all, Colonel. The tie to Longstreet continues. Our Mr. Harrison was paid two hundred dollars in United States currency in early June of that year. This was charged to the secret service fund by order of Lieutenant General Longstreet."

The captain grinned. "And . . . on the nineteenth of July, Harrison was paid three hundred dollars more, one hundred and fifty per month, for 'scouting within the enemy's lines for General Longstreet's Corps.' The dates run from May nineteenth through July nineteenth, same year!"

Mosby went from document to document, shaking his head. He grinned back at the assistant adjutant general. "There is no doubt that our Mr. Harrison was thick as thieves with Old Pete during the Pennsylvania campaign."

"I can have true copies made of these documents if you wish, sir."

"Thank you, but without our missing scout, I'm afraid it won't do much good. Still, it's something. Go ahead."

"Very well, sir."

Mosby started to go, looked back over his shoulder. "By the way, don't you normally work for Colonel Axline when he isn't playing lawyer?"

The captain grinned broadly. "Yes, sir. That's exactly why I want to give you all the help I can."

Walking out, Mosby felt good. It was all coming together. Now he had to go see Jubilo. Were things ever going to settle down into normal humdrum? Maybe one of these days he could take Spring down to meet his mother . . . maybe one of these days he could just be alone with her . . . and why not this afternoon? A nice lunch, send the servants away. Great idea!

★   ★   ★

I T WAS one of those fresh, clear days that follow a stormy night. A brisk breeze was hustling the gray-white clouds along to the east, leaving plenty of room between them for the blue sky and bright sunshine to burst through like eager visitors.

Mosby and Jubilo walked along the wharves on Water Street, talking quietly. "You're getting famouser than ever, Cunnel. Every time I see a newspaper, there's your name plastered all over the front page," the huge man said with a grin.

"I'd trade every iota of that fame to clear Jeb Stuart."

"Sounds like the general just likes to win wars all by himself. I'm not so sure I would've liked soldiering under him."

"You know you would have. Speaking of wars, Jubilo, it seems there are some people trying their damnedest to get the last one started all over again."

Jubilo glanced at a sailboat gliding in from midstream. The captain of the brightly painted craft was busy with a pale yellow sail, while two small boys tried vainly to help. "That so?" he replied.

Mosby, too, turned to watch the boat. "You know," he said, "that reminds me of what's going on with the abolitionists—the owner of a boat has a certain way to sail it, but there are those who want to help, and merely get in the way."

Jubilo just nodded as they strolled on.

"Right now, my friend," Mosby continued, "there may be some

people up North, and maybe down here, who are trying to capsize us. Before that happens, and an awful lot of people get killed, it has to be stopped. We talked along this line the last time I came down to see you. But now, there are some pretty heavy threats being made."

Mosby stopped, looked at the big man's expression. "Is Abraham involved in anything destructive right now, anything involving the Northern abolitionists, or the government of the United States?"

Jubilo shook his head. "Lordy, Cunnel, you sure do put some big questions all together at once."

"I can ask them one at a time."

"I don't really know much about this Abraham, but I can rightfully say I don't know of any such goings on that involve my people."

Mosby looked at him closely, nodded. "You know what it would mean, don't you? A curfew, martial law, loss of what freedom you've got. Lots of people going to prison, many executions. I don't have to spell it out."

Jubilo's eyes hardened. "No, you don't, Cunnel. I've been preaching moderation in my church all along. You don't believe me, you come on down to my services whenever you feel like it."

Mosby chuckled. "If you saw my white face coming in there, you'd switch your sermon in the blink of an eye. I'll bet you've got dozens to suit the occasion."

Jubilo blinked, a slow smile working its way around his mouth. "All right, Cunnel, you're all involved with Gettysburg. Here is a man's sermon that came from that place . . . 'Four score and seven years ago, our fathers brought forth upon this continent a new nation, conceived in liberty, and dedicated to the proposition that all men are created equal' . . . and then that man went on to say about those who fought there, 'that we here highly resolve that these dead shall not have died in vain; that this nation, under God, shall have a new birth of freedom, and that government of the people, by the people, for the people, shall not perish from the earth.' "

Mosby nodded. "Lincoln at his best. Very good, Jubilo. What are you trying to tell me?"

"Maybe the story of General Stuart and Gettysburg is riling everybody up in the North, reminding them that their boys *did* die in vain. There's sure as hell no government down here *by* the black people, *for* the black people."

Mosby walked several steps before replying. "That's a remote possibility. I suppose the abolitionists could use that speech for fodder.

Maybe even incite some hotheads into violence ... yes, I'll give that some thought. Oh, by the way, have you seen a strange white man hanging around Rocketts, maybe even in your church?"

Jubilo turned back into the sun for the return walk. "Can't say as I do, Cunnel. They come and go. Sometimes one drops in for some rousing nigger spiritual music to save his soul when he's been drinking too much."

They walked on. Finally Jubilo asked, "You've mentioned change to me before, Cunnel. Is there anything new coming forth in the government that I can tell my people, or is everyone supposed to sit on his hands for another hundred years?"

Mosby stopped, held up his hands in protest. "All right, so what Lincoln said should be the way everywhere—I admit it! But this is the *South*, and you know how it is. And it isn't going to change overnight, no matter *what*. You know that, Jubilo."

Jubilo just nodded as they continued toward his store. When they reached the steps, he said, "Look up Ecclesiastes Twelve, Cunnel. It says 'In the day when the keepers of the house shall tremble, and the strong men shall bow themselves ... and those that look out the windows be darkened ... Then shall the dust return to the earth as it was.' "

Mosby smiled as he shook his head. "Never try to argue with a preacher. He can twist Bible passages around until your head swims, and you don't ever know if he's right." He sobered, touched his hat brim in a casual salute. "Take care, my friend. Our country needs you more than you know. And if you hear of anything destructive, send word. You hear?"

Jubilo watched the white man get into the waiting hack. He wished he could truly trust Mosby, but there was no way. Not yet, maybe not ever. No matter what, they would always be on opposite sides of the fence. . . .

★   ★   ★

VERITA stepped gingerly down from the hack, avoiding a large puddle of water. "Wait here, please," she said to the driver. "I shouldn't be over fifteen minutes."

"Yes ma'am." The driver reached for his dime novel and settled back on the seat.

Salmon nodded from the front doorway of the warehouse. "Good day, m'lady, please come in. The merchandise you mentioned in your letter came in yesterday afternoon."

As soon as he closed the door, Verita looked around, nodding in approval. The large room was set up with rows of boxes simulating the benches in the courtroom. At one end a higher row of boxes represented the judges' bench; others the counsel tables. Open door frames at the other end and to the right of the judges' bench simulated the exits; windows were drawn with chalk on the floor, as were the positions of the inside sentries. "Everything is as close to the actual measurements as I can guess," Salmon said. "We set it up last night after Jubilo walked out on us."

He took her through the same rehearsal he had conducted with the others the previous night. Then once more. When they finished, she asked, "What's this about Jubilo?"

"The boys got a little bloodthirsty in their talk and he gave us a sermon about the meek inheriting the earth."

"That's what you get for dealing with preachers. Do we really need him?"

"Yes—for two reasons. One, we need a diversionary force, and that means his people. We'll all be at the courthouse. Two, we must have the participation of Abraham people to show the world it's a united effort, supported by the North. And Higginson wants him in."

"Maybe there's someone else."

"No, he pulls all the strings."

"What if he stays out—can you recruit anyone? Hire them?"

"I doubt it. You really don't know how strong Jubilo is, do you?"

She smiled ruefully. "How could I? I'm living in the hallowed and rarefied air of the wealthy whites." She saw him stiffen. "Have you ever been around any really *rich* people, Salmon Brown, I mean *shamefully* rich? Why, I'll bet Bessica Adams Southwick makes enough money in one day without lifting one little finger to feed half of Rocketts the slop everyone down there is forced to eat."

"Verita—" He moved closer to her. "I don't want to talk about rich white people." He touched her hand. "You're something special to me. When this is over, I, well, I'm not very good at this, you know ... I would like for us to be close."

Her eyes widened. She had detested this strange man at their first stormy encounter, because of his rejection of her and because she knew he had turned down the chance to be a true revolutionary like his father. But gradually she had grown to respect him, even liked him at times. Now this. She had seen it coming, knew this violent man, who was quite awkward and insecure with women, was groping. Somewhere, sometime, a woman had hurt him badly, and now he was wary . . . wary and unsophisticated. She'd have to be blind not to see how much he wanted her. He was like a wounded lion cub circling her, just out of reach, but making pleading little noises . . . and it gave her a warm feeling. Her voice was low as she looked into his eyes. "I thought you said we would go straight to our goal without any entanglements."

"Uh, yes, I did say that. But what I mean is afterward, when we go on our next mission."

"There may not be a next mission." Her hand went to his cheek, touched it softly. She leaned up and kissed him lightly on the lips, looked again into his instantly troubled eyes.

He turned away, releasing her hand as if it were burning him. He cleared his throat, cleared it again, said gruffly, "Of course there will be a next mission. I've even picked the target."

She didn't want this tender, unique moment to pass. Always men were a combination of passion and challenge to her. With Salmon, she was beginning to feel a strange sense of affection, of warmth. "Why are you afraid of me?" she asked.

He pulled away. "Damn it, I'm *not* afraid of you. I just . . . no entanglements!"

She shook off the emotion. "Tell me about the escape."

He collected himself, moved to the map. "Here. We scatter in different directions when we come out of the courtroom and get to the horses that have been tied close by. The colored men should have no trouble getting rid of the mounts and slipping back into Rocketts. The three whites will come here, where we'll change clothes. Then we'll go to the boat and sail down the James past Drewry's Bluff, eventually reaching Norfolk.

"There, we'll take ship for Tampico in Mexico, where the others will join up with us when they can. Higginson has arranged that part. I suspect martial law will be declared, and troops and police will be checking everyone everywhere. We whites will all be known because they'll find out our identities. . . . Fact is, I want everyone in the world to know that I'm *Salmon Brown!*"

She nodded. "Yes, it sounds good. But why did you say *three* whites? Did you pick up another white somewhere?"

"You know what I mean—you're the third white."

"You know damned well what I am—a mulatto, a Negro!"

He stiffened again. "You are *white!* Now I don't want to discuss it any further." He turned away.

She caught his arm; her eyes were brittle. "Wait, Salmon Brown. Aren't you about to become one of the greatest of the abolitionists? Won't your name echo around the world when this is done?"

He shrugged.

Her eyes narrowed. "All right, supposing I were to move in down here in Rocketts. And supposing you came to see me on a day like this and I was scrubbing clothes—wearing a stained old hand-me-down calico dress, and had a mammy bandanna wrapped around my head. Maybe I had a little black child playing at my feet, calling me 'mama.' And there were nothing but colored folks all around—all colored, middle colored, and a little colored. Mulattoes of every shade.

"What would you do then, *Salmon Brown?* Would you take my hand gently, like you just did, and want to lay with me? Hold me and tell me how much you think you love me? Would you do that, Salmon Brown—right there in the middle of Rocketts? Or would you do like you did just now—turn into a board and stare at me as if I were just another *nigger?*"

Salmon's eyes widened as he shook his head. "I don't want to listen to such damned nonsense. You are a beautiful, educated woman. Never in hell would you be down here washing clothes like that."

"Except for my having a father who cared, that's right where I might be—married and having a string of kids, and growing old fast. I'm just lucky. But you don't know about such things because you're *white*. Well, you'd better damn well get it all straightened out before you talk to me about anything between us."

He shook his head. "I don't want to discuss it. Now c'mon, you have to be going or that hack driver will get impatient and drive on."

"Yessuh, Cap'n Brown, *suh!*" she replied sharply, rolling her eyes and stomping toward the door.

★ ★ ★

"JOVE, Jove! this shepherd's passion . . . Is much upon my fashion." Spring Blakely smiled pertly as she delivered the line.

Mosby scowled at his coffee cup. "I know it's Shakespeare, I just don't know what—for the moment."

"Thou speak'st wiser than thou art ware of."

He shook his head.

"Peace, fool; he's not thy kinsman."

He tugged at his neat beard. "Damn, it's right there at my fingertips. Give me another moment."

She laughed. "Spoken like any unprepared student. Very well, I simply must give you a failing grade, sir . . . 'From east to western Ind, no jewel is like Rosalind. Her worth being mounted on the wind, through all the world bears Rosalind. All the'—"

" 'Pictures fairest lined are but black to Rosalind'—'As You Like It.' I knew it all the time."

"Certainly—as soon as you heard 'Rosalind.' "

They both laughed. They had played the literary game all through lunch at his house. Still at the dining table, they were both suddenly quiet, as if to catch a new breath. The light from the bay window played over their faces. She sipped the last of her brandy, said softly, "The one line is most appropriate, you know. 'Peace, fool; he's not thy kinsman.' "

It was a moment before he replied. "If you're speaking of Jeb, you're wrong, my dear. He is my kinsman, just as surely as if we were born in the same litter."

"It just seems that no matter what you do, how well you present his case, it gets more hopeless, John."

"Wrong, pretty lady. I have them right where I want them."

"It isn't a jesting matter."

"No, it really isn't." He was enjoying this interlude to the utmost and wasn't about to let their light mood slip away.

"But what will you do? You can't fight the whole army and Davis too. My uncle has already made a noise about you becoming the oldest lieutenant colonel in the army some day."

Mosby chuckled. "That's better than being the oldest private."

"You didn't answer my question."

Mosby sipped his brandy, the remainder of a fine French cognac he had liberated from a Yankee colonel in Loudoun County just before the end of the war. He smiled. "I don't know if I can tell you."

"What do you mean?"

"Because, pretty lady, you were once a spy. And this whole thing of you pursuing me could be a ploy of the enemy to extract all of my secrets."

"That's ridiculous," Spring said. "And I'm not pursuing any more, just doing all I can to preserve my virtue."

"Drat! There goes my plan for this afternoon."

"What do you mean—plan?"

He poured more brandy for each of them. "Have you seen a servant since the coffee was served?"

Spring looked around in the direction of the kitchen. "No. What are you talking about?"

"I sent them off on enough errands to keep them busy until sunset. You, my dear, are all alone with me in my lair."

"Are your intentions dishonorable?"

"I'm not sure. It's been so long since I seduced anyone, I really don't know where to start."

She reached across the corner of the dining table for his hand.

He drew her hand to his lips, held it for a moment. "You know, Spring," he said softly, "we can joke around about this just so long and . . . well, I really do feel like a schoolboy. Feel that tremor in my hand?"

"That's in my hand, not yours."

"Thanks, but I know. Spring, I—" *Why couldn't he just sweep her up and take her to bed?* "You know how I feel about you. I wake up in the middle of the night with you all around me. Sometimes, even in court, my mind drifts back to you, and I want to turn around and just look at you. It's just that it takes time for me. I thought bringing you here to lunch today would break down the last barrier, but here I am— pussyfooting around like a milksop."

Her dark eyes were wide. "How *do* you feel about me, John?"

His brief smile had a touch of pain in it. "I love you. Yes, that's what I've been afraid to say. I'm afraid because I don't know if I can give all of myself. . . . Do you understand?"

She squeezed his hand tightly. "Say it again."

"I love you."

"Again."

"I love you, Spring."

She brought his hand up to her cheek, kissed it. "That's all I need to know, my darling. I love you so much I could *burst!* That'll take care of the rest."

He pushed his chair back, got to his feet, and drew her into his arms. Their lips met softly, then more urgently. Her hands found the back of his neck as their tongues hurried through their first truly passionate kiss. She kicked away her low-heeled satin slippers, pushed herself closer against him, unable to hold still. She broke the kiss, brushed her lips against his chin, held his cheeks in her hands, looked into his wide blue eyes. A gentle smile was in those eyes. And the passion, the lust she so wanted to ignite.

His lips came back to hers, eagerly, his tongue hurrying around the inside of her mouth, stroking hers, his arms gripping her tightly, his hand slipping to her buttocks, pulling her fully into himself. His mouth dropped to her neck, continued to her décolletage as he murmured, "I love you, I love you, oh, I do love you."

Her fingers gripped the back of his head tightly as she threw her face back and closed her eyes. She arched even more tautly up to him, moving against his erect manhood, whispering the senseless words of love that tumbled out of her mouth—the same words of love that she had babbled into her pillow so many times in the past few weeks.

His mouth found her ear, nibbled a moment, kissed, and whispered, "I have a new book of Poe poems on my bedstand. I bought it for you this morning."

She blew out a deep breath against his chest, found her voice, "That means you knew we were . . . I'm very glad, my darling."

He smiled, encircled her waist with his arm, and led her from the dining room.

★　★　★

SHE leaned back in his arms as the closed hack turned up Sixth toward Clay. It was so fresh and wet after the big storm. The uncobbled streets were quite muddy, and quite empty in the residential area. "Hmmm," she sighed, closing her eyes, "I could spend the rest of forever right here."

He smiled. "You said that back in bed."

"There too. Oh, John, I love you so much." She sighed again, then suddenly jerked upright, looking intently into his face. "I forgot to tell you about Marie Jolie. Do you know that she's a real *communist*? You know, that Karl Marx revolutionary thing. And she's also an abolitionist. Can you imagine, a French abolitionist!"

"With *their* colonial policies, she should have an ample cause."

"I mean here. She's well-informed. Why, she has even met Sojourner Truth."

"Good." He wasn't the least bit interested in the French actress or her politics. All of the pressures that had been piling on his head during the past week had been washed away in a massive gusher of emotional and physical releases, and he was too drained to care about such nonsense. And his mind was drifting back to the court. The answers to his telegraphs should be back soon. . . .

"We had such a delightful lunch. She is a very bright lady. Kind of makes me feel like the dumb little farmer's daughter from the backwoods of Kentucky."

"Uh huh." Maybe there was something from Ogg.

"Anyway, it's too bad our get-together is tonight when she has to be on stage. I did mention the meeting, didn't I? Oh, you will come with me, won't you, darling? We should be there about eight. Twelveten East Marshall. Will you pick me up shortly before that, or should I meet you somewhere?"

"That's okay."

"Meet you?"

"Uh huh. Spottswood lobby. Uh huh."

"You'll like these people. I know you don't feel the same way I do about slavery, but I want you to just listen. Okay?"

"Yes, if I don't have to stay too long." He kissed her. "I would rather just be alone with you."

She leaned against his cheek. "We can do that too. Oh, here's my uncle's house. See you tonight . . . and, darling—"

"Yes."

"You've just made me the happiest Kentuckian in Virginia."

★　★　★

T HE message was waiting at the desk when Salmon Brown returned to the hotel at five-thirty. It was from Verita: "I have just found out from Mrs. S. that the St. Court will end on Tuesday afternoon. She heard it from St. Everyone will be there. Will we?—V."

Salmon could hardly contain himself as he reread the message. Throwing a fist in the air, he shouted to himself, "You're damned right we will, lady! We'll be there in all our glory, with our keenest shooting eyes, firing shots the whole world will hear!"

He hurried up the steps and as soon as he was in his room, he jerked the Whitney revolver from its holster under his arm. Springing into a shooting position, he pretended to blow away the faces of each of his targets. *"Bang! Bang! Bang!"* he shouted, picturing their faces disintegrating and the red wet blood bursting out of their shattered veins like massive raindrops.

"Now, Old Man, now we'll make up for Harpers Ferry! They'll be singing your song all over the world, and singing my praises even louder. The Brown family will be remembered for a thousand years, Old Man! That's right—I'm going to finish what you started because I'm not going to *dally!*"

"Bang! Bang! Bang!"

They had a target date!

★ ★ ★

J OHN Rawlins stared at the note, glanced again at the colored boy standing hat-in-hand outside his hotel room. It was on heavy rag stationery with Bessica Adams Southwick's embossed heading. It read:

> Please forgive my intrusion, but
> I would like to talk to you.
> Hopefully,
> Marie Jolie

"The lady, she's in a hack buggy downstairs, Gennul, suh," the messenger said. "Up the street a tad."

Rawlins's pulse quickened as he wondered what this could be about. This enchanting young Parisienne had been on his mind for two days now—intruding on his thinking, creating moment after moment of desire. He had even gone back to the New Richmond the night before, paid an exorbitant price for an obscure seat, and been fascinated by her. Now this. He nodded, reached for his hat.

She was seated on the right side of the covered hack, wearing a light peach-colored silk dress, topped by a wide-brimmed hat worn low over her face. She held out her hand to be kissed, a gesture that made him uncomfortable. "How may I help you?" he asked.

"I just want to see you. Perhaps ask you something."

Her eyes reminded him of a Siamese cat's, but golden, with long, dark lashes and humor. Exciting. "Ask away," he replied.

Her white teeth flashed in a quick smile. "Not yet, *mon général.* I want to look at you first. You are a very handsome man, you know."

First the hand and then the flattery. Very disconcerting. His knee touched hers as he climbed inside the hack, exciting him more. "Uh, thank you, Mademoiselle. Now what—"

"Ah, you American officers, you are so impatient," she laughed. Leaning forward, she said, "Driver, please take us to Gambles Hill." As the buggy started forward, she put her hand over his in a casual way. "Have you ever been there before? It's a delightful place overlooking the river. Bessica told me about it."

Her hand remained on his.

"No, I haven't heard of it." He paused. "I came to the theater again last night. In fact, I saw Judah in Bessica's box."

Her eyes smiled, teased. "Why didn't you join him?"

He shouldn't have mentioned it. "Well, I didn't know he was going. And I didn't intend to stay for the whole performance." What a limp excuse, he thought. He should've just told Judah.

"It's a big box, plenty of room for two." She squeezed his hand, still smiling but not mocking him. "I understand, *cheri.* And I looked for you."

"Oh?"

"*Oui.* I told you the other night how I like to be free like the breeze, to pursue my fancies wherever I wish."

He was becoming fully aroused.

"And you are my present fancy," she murmured, moving closer to him, looking into his dark eyes. "I love strong men, men who can take what they want, when they want it."

Her face was close, her lips parted, taunting. *To hell with everything!* He took her in his arms roughly, kissed her hard, met her hungry tongue and overpowered it. Forcing her down into the corner, he buried his face in her décolletage, reached inside her thigh. But he suddenly felt the cough coming, fought it, managed to hold it off. The *clip clop* of the horse's hooves as they crossed a cobblestone street rang in his ears, and all at once he was angry—at his disease, at this alluring damned French temptress who had him half out of his head, and not least, at himself.

He sat up, gripped her arms tightly, looked directly into her eyes. "Don't play with me, lady," he said harshly. "If you want to jump in bed with someone who makes your goddamned nipples hard, I'm all for it. But tell Judah *first!*"

Verita looked as if she'd been struck across the face. Her eyes blazed. "How dare you speak to me so coarsely? I don't discuss my lovemaking with *anyone!* You Americans are such *boors!*"

Rawlins leaned forward. "Driver, take us back to the Spottswood Hotel."

The hack driver stole a look over his shoulder. "Yes, sir. Right away, sir."

"Why did you tell him that?" Verita asked.

"Because I don't need any more of this silly game. You're going to drop me off and go on your merry way."

She smiled, but only with her mouth. "Whatever you wish, *mon général.*"

In that moment, in the midst of his turmoil, he was once more struck by the feeling that he had seen her beautiful face somewhere before, but the expression had been more animated.

★   ★   ★

WATCHING him disappear into the hotel, Verita shook her head. She wasn't used to being rejected and talked to in such a crude manner. The bastard. Still, he had really aroused her. God! he was *strong*. Those eyes of his were like hard black diamonds. She could make him change his mind, she knew it! But she couldn't estrange Judah, not yet. She still hadn't found out whether he knew anything about his brother Jews. Everytime she tried to steer the conversation toward the right questions, he skillfully evaded her.

It was too bad about this harsh Yankee general. There wouldn't be time to implicate him in public now. Maybe there was some other way. It was just too perfect to miss. She could see the Richmond newspapers now—screaming about the plot coming directly from Grant's office, from McClellan. Rawlins and Benjamin, a *ménage à trois* with the notorious Verita!

She laughed. And then she thought of Rawlins's rough face on her breasts. He was so different from Judah, so harsh, unpolished, unrelenting. A wild one perhaps—

Maybe another time.

She told the driver to proceed.

★   ★   ★

MOSBY'S buoyancy slipped the moment he walked into his office and found the telegraphs on his desk. The first was from Harry Sellers, Hood's former adjutant, in San Antonio: "Impossible for me to leave before Sunday. Could not arrive Richmond before Weds. Sorry." Mosby nodded; he'd expected something like that. But Sellers wasn't important; Lafayette McLaws was crucial.

The telegram from Savannah, Georgia, was from his wife: "General McLaws is fishing in the Tennessee Mountains somewhere west of Chattanooga with some of his old army friends there. I have no way of contacting him. Sorry."

Mosby threw the telegraph on his desk. *Damn!* He looked at a map on the wall. Chattanooga was damn near a two-day train ride away. And he didn't even know where the man was! Of all the damned times to go fishing! Chattanooga. There was a military district headquarters there . . . he could wire the commander, maybe he would know. It was his only chance. He looked at his watch. 3:21. God, it was late on a Friday afternoon.

After sending the telegraph to the Chattanooga commander, he went to Jeb's office and told him the problem.

"Is there anything I can do—take the stand and tell it all from my side maybe?"

Mosby shook his head. "Won't help."

Stuart frowned. "Then what *can* I do? I told you, I'm tired of being a bump on a log."

"Like I said, be patient. I have a couple of ideas spinning around in my head."

"Like what?"

"Going to Arlington."

"To see the general?"

"Yup."

Stuart's eyes lit up. "Now, *that's* something I could do."

"Not as well as I can. It's possible, Heaven forbid, that he's part of this damned conspiracy. In that case, someone has to talk to him directly. And you can't do that."

"That's impossible." Jeb's face grew red. "I don't ever want to hear anything like that from you again, John. He is the greatest man this continent has ever known, and his integrity is unassailable!"

"That's why you can't go."

Stuart was still perturbed. "And I don't want you accusing him of anything, either. That would be just like it was coming from me, and I won't have it!"

Mosby nodded, smiled softly. "Sometimes, Jeb, you are the most innocent of innocents."

"I mean it."

"I won't in any way infringe on your friendship with him. I promise."

"What are you going to ask him?"

"I don't know for sure. I haven't even made the decision to go yet."

"Well, if you do, just remember what I said."

"I will." Mosby watched his friend for a few moments before asking, "Jeb, have you ever considered what you might do if this all blows up in your face?"

The answer was soft, measured. "I've thought about it. I could get a king's ransom to command cavalry in several places around the world. Three good offers have come in since this mess started. But I'm a Virginian, John, and I want my kids to grow up here. So I suppose it would be business or politics. Trouble is, I don't know anything about business, and I think I'm too honest to be a politician."

He found a chuckle. "You don't suppose Phil Sheridan would hire me in the Union cavalry, do you? And let me come home on weekends? I'll have to ask John Rawlins about that." He got to his feet. "Fact is, I don't want to be anything but what I am—the cavalry leader of the C.S. Army. And I don't know if I could stand to have that taken away from me."

He paused, suddenly feeling sentimental. "You know, John, I had a trooper once who always managed to sing a little ditty when things got tight. It went like this: *'Now let the world wag as it will; I'll be happy and gay still.'* Maybe I ought to remember some of the good things." He cleared his throat. "If you see the general, say 'hello' for me, will you?"

★   ★   ★

JOHN Mosby couldn't remember exactly what kind of a get-to-gether Spring was taking him to, just something with her abolitionist acquaintances. It would be a strain, but he should at least go through the motions. One of these days, there might be time for a good long talk on the matter. Certainly, it was something they needed to settle between them. But with so many other things pressuring him, he didn't have time now.

Waiting in the Spottswood lobby, he played mind games with the black-and-white marble squares that made up the famous floor of the hotel. He tried to picture huge chess pieces with the uniforms and faces of the members of the drama known as the Stuart Court. But it didn't work—he kept seeing too many pawns. . . .

"Hello, darling!" Spring looked somewhat prim in a looped-up damask plum skirt topped by a white blouse with a black lace Victoria tie that reached to her slender waist. She kissed Mosby's cheek. "Have you waited long?"

He grinned. "An eternity." He glanced at the top of her head. "Where do you get those funny little hats?"

"I stopped at William's in Washington City in June, and bought four different styles. You might say I sort of pattern the others from them."

"Do you mean to say I'm in love with a lady capable of making her own hats? Now, that's a special kind of dowry."

She fluttered her fan in the gesture that gave off a modesty signal. "Oh, I have all sorts of specialties. Did I hear you mention a dowry? Doesn't that have something to do with a bride?"

He shook his head. "My tongue must've slipped. Where is this party we're attending?"

She looked at him sharply. "Party? John, we're going to a meeting at twelve-ten East Marshall. It's with some acquaintances I've made —some people interested in the universal freedom of—"

"Colonel Mosby, how are you tonight?" It was John Rawlins. He raised his hat, nodded to Spring, "Miss Blakely."

"Evening, General. Is the Yankee mail still interesting?" Mosby replied.

"It does tend to keep Little Mac from being bored. He doesn't like the word 'Armageddon.' "

"It's a threatening word."

"Can we talk tomorrow?"

"May have to wait until Sunday, General. I'm considering a trip out of town tomorrow. Would sometime in the afternoon do? Or is it too urgent?"

"That should be fine." Rawlins touched the brim of his hat. "Have a pleasant evening, folks."

As they headed for the door Spring asked, "What was all of that talk about Armageddon and mail?"

"Army talk, ma'am."

"But I'm part of the Army, remember?"

"It's secret stuff—I can't talk about it, darling."

She frowned as they reached the street and he pointed to his rig parked about twenty yards away. "I don't believe General Rawlins is down here just to observe Jeb's court. If you won't tell me, I'll just have to ask Uncle John."

He grinned. "If Uncle John wants to tell you, that's fine."

As they turned on the north side of the Capitol, Spring suddenly asked, "Where are you going out of town?"

"Up to Arlington to see General Lee."

"About what—can you tell me *that?*"

"Uh huh." He told her about McLaws's fishing trip. "The only way out may be for Lee to testify."

"Will he do that? Uncle John said the president has asked him to stay completely out of it."

Mosby frowned. "I guessed that, but I didn't want to believe it had really happened. *Goddamnit!*"

"You going anyway?"

"Yup."

★　★　★

"TELL me, Colonel Mosby, how is Stuart going to come out?"
The questioner was a Reverend somebody, a young Methodist
minister.

"If there is any justice, General Stuart will be cleared of all allegations." It was a relief to hear a name other than Wendell Phillips
or William Lloyd Garrison, Mosby thought, trying to remain tolerant.
Why in the hell had she brought him here?

An older woman asked, "I've often wondered—how did the slaves
of soldiers fare during the war? I mean did they fight too? We always
hear about how our brave white boys were shot up, but what about
the poor slaves?"

Practically all of the fourteen people in the parlor turned to hear
Mosby's answer. Spring smiled, listening from where she was pouring
each of them a fresh cup of coffee.

"Well," he replied, "only those sons from slave-holding families had
servants in the war, and the preponderance of them were officers.
There were, however, many instances of privates having as many as
three horses and a servant. No, the servants did not fight, although
there were occasions when they had to for survival. And there have
been instances of servants saving their masters' lives. But never in
ranks, formally.

"They usually rode along in the rear of any column, taking care of
extra horses and the belongings of their masters. When a campaign
was hard on the masters, it was hard on the servants, and vice versa.
And medically they were well taken care of by our surgeons when
there was time."

"What do you mean—when there was time? Did you just let them
die like vermin when time was of the essence?"

Mosby sighed. "Of course not. I meant that there were times when
nobody was well taken care of. Can you imagine how many wounded
soldiers were left behind on the slope of Cemetery Ridge at Gettysburg
after Pickett's Charge?"

"Did you have a servant during the war, Colonel Mosby?"

"Yes. Aaron went through the whole war with me."

"And did you free him out of gratitude when it was over?" asked
a man with a Maryland accent.

"No. He and his wife manage my house."

"Do you mean you *still* have slaves?" This time the questioner was
a young woman with blond hair in a plain black dress.

"I have two servants."

"Don't you feel any guilt about that—I mean in this day and age?"

Mosby glanced through narrowed eyes at Spring as she moved close to him with the fresh coffee. She said nothing. He turned back to the blond woman. "No."

She persisted. "What do you mean, 'no,' Colonel Mosby?"

His smile was tight. "No, ma'am."

"You have no consideration for the liberty of a man and his wife, human beings just like yourself in God's eyes—a man who followed you through thick and thin in the war?"

His voice was even, measured. "Madam, I have the utmost consideration for my servants. And I don't think you have a right to ask me such a question."

"Then what are you doing at an anti-slavery meeting?"

Spring broke in, "Colonel Mosby is here as my guest, and I think we should get on to our lecture."

Everyone began to talk at once, glancing back at him as they turned away. He shook his head as Spring handed him his cup. "Why the hell did you bring me here?" he asked through clenched teeth. "I'm no goddamned abolitionist."

"I told you what it was. I—"

"I want to talk to you outside."

"But, John—"

He headed for the hallway, went out the front door, so angry his hand was shaking. She reached him moments later where he stood by his rig. "John, you have to listen to me. This is a big part of me, and I want you to understand it. I want you to see that we can't go on in the South as before. This is a new age and the colored people have heard about the life and freedom Lincoln promised them. We have to see with an open mind. Change simply can't be denied."

"You had no right."

"If you love me as you say, I have a right to share my feelings with you."

His eyes blazed. "You didn't have one single goddamned right to do this to me. I'm a Southerner, and I'm damned proud of it. I have a *right* to own slaves if I so wish, and I won't have a bunch of malcontents deriding me for it!"

"Is that what you think I am—a *malcontent?*" Spring snapped back.

"No, you're just a little mixed up. Kentucky and all. When you get over this game and come back to your senses, you'll be all right."

"A game is it?" she flared. "Is wanting four million people to be freed from their chains a goddamned *game,* John Mosby? You're no better than the rest of the bigots, the last dregs of the cotton aristocracy that want to preserve the status quo of having negroes do everything for them but eat and make love!"

"I don't want to talk about it any more tonight. Get in the buggy and I'll take you home."

She stamped her foot. "I wouldn't ride with you if this were the last horse in the goddamned Confederacy!"

"Don't be silly. Get in."

"Silly, am I? I don't ever want to see you again, John Mosby!" She spun on her heel and stomped back to the house.

★   ★   ★

THE three-storied house at 9 Main Street was totally quiet as Verita sipped her brandy and regarded Judah in the candlelight. He had attended the play again and brought her home for a late supper.

Judah's dark eyes smiled. "A bright copper penny for your thoughts, my dear."

"I heard about this Negro cause known as Abraham today."

"Now, where did you hear about that?"

She raised an eyebrow. "We liberals have our ways."

Judah smiled, shook his head. "You certainly do."

"Well, are you going to tell me about it?"

"I don't know much. It's supposedly some kind of movement among the Negro people to gain their freedom, as you already know. What did you hear today?"

"That the coloreds may rise sooner than anyone thinks. Does that make any sense to you?"

"No—they have neither the means nor the organization. As you know, revolution costs a lot of money."

That was precisely what she had wanted him to say! "So . . . there must be ways of getting money for such a noble cause as freedom."

"Yes, I suppose there is Northern money available from all those rabid abolitionists up there. And probably money from France and Great Britain . . . Canada. But it takes exceptional organization to gather and best use such monies. I don't believe that kind of structure exists. Remember that classic old story from the French Revolution: It seems these two men were having a glass of wine on the Champs Élysées when a mob rushed by. 'Oh, I must go,' one said, getting slowly to his feet. 'I'm their leader.' "

She frowned. "I don't think that's particularly amusing. Aren't there people here in the South who can do this organizing?"

"Perhaps a few, but you don't understand what a massive problem it would be. Just to keep from getting shot would be—"

"What about your sympathetic Jews? Certainly some of them have the capability to organize such a venture."

"Of course, but that would be terribly risky."

"*Are* there any Jews who are sympathetic to this cause?" she persisted.

"I'm sure there are. It's in the Jewish nature. But you must understand the Jewish assimilation situation in the South."

"If they wouldn't manage such a risky enterprise, would they at least support it financially?" She held her breath, watched him closely.

He smiled, got up from his chair and came around the table without answering. Leaning over, he kissed her and drew her into his arms. Moments later, he said, "*Cherie*, we've talked enough about revolution and money. Come, let me take you to bed and shut out the cares of the cruel world."

Damn him!

DAY 6

MOSBY looked up in wonder as he turned off the road and up the long drive that led to Arlington House. The tall white-columned mansion had never failed to impress him, whether he was looking west from the U.S. Capitol, up from the river, or from the road below. Set against the dark green trees that provided its back-drop, the stately structure was even more imposing, he thought, than the Confederate Capitol building. Perhaps it was the setting, the majestic defiance the mansion provided sitting there on its promontory, an-nouncing to the North that it had survived. Announcing that the man most instrumental in saving the Confederacy lived right there, right across the Potomac.

Mosby was familiar with Arlington House. He had written a paper on the place when he was a student at the University of Virginia, and recently he had read an article in the *Southern Literary Messenger* about it. The mansion was constructed early in the century by George Wash-ington Parke Custis, the foster son of the first president, and the father of Mary Custis Lee, the general's wife. Upon her father's death, the eleven-hundred-acre estate was willed to Mary, to pass on to his eldest grandson, Custis, upon her death.

Soon after his father-in-law died in 1857, Robert E. Lee took an extended leave of absence from his regiment in Texas to administer the will and bring the farms of Arlington back into full production. One of his requirements was to free the huge number of slaves be-longing to the Custis family. Knowing he couldn't turn them loose to fend for themselves immediately, he conducted a unique experiment and educated them before creating the community known as Freedman's Village—where some seven hundred free negroes now lived.

Soon after making his difficult decision to resign from the U.S. Army and go with Virginia in 1861, Lee brought his crippled wife to Richmond. A short time later, Union General Irvin McDowell made Arlington House his headquarters. And not long after that, the U.S. Congress passed an atrocious bill that enabled the U.S. government to confiscate land held by Southerners, men or women.

Mosby still got angry when he thought about it!

An owner had to pay the taxes *directly*—no intermediary could pay them. And since Mary Custis Lee was in a wheelchair, and obviously General Robert E. Lee wasn't about to present himself to Federal authorities, the estate was sold to the government in lieu of a tax of $92.07, plus 50 percent of that sum, for a *pittance* of its real worth.

And in June of 1864, two hundred acres of the estate had been turned into a Federal cemetery. Now thousands of graves—Union, Confederate, and contraband—dotted the beautiful grounds, a stark reminder of the terrible conflict. But they weren't the only reminder: the mansion and outbuildings had been allowed to run down considerably during the war, and General Lee had not yet been able to get rid of all the scars.

Mosby rode slowly, taking in the massive white Doric columns that overwhelmed the sixty-foot-long front portico. There were eight of them, eight huge guardsmen overlooking the broad Potomac below. He turned, was greeted by the sight of Washington City on the other side of the river. What a breathtaking view!

"May I take your horse, sir?" a well-dressed servant asked as he reached the mansion.

"Yes, thank you. I am here to see General Lee."

"Yes, sir. Of course, sir. The butler will meet you at the main door, sir."

Mosby nodded. He had taken the early train north to Alexandria, where he rented the sorrel mare. Before leaving, he had considered sending a telegraph to the general, but had instead decided to just take his chances on finding him at home. But walking by the huge columns on the portico, he felt a sudden pang of nervousness. This was not an escapade behind enemy lines, nor was it a meeting with Beauregard. *He was infringing on the privacy of Robert E. Lee!*

The butler took him to the formal drawing room off the main hall and indicated a chair by the cold fireplace. It was a large room, one that had probably seen many important people, he thought as he waited and tried to calm his jitters. Washington, Custis, Lee—the names that rang through Virginia history—the old quality, the nobility of Virginia. He wondered if the general would even see him. . . . He remembered a story he'd heard about Lee in the war—that Lee's aides always shielded him from complainers because the general hated to say "no" to anyone.

And he remembered the first time he went to see the general. It was a hot, dusty day in the early summer of '62, and he had trudged several miles sucking hard-to-find lemons that he had obtained at Fortress Monroe. He had just been exchanged as a prisoner and had discovered intelligence that General Burnside was moving his corps north to reinforce Pope. It was information Lee should have, and the fact that its bearer was a lowly, dirty private made no difference. After all, hadn't he just ridden around McClellan with Jeb a few weeks before?

He was at first rebuffed at Lee's headquarters, but somehow he finally got in to see the gray-bearded commander. The general remembered his name, was delighted with the information, and got word off to Stonewall Jackson immediately. He recalled how the commanding general had smiled when the dusty scout offered him a lemon—

"I'm sorry to keep you waiting, Colonel Mosby," Robert E. Lee said as he strode into the drawing room, hand extended, wearing a light blue cotton suit. And boots, as if he'd been riding.

Mosby shook hands, noting how white the general's hair and beard had become. He said, "I sincerely apologize for not contacting you prior to coming, sir, but things are reaching such an abrupt head with the Stuart court that there wasn't time."

Lee nodded, indicated that Mosby should return to his chair, and sat beside him on the edge of a straight-back. "I understand, and it's quite all right. How is Jeb holding up under the strain of keeping quiet?" He smiled.

Mosby thought he seemed shorter, but that was always the case when the general was out of the saddle—he had such short legs and tiny feet. And Lee didn't look well. Grayer in the face, new lines, the flesh beginning to sag around his eyes. A sick man, the heart disease had even bothered him back at Gettysburg—that and the old soldier's disease from some green fruit, Mosby had heard. But no illness could rob Robert E. Lee of that special bearing of his, that unique nobility that could make soldiers cheer and wave their hats, often sing, when he rode by—even if they had just been thrashed in battle. No sickness could rob those clear black eyes of their ebony sharpness, their warmth, and their sadness. Mosby acknowledged the joke with a smile. "He's okay at this point, sir."

"And how is our regal, zestful old capital—still winding down into respectability? I haven't been there in weeks."

"It's a bit of a circus right now, sir—what with all of the visitors for the court."

"Yes, I read in the *Dispatch* where they've come all the way from Texas to get their two cents in. That's what can happen when a man as exciting as Jeb is challenged." His eyes drifted away to a bright scene in the past. "I remember when I first met him . . . it was right here in this room, the day of John Brown's raid on Harpers Ferry. He was young and breathless, a lieutenant on leave from Kansas, just dying to get in on some excitement. He had just rushed from the War Department to tell me I was to command the troops heading for Harpers Ferry. I was on extended leave, you know . . ."

Robert Lee smiled, the black eyes crinkling at their corners. "Jeb's exuberance never did wear off, you know. If he'd had his way up there, he would have stormed that firehouse single-handed the moment we arrived. I had no idea that within three years he would be one of my most valiant generals. . . ."

A look of pain crossed his face, didn't linger. He massaged the fingers of his left hand, turned away.

Mosby wondered if it was physical or for Jeb. He wanted to break in, bring up his request, get the hell out—but it didn't seem right. He had rehearsed his opening comments to the *clickety-clack* of the railroad wheels all the way up from Richmond, but right now, in the still presence of this regal man, he was somehow . . . intimidated? No, it was something else, something he couldn't put his finger on. Spiritual, that was it—being with this extraordinary man was a *spiritual* experience. And what he had to say would be an intrusion into that indefinable spirituality—

"You don't know how this court has troubled me," the general said, turning back with eyes that were now softer, like India ink. "I've read every word from all of the Richmond papers. It must be dreadful for him."

Mosby found his voice. "It hasn't been pleasant."

"How does it look?"

Mosby took a deep breath. He *had* to get on with it. "I'm worried about the outcome, sir."

"And why is that?"

Mosby told him about Bragg and the order to shorten the proceedings.

Lee shrugged. "Perhaps they've heard enough to make a decision."

"Unfortunately, I think that decision was made before the court ever opened."

"Why do you say that?"

"Because I think there is a conspiracy to nail Jeb to the wall, General."

"That's a harsh accusation, Mosby." The black eyes were now cold.

"There are obvious signs."

"Braxton Bragg has always been choleric, but he is a fair man."

"Was. I don't trust him this time, sir."

Lee frowned, obviously uncomfortable. "I don't like to hear such an accusation, sir."

Mosby couldn't stop now; he held Lee's stern gaze. "It's not intentional with him, sir. I think it comes straight down from the top."

Lee just shook his head.

Mosby went right to the point. His words were low, clear in the large room, "And there is only one way the truth will be accepted . . . and that is for you to testify, sir."

It was utterly silent for several moments. Finally Lee said softly, "I can't."

Mosby saw the pain in his eyes, knew how difficult this was for him. But he couldn't stop. "Why not, sir? Do you know that Jeb almost forbade my coming here? Do you know how much he loves you?"

"There are reasons, Colonel. I must ask for your confidence for twenty-four hours in what I'm about to tell you."

"Certainly, sir."

"It will be officially announced by President Davis tomorrow that I will be his running mate in the coming election. And he has asked me to remain aloof from this court."

Mosby nodded; he had expected it. "Congratulations, sir! Our government will be in safe hands with you there . . . but as far as the court goes, that's coercion."

Robert Lee frowned like a schoolteacher. "There are times, Colonel, when one has to weigh the values. President Davis has great plans for this young country of ours, and I am quite enthusiastic about them.

This inquiry into Jeb's sometimes impetuous actions doesn't balance with their magnitude."

Mosby shook his head, got to his feet. "Are you saying, sir, that Jeb is expendable, that you are involved in the conspiracy as well?"

Lee seldom raised his voice; his face just got red. "Sir," he said coldly, "I know of no conspiracy."

"I know that. You are above any such skulduggery."

"I see nothing to be gained by testifying. Those court members are all honest men."

"Undoubtedly. But if you speak, sir, the world will know it's the truth."

Lee shook his head. "I still see nothing to be gained."

The former ranger spoke softly, "Nothing but honor, sir."

The general gathered himself, gave his visitor a bleak look. "You are welcome to stay the night, sir. But I'm afraid I'm too busy to talk with you further. Good day."

Mosby watched the erect figure leave the room.

He had failed.

★ ★ ★

"MAY I join you for a wee glass of beer, sir?" Mosby looked up from his corner table at the Irish brogue. A medium-sized man of uncertain appearance was standing three feet away, holding his hat in his hands. The man's name was Mark and he was Mosby's Washington agent. "Yes," he replied. "Have a seat."

After the man took a chair and ordered a large glass of beer from the buxom waitress, he asked, "You from Alexandria, sir?"

"No, Winchester."

"You come here often?"

"No, only when I wish to buy a rare book."

"Sure and it's strange you should say that, with me being a rare book dealer and all. Fact is, I have a title here that might interest you, and the price is surely right." The agent named Mark rummaged through the bag he was carrying and brought out a faded brown book. "Here, mate, feast your eyes on that."

Mosby nodded, sipped his beer, leafed through the pages. At page thirty-eight, there was a thin sheet of paper filled with neat handwriting in a dark blue ink. Mark's written report. "Ah, what is the background here?" he asked appreciatively.

"The author was a novelist before the War of the Revolution in this country. And a fine one he was! It's a story about the rising of negroes and the killing of white leaders in this new country. A bit far-fetched, but intriguing." Mark drank deeply from his beer glass.

Mosby nodded. "Sounds interesting, but I have to leave. Would you like to walk with me and tell me more?"

"If you'll buy me book?"

"I think there's a good chance."

Moments later, on the brick sidewalk outside the tavern, Mark dropped his accent. "It's in some way connected with the damned abolitionists, but we don't know how. It's a special radical group of no more than a dozen members with a special mission of inciting the Southern negroes to revolt. They are calling it *Amistad,* for that slave ship."

Mosby frowned. The crumbs, the pieces, and the pie—starting to come together in reverse order as it always was with intelligence. But several bits were still missing. "Does this Amistad have a specific goal?"

"Something big against the Confederate government, maybe big enough to bring us back to a state of war."

Mosby stared at his agent. "How reliable is this information?"

"My man has been inside the anti-slavery movement for a long time and hasn't lied to me yet."

"Is there anything he could gain by concocting a story like this? Money or anything?"

"No, I trust him completely, sir."

"And no names?"

"No names, just excited whispers."

"Any more?"

"Yes, this Amistad supposedly has been training here in the Washington area—or at least staying here."

"Any leads on that?"

"Not a one, sir."

"Anything else at all?"

"No, sir."

Mosby nodded. "All right. Use all of your resources among the negroes, the malcontents, the anti-slavers, and the warmongers. Money is no object. I'll wire queries to all of our other people. *Someone* will know something about this Amistad. It's too exciting to keep quiet."

★ ★ ★

I N THE late-setting sun of Rocketts, two black men were paying more attention to their drinking than to pulling any fish out of the James River. But only one of them was really imbibing.

"Where do you get such good corn whiskey, nigger?"

"I got this here friend with his own still," Israel Jones replied, trying to keep a straight face. "He sells it to me for only twict as much as he does to his enemies. *Haw!*" He slapped his leg and roared with laughter.

Willie Burns choked laughing, spewing whiskey out like spray. He lowered the jug and threw his head back in a fit of hilarity. "Tha's good, tha's good—for only *twict* as much as his enemies. Israel Jones, you's de funniest nigger in this whole town, you know that?"

"Here, Willie, you let me have some of that. Just cuz I gets it so cheap doesn't mean you have to drink all of it." Israel Jones tilted the jug back, faking another big swig.

"You really is funny, Israel, you know that?"

"My wife don't think I'm so funny mostly. *Haw!*"

Willie Burns was taken by another fit of laughter. "Ain't a woman in Rocketts thinks her man's funny," he gasped.

"What's your woman say when you go to Jubilo's meetings?"

"None of her damned business. That's *Abraham* business!" Willie Burns took the jug from Israel and tipped it back.

"I sure wish I could get in your guards company—I hear tell you got guns and uniforms and everything just like during the war."

Willie Burns looked from side to side in mock secrecy. "We's got black uniforms, like *death,* and *carbines*—good uns. I'se a corporal!"

"Think you could get me in?"

" 'Course I could. They's only 'bout forty of us training like soldiers, you know. We what old Jubilo calls his core corps. Ain't that funny —*core corps!*" Willie Burns threw his head back and nearly choked laughing again.

Israel Jones slapped his back, cackling. Finally he asked, "You fellas ever gonna do anything for real?"

Willie Burns nodded, sobering. In nearly a whisper he said, "They say soon we's gonna go to war. Nothing for sure, but since de man come, we's training harder and tha's a fact."

Israel Jones laid his fishing pole on the river bank and leaned back on his elbows. "What *man* you talking 'bout? I been hearing about some man come to town, but I don't know nothing 'bout him."

Willie Burns tipped the jug back, wiped his mouth. "De *man!* He de new John Brown come to set us free! Where you been, nigger, up there shoveling that there horse shit so much you don't know nothin?"

Israel Jones assumed a look of awe. "John Brown come back from de grave, huh? Say, when can you talk to old Jubilo 'bout me getting in? I sure would like to meet old John Brown. You ever seen him?"

"I seen him in Jubilo's church last Sunday. Least most folks says that was him."

"What 'bout old Jubilo?"

"You meet me at the church 'bout a half hour before the service, and I'll tell him I axed you in. You say you can get us horses if we goes to war?"

"I works right there in de stable where they all is."

Willie Burns reached for the jug. "You know, Israel, you's a case, and that's a fact."

★ ★ ★

S PRING Blakely couldn't remember ever feeling so dejected. She had tried to read, tried to crochet, tried to write in her journal, had even gone for a ride late in the afternoon. Now, as she ambled along on a late evening walk near her uncle's house, she had about expended her avenues of occupation. She felt dreadful. She had absolutely no one to talk to. Not a single one of her abolitionist friends would understand—all they would say was "he's just another typical slaver; get used to it, or forget him." And she hadn't been in Richmond long enough to make any other friends. Verita might understand, but she was at the theater. Her uncle was on John's side, like almost everyone else in the whole country.

She was ready to grab the next person coming down the walk and shout, "But I love him!" But what good would that do? The voice still lingered, the one that whispered, "It'll never work—you are at opposite poles on a problem that can never be resolved."

She heard the katydids beginning their Saturday night song, saw the first of the fireflies. Magnolias and hoop skirts on the old plantation, peach blossoms and broad leaf tobacco, cotton bales and the *toot* of the riverboat's horn, spirited horses and Shakespeare; the darkies a-singing down by their cabins in the velvet summer nightfall; ante-bellum forever.

Was it ante-bellum forever? Would the evils of the old South persist? Surely such a terrible social ill was wrong in the eyes of God. Why didn't He, in all of His omnipotence, rectify the wrong? Were the colored people, in spite of everything, the misbegotten sons of Ham who were forever cursed to be the hod carriers of civilization?

A couple drove by in an open carriage, the young woman sitting close to the handsome young man and laughing gaily. *They* weren't squabbling over the imbalance in the social structure. *Damn you, John Mosby!*

Shortly, she realized she was in front of the yellow brick mansion on East Clay—maybe Bessica would talk to her! But it was Saturday night, and she was probably busy. She started to turn away, then shook her head and strode briskly up to the front door.

"Why of course I'd just love to talk to you, my dear," Bessica said moments later. "I'm just sitting here alone reading. Who would ever guess that I'd be doing such a terrible thing on a Saturday night? Why, honey, you just come right on in—would you like some coffee, or maybe some wine?"

"Do you have any bourbon whiskey?"

Bessica raised an eyebrow, smiled. Southern ladies didn't drink such things. "Certainly." She went to a sideboard in the parlor.

"The best of Kentucky women sometimes drown their sorrows in good sour mash," Spring said, feeling awkward.

Bessica poured two glasses neat and handed one to her guest. "And what are you sorrowful about, my dear?"

Spring sipped, said, "I guess, since you probably own about a thousand slaves or more, you're the last person I should talk to . . . but, Bessica, I'm so blue I could just put my head down on your shoulder and bawl my damned eyes out."

Bessica smiled. "Honey, when it comes to crying, it doesn't make any difference whether you own slaves or elephants. Is it that John Mosby—has he been bad to you?"

The tears let loose, running into Spring's bourbon. "I must tell you first that I'm an, an abolitionist. Now, maybe you'll change your mind. I, I—" she dropped her head and sobbed.

Bessica was at her side instantly, taking her in her arms and holding her head against her breast. "Now, honey, you just go right ahead and let it out. I don't care if you're John Brown. I've been doing a little crying myself lately, so I know what tears feel like."

Spring blinked, pulled her head up. "What have you got to cry about?"

"That case, Jeb Stuart. I love him so much I can hardly stand it, but all I am is the scarlet woman. I . . . but tell me what that dreadful John Mosby did to you."

Spring poured it out, letting the tears flow throughout. And when she was finished, Bessica handed her a fresh hanky. "You poor dear. He had no right to be so mean about it . . . but you do know what a hard subject it is. Honey, you're a Southerner—you should know that. It's the way things are down here. 'Course, you're welcome to your own opinion, that's why we have a free country."

Spring drained her bourbon. "I *know*, but I love him so much, and he just has to understand how I feel. I'm *different,* and he just won't take the time to realize it! He doesn't care!"

Bessica poured each of them another neat whiskey. "He cares— just don't crowd him. Honey, he'll be kissing your feet and *begging* forgiveness for being such a boor."

Spring tossed off her whole drink. "He'd better. Now what can we do about Jeb? Oh, that's right—he's married. I've never met his wife so I can't say anything. . . . Oh, how dreadful, Bessica, you *are* the scarlet woman. How long has your affair been going on?"

Bessica's eyes brimmed. "That's just it, Spring, it isn't even a real affair! I throw myself at him like a shameless hussy, and he just about slips, and then he draws his damned Sir Lancelot cloak about his shoulders and fades away in his precious honor." Bessica drained her glass. "And I'm almost beside myself. That's why I'm not out at a party somewhere tonight—I'm hoping he'll come by and say, 'Bessica, honey, I love you and I'm taking you straight to bed.' I tell you, darling, I'd make love to him on the *front lawn!*" The tears broke and ran down her cheeks. "But he won't do it, I know I won't see hide nor hair of him tonight."

Spring held her tightly for a moment, then went to the sideboard and refilled their glasses. "Let's drink a toast," she said, "to the two least understood women in Richmond."

Bessica's tongue was already getting a bit thick. She licked away a salty tear and raised her glass. "Hear! Hear! And to slavery and anti-slavery, and uncaring men, and every goddamned scarlet woman in *history!*"

★　★　★

JUBILO peered into the darkness of the covered hack waiting outside his store. There was plenty of moonlight for him to make out the sharp, handsome features of his former commanding officer. "That you, Cunnel Higginson, suh?"

The clergyman leaned forward, extended his hand. "Most certainly is, First Sergeant Jubilo. How are you?" He grinned broadly.

"Tolerably good, suh." Jubilo came automatically back to a position of attention, remembering that first time so long ago when the colonel had noticed him and called him aside at the rifle range. The next day he was a corporal. It had been his first step into power.

"Get in, my friend, get in. We have much to talk about."

"Yessuh, Cunnel, suh." He wanted to speak correctly, not like some shiftless darky. He hadn't seen the colonel since the day he left the regiment. He crawled inside the buggy.

"Any place you'd like to go?" Higginson asked.

"Maybe drive on down by the river where there ain't no one around and we can maybe walk a spell." He gave the driver instructions.

They talked about the old days during the war in South Carolina in the first negro regiment on American soil, and of the problems of organization and early training. They both chuckled at some memories, laughed aloud at others. And before long they were well out of town, standing on a low knoll overlooking the river. The reflection of the new moon struck the water directly in front of them, adding to the blue-gray brightness of the landscape.

"Almost like daytime, isn't it?" Higginson said softly, watching a rather large boat with a lighted cabin float by a couple of hundred yards away.

"Yes, sir, mighty bright. How long will you be here, Colonel?"

"I'm going back on the late train to Washington tonight. I wouldn't even have come down now if it weren't for the problem Mr. Smith is having with you."

Jubilo just stared at the river, saying nothing.

"Amistad really needs you, you know."

Jubilo nodded imperceptibly.

"Salmon told me the men were talking kind of crazy the other night when you went to their meeting. Well, I figured it was time for me to come and see you anyway, so here I am, First Sergeant."

Jubilo recognized the ploy of using his former rank to remind him that he was a subordinate.

"I'm sorry they did that," the minister went on, "but sometimes when you sharpen the skills of men like that they talk strange, fool around. These are good people, Jubilo, very good people. I recruited every one of them myself, and they will be superb in their mission." He paused, watched another lighted boat go by. "Thing is, they really need your people as the diversionary force on this, Jubilo. The whole mission and those that will follow depend upon it. I don't have to tell you the importance of this first mission, do I? If we manage to get Davis, there will no stopping us. It'll be like a broken dam!"

"Yes, suh," Jubilo replied. The colonel certainly hadn't lost any of his old persuasive powers.

"Therefore, my friend, I beseech you to do everything in your power to help them. Whether you like it or not, we are *all* brothers in arms. They are placing their very souls on the block for the same things you so fervently believe in. . . .

"*No* one will be satisfied until every one of God's people is free. And it is *most* important for Abraham to be a part of this very first mission. The Southern negro will then be able to stand tall and say, '*There*, you white folks, that's what will happen if we don't get our freedom!' . . . Don't you see, Jubilo, your people *must* be a part. The Cause will then gather momentum and size like a giant snowball coming down from Mount Sinai—*unstoppable!*"

Higginson lowered his voice. "And most important, everyone in the North will know about Abraham, and that it's a fighting force. And then, my friend, *then* the march to a new war will begin. The Union Army will be marching across the Potomac in no time at all!"

Jubilo broke away from Higginson's glowing gaze, walked away a few steps, then returned. "Cunnel," he said quietly, fingering the scar on his cheek. "I been over all of that with myself. And I had a sign that told me to go ahead. But I just don't know if it's time yet. I just don't know."

A dog barked off in the distance, sharply, with distress.

"Trust me, Jubilo."

The huge black man nodded, sighed. After a long pause, he said, "I'm still getting bad feelings about Salmon Brown and those others, though. But I truly want to please you, and that's the God's truth, Cunnel."

"It's more than pleasing me, it's the future of your people."

Jubilo sighed again. "I'll do it only on condition that Salmon Brown's plan meets with my approval. Anything crazy, or anything that isn't fully in keeping with my overall goals, and I'll pull out. I don't want no Harpers Ferry here, Cunnel."

Thomas Wentworth Higginson stuck out his hand. "Fair enough. I'll so instruct Captain Brown."

DAY 7

JOHN Rawlins opened the door to his hotel room shortly after Mosby's knock. "Come in, sir. Thank you for being so prompt."

"I just found your note a few minutes ago when I got in from Alexandria." Mosby removed his hat, took the chair the general indicated. The ornate room was large, comfortable, certainly befitting a visiting foreign general. But that was why the Spottswood enjoyed such an excellent reputation.

"Yes, I thought you should see this message that came in last night from Washington. Our friend at the Washington *Star* discovered this letter to the editor." He handed over a yellow sheet of paper.

Mosby read quickly:

As a negro journalist who wrote for major Canadian newspapers, I have a special offer for you. I have joined an elite radical group, as second in command, that will in the immediate future destroy the top of the Confederate government. But that is only the first step, for the revolution in the South will blossom like a giant thunderhead until every colored man in America is free from the white man's yoke. I am planning a series of articles that will bring the reader *inside* with a palpitating heart. What is your bid for such a series?

—Crispus Attucks
Box 341
Richmond, Virginia
C.S.A.

"Crispus Attucks—James Grace," Mosby murmured. "Our murdering abolitionist sure does like to write letters, doesn't he?"

Rawlins nodded. "I assume you can put a guard on that post office box, right?"

"Yes, sir. When it opens tomorrow. What have your people come up with on Grace?"

Rawlins handed him another sheet of paper. "That's his service record from the Army. And arrest record. Three times for assault and battery. Seems to be an unfriendly chap. Even have a picture."

Mosby grabbed the photograph. It wasn't clear. "The bastard could be anywhere in Rocketts, you know." He told Rawlins about the previous night's meeting with his agent, Mark, in Alexandria.

"*Amistad,* huh? *Crispus Attucks?* They seem to have everything worked out along historical lines. I'll get that off by telegraph to Grant himself. John, I think we can quit surmising anything. This sonofabitch is a reality!"

★   ★   ★

ISRAEL Jones summoned up his last reserve of courage at nine-thirty and walked up the path to Jubilo's church. If he kept his hands in his pockets, maybe no one would notice how much they shook, he thought as he went inside the front door and looked around for Willie Burns. He just *knew* that no-count Willie wouldn't be there; it was all corn whiskey talking the night before. Well, that was all right too, because he just couldn't go through with this. No, he'd go back and tell Colonel Mosby to just stick him back in jail if that was the way it was—but he just wasn't cut out to be no spy!

"Hey, Israel Jones. C'mon up here, boy!" It was Willie Burns, sticking his head in the door by the pulpit.

Israel waved, hurried forward. It was too late now. "Oh, Lord," he whispered, "just get me through this morning and I'll be good the whole rest of my days. I promise!"

Jubilo nodded from the cluttered table that served as his church desk when Willie Burns introduced them. "Yes, I've seen you around, Mr. Jones. In fact, in my congregation a couple of times. Mr. Burns, here, tells me you want to join my special guards company. That right?"

"Yessuh."

"What did you do in the Army, Mr. Jones?"

"I was a soldier in the infantry, suh."

"You do anything special? You shoot good?"

"Yessuh. And I was a scout."

"How good did you shoot?"

"I could hit a man at over five hundred yards with de big rifle."

Jubilo nodded. "That's good. Why do you want to be in my guards, Mr. Jones? You might get killed."

Israel felt as if the water was running straight out of his armpits. "I wants my chilluns to be free, and their chilluns," he said with surprisingly strong conviction. "I jes' thinks it's time to do something, stead of jes' talking. You know what I mean, suh?"

Jubilo nodded, fingered his scar. "I know. All right, we're having a special training meeting tonight down at the old tobacco warehouse next to the Powhaton wharf. Just as it's a-getting dark. Nine o'clock. You be there. And I don't stand for nobody being late."

"Yessuh, Parson Jubilo, suh. I'll be there." Israel found a smile for Willie, then suddenly decided he should salute. He stiffened to attention and brought his right arm up.

Jubilo nodded, a brief smile touching his lips. "We don't salute except at meetings, Private Jones."

As Israel Jones hurried out from the interview he bumped directly into Crispus, who had been eavesdropping. As each tried to get out of the other's way, Crispus frowned directly into Israel's sweating face.

"Reverend Jubilo," the Amistad second-in-command said smoothly, "may I have a spell of your time?"

The big man nodded, motioned for Willie Burns to leave. "Make it short, mister. And I don't want to talk about killing women."

Crispus manufactured a smile. "Sir, I feel responsible for upsetting you the other night at the Amistad meeting. And I want to fix that bridge, if I can."

Jubilo eyed him warily.

"We folks at Amistad also have a holy mission, Reverend. And we're willing to lay down our lives any time of the day for it. And it's exactly the same as yours—liberty for the Negro in America. I would like to persuade you to join us, suh."

Jubilo looked coldly down at the smaller man. "I already am. Sent a message to Mr. Smith early this morning. What's wrong, don't you folks talk to one another?"

Crispus blinked, stiffened. "Yessuh, we do. I didn't see him yet. Uh, excuse me for taking up your time."

★　★　★

WALKING out the front of the church, Crispus felt the heat on his cheeks. *Nobody talked to him like that!* And certainly no half-educated common nigger who belonged back in the fields! When the revolution was over it would be different, for damned sure!

He kicked a cracked glass jar lying in the dusty street, breaking it into bits. James Grace didn't have to take that kind of damned abuse. His name would blaze across the sky before this was over, bigger than them all! Yes, they'd all rue the day when they treated him like baggage. All of them. 'Cause they couldn't tie his shoelaces, that was why.

And he always got even.

He'd dug himself out of the garbage of New York City and made something of himself. Learned to read and write toting newspapers when he was little. Never had a daddy, never was sure how old he was. Always had to fight because everyone was against him. Like now; same thing. And always, they weren't as smart as he was.

Always against him.

Even in Toronto where he passed off an old knife scar as a war wound, and got a job on the newspaper. They thought he was a big hero . . . James Grace, he was then . . . a brilliant colored journalist.

Until he killed that girl and had to leave.

It wouldn't be long now. When the smoke cleared from the attack on the court, he'd be fast on his way. Soon the Washington *Star* would offer him a lot of money for that series of articles. And then it would be time for the big book, the one that would tell how he taunted and outwitted the president of the United States!

And then he would not only be the most renowned Negro in America, but the most celebrated revolutionary in the world! He would dwarf everyone who had gone before him . . . even the real Crispus Attucks.

And he would be a power in Abraham . . . and kill all the damned Salmon Browns and the arrogant Jubilo's . . . just as if they were ants.

★ ★ ★

"ALL right, boys, that should do it for tonight," Salmon Brown said from the front of the courtroom mock-up. "We've covered just about every problem that might pop up. We should be in, hit our targets, and out within the three minutes we've practiced. You all know your individual escape plan and each of you has plenty of money.

"Barring any unforeseen change, we should be finished and out of Richmond by this time Tuesday. And the free world will be on its feet shouting our praises. Any questions?"

Beecher Lovejoy, the white man, spoke up. "I still don't like the idea of having Verita in on the final show without practicing with us. Crispus was right about that." There was a murmur of agreement from the others.

Salmon held up his hands to quiet them. "That really isn't a problem. She'll walk through the whole thing with me tomorrow. Besides, that is a command decision, not yours. *I* have planned everything so there can be no error."

Beecher Lovejoy arched an eyebrow toward Crispus over Salmon's growing imperiousness.

Crispus just shrugged imperceptibly.

"What you must keep uppermost in your minds is this glorious opportunity God has offered you," Salmon went on. "When the name Brown is again sung from the rafters, your names will be added in following stanzas. And some day we will *all* be saints. . . . Now, are there any more questions?"

"Yes." It was Nat Turner. "What if old Jubilo decides he ain't gonna be there for that there diversion."

"He'll be there. Crispus and I are going to pay a little visit to him shortly. Anything else? Very well, I'll see you here tomorrow at six."

★   ★   ★

FIFTEEN minutes later, Salmon and Crispus approached the old
tobacco warehouse that served as Jubilo's armory. After being
challenged by a sentry, they entered by a side door. Crispus sniffed
the aromatic old tobacco smell, then glanced up at the large hole in
the roof where the fire had left its signature. Now the bright moon,
already aloft and busy, was adding its presence to the assemblage on
the damp floor below.

Thirty-six negroes in black uniforms with red piping stood at ease
in four ranks of nine each, while four others—officers and non-com-
missioned officers—stood in front of the formation. Another was
lecturing, while Jubilo stood facing them a few feet behind the center.
Everyone except Jubilo had a late-model Spencer carbine.

Salmon and Crispus stopped a few yards to the side and listened
quietly.

"Now as I said," the instructor went on, "I ain't a-telling you what
this building is until de day we hits it. And I ain't a-telling you when
we's gonna hit it until we knows for sure." His dark frown broke
momentarily into a wide smile. "But one thing's a fact—everybody in
this here country knows what it is!"

As the instructor continued, Crispus noticed Israel Jones staring at
Salmon from the near end of the rear rank. He recalled overhearing
the man's conversation with Jubilo that morning at the church, and
how scared he'd looked. He could see the sweat glistening on the
man's cheek, and it wasn't even hot in the old building. Why did he
keep staring so wide-eyed? Everything about him sent off a danger
signal; he was simply too nervous, too shifty and unlikely to be a part
of Jubilo's tough core guards.

"Just before we ignites de dynamite," the instructor said, "you'uns
with de torches will light them with a match and set de curtains to
burning. When this is done, everyone clears out of de building. And
then you dynamiters strikes de match, and *boom!* de whole world
knows de colored folks has stood up on their hindquarters and said,
'No more!'"

Everyone in the ranks grinned and nodded his head as the instructor added, "Y'all who will be going will be told when we knows what day. And now here's your commander, Cunnel Jubilo!"

The big man spoke clearly. "You all know this will be our first real mission as a military group, as a genuine force in Abraham. I'm sure you will all be proud of our part. Now, I know you want to meet our visitor—the son of the famous man from Harpers Ferry whom you've been whispering about . . . his name is Captain Salmon Brown. . . . Sir, would you like to say a few words to these soldiers?"

Salmon nodded, stepped closer, cleared his throat. "Yes, sir, I would." He paused, letting them take him in. "Men, you are about to take part in a divine cause, a mission that God himself has ordained and is overseeing. For the second time in seven years, He has sent a Brown to free the slaves. But this time, the colored man is going to help. And you who are taking part now will be remembered centuries from now in the history books as the first heroes . . . the first saints . . . I'm just proud to be here." He stepped back.

The men in ranks watched him soberly for several moments, sorting out their feelings of awe, fear, and superstition. Finally, one of them said, "Praise de Lord!" and others joined in. "Praise de Lord! Praise de Lord!" When the reaction ended, Jubilo began his half-lecture, half-sermon.

Crispus, immediately bored with the speeches, kept his eye on Israel Jones. The more he watched the man's shifty eyes wander about, the more he was convinced the man was here for some ulterior purpose. He would bear watching. . . .

As soon as Jubilo finished, he walked with Salmon to a corner of the large room where they could have some privacy. "Thank you, Colonel," Salmon said, "for introducing me like that. Some day those men will tell their grandchildren about tonight."

Jubilo looked at him sharply, but Salmon had his eyes cast upward, his hands clasped behind his back. "And their grandchildren will tell *their* grandchildren . . . that this was the night their saviour walked in their midst and spoke to them."

Jubilo was speechless—did this man actually think he was divine? He blinked, wanting to ask him if he had any bread and fishes for the hungry.

Salmon turned his attention to the negro leader; his tone was less lofty. "And now I think we should talk about your part in the Amistad attack, Colonel. Reverend Higginson told me that you are ready to join our cause. I—"

"I've made no such decision, Mr. Brown. I told the cunnel that I must first pass on your entire plan. I've yet to be told precisely what it is."

Salmon kept his displeasure from showing. The inside part of the attack really had nothing to do with the diversion, and it was—to be frank—none of Jubilo's concern. He didn't mind buttering up to the man when it was necessary, but to seek his approval on a plan that he had worked out to perfection? Why the man was really nothing more than a sergeant, a sergeant in a Negro regiment . . . and everyone knew they never did any fighting. Why should a former Negro sergeant pass on his plan? It was arrogant of him to make such a demand. He might rule Rocketts and tell part of Abraham what to do, but by God, he didn't command Amistad! And he didn't give a damn what Higginson had told him.

"Well?"

Salmon frowned. The very idea of knuckling down was repugnant. "When the diversion commences," he replied, "we'll burst into the courtroom and kill our assigned targets. We have rehearsed each step repeatedly and can do it in our sleep. Our targets will be dead and we will have fled in the confusion before they know what hit them."

Jubilo nodded. "That's the mission, Mr. Brown. I want the complete plan."

Salmon's brown eyes grew flinty. "Sir, it must be kept secret. We can't take a chance on anyone talking."

"Are you implying that I will give away the plan, suh?"

Salmon stood his ground. "No, but I must insist on keeping our exact movements and escape plan to ourselves."

"Then, suh," Jubilo growled. "I will have no part of it. Kindly take your man and leave!"

★ ★ ★

VERITA had to admit that it was most charming of Bessica to let her use the carriage at night. Of course her hostess was a hopeless romantic and was convinced she was meeting Judah again. Now, as she waited for Salmon on Ninth Street near the Washington monument on Capitol Square, she thought again about killing the lady. No, it wouldn't be necessary—the staggering mortification of having taken a murdering revolutionary under her roof and to her breast would be enough to send Bessica Adams Southwick off to a cage on a South Sea island.

Salmon's note had come to Bessica's house by messenger shortly after six o'clock, telling her to meet him at the monument at ten-thirty P.M. He was late.

She was about to tell the driver to drive around the square when Salmon stuck his head inside the cab. "Would you like to take a walk with me, mademoiselle?" he asked pleasantly.

They moved well away from the carriage to the base of the statue. "I was held up at Jubilo's meeting," he explained. "That man sure does like to sermonize."

"First, let me tell you about Benjamin. I simply can't pin him down about the Jewish sympathizers. One minute I don't think he knows anything, the next, I thinks he's avoiding the issue. Will you send that information on to Higginson?"

Salmon frowned. "Far as I'm concerned, you don't even need to see him again."

"Can't change anything now. We're too close. Now, tell me about your friend, Jubilo. Is everything all right with him?"

"He's being difficult, thinks he has to approve my plan. Can you *imagine?*"

"What's wrong with that, if it makes him happy?"

"I can't take the chance of any word leaking out."

"Will he talk? I thought you told me he was the king of trumps in Rocketts."

"He is, but that doesn't mean he has the right to question me. After all, he's only a—he's only involved with the diversion."

Verita picked up on the slip. "He's only a what, Salmon, only another negro pretending to the throne? Is that what you were going to say? Is it?" Her eyes were hard.

"No, as I said, he's only a small part of our mission, and I will not take any unnecessary chances. That's all there is to it."

"Don't pontificate with me, Salmon Brown! What are we going to do without him—have you thought of that?"

"Certainly. We can handle it."

She moved close to him, unable to resist the taunt. "Why don't I go see him, Salmon? Let me spend one night with this big bad black man, and he'll see the light, believe me!"

His open palm caught her flush on the cheek, snapping her face around to the side. His other hand siezed her wrist before she could pull her stiletto. "Don't talk such trash to me!" he barked. His face was only inches from her blazing eyes. Twisting her arm behind her back, he groped for her lips, found them . . . and suddenly pulled back, released her, and turned away.

She wanted to jerk him around, slash his face . . . but for some reason his stillness stopped her.

"I'm sorry," he murmured, still not looking at her.

Her anger began to subside as suddenly as it had erupted. What was wrong with this strange obsessed man? Her hand went to the hilt of her dagger. If she had any sense whatsoever, she would kill him and take over Amistad herself. But of course she couldn't. "What is wrong with you, Salmon Brown—are you crazy?" she asked.

He turned, his eyes dark pinpoints in the moonlight. His voice was low, toneless. "Don't you ever say that again."

She looked into those eyes and nodded. "All right, then start making sense. What are you going to do about Jubilo?"

His voice was still flat as he turned to go. "I might kill him."

As she watched him walk away, she again felt a tug of tenderness, an urge to hold him close and tell him it would be all right . . . hold that sometimes fierce, troubled face against her bare breasts and kiss away its demons until it softened into peacefulness. She wondered what he had been like as a boy—probably a pretty child. She knew John Brown had fathered a big brood . . . could Salmon have been cheated of affection when he was young? Maybe someday she could talk to his mother, find out these little things about him. But such thinking was *nonsense,* the kind of inane maundering a lovesick girl might get caught up in. Still, it would be nice to hold him against her breasts and gentle him. . . .

★ ★ ★

I N ROCKETTS, Mosby's spy had silenced his fears enough to carry out his part of the bargain. "Now, boy," Israel Jones said earnestly, "I want you to go straight to Colonel Mosby's house. The same place as before, and you tell him or his servants—don't matter none which—that I has to see him fust thing in the morning at the stables. I has de important information. Now, you tell me what I said."

The Negro boy, a fourteen-year-old by the name of Harpy whom Israel had used as a messenger before, nodded and repeated what he had just heard.

"Good," Israel said. "Now, take this here piece of paper, and you give it to them also. But no one else. Anybody else gets this here piece of paper, I don't never hire you again. You understand, boy?"

Harpy shook his head, rolled his eyes. "Yassuh. I'll eat it 'fore I gives to anyone else."

"Good, now say de message for me again."

Harpy repeated the message with a grin.

"All right, here's your money," Israel said. "Now you hurry, you hear?" He handed him a quarter and watched as the boy moved away at a slow trot.

As soon as he turned the first corner, Harpy slowed to a walk and began repeating the message, over and over, so he wouldn't forget. He liked walking in the moonlight, even though it was quite a piece uptown to Colonel Mosby's house. Two-bits! Lot of money for a colored boy his age to lay his hands on these days, 'specially for not really working. He began to whistle "Rock of Ages," his favorite hymn, as he turned up Bloody Run Street toward Main. Yassuh, he told himself, he might even open a whole messenger service pretty soon, hire himself some other colored boys to—

"You hold it right there, boy!"

He froze, stared wide-eyed at the man who had jumped in front of him.

Crispus grabbed his shirt front. "Where you going, boy?"

Harpy was so scared he couldn't answer.

"You hear me, boy?"

"Y—yassuh."

"Then answer me. I saw you talking to Israel Jones. Where's he sending you?"

"I—I can't tell you. It's a secret."

Crispus whipped out a knife and held it right in front of his nose. Its blade flashed in the moonlight before Harpy's crossed eyes. "Tell me or the fish'll be eating your carcass." Crispus snarled.

Harpy groaned, closed his eyes. "He sending me to Colonel Mosby's house uptown."

"What're you going there for?" Crispus touched the tip of Harpy's nose with the knife.

"Don't cut me, suh, don't cut me! I'se to tell 'em that Mr. Israel

Jones wants to see Colonel Mosby fustest thing in the morning at de stables. That he has important information. That's all."

Crispus studied his eyes, nodded, finally let go of his shirt front. "All right, boy. Now, you just forget we even had this little talk. It's a secret thing for Abraham. You know what that is, boy?"

"Yassuh, I knows."

"Then you know how important it was for me to find out, don't you?"

"Yassuh."

"All right, now you go on home and go to bed."

★ ★ ★

I T WAS just another shack like so many the colored people lived in, possibly a little bigger, on one of those dirt lanes off Nicholson Street. But this one had tables outside in the front yard for when there were too many customers to handle inside. A fat woman ran the place and called it the Brown Turtle. It was the favorite hang-out for the guards company, and they all met there after their drill nights.

Israel Jones was sitting at one of those outside tables with his friend, Willie Burns, when Crispus arrived a short time later. The Amistad member slipped behind a stand of bushes across the lane and quietly settled down for the wait. The men were noisy, drinking and laughing, as they talked about the earlier meeting. Crispus watched Israel pour down two fast drinks, then order another from the fat woman. Now he knew why the man acted nervous.

The time passed, ten minutes, fifteen, a half-hour.

And Crispus never took his eyes off Israel Jones.

Finally, Israel got to his feet and vigorously shook the hand of Willie Burns. Then he made his way a bit unsteadily away from the tables and into the lane. Crispus nodded to himself and fell in behind when the man turned right and headed toward the river. When they were out of earshot of the Brown Turtle, Crispus picked up his pace. Just before Israel reached Nicholson Street, Crispus called out, "Mr. Jones!"

Israel stopped, turned, blinking his eyes. He hiccuped. "Yassuh, what can I do for you, suh?"

272

Crispus moved up close, jammed the barrel of the Allen revolver into Israel's stomach. "You can turn around and march straightaway to the river," he said flatly.

"But what—"

"*Move!*"

"Yassuh, yassuh!" Israel turned and stumbled forward.

Three minutes later, on the pier at Pleasant's Wharf, Crispus slit Israel Jones's throat from one ear to the other and threw his blood-spewing body into the James.

★   ★   ★

"MISTAH John, they's a man from the telegraph office," Aaron said from the doorway to the small study.

Mosby jumped to his feet so fast he nearly knocked over the cup of half-cold coffee. "Send him right in!" He had been anxiously waiting all day for some kind of word, had even sent a follow-up telegraph to the commander at Chattanooga that morning.

There were two wires. The first was from Ogg and read: "Located the right Harrison in Baltimore. Be there Monday."

Finally! But the spy was only frosting now—he needed the *cake*. He opened the second telegraph and heaved a massive sigh of relief. It read: "Departing Chattanooga this afternoon. Should arrive in Richmond by noon Monday if the trains run on schedule. Lafayette McLaws." It was dated that morning.

"Where has this been?" he asked the telegraph clerk. "I left word for any wires to be delivered to me immediately."

The young man shrugged. "Don't know, sir. Must've gotten mislaid."

"Well, you tell your sergeant if it happens again, he'll be working for *you*."

"Yessuh." The man grinned, saluted, and hurried out.

Mosby reread both telegraphs and smiled. He couldn't believe he was really going to have both of his prime witnesses. God, was he finally getting a share of the good side? He shook his head. The way things had been going, the trains would break down or run late . . . and Bragg would never give him another delay.

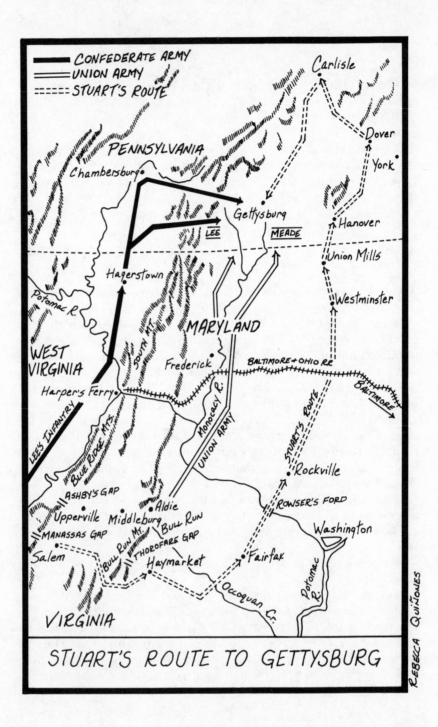

STUART'S ROUTE TO GETTYSBURG

REBECCA QUIÑONES

Above the bayonets, mixed and crossed,
Men saw a gray, gigantic ghost
  Receding through the battle-cloud,
  And heard across the tempest loud
The death-cry of a nation lost!
          —Will Henry Thompson

DAY 8

S ERGEANT Reverdy Ogg was reading the *Examiner* in the Intelligence Office when John Mosby arrived a little after seven. "I've
got our spy, Colonel," he said. "It was so late when I got in last night
I didn't want to bother you."

"Good. Where is he?"

"Over in my room at the boarding house."

"Why didn't you bring him along so I could talk to him?"

Ogg shifted his weight, sighed. "He, uh, ain't too healthy, Colonel."

Mosby looked at him sharply. "You didn't bring him here forcibly,
did you?"

"No, nothing like that. I offered him a little money. He's a drunk,
Colonel. A *sot*."

Mosby stared at him a moment, then winced. And after all of this
trouble finding him. "Damn! How bad is he?"

"Shaky when he ain't got a drink in him. I left him locked in my
room with a quart of beer. Told him I'd be back directly."

"And you're sure he's the right Henry Thomas Harrison?"

"It's him, Colonel. He told me the whole story about him and Longstreet and Gettysburg. It's him all right."

Mosby shook his head. A damned drunk—if Axline picked up on it, the man's credibility could be shot full of holes. "Okay, Reverdy," he said. "Nice work. Now I want you to go back and stick to him like glue. Don't even let him go to the toilet without you. And take him some pure garlic to chew on. The court convenes at ten. He'll be my third witness, if you think we can put him on the stand."

"Yes, suh. He won't be any better tomorrow."

"Well, keep going over his story with him. Things are going to be nip and tuck today." Mosby told Ogg about General McLaws, ending with, "All right then, get Harrison in the best shape you can."

Going into the inner office, Mosby shook his head—it seemed like every damn step he took forward was blocked by something. He was almost afraid to wonder what else could go wrong.

★　★　★

AS Brigadier General George Pickett adjusted his long auburn curls before a small mirror in the judges' chambers, he looked back over his shoulder and said, "Just two more days of this, huh, Sam? Then Gettysburg'll be put away forever. I'll tell you for sure, it won't be soon enough for me."

John Bell Hood just nodded as he got to his feet and checked the fastener on his pinned-up right pants leg. He had rented a buggy and driven away from Richmond for the weekend, visiting old battle sites and reliving some of the glories he'd shared with his beloved Texans. And on Saturday night, he too had gotten rip-roaring drunk. He'd found a little country inn outside of Petersburg, run by a buxom widow who took care of every single one of his physical needs. But when the rooster crowed on Sunday morning, the jug was empty, the widow looked fat, and his problem hadn't gone away a solitary inch. He was still acting out a goddamned lie. But George was right—just two more days.

Braxton Bragg looked at his watch. "It's three minutes before ten. You boys ready?"

With Hood leading the way on his crutch, they headed for the courtroom and took their places behind the bench. "Quiet in the courtroom!" the provost sergeant shouted. As Sam Hood settled into his chair, he glanced out at the audience and found Bessica Southwick Adams in the mass of faces. She seemed to sense that he was looking at her, for she smiled back.

★　★　★

BRAGG banged his pistol butt. "This court of inquiry is re-opened!"

Mosby drew in a deep breath. Again he was about to plunge into the final dash to the finish line, but this time there would be no reprieve. He got to his feet, cleared his throat. "Gentlemen, when this court recessed last Thursday, testimony had just been given placing General Stuart at Gettysburg. Now I think the record should show what he did on his much discussed ride, and the severe obstacles he overcame."

Mosby went to the map and pointed. "After getting through Hooker's army and completing a nearly impossible crossing of the Potomac at Rowser's Ford, he headed north toward Pennsylvania. By this time, his command was dead tired, but he pushed them on. . . To tell you the rest, I would like to recall Major Henry McClellan to the stand."

Stuart's former adjutant seated himself once again in the witness chair, and was reminded by Colonel M. R. Axline that he was still under oath.

Mosby spoke from his table. "Major McClellan, will you please describe the march on to Gettysburg?"

Henry McClellan nodded. "Yes, sir. Near Rockville, Maryland, our horses were about to give out from lack of forage when we captured a Yankee wagon train loaded with oats and other goods. About one hundred and twenty-five of them, if I recall. The wagons slowed us up some, but without them we wouldn't have had anything for our horses to eat. Anyway, we rode north to a place called Brookeville, where we stopped to make out parole papers for four hundred prisoners that Jeb wanted to be rid of. We moved on about one o'clock in the morning, so tired we could hardly stay awake in the saddle."

McClellan smiled sheepishly. "Fact is, I was caught snoring about three o'clock in the saddle in front of a roadside store where my horse had taken me. But we woke up when we ran into Kilpatrick's Union cavalry at the town of Westminister. After winning a sharp fight, we crossed the Pennsylvania state line and went northeast to Hanover, where we ran into a real Yankee hornets' nest."

McClellan paused, smiled at Jeb. "I guess it was Kilpatrick's whole division. I know I twice saw that glory-seeking, yellow-haired Custer in the middle of the fray. I even toyed with a plan to capture him, but we were too busy fighting a hard battle—oh, I forgot to mention that well before we got into Pennsylvania, we were no longer moving through Hooker's army. As everyone knows, it was by then *General George Meade's* army. He took command on the twenty-eighth, when Hooker got relieved.

"Now it was the thirtieth, and as I said, our cavalry force had gotten itself tangled up with a buzzing hornets' nest at Hanover. The fighting was terribly fierce, and as usual, General Stuart was right in the middle of it. But we won out."

McClellan paused again. "It was night before we withdrew from Hanover. We were extremely weary and still burdened by the wagons, as well as another four hundred prisoners we'd taken. But we had stung Kilpatrick enough that he broke off and left us alone.

"Nearing York, General Stuart found that General Early had left there, moving westward, so he sent Major Venable of our staff to find General Lee and get new orders. We then moved on north to Carlisle, looking for food and forage."

Major Henry McClellan shook his head. "No rest for the weary, though. Union General Baldy Smith had two brigades of militia staunchly emplaced at the town of Carlisle, and he jeered at General Stuart's demand that he surrender. Whereupon we shelled the town and burned the old military post to the north—the Barracks.

"About midnight, Venable returned, bringing us the first news that a major battle had begun at the little town of Gettysburg, about thirty miles to the southwest." McClellan looked down at the floor, paused again. In a quiet voice he said, "Little did we realize at the moment that an event so massive, so staggering in violence and casualties as the battle of Gettysburg, had gone through its opening round. And we were winning, Venable said. I remember thinking with elation, '*This could be it—the finish, the finale of the war!*'

"We started for Gettysburg about one A.M., dragging along in column, asleep on our horses, until we finally halted for a couple of hours rest. We had been in the saddle steadily for eight days, and done no small share of fighting. Even our hardiest troopers were on their last legs. At that, Hampton got into a sharp fight with Kilpatrick on the way."

The former adjutant turned, looked into Bragg's eyes. "We arrived at Gettysburg on the afternoon of July second, ready to fight—which we did the following day. And now you say what General Stuart did was wrong. How can that be? If our army had won that battle, Stuart would have been hailed as a great hero for such an accomplishment."

His voice trailed away, caught with emotion. "I find that charge unbelievable."

"Major McClellan," Mosby said, going to the witness stand. "Would you say the Union commanders were adversely affected by Stuart's action?"

The witness cleared his throat. "There is no doubt about it, sir. Their cavalry that had to be deployed to counterattack our column could have been used effectively elsewhere—as could the other troops whose dispositions were dictated by General Stuart being east of the Union army."

Mosby nodded, slowly walked the few steps to the front of the bench, where he looked solemnly up at the members of the court. He looked for a moment into Pickett's eyes, then into Hood's. "I'm sure this account brings mixed memories and emotions to you gentlemen who were there at Gettysburg at that terrible time. Would you like to ask the witness any questions?"

One by one, each of the generals shook his head. Sam Hood stared at the paper in front of him and doodled with his pencil.

Mosby nodded, turned to Axline. "Your witness, sir."

The judge-advocate stood at his table, said, "This tale of a heroic ride by bone-weary troopers under the command of General Stuart is touching, and every single one of those men should spend the rest of his life in great pride . . . but it has *nothing* to do with the poor judgment that took them on it."

He shook his head. "General Munford has already testified that General Lee had no use for those wagons and worn-out mules, and that General Lee nearly struck General Stuart for having been gone. I think that fairly sums up everything. No, I have no questions, Major McClellan."

Mosby groaned inwardly. Munford was still the most damaging witness of the whole court.

★　★　★

MAJOR General John Rawlins was just about to walk out the front door of the Spottswood when he saw Verita in the open hack. As the man with her stepped down and leaned forward to talk to her, Rawlins pulled back inside the entrance and watched, wishing he could hear their conversation. There was something familiar about the man, something tied to Verita. . . .They seemed quite well acquainted. What the hell was she doing with this man?

Again, he had that feeling that he'd experienced the first time he met her—that he'd seen her somewhere before.

Rawlins watched Salmon walk past him on his way to the lobby, then turned in time to see Verita's hack pull away. And all at once, he remembered where he had seen them! *It was at that Anti-Slavery Society convention in that old theater in Washington a couple of weeks earlier. The two excited young people who sat near him—the ones who cheered so lustily and sang "John Brown's Body" so loudly!* He shook his head. Now what in the hell?

He turned to catch up with the man, but he had disappeared. He hurried to the bar, but couldn't see him in there. He wasn't in the dining salon. Could he have a room here?

A lot of damned questions.

What was Verita doing at the Anti-Slavery Society meeting in Washington? And what was she doing with the same man here? What in the goddamned hell was going on? He coughed, and one of his hacking sieges began. Finally, red-eyed and heaving, he wiped the blood away from his mouth. *Sonofabitch!*

He got into a waiting hack and told the driver to take him to an old tobacco warehouse on the river in Rocketts. Pulling his watch from its pocket, he checked the time, then reread the note.

General R,
> I have an answer to your question.
> Please come to see me this morning.
> The boy will give you directions.
>
> J.

He had written a carefully couched letter to Abraham Lincoln two days before, describing his earlier meeting with Jubilo. But there had, of course, been no answer.

Fifteen minutes later, a Negro opened the side door to the fire-scarred old warehouse and led him to the long room that served as an office and a storage place. "Afternoon, General," Jubilo said from the doorway. "Glad you could come." He was wearing a long coat.

"My pleasure, sir." Rawlins stuck out his hand.

"Would you like a glass of whiskey, General?"

"Never touch the damned stuff."

Jubilo nodded, offered a chair.

"This your place?" Rawlins asked, looking around at several forms covered by blankets.

Jubilo fingered the scar on his cheek, replied, "It belongs to a cause known as Abraham."

Rawlins nodded, waited.

"It is just one of many places that are springing up secretly around the Confederacy, General Rawlins." His voice was strong, proud, as it was when he was in the pulpit. He went to the nearest form and jerked off the blanket. It was an arms rack and it held twenty late-model Spencer carbines on each side. "This is what your friends' money can buy. Abraham doesn't have too many around the country because colored people can't purchase them legally."

"Where'd you get these?"

"These are mine. I am the exception." He removed the long coat and placed the black officer's slouch hat on his head. He was wearing his colonel's uniform. Coming to rigid attention, he saluted. "Suh, the commander of the First Abraham Guards Regiment is at your pleasure."

Rawlins returned the salute, concealing his complete surprise.

"The regiment consists only of my headquarters company at the present, General, but soon it will have companies in other locations. We hope there will be a regiment in each state one of these days. Military organization provides control over the fanatics who want to burn everything in sight." He nodded, smiled briefly. "Yes, we can use the help of powerful friends up north . . . but they have to be the right friends."

"What do you mean by that?"

"There are those who wish to strike now, and we aren't near ready. Matter of fact, General, I just said 'no' to some people last night."

"Can you tell me who they are?"

"No, suh, I do not wish to discuss them."

It was this Amistad! Rawlins knew it! But he had to tread carefully with Jubilo. "All right," he said. "Can you tell me how many members you have in Abraham at the present?"

"We don't have a membership, suh, the people just come to meetings whenever and wherever they can. Many times, an organizer, he rides into a plantation or big farm under the guise of a circuit rider. Often he is. And he spends the night and spreads the word quietly among the slaves. The freedmen, like here in Rocketts, they have an easier time of it."

"How can the people I represent best help—aside from providing weapons?"

"General, we're gonna need books and teachers, and medical care. As you know, there ain't hardly any education among my people. And do you know there can't be more'n a half dozen Negro doctors in all of the South—and naturally, they've come from up north or some other country."

Rawlins scowled. "Yes, and when the revolt comes, an awful lot of white doctors are going to forget their oath to Hippocrates. And you'll need all kinds of medicine and the like."

"And we'll need your army people down here helping us."

"Possibly some civilians as advisors."

They talked on, until finally Rawlins had to go. "I'll be leaving here the day after the Stuart court ends, Colonel Jubilo. But you've provided me with enough valuable information that I can render a full and favorable report to my friends when I return to the United States. And that will include Mr. Lincoln personally. He'll be extremely pleased. We will be back in touch with you, sir."

As he was leaving, Rawlins made a final attempt to find out something about Amistad. "Are you sure, Colonel Jubilo, that you can't tell me about these troublesome friends up north?"

"No, suh, I can't."

Jubilo watched through a window as Rawlins rode away. A big grin creased his face. An important major general was going to talk to Mr. Lincoln about him. It was a big step in his plan. . . .

But there were unpleasant steps too, and he had to make one.

★ ★ ★

"ARE you serious, Mosby?" Colonel Axline asked incredulously as he read the name on the piece of paper.

"Deadly so, Colonel."

The judge-advocate shrugged, turned to stare at the back of the courtroom where Mosby's surprise Yankee witness was waiting.

"Are you gentlemen ready?" General Bragg asked icily.

"Yes, sir."

"Then let's proceed. Remember, we're heading toward the close."

Mosby spoke loudly. "Major General Joseph Hooker, will you please take the stand?"

There was a sudden silence, and then a murmur that quickly grew in volume as all heads in the courtroom craned to see if their ears were playing tricks. Surely that hated Yankee general wouldn't be a part of this! Even the three generals on the bench stared up the aisle in surprise.

Sure enough, Major General Joseph Hooker, wearing a sober dark suit, was making his way down the aisle. But he walked with an uncertainty of gait and a slight slump that was a distinct departure from his once erect carriage. The handsomeness for which he had been famed in his youth was now gone—replaced by a red face with a mouth that had seen firmer days, and a lackluster eye. The man who had been dubbed by a newspaperman just a few years earlier as "Fighting Joe" was obviously not well. He was clean-shaven; his hair was quite gray.

Braxton Bragg watched gravely as he saw the shadow of the man who had graduated from West Point with him, the other heroic artilleryman who had also gotten three brevets in the Mexican War— his one-time rival . . . the man whose many camp followers were known as Hooker's girls, or sometimes just Hookers. There had been whispers about a stroke.

General Hooker's voice, with its Massachusetts accent, was hoarse as he took the oath.

Mosby approached him in the witness box with a respectful tone. "Thank you for coming all the way down here from Philadelphia to help us find the truth, General. As you know, your name has been bandied about this courtroom almost as much as General Stuart's has. I understand you are no longer on active duty, sir."

"That's correct."

"Merely for the record, sir. You were in command of the Army of the Potomac in June of Eighteen-sixty-three, weren't you?"

"Yes, sir, I was."

"When you first ascertained that General Lee was moving his army north, what was your guess as to his intentions?"

Hooker cleared his throat, but his voice was still grainy. "Of course, I, or I should say we, since President Lincoln and General Halleck— then the Union general-in-chief—thought Lee would make another attempt on Washington. Therefore, I moved my army out of its camps around Fredericksburg and began displacing toward the Potomac. You might say we were like a huge chess piece, constantly moving in a blocking position."

"After the Battle of Brandy Station, you sent your cavalry into the mountains to find out what Lee was up to. They were met by Confederate cavalry in the area of the Bull Run Mountains. General, did they ever really *know* what Lee's strength and intentions were?"

Hooker started to speak, coughed. His face turned a mottled red, but he answered at length. "Not then. At that point, we didn't have any observation posts, and we still thought he would wheel and head for Washington."

"When you decided to cross the Potomac about the twenty-fifth, only to find that General Stuart's cavalry had cut through your trailing corps—was this a problem for you?"

"Most certainly. You don't let a man like Stuart loose in your rear or on your inner flank without worrying."

"Did you make dispositions to counteract him?"

"Yes, of course. I was forced to keep my cavalry corps in the rear of my army. And later, a whole division of cavalry under Kilpatrick was sent to stop him in Pennsylvania."

"And were other troop dispositions made to guard against him raiding to the east?"

"Most certainly." Hooker pulled out a handkerchief and wiped his moist face. "There are newspaper reports that the capital went into a panic, like a city besieged. And Baltimore as well."

John Mosby walked back to his table, turned. "General Hooker, were you aware of General Lee's movements and location prior to General Meade assuming command of the Army of the Potomac on the twenty-eighth of June?"

"Absolutely. We knew Ewell had moved into Pennsylvania and we had taken steps to block him at Harrisburg. And our signal people up in the hills had been constantly tracking the movement of Lee's main body." Hooker fumbled in his coat pocket, pulled out a yellow page. "This is a copy of a message from General Howard, one of my corps commanders, dated June twenty-sixth at five-ten P.M. It ends with ' . . . Lee in person crossed the Potomac last night. His entire force came up yesterday—reported to be between sixty and seventy thousand men.' "

Mosby nodded his head. "Then Confederate cavalry could not have kept you from knowing where Lee was, or his strength. Is that correct?"

"Not unless they could have ferreted out our observation posts, and that would have taken them weeks."

"Did you, or did General Meade, plan in any way on a great battle being fought at Gettysburg?"

"No, the location was a total accident."

Mosby paused for effect, then said, "Thank you, General Hooker. That's all I need from you."

Hooker looked suddenly blank, confused. "But we haven't, that is, we haven't talked about my troubles with Lincoln and Halleck yet . . . the conspiracy against me . . : how I resigned in protest. We have to talk about that. The world has to know!"

Mosby had a sudden sinking feeling. It had never dawned on him that Hooker might not be himself.

Axline pounced immediately. "General Hooker, isn't it true that you spent those last days of your command of the Army of the Potomac just squabbling with your superiors—Lincoln, Halleck, and Secretary of War Stanton? In fact, it's a matter of record that you were *fired* by the president himself! Isn't that right, General?"

Hooker looked up like a wounded animal. "No, no, I was fully informed. And I didn't get fired, I resigned. It's a matter of record. Everyone knows that! Ask anyone, they'll tell you. Why, I went on out later that year and won my great victory above the clouds at Lookout Mountain. No . . . I wasn't fired." He sobbed, suddenly staring at the floor.

Braxton Bragg looked down at the broken remains of his old associate and antagonist. "That will be all, General," he said quietly.

Hooker looked up at him with a dazed expression, nodded finally, and stepped unsteadily from the witness box. The courtroom was quiet as he made his way out.

Mosby drew in a deep breath and expelled it. He shook his head at Jeb and pulled out his watch. It was a quarter to twelve and he still had no word of McLaws's arrival. And the only other witness he had was the drunken spy. With relief, he heard Bragg close the court for lunch.

ROBERT SKIMIN

★　★　★

THOMAS Wentworth Higginson enjoyed his infrequent visits to the farm Liberty, north of Washington City. Its lush greenery and remote stillness were a more relaxing setting for his writing than the hubbub of Boston. And within a few days, the first mission of Amistad would be over. He patted the rump of a sleek saddle horse at the edge of the meadow near the main barn. There was so much riding on this first mission, perhaps more than even he had dreamed. . . .

He wondered how much bearing that Confederate court of inquiry had had on recent events.

In just the past few days, the political climate in the United States had grown considerably belligerent. The Northern press was getting more vociferous by the day . . . the New York *Herald* was running Lincoln quotes constantly . . . the Gettysburg address appeared somewhere daily. He shrugged—maybe the Stuart court *was* a primary tool for the abolition cause in the North, as a major journalist had suggested.

"Reverend Higginson!" It was Bertha Friar hollering at him from the back door of the house. "There's a man from Richmond here to see you!"

He frowned. He'd just left the place last night.

The man was a negro who touched his hat brim as he said, "My name's Murphy, suh. I served in your regiment during the war—C Company. Jubilo sent me first thing this morning, suh, to give you this personally." He handed over an envelope.

Higginson read the letter quickly: "*I hate to go against your wishes, but I cannot cooperate with your man Smith. I believe he is not well in the head, or he is hungry for power. Either way, your plan is wrong at this time. You must call it off, or I will be forced to tell all of Abraham never to cooperate in the future. I am sorry, sir. Your obedient servant, Jubilo.*"

Higginson reread the letter, felt a deep wave of disappointment. What could Salmon have done? He had been perfectly normal during their talks the day before . . . a bit pretentious, but he expected the Old Man-influence to take over to some extent. He had anticipated that back in Oberlin—it was part of the allure of Salmon. The debt, the obligation, the fanaticism element. Had it all gone too far?

He looked at the man, Murphy. "Did Jubilo tell you anything about this letter?"

The Negro answered quietly. "Only that I was to tell you, suh, that they ain't no way he was going to change his mind."

Higginson drew in a deep breath. "Come walk with me a bit, Mr. Murphy. Tell me what you think of Reverend Jubilo."

"Suh, I can do that without walking. Jubilo is the *man*—he is already the most powerful colored man anywhere. And we'uns will go anywhere he tells us, even to the death. Does that answer your question, Cunnel?

Higginson breathed deeply again, nodded his head. "Quite emphatically, Mr. Murphy. Let's go on back to the house where you can get something to eat while I write a reply to Jubilo."

★　　★　　★

MOSBY was about to leave his office and head on back to the court house when Aaron, his servant, walked into the outer office.

"Colonel, suh, I'se got a message for you. Boy brought it from Rocketts. That same boy what brung de other message. He was mighty scared, Colonel. Wouldn't tell me nothing a-tall, just give me this here slip of paper."

Mosby took the scrap of paper. In crude printing it read: "Saman Brown." Strange. And he didn't like the part about the boy being scared. Not at all.

He frowned. "And this boy wouldn't tell you anything else?"

"No suh. He just skeedaddled. But he de one who come from that Israel Jones de last time. I knows that, Colonel."

"All right, Aaron. Thanks."

Mosby hurried to the stables, but Israel Jones was nowhere to be found. And the sergeant who ran the place was apparently out to lunch. He had just started a note to the man when a colored stablehand walked up. "You wants something, suh?"

"Yes. Do you know a man named Israel Jones?"

"Yassuh."

"Good. Do you know where he is?"

"No suh. He ain't come in this morning."

"Is he sick or something?"

"I don't know, suh. Might be, 'cause he pretty steady here at work."

Mosby had a hollow feeling in his stomach. He said, "If he comes in, you tell him to stay here until Colonel Mosby comes to see him this evening. All right?"

"Yassuh, I tells him."

Mosby left hurriedly. He had to see Rawlins before the court reconvened.

And there was still no sign of McLaws.

★ ★ ★

"SO WHAT do you make of her being in the company of this man again here in Richmond, Judah?" John Rawlins had just finished telling the ambassador about his encounter at the hotel. They were standing in the aisle beside their bench at the court house.

"I don't know, John. I know she has abolitionist leanings, and it's plausible that she attended that meeting if she was in Washington City at the time. And it's just as logical that this man is merely an old friend who accidentally ran into her down here. Or maybe he lives here and is one of those secret abolitionists. I'll ask her about it tonight when I see her."

"General Rawlins!" John Mosby said, hurrying up. He nodded his head to Benjamin in greeting. "I'm glad you're here also, Mr. Ambassador. I'm afraid my spy down in Rocketts may be in trouble. This was delivered at my house a while ago." He handed over the slip of paper that said "Saman Brown."

"Does that name mean anything to either of you?"

Rawlins said, "No." Benjamin shook his head.

"Will you telegraph that name up to your people, General?"

"Certainly." As Judah turned to speak to a friend, Rawlins lowered his voice. "John, do you know anything about Marie Jolie—I mean about any abolitionist connections?" He described his encounter at the hotel.

Mosby nodded his head. "She's an anti-slaver, and I think she's a French communist or something. I'll check into it." He saw the members of the court filing in. "Got to go."

★ ★ ★

H ENRY Thomas Harrison was a slender, wiry fellow of about five feet eight; thirty-three years old. He had dark hair and bleary hazel eyes that he tried to fix on an object at the back of the courtroom so they would look steady. His brown beard was long and scraggly; his suit was rumpled and stained. He kept his legs firmly crossed on the witness stand, and continued clasping and unclasping his nervous hands when he wasn't wiping beads of sweat from his brow. He did not present the most reliable picture of a witness Mosby had ever seen.

But he was Harrison, the spy.

After Axline gave Harrison the oath, Mosby walked to the front of the bench. "Gentlemen," he said, "it has been an assertion in this investigation that General Stuart's actions on the march to Gettysburg were to blame for the outcome of the battle. I contend, unequivocally, that the cause can be pinpointed elsewhere."

"Colonel Mosby," General Bragg said sharply, "we are not here to determine blame for the outcome of that battle."

"Sir, you may wish to change your mind when you have heard this man's testimony."

"I *never* change my mind, sir!"

Mosby turned to the witness. "Mr. Harrison, to whom did you report for orders in the spring of Eighteen-sixty-three?"

"General James Longstreet, sir." The spy's voice was surprisingly low, raspy. Mosby thought it was probably from cheap corn whiskey.

"What were your duties for General Longstreet?"

"I was a scout, sir. Some people liked to call it spying, but officially it was scouting that I did. I went back and forth through the enemy lines and gathered information in his rear. Sometimes I even went into Washington City and got into War Department files. I've even seen documents in Secretary Stanton's file."

Even Mosby was impressed. "I would say you were pretty capable, Mr. Harrison. Would you please tell the court your connection with the Gettysburg campaign?"

Harrison nodded, wiped his forehead with the moist handkerchief, and wrapped it around his clasped nervous hands. "The general summoned me to a meeting at Culpepper, prior to the march to Pennsylvania. Said he wanted me to go into the Union camp, and Washington as well, and bring back any worthwhile information.

"Well, I went on into Washington City and picked up everything I could—you know, in saloons and places where men loosen their tongues. And finally the Army of the Potomac began to move, and I stayed with it as it headed toward the Potomac. When Hooker had it across the river into Maryland, I decided I'd better think about getting back to General Longstreet.

"That was the twenty-eighth of June, and before you know it, the word flew around the camps that General Meade was replacing Hooker! And I knew right then and there, that I had to skeedaddle after the Rebel army and find Old Pete. I got me a fair horse and headed west, cause Old Pete had told me he'd always be near General Lee, and all I had to do was ask questions and keep moving toward Pennsylvania."

Harrison took a deep breath, mopped up his face again, and went on, "I found Longstreet that night, near Chambersburg, and told him my news—him and Colonel Sorrel, and Old Pete got real excited and sent me on with a major by the name of Fairfax to see General Lee. Well, sir, Old General Lee, he listened to me real close and asked some good questions. You see, he didn't know the Bluebellies were north of the river, and also he didn't know anything about Meade replacing Hooker."

Mosby broke in. "Lee knew nothing about the disposition of the Union army, nor that Meade had replaced Hooker?"

"That's right, Colonel. I showed him on a map where all the different Yankee corps were located, and told him I estimated they was over a hundred thousand strong."

"And when he finished his questions, what happened to you?"

"This Major Fairfax took me on back to Longstreet's camp and told me 'the information you have just given us is more valuable than all the cavalry in the army could have provided.'"

"Would you please tell us again what Major Fairfax said?"

Harrison cleared his throat, spoke loudly. *"He said the information I had just given them was more valuable than all the cavalry in the world could have provided."*

"Thank you, Mr. Harrison," Mosby said thoughtfully. He turned to the bench. "Gentlemen, if you think it is necessary to get their direct testimony, we can suspend the court long enough to bring Sorrel and Fairfax in. General Sorrel recently tried to help us find Mr. Harrison, so I know he is familiar with this situation."

"No, that won't be necessary," Bragg replied.

"Then I would like to summarize, General. On the twenty-eighth of June, General Lee knew the disposition of the Army of the Potomac, and he knew that General Meade—a more respected foe than Hooker—was to be reckoned with. He could anticipate that the Union host might come after him."

"Colonel, that is an *assumption!*" Bragg snapped.

Mosby nodded. "Yes, sir, but a logical one. And the information this scout provided—according to a senior staff officer—was more valuable than all the cavalry in the army could have provided." He paused, continued. *"Therefore, whether General Stuart and his cavalry force were on the army's immediate flank or not, General Lee did get the information he needed about the enemy."*

Once more, the courtroom was completely silent.

"This being the case, there is no possible way General Stuart can be found responsible in any way for what followed."

The stillness still hung over the huge room as everyone's eyes remained on the former ranger.

"Gentlemen," he said quietly. "We all know there is something very delicate that is being side-stepped here. A previous witness has at best *conveniently forgotten* that the man sitting here on the witness stand had brought him the most *vital* news of the march north . . . that he considered that man's news so *vital* he sent him *straight* to General Lee . . . and I am perfectly willing to examine his intentions in doing so." He was obviously careful not to use the word *perjury.*

Bragg's face grew red once more. He cleared his throat, frowned and said, "Such a course is not necessary."

But every single person in that courtroom was picturing Lieutenant General James Longstreet sitting right there in the witness chair saying that he didn't remember why Harrison came to him.

The journalists scribbled furiously.

Mosby glanced at Hood, back to Pickett, wondering what they could be thinking. Nothing showed.

"Judge-advocate," Bragg said, "do you have any questions for the witness?"

"Yes, sir, I do." Axline hauled himself out of his chair and approached the stand. He leaned into Harrison's face, sniffed, and made a face. "Tell me, Mr. Harrison, have you been drinking? I must remind you that you are under oath, and that perjury can put you in prison."

Harrison cleared his throat, tried not to look at Axline's glaring eyes. "Uh, yes, suh. I had some beer this noon when I ate."

Axline moved closer, leaned into the former spy's face. "Does garlic hide the smell of drink? Do you drink all the time, Mr. Harrison?"

"No, no, suh, I do not."

"How much do you drink in a day?"

Harrison brought his hand to his mouth and everyone could see the severe tremor. "I don't measure it."

Axline turned to the court. "I would guess a lot." He wheeled back to the witness. "*Were* you drinking all the time when you arrived at General Longstreet's camp and went to see General Lee with Major Fairfax? Isn't your recall of Major Fairfax's statement about the value of your information in fact something that Colonel Mosby planted in your drink-sodden memory?"

"*Sir!*" Mosby shouted.

Bragg replied instantly, "Colonel Axline, you know better than to ask such a question." He turned to the court reporter. "Delete that part of the testimony relating to the witness's drinking, Sergeant."

Axline nodded, turned back to the witness. "Tell me, Mr. Harrison, what information did you provide during the two days *after* you saw General Lee?"

Harrison wiped his face. The tremor in his hand was more pronounced, his voice more gravelly as he replied, "Why, uh, nothing much of anything, Colonel. I just hung around Old Pete's camp, like I was told."

"Who *did* provide information to General Lee during that time?"

"Why I don't know, sir. Probably nobody, since they didn't find out until late on the thirtieth that Union cavalry pickets were at Gettysburg."

"Yes, that's right, Mr. Harrison, *nobody* was providing information because there was *no cavalry* to do so! There was no General Stuart and no cavalry for General Lee to send out *after* he received your timely report. No cavalry to feel Meade's army and tell Lee where he was heading."

Axline moved the few steps to Stuart's table, looked down into Jeb's angry eyes and said harshly, "All along, we have been talking about the period of the *march* to Gettysburg. Now, Lee's army was *there*, at least near—since Chambersburg is only some twenty-eight miles away, and some of his regiments were much closer."

Axline stabbed his finger toward Stuart. *"That was when Lee needed you most, General. That was when you were most derelict for deserting him!"* His voice dropped to a harsh, contemptuous tone. "That was when you most let him down. It's no wonder, sir, that the most gentlemanly and chivalrous man in the South nearly struck you when you finally returned."

"NO!" Jeb's cry was naked, wounded, as he jumped up and grabbed Axline's coat front. "No! You're making it all so wrong! I would never let him down!" He raised his fist.

"Jeb!" Mosby grabbed his arm. *"Sit down, Jeb!"*

As Bragg's revolver slammed into the bench repeatedly, Jeb slowly released the judge-advocate and with an effort returned to his chair. The courtroom broke into an uproar of shouting voices as the mounting tensions of the partisan audience found a common escape valve. And finally it happened—the big Navy Colt *roared* as Bragg fired it into the ceiling.

"General Stuart!" Bragg said moments later as quiet returned. "If you lose control one more time, I shall have you manacled and chained to your chair. *Do you understand, sir?*"

Jeb slowly looked up, gritted his teeth, and nodded. "Yes, I do," he replied flatly.

Bragg turned to the witness. "You are excused, sir."

Mosby shook his head inwardly as the sweating Harrison practically jumped out of his chair and hurried from the stand toward that stiff drink Ogg had promised him. All that damned work to find the man, and he had all but discredited himself! Both of his last two witnesses had been losers. He might as well—"

"Colonel Mosby?"

He turned to find a captain from Stuart's office kneeling at his side. "Sir, General McLaws is here."

Mosby turned, saw his witness at the back of the courtroom, and blew out a big sigh of relief. *Oh, thank God!* He told the smoldering Jeb.

"Now, do you have further witnesses, Colonel Mosby?" Bragg asked wearily.

"Yes, sir."

Mosby nodded, stood. It was time to shoot the whole roll. He would play this trump as much to the press and the audience as to the court.

He quietly quoted Francis Bacon: " 'What is the truth?' said jesting Pilate; and would not stay for the answer." He paused, went on, "We cannot play jesting Pilate, gentlemen. No, we must stay for the truth, as uncomfortable as it may be."

He drew in a deep breath, exhaled it, began:

"Since it has been falsely charged that General Stuart is to blame for Gettysburg, it is necessary to prove who was primarily at fault. With the court's permission, I would like to provide this map of the Gettysburg battlefield." Mosby went to the easel with a large drawing and placed it over the other map. He nodded toward General Pickett, who was closest. "I'm sure, sir, that you and General Hood will never forget the terrain."

Using a pencil as a pointer, he drew an imaginary line south from the town of Gettysburg past Cemetery Hill, down the long crest of Cemetery Ridge to two hills known as Little Round Top and Round Top. "As the sun came up on the second day, Meade's army occupied this three-mile-long high ground, as well as Culp's Hill to the east of Cemetery Hill—forming an inverted fishhook. The day before—as we all know—had been victorious for Lee, as the two armies more or less ran into each other and the battle accidentally began to take shape.

"Unfortunately, Ewell did not follow up well enough from the north side of Cemetery Hill and Culp's Hill. This was the first major mistake of the battle. Had General Ewell been decisive when he had the momentum, Meade would never have been able to occupy this magnificent, dominating terrain . . . 'good ground,' as we like to call it."

Mosby nodded, smiled fleetingly, continued, "There were many other errors committed by Confederate leaders in the next two days, but none were as pronounced as those by General James Longstreet, the commander of the First Corps."

He looked up into the frowning face of Old Pete in the third row; it was white as a faded bedsheet, the eyes dark and hostile, glaring back at him.

"By the time of the Pennsylvania campaign, General Longstreet had built a substantial reputation for defensive battle strategy, and he didn't like the idea of fighting the enemy anywhere except on ground of his own choosing. Fact is, he made no bones about being against the Pennsylvania campaign to begin with. Now, he quite strenuously objected to fighting Meade at Gettysburg.

"By the second day of the battle, two of Longstreet's three divisions were close enough to take part; these divisions were commanded by

General Hood and General Lafayette McLaws. General Pickett's division, which had been given a rear guard assignment, was still too far away to join in."

Mosby shrugged, spread his open palms. "Obviously, I can't call either General Hood or General Pickett to the witness stand, so the facts of what occurred in General Longstreet's First Corps must be recounted by the other division commander . . . I call Major General Lafayette McLaws to the stand."

A murmur went through the crowd as McLaws made his way forward. He was a stocky man, burly, with thick dark hair that waved generously, and a fierce beard to match.

He took the stand and was sworn by Axline.

"General McLaws," Mosby said, "will you describe the events of the second day at Gettysburg as they relate to the attack by the First Corps?"

"Yes, sir, I will." McLaws had handsome dark eyes under surprisingly delicate black eyebrows. He spoke in a deliberate deep voice. "Since both Hill and Ewell had fought heavily the day before, and since Longstreet was General Lee's most trusted corps commander, following the death of Stonewall Jackson, it was the First Corps's turn to go after Meade. We had been last in the line of march from Virginia, but my division and Sam Hood's were in position to fight.

"Well, Lee wanted us to attack the southern end of Cemetery Ridge, down where it petered out and ran into those rocky hills that we later found out were called the Round Tops. He wanted us to attack in echelon from right to left, meaning—" McLaws looked out at the audience, "not only by divisions—first Hood, then me, then the two divisions from the Third Corps—but by brigades within those divisions, so the attack would snowball as it rolled northward."

He turned in the witness box to look at Hood and said, "This is pretty awkward, Sam, me quoting things you said, to *you*, but I'll be hanged if I know any other way." He glanced at his notes, paused.

"It was quite early that morning and General Lee had just stated, 'The enemy is here, and if we do not whip him, he will whip us.' Everyone knew Lee wanted to attack as soon as possible, yet shortly Longstreet drew Hood aside and said, 'The general is a little nervous this morning. He wishes me to attack, but I do not wish to do so without Pickett. I never like to go into battle with one boot off.' "

"General Bragg," Axline said sharply. "That is *hearsay!*"

"Sir," Mosby countered, "the man he is quoting is sitting right beside you. If what the witness is saying is wrong, I'm sure General Hood will intervene." He lifted an eyebrow toward Hood. "Isn't that correct, sir?"

Hood nodded.

"Proceed, General McLaws," Bragg growled.

"Later, about eight o'clock, Lee showed me where he wanted me to place my division. When I told him I would like to see the terrain first hand, General Longstreet, who had been pacing up and down like a nervous bear, broke in and told me that I wasn't to leave my division for any such reconnaissance. He then leaned down and traced a line on the map perpendicular to the one Lee had drawn. 'I wish your division placed so,' he said emphatically. Lee intervened, 'No, General, I wish it placed just opposite.' "

"I can't tell you how embarrassed I was. After Longstreet once more told me I could not go forward to personally look at the ground, I saluted and left them to work out their problems. It was the beginning of a long day of Longstreet dragging his feet like a petulant little brother, keeping us right in our first assembly positions until Lee returned from the Second Corps at eleven o'clock—a fact that annoyed the impatient Lee considerably."

McLaws shook his head. "Shortly we began one of the most disorganized marches to do battle I've ever experienced. We started down the west side of McPherson Ridge, which masked us from Union observation on Cemetery Ridge and the Round Tops. But just as the head of our column reached a point about a thousand yards from our destination, Longstreet decided the cover was too thin, and that Meade would see us . . . and he had us *countermarch* back the way we had just come, to march down the west side of Seminary ridge, wasting two hours to bring us back to the starting point! And by this time, the bluecoats had occupied the nearby peach orchard, as well as Little Round Top and the Devil's Den on its slope, effectively blocking the path of our planned attack. . . .

"And that was only the beginning of Longstreet's stubbornness! As Hood and I reached our jump-off positions, we realized the situation had changed drastically in the hours since Lee had made his plan. Instead of open terrain, a sea of bluecoats faced us! If I were to attack up the Emmitsburg Road as ordered, my flank would have been *devastated* by enemy fire!"

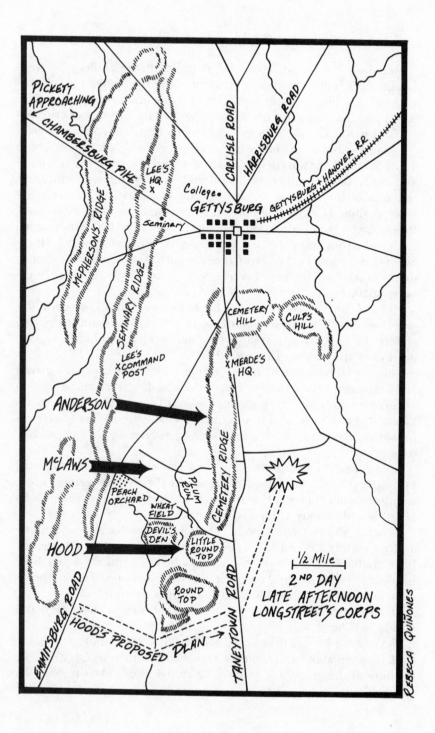

PICKETT
APPROACHING

CHAMBERSBURG PIKE

McPHERSON'S RIDGE

LEE'S
HQ.
X

College

Seminary

GETTYSBURG

CARLISLE ROAD

HARRISBURG ROAD

GETTYSBURG + HANOVER R.R.

SEMINARY RIDGE

LEE'S
X COMMAND
POST

CEMETERY
HILL

CULP'S
HILL

X MEADE'S
HQ.

ANDERSON

McLAWS

PEACH
ORCHARD

WHEAT
FIELD

PLUM RUN

CEMETERY RIDGE

DEVIL'S
DEN

HOOD

LITTLE
ROUND
TOP

ROUND
TOP

TANEYTOWN ROAD

EMMITSBURG ROAD

HOOD'S PROPOSED PLAN

½ Mile

2ND DAY
LATE AFTERNOON
LONGSTREET'S CORPS

REBECCA QUIÑONES

McLaws's jaw jutted out as he glared into the audience to find Longstreet's stolid expression. He went on coldly, "When I told Longstreet about this, his reply was 'The orders cannot be altered.' *Three times* I protested, and three times the man told me to attack as ordered.

"And it was the same story with Hood. But Sam had a powerful alternative—his scouts had discovered that Meade's left flank south of the Round Tops was completely unprotected! He could swing around and easily fall on the enemy flank and rear! Swiftly reporting this remarkable information to Longstreet, he was amazed to receive a reply stating, 'General Lee's orders are to attack up the Emmitsburg Road.' Again Hood requested a change of orders, only to get the same reply. The third time, he sent his respected adjutant general, Harry Sellers, to personally try to convince the corps commander. And once more, Longstreet replied, 'Lee's orders are to attack up the Emmitsburg Road.' "

McLaws shook his head, glanced at Hood, went on, "Longstreet did ride down to see Sam, but when Hood tried one more time to get the orders changed, all our great corps commander could say was, 'We must obey the orders of General Lee!' "

General McLaws raised his fist, came half out of his chair, glared at Longstreet. "With the door open to Meade's rear, and a golden chance to smash him into retreat, General Longstreet steadfastly refused, like a pouting child, to request a change in orders from Lee! *In that one decision alone, he single-handedly threw away the Battle of Gettysburg!*"

In the rear of the courtroom a woman shouted, "Court-martial Longstreet!" And the crowd erupted. As the newspapermen wrote rapidly on their notepads, and Bragg tried to quiet the uproar, Sam Hood stared blankly at Longstreet.

General McLaws continued, "The bluebellies fought tenaciously and we suffered over fifty percent casualties. Brigade commanders, field grade officers, Hood was nearly killed . . . and we didn't have hardly any real estate to show for it. Were those big rocks in the Devil's Den, or a worthless peach orchard, a proper receipt?"

McLaws turned to look into George Pickett's stern expression and nodded his head.

Pickett sat rigid, as if he could tell McLaws was coming after him, as if he were about to become a target rather than a judge . . . the opening of the grave. He made a fist so tight he broke the comb he was holding.

McLaws continued, "During that night, General Lee made the difficult decision that led to the battle of the third day. Ewell had launched a hard Second Corps attack at sundown to threaten Meade's left. Now, it was time for the center. Pickett, who had been chomping at the bit for action, was in position with his fresh division now—prancing around on his beautiful black charger, in his curls and perfume, laughing, reaching for glory.

"With Longstreet, it was more of the same. He went to Lee at dawn with a plan to move the whole army around Meade to the south, pick some good ground, and lure the Union commander into attacking us. But Lee reportedly pointed to Cemetery Ridge and said, 'The enemy is there, and I am going to strike him.' We were going to assault the ridge directly in its center, just as the French had done when they crushed the Austrians at Solferino years earlier. In fact, General Pettigrew, the brilliant North Carolinian who was to command the division on Pickett's left, had written about that battle. . . ."

McLaws paused, frowned, went on, "Now Pete was in a blue funk again. Lee had refused his plan, then placed him in command of an attack he didn't believe could possibly be successful, and had given him, in addition to Pickett, two understrength divisions from Hill's Corps. Granted, the attackers had to cover a long exposed area and then march uphill into the fiercest fire, but our artillery, over one hundred and forty guns, would lay on the greatest concentration of fire before the attack the war had ever seen. The Union artillery and troops on the ridge would never be able to withstand it.

"But let's go back to Longstreet. I wasn't there, but there are ample affidavits that will back up my statement. The corps commander was in some kind of a deep depression, more intent on finding a reason to stop the attack than in adequately commanding it. It was noon on this terribly hot and windless day, and Longstreet did something so totally unprofessional that he should have been relieved and shot on the spot. . . .

"He laid the responsibility for the attack on his twenty-eight-year-old chief of artillery, Colonel E. P. Alexander! He sent the young artilleryman a puzzling note informing him he was not only to make the decision *when* the infantry was to attack, but *if* the attack should be commenced at all!"

McLaws shook his head angrily. "Knowing he would have no knowledge of the effectiveness of his fire, Alexander questioned this order, stating that he would be out of ammunition for any second effort.

But Longstreet didn't budge—he insisted that the artilleryman advise Pickett of the right moment to begin the assault. The most valorous charge in the history of the war was to be launched by a young colonel while a lieutenant general was lost in his own *ineffectiveness!*

"With this terrible ax over his head, Alexander opened the massive artillery barrage at just past one o'clock. . . ."

McLaws turned, frowning directly at George Pickett behind the bench. "General Pickett should give you this account himself, but he can't because he's a member of the court. And besides, he always was Old Pete's favorite. So I'll tell it as I know it. . . .

"George Pickett, eager to eke out some glory with his well-rested division, which hadn't yet fought a lick at Gettysburg, was poised with his brave Virginians, waiting for the word to attack from Colonel Alexander. And finally, at just past two-thirty, it came. And General Pickett gave the order to move out. Like well-drilled troops on parade, his proud regiments headed for Cemetery Ridge and the devastating fire the Yankees began to lay down. They soon joined with Pettigrew's North Carolinians on their left. Falling like flies as they continued to march, they filled in the holes as best they could. Every time a regimental flag went down, some brave lad picked it up and kept going right up that murderous slope."

McLaws's voice broke momentarily. "All of his generals went down, two killed, one terribly wounded. Yet still those proud colors staggered upward . . . until finally the reeling ranks broke and those who could still walk turned dazed from the hell they'd faced, and began a stumbling, broken retreat. One proud sergeant who refused to run, walked backward, unblinking, erect, until he was out of range of that savage carnage. But mostly, gentlemen, the withering fire from Cemetery Ridge had drenched that Pennsylvania ground with heroic Southern blood that could never be replaced. And suddenly it was silent. It was as if one massive artillery shell had exploded and left broken bodies and the foul breath of death in its wake."

McLaws paused again, looked at Pickett, who sat staring through brimming eyes as he plucked absently at one of his dark curls. "They called it Pickett's Charge, and it was one of the finest examples of heroism in the history of warfare—but in reality, it was the decimation of a fine division . . . seventy percent casualties, loss of all his field officers, a slaughter for nothing. . . .

"And there it is," McLaws said quietly in the hushed courtroom. "It wasn't even Pickett's Charge any more than it was Pettigrew's. It was really *Longstreet's* Charge, but he wasn't capable of handling the responsibility. . . But there shouldn't even have been a third day on those damned hills, nosiree! If Longstreet had listened to our warnings—Hood's and mine—on the Emmitsburg Road the afternoon before, if he had only taken Hood's plan to Lee, the plan to go around south of Round Top to Meade's unprotected rear . . . then, *then*, gentlemen, Gettysburg would have been ours."

McLaws rose in the witness box, raised his right hand and pointed toward General Longstreet. "There is your villain, Colonel Mosby. Jeb Stuart may have taken a little license with his orders and done a little joy-riding, but there were all kinds of cavalrymen around in his absence. He's no more guilty about Gettysburg than Sam Hood is back here behind this bench, or George Pickett, or, by God, Braxton Bragg—and he wasn't even there!"

The courtroom exploded in an absolute uproar!

In the midst of the pandemonium, Jeb Stuart rushed forward to shake Lafayette McLaws's hand as the Georgian continued to stand in the witness box.

★   ★   ★

FOLLOWING a short intermission in which the crowd was brought back under control, Hood watched coldly as Axline went after McLaws. It was out in the open now. "Is it not true," the judge-advocate asked the stocky Georgian, "that you had trouble with General Longstreet . . . that he in fact *court-martialed* you later in the war? Wasn't it for lack of cooperation in the Knoxville campaign?"

Lafayette McLaws glared into Axline's red face. "Aw, c'mon, Colonel, surely you read far enough to find out that he preferred charges against Law and Beverly Robertson too. Called it mutiny at first, then, in my case, changed it to 'improper preparation' when I demanded a court-martial. That's right, *I* pressed for the court-martial over Knoxville. Fact is, when its results were finally released in Sixty-four, it took President Davis just three days to reverse them! Did you find all that in your reading, Colonel?"

Axline's color bleached, but he went on, "The fact does remain that you are prejudiced against General Longstreet. Isn't that correct?"

McLaws leaned forward, looked him directly in the eye, said in a low flat voice, "You're damned right I am."

"Which would tend to influence your—"

"That's *enough*, Colonel Axline!" Sam Hood said sharply, his great bloodhound eyes narrowed. "This witness does not need to be hectored. Not one bit!" He broke the pencil in his good hand.

Axline started to say something, saw instantly that it would be a waste of time. "You are excused, General McLaws," he murmured, returning to his table.

As the witness made his way from the stand, Bragg asked, "Do you have anyone else, Colonel Mosby?"

"Yes, sir, I do—"

Everyone in that courtroom knew who it was going to be.

"—I call General James Longstreet to the stand."

The heavy-shouldered general walked slowly from his third-row seat to the witness box, where Axline reminded him that he was still under oath. Looking up for an instant at Pickett, he blinked his eyes, then settled into the chair like a great bear readying himself to fight a pack of wolves. His expression was blank, the poker face so many of his old cronies knew.

"General Longstreet," Mosby began, "as a spectator, you have heard most of the testimony that has been presented in this court, and particularly that of General McLaws. How do you explain his charges?"

Longstreet shifted his weight, spoke in a low, slow voice, "First of all, the man hates me."

"He didn't hate you before Gettysburg, did he?"

"He was jealous because we came from the same class at West Point, and I was always ahead of him in rank. And then there was that trouble in the Knoxville campaign when he didn't want to fight." Longstreet's eyes wandered off, out of focus, to the troubles of that time. He took a deep breath, but added nothing more.

Finally, Mosby said, "But let's go back to Gettysburg. Why didn't you listen to McLaws and Hood—particularly General Hood—when they informed you that the second day's attack just couldn't be effected as planned?"

Longstreet's eyes focused. "I told them we had Lee's orders and they couldn't be changed."

Mosby moved close. "Come now, General. Everyone knows orders can be changed if the survival of a major command is at stake. And

Hood presented you with a remarkable opportunity—to go around the open end of Meade's army and strike him a mortal blow in the rear. If your entire corps had followed, Meade would have had to divert half his army from the ridge to counter the threat. You would have had him in a vise. Even if you hadn't soundly defeated him then, he would have been forced to withdraw from the field and give Lee a great victory. Isn't that true, General?"

"You don't understand, Colonel."

Mosby tasted blood. "From what I hear, you never were afraid to speak your mind to General Lee. Why not then? Why did you refuse, after repeated demands from two trusted subordinates, to even go *talk* to Lee?"

Longstreet stared at his knees. "He had already refused my advice repeatedly. Why bother? The general was simply intent on going right at them, no matter what."

"Do you honestly mean to say he wouldn't have considered Hood's proposal?"

Longstreet looked up, the poker mask suddenly gone, replaced by a haggard look. A cross between anger and guilt. "No, he wouldn't! He wouldn't listen to *anything* I had to say. I was a fifth wheel to him, just another lackey."

Mosby shook his head. "He thought so much of you that he gave you command of his major thrust the next day."

Longstreet slumped, diverting his eyes back to his knees. "Yes, to the slaughter. Poor Pickett, those fine lads, so many . . . and after my poor babies had died earlier in the year . . . my poor babies." He looked up, his eyes brighter, wet. "Did you know about my three babies dying, Colonel, did you?"

Mosby nodded. If anyone knew about such a thing, he did. He waited. . . .

Finally Longstreet went on, staring down, "I've been riding up and down that ground at Gettysburg in my dreams for three years now, you know. Up and down in front of that ridge, those Round Tops, that ridge. All night long at times . . . seeing the ghosts, counting the bodies . . . white bones glaring in the sunlight, a horse's gleaming skull with its hideous teeth grinning at me. A rusting carbine, a broken saber. A face, a butternut figure, a fife playing 'Camptown Races,' a corpse laughing at me. I can hear the rattling of musketry, the crush of artillery. Smell the odor of burning gunpowder, rotting bodies, the sweat of fear. . . ."

He looked up briefly—searching momentarily for a tender word of reassurance, understanding. "You see, no one knows what it's like to be blamed for something as ghastly as Gettysburg . . . the voices behind my back—oh, I heard them all right."

His gaze came up, centered on Jeb. He pointed. "That's who they should've been after—I said back then he was to blame for everything, and should have been court-martialed as soon as we got back to Virginia. Joy-riding, that's what he was doing when we needed him. They should've named him Mars, because he thinks war is God's greatest game. Under his fancy clothes and big smile, he is an ogre—*a damned ogre!*"

Longstreet's eyes dropped once more, centering on his wringing hands. "Sometimes when I'm at Gettysburg, it's raining—as it was the day we left. And those skulls with the holes for eyes, they have bright raindrops on them, reflecting back the sight of shells bursting, and blood-covered butternut figures falling, the bonnie blue flag lying in the dirt. Oh, God!"

Mosby suddenly wanted to reach out and touch his cheek where the tears were flowing, the tears that may have waited an eternity to flow. He cleared his throat, spoke softly, "I have no more questions, General."

After a moment, James Longstreet looked up, blinked in confusion. "Sir?"

"You may step down, sir."

As Longstreet made his way back toward the hushed audience, Braxton Bragg announced, "This court is closed until tomorrow morning at ten o'clock."

★　★　★

WHEN the crowd caught its breath and let out its exultation, several people rushed forward to congratulate Jeb, but Mosby held back, by the bench. He caught Spring's eye for a moment, saw Rawlins smile his congratulations. He turned, looked up at the bench, and slowly nodded his head as he met Sam Hood's gaze.

Imperceptibly, the general nodded back.

Then, as the crowd began to leave, he went slowly to the table, where Jeb detached himself from Bessica and the other well-wishers.

Stuart extended his hand, grinned broadly. "You did a marvelous job, John," he said. "I hated to see Old Pete come apart like that, but he's a tired man with a lot of misery on his mind. Tomorrow morning should be perfunctory, shouldn't it, the epilogue?"

Mosby raised an eyebrow. "I'm not counting on *anything* until it's over. As we've all said from the beginning, a court of inquiry can be an unwieldy procedure." He picked up his papers. "In the meantime, I have to turn back into an intelligence officer and stop this Amistad thing."

The French actress—a perfect excuse to work things out with Spring! He caught up with her as she was making her way out. Her smile was cool. "You really are a good lawyer, John Mosby,"

He felt awkward, wanted to take her hand, hold her. "Thanks. May I ask you something important?"

"Of course."

"It's about your friend, Marie Jolie. Will you find out something for me?" How he loved her dark eyes, even when they were guarded.

"What do you want to know?" she replied in a cool tone.

"Remember that alleged plot I told you about—the wild story about some kind of an attack on our government?"

"Vaguely."

"Well, there have been some positive developments." He sketched Rawlins's encounter with Verita at the Spottswood.

"I also attended that Anti-Slavery Society convention in Washington," she replied caustically. "Does that make me a radical, an *enemy*?"

"No, but I haven't told you all of it. There is a definite abolition connection to a very real plot. Will you meet me for an early supper so I can tell you more about it? Maybe at the Exchange dining room?"

"All right—six o'clock?"

"Yes," he smiled, touched her hand. "Thanks, Spring."

This time her smile was real, dimple and all.

★ ★ ★

JOHN Mosby hurried from the courthouse to the stables, weaving through the elated crowd that still hung around the front of the building. He guessed there were over twenty people carrying signs, and maybe fifty ex-soldiers wearing some item of a uniform or piece of equipment—a faded old slouch hat, a cartridge belt, a canteen. And there were probably another hundred civilians, including a majority of happy women. A few tried to stop him, but most just wished him well. "Give 'em hell tomorrow, Mosby!" "You just say the word, Colonel, and we'll take care of old Bragg!" There was even one small group chanting, "Jeb for president!" to the accompaniment of a banjo. Mosby squinted into the hot afternoon sun and smiled back.

At the stables, he was told that Israel Jones still hadn't been seen, so he hastened on over to the city jail. A captain met him, told him that no one, not even the man's wife, had seen Jones since the day before. "Well, Colonel, we went on the assumption that he met with foul play and there are two nigger males that have been fished out of the river today. One might be him. You want to go to the morgue and take a look?"

"Yes." Mosby had that cold feeling that he remembered from the war—the one he always got when one of his men was killed. The chill of blame.

The morgue was a sterile place, recently repainted white, smelling of disinfectant, unfeeling and depressing. The first body they showed Mosby was a middle-aged man who had choked to death from one means or another. The second body had just been cleaned up. The throat had been slit from one ear to another, and the head had bloated hideously. Mosby's stomach knotted. It was hard to recognize him, but it was Israel Jones.

★ ★ ★

"I BELIEVE I'll wait in Ambassador Benjamin's study," Verita told the butler.

"Yes'm, most certainly, ma'am," the man replied, leading her to the small study off the parlor. "Would you like some cool lemonade, ma'am?"

"No, I just had some. *Merci.*" She had to hurry and didn't want to be interrupted.

The book-lined study contained a large desk with files in its drawers. As soon as the butler left, she went to the files and quickly began to skim through them. They were well-organized, mostly about politics and his private business holdings—his New Orleans correspondence, articles he'd written. She looked under "A" for Abraham, found only a short memorial about its present stage of ineffectiveness. She moved on to "J," but found nothing.

She glanced up at the clock on the wall. He'd be along any minute now!

She tried "H" for Hebrew and drew a blank. *If he knew about the contributors, how would he file any written information?*

She looked for "spy" and found nothing; tried "rebellion." And just as she was leaving "R" she saw a page on which Judah had scribbled "revolt and sedition." It was followed by:

> The following men of Jewish lineage are thought to be sympa-thetic to the Negro cause in the South. There is also a possibility that they are contributing money to the movement known as Abraham. They may be a key to other contributors. Perhaps I should have turned this list over to someone—probably Mosby —already. But it is such a sensitive matter! Here I am, a Jew, compiling a list of my fellow Jews who believe in freedom. God, this puts me in a terrible position! But my duty is clear. I will take their names to Mosby when the court is over.

Five Jewish names from three different cities followed. *Benjamin was onto them, but he had told no one!* If she took the list and killed him, no one would know about them ... and their money could keep flowing into the Cause. And kill him she would, with pleasure! But now she had to get word to Higginson for these men to lie low.

She folded the sheet of paper and slipped it into her purse just as she heard the butler greet Benjamin at the front door. Smiling to herself as she hurried to the wall, she pulled a book from the shelf and scanned its first page as Judah strode into the room.

★ ★ ★

M OSBY got to his office just before five. Pushing aside the pile of routine paperwork on his desk, he swung his feet up and closed his eyes. He sure would like to just conk out for a couple of hours. Too much was closing in on him: the pressures of the court, this Amistad plot, and Spring Blakely. The court alone had been driving him to the end of his wits—and he refused to guess at what the precise findings would be. Well, he'd done all he could, pulled out all the stops. One thing was certain, he hadn't made many new friends through the run of the court. . . .

He might be looking for a job, himself, before long.

Like Longstreet. He couldn't help feeling sorry for Old Pete; a proud, brave officer caught up in the whirlpool of war and tragedy, trapped by his own ego, author of an off-balance series of decisions that would forever leave a stain on his name and the lives of thousands on his conscience. He would have to go see Old Pete when this was all over, try to offer some kind of comfort.

And now this Amistad thing. Seeing Israel Jones on that slab, with his head nearly sliced off, made the plot about as real as anything. He'd have to find some money in a contingency fund for the widow . . . *goddamnit!*

And Spring—how could he do anything with her chasing through his thoughts constantly. A hundred times he'd told himself to forget her, but she had saturated him and wouldn't go away. Why did she have to be such a damned radical? What was it Shakespeare said about a radical—"He has everything that an honest man should not have . . . What an honest man should have, he has nothing."

Well, Spring wasn't a true radical, not really. She just believed in something and was making it a cause. The trouble with people who get involved in causes was that they too often forget to see the other person's view. They get in that tunnel with blinders on and often get so unseeing they miss the way out.

God, how he loved her!

But he had to push her away, keep her in perspective. Amistad— he had to think about Amistad! There was just too much information coming in for it not to be a viable problem . . . the letters to President McClellan, the negro journalist junk, Mark's information, Amistad, Saman Brown, the savage death of Israel Jones.

Saman Brown—who in the hell could that be? If Israel Jones sent that name to him just before he was killed, Saman Brown had to be a vital cog.

He should concentrate on that name alone, shut everything else out. The key: *Saman Brown. Saman Brown.* There was something back in there in the cobwebs of his memory. Where had he heard that name? Saman Brown. What about abolition—that was the root of this whole Amistad thing. Of course, there was Old John Brown. *Always* there was Old John Brown—whose body was supposed to be a-moldering in the grave. But it wasn't, no sir, not with the abolitionists singing about it from morning 'til night. It was worth a try.

Mosby swung his legs down and went to his filing cabinet. He had some old clippings about the raid on Harpers Ferry in '59, some of the plethora of nonsense that had flooded the newspapers and magazines while the old zealot waited for the rope. Every reporter and writer in the country had run out of ink on that one.

There was an article from the *New York Herald* about John Brown's murderous spree out in Kansas: "John Brown formed a vigilante squad of his own choosing for a very special duty. It included his sons Frederick, Oliver, Salmon, and Owen, as well as his son-in-law, Henry Thompson and an Austrian-Jewish immigrant by the name of—"

Salmon Brown! It had to be! Mosby flipped hurriedly through the clippings. Which of the Brown sons survived Harpers Ferry? There was the old poem written to ridicule the South:

> *There's a flutter in the Southland, a tremor in the air,*
> *For the rice plains are invaded, the cotton fields laid bare,*
> *And the cry of 'Help' and 'Treason' rings loud from tongue and pen,*
> *John Brown has crossed the border with a host of fifteen men.*

Mosby read on—the names of Brown's "soldiers" were scattered throughout. Finally he found a statement about the Brown sons: only Oliver, Watson, and Owen had gone on the raid. He double-checked—no Salmon Brown! *He had to be the man!* Now it came back—hadn't Israel Jones mentioned something about a special white man coming to Jubilo's church? Salmon Brown. He'd have to get some wires off immediately. He looked at his watch—God, it was already five minutes after six; Spring would be even angrier.

And he still didn't know what Amistad intended.

He locked the office and trotted to the telegraph office, where he told the telegrapher on duty to get the messages off at once. They went to all of his agents in the field, requesting any available information on Salmon Brown of the Harpers Ferry Browns.

★　★　★

I T WAS twenty after six when he hurried into the dining room at the Exchange Hotel. Before Spring could say anything, he quickly explained what had held him up. "Now, c'mon. Dinner will have to wait. I have to see General Rawlins at once!"

"But I don't—"

He grabbed her hand as she got to her feet. "We have to hurry. I'll tell you all about it on the way."

She held her hat with the other hand and had to run to keep up. "It's a good thing you've got such long pretty legs," he said as they left the lobby and hurried along Fourteenth toward Main. "I have to confess—I really only spoke to you about your friend, Marie Jolie, as an excuse to talk to you this afternoon . . . but now, it's just possible that she really is a part of this whole crazy scheme. She did arrive just as all of this information started coming in, you know. Will you talk to her, find out what she was doing in Washington, and all?"

"I still don't think it's right."

Mosby stopped suddenly, took her by both arms and looked directly into her dark eyes. "Listen to me, Spring Blakely. There are people who may be trying to assassinate some of our leaders this week, and your uncle might be one of the targets. Now it's time for you to get your priorities in order, young lady. You are a Southern woman, and your country is in danger from some unknown fanatics. *Now* will you do as I ask?"

She looked back into his stern expression and saw no room for argument. "Yes, John," she replied quietly, "I'll talk to her first thing in the morning."

"That's not good enough. Go to the theater on some pretense before the play starts tonight."

Spring nodded in agreement. "Any ideas about *what* pretense?"

Mosby grinned. "You're an ex-spy. Dream something up."

"Yes, sir!" She smiled, leaned forward, and kissed him on the mouth.

★　　★　　★

J OHN Rawlins was in his room at the Spottswood. Mosby quickly told him that Spring was going to help with the French actress, then he sprung his premise about Salmon Brown.

Rawlins's black eyes lit up. "By God, I think you're right. Huh, now why in the hell didn't *I* think of that?"

"Can you get somebody on this right away? He might have been in the Union Army. If not, surely someone knows something about him in Ohio, or upstate New York where the Brown farm was. But we've got to do it fast. I have a feeling that whatever they're planning is going to come off pretty damned soon!"

Rawlins reached for his coat. "I'll wire Grant personally. Anything new on our Crispus Attucks?"

"No, we're still watching his mail box."

Rawlins nodded his head. "Let's go!"

★　★　★

S ALMON Brown had been out on the river practicing with the boat most of the afternoon. Following that, he worked out a plan that would be independent of Jubilo's support. Now, he looked forward to a good bath at the Spottswood. "Do I have any messages?" he asked the desk clerk.

"Yes, sir," the young man said, pulling a telegraph envelope from the guest's box. "This came in the middle of the afternoon." Salmon tore it open eagerly, but his face flushed as he read it.

Mr. Smith. It is with deep regret that I must order you to stop the Richmond operation of the American Importing Co. Ltd. for the time being. The business with Stuart Court is canceled. Repeat. The business with Stuart Court will cease until further notice. A courier will bring handwritten verification and I will be in Richmond the morning of Tuesday August 14. Higginson.

Salmon blanched, felt an emptiness in his stomach, and then sudden anger. What had gone wrong? They couldn't stop now! It was all set. *He couldn't do this!* Higginson simply could not cancel this great magnificent blow. It was too well-organized, too well-planned.

He read the message again, shook his head. His skin felt prickly, his hand shook. Maybe a whiskey would help.

Moments later at the bar, he gulped down two fast bourbons, felt their heat spread. But it didn't help. What in the hell was wrong with

311

the reverend—cold feet at the last minute? He blinked his eyes, glanced down at the front page of the *New York Herald*—a worn copy that had been discarded. Only a few words registered with him: "Jeb Stuart Court a Guilty Reminder of Gettysburg . . . Does it take a Rebel court to tell *us* it was all in vain?" The column heading shouted, "March on Washington, Then to Richmond!"

But Salmon didn't want to read what ordinarily he would have devoured. He didn't want to read anything, couldn't, in the red haze that enveloped him. *How could Higginson do this to him?* It was less than eighteen hours before the name Brown would again blaze across the firmament, declaring liberty with a deed so magnificent that school-boys would be shouting it! Higginson couldn't take that away from him, he wouldn't let him!

He had one more quick shot of whiskey and went to look for a messenger. There were changes to be made, and people to be rounded up. To hell with Higginson and be damned—Salmon Brown was still in command of Amistad and, by God, *they would hit the Stuart Court as planned!*

★　★　★

FLORA Stuart stared at the editorial in the *Examiner*. She had read it five or six times since the newspaper came late that morning, and now she had to read it just one more time.

> **Situation wanted. Heroic cavalier, major general of cavalry experienced in glory-earning operations not relating to other parts of an army. Superb at exceeding authority and orders, dancing with and kissing the ladies, and riding around enemy armies at a given whim. Should be available after Tuesday, August 14th. Will probably travel. Quote salary offer and rank. All correspondence should be directed to: Knight of the Golden Spurs, *The Richmond Examiner*.**

Flora flung the newspaper aside and shouted, *"Mama!"*

Moments later, Elizabeth Stuart came running into the bedroom. "What is it, child, what's wrong?" she asked with alarm.

"I've made up my mind. Jeb is going to need me in Richmond!"

"But you haven't even been out of that bed in weeks. And the doctor said—"

"To *hell* with him!"

"But you won't be able to walk!"

Flora was already pulling at the loose straps that held her to the board. "We've got a wheelchair and a wagon that'll get us into town, don't we? What time is that early morning train to Richmond?"

"There's one at eight-forty that gets in there about noon or a little after."

"That's plenty of time."

Elizabeth Stuart looked closely at her daughter-in-law. "You sure you want to do this? We might not even be able to get in."

Flora gritted her teeth to shut out the pain as she tried to swing her legs over the side of the bed. "I'll get in. Now, Mama, help me. Pick these legs of mine up and sit me up."

Elizabeth nodded her head as she gently complied. "I'm glad. It's about time the Stuart women showed those uppity Richmondites our mettle. Yes, and I'll remind them of what a proud Letcher lady looks like when her favorite son is being maligned. You sure you're going to be all right, darling?"

Flora cried out at the pain as she sat upright and touched her toes to the hardwood floor. "It may take all night to get this sick room smell off me," she said gripping Elizabeth's arm tightly. "And maybe I won't be as pretty as that Southwick woman. But I'll be in that courtroom tomorrow if I have to crawl."

★　★　★

"I HAVEN'T been backstage at a big theater like this before," Spring Blakely said as she smelled the white roses sitting on the end of the dressing table. "It's exciting, isn't it? Who are these from, a special admirer?"

Verita smiled into the mirror. "Very special. Monsieur Benjamin, in fact. He sends them every night, red ones, yellow, white. I love them!"

"I was in a couple of plays back home in Kentucky."

"I'll bet you were good at acting."

"Oh, I don't know," Spring lied. "But I played a Northern spy in one of them, and I was told by a professional actor that I should go on stage."

Verita pinned the little hat to her hair. "Perhaps you should take some acting lessons."

"I wish I could play a powerful abolitionist—that would be a part I could really enjoy. You know, something highly dramatic, where I die for the cause. I was at that wonderful conference in Washington recently—the Anti-Slavery Society meeting—and I sat there in that audience enthralled to my very bones! Now that was a good setting, just like a huge play itself."

Verita nodded her head, brushing on a bit more eye makeup.

"Did you get that feeling?"

The warning shot through Verita. Looking through the mirror, she said, *"Pardon?"*

"You know, the Anti-Slavery meeting, where all those abolition leaders gave speeches. I didn't know you then, but General Rawlins mentioned this noon that he recalled seeing you there with some handsome young man."

Verita nearly dropped the little eyeshadow brush. *Rawlins recalled seeing her with Salmon?* She managed a smile. "Yes. Oh, that was so stimulating. I thought Frederick Douglass was most impressive."

Spring sniffed another rose. "Yes, but I liked that handsome Higginson. Now that man is truly elegant!"

"Did your uncle know you went?" *What was Rawlins up to?*

"I just told him I was going on a shopping trip. What about you?"

What kind of a game was this? "Oh, I was visiting from New York for a couple of days. That young man I was with is an old lover."

Spring grinned. "How exciting! A lover who's an avid abolitionist. Golly, that must be fun. Do you still see him?"

"Not since then. He's married."

"Oh."

Verita watched her expression carefully. "Yes, we used the meeting as an excuse. But I ended it then. He wanted me to be his full-time mistress and I refused. Ha! Can you imagine me being chained to one man?" She chuckled. "Well, *merci* for stopping. Perhaps we can have that lunch soon."

Spring smiled. "Yes, by all means. And I hope the play goes well tonight."

Verita caught her sleeve, handed her a rose. "For luck, *cherie.*"

As soon as Spring Blakely was gone, Verita withdrew paper and a short pencil from her purse. She scribbled the note to Salmon quickly, folded it into an envelope and called out to the colored boy who ran errands for the cast.

★　★　★

A S THE sky to the west began to lose its scarlet blush and ease in its violets, John Mosby, accompanied by three uniformed city policemen, arrived in front of Jubilo's store in a police wagon. Hurrying up to the front door, he knocked loudly, waited, knocked again. Finally, the minister's wife opened it. "I wish to speak to Reverend Jubilo," Mosby said.

Jubilo, who was about to leave for the guards' warehouse, came to the door, eyed the policemen. "What may I do for you, Cunnel?"

"I want to talk to you. Do you want to come along, or is there another place that's convenient?"

Jubilo glanced down at the slender officer. "Come on in, suh. We can go on back to my store office." He looked back at the policemen. "Uh, you planning on arresting someone, Cunnel?"

Mosby removed his hat, entered, nodded to the woman, and followed the burly negro to his office. The big brown dog sniffed at his trousers, accepted a brief pat, and returned to watchful repose by Jubilo's desk.

Refusing a proffered chair, Mosby eyed the huge negro and said, "A grave situation exists, Reverend Jubilo. I told you both sides of the fence had to start communicating, but all I got out of you was a sage shake of the head and some mumblings that nothing rebellious was going on down here. Since I knew you were lying, but didn't want to do anything about it, I sent a man to spy on you. His name was Israel Jones before someone slit his throat last night."

Jubilo shook his head, frowned. He didn't like any of this. "I have a parishioner named Israel Jones, but I know nothing about his death. Absolutely nothing, Cunnel. I'll swear on the holy Bible."

"I may ask you to do that. The second matter is even more serious. We have reason to believe some kind of a sinister plot is afoot to murder some of our government leaders, or something similar. Have you ever heard of a colored newspaper reporter who calls himself *Crispus Attucks?*"

Jubilo pursed his lips, shook his head. "No, suh, can't say as I have."

Mosby leaned forward, peered intently into his eyes. "How about a man by the name of *Salmon Brown?*"

"No, don't know him."

"How about something called *Amistad?*"

"That was the famous slave ship. Everyone knows about that."

"No, something new. A group of radicals. They would probably come to you since you are head of the Abraham movement in this part of the country."

Jubilo drew himself up, frowned. "Suh, I know nothing of any of this. You been smoking some of that good opium again?"

Mosby got to his feet. "I can have you arrested right now on suspicion, you know. In fact, I can have you locked up and throw away the damned key. Grounds of *sedition.*"

Jubilo didn't budge. "Then why don't you do it?"

"Because I have the maybe foolish notion that you have too much sense to get involved in anything crazy. Everything I know and feel about you indicates that you truly have the best interests of your people at heart. Oh, you make a little money off them, but you really care."

Mosby slowly lit a thin cigar in the stark silence. ". . . I would hate to be wrong."

"I know of nothing about which you speak, except the fact that I do care about what is in store for my people. You know, Cunnel, this country can't go on forever keeping them in chains. The day may be coming when something like this is a reality. Yes, suh!"

Mosby's voice softened. "I agree, but change takes time and the use of the law. It'll come about some day, but not by bloodshed." He turned to go. "If you hear anything of these names, let me know immediately—at the War Department, the police station, or at the courthouse. It's most urgent!"

★ ★ ★

My captain went a-scoutin'
And took my brother Jim;

> *He went to catch the Yankees,*
> *But the Yankees, they catched him.*

The stanza from "I'll Lay Ten Dollars Down" kept running through Jeb's head as he tried to occupy himself. The evening meal was long over and he had agreed with Mosby that of all nights, he should be out of the public eye on this one. And there had been three invitations to dinner.

He had tried fruitlessly to read, even attempting the racy old novel, *Tristam Shandy*. And he had written four letters, including one to Flora and a reply to the Shah of Persia's secretary in regard to an offer of cavalry command. He snorted to himself as he walked around his small study, coffee cup in hand. He should send some of these letters to that damned Pollard at the *Examiner* in response to that day's caustic editorial about job openings.

He picked up a copy of the *Southern Literary Messenger,* turned to the article about the court of inquiry. It began, "Will one of the most romantic figures ever to grace American soil be ground to dust by the heel of political exigency? Or will a heroic but spoiled general who could not control his passions be chastised for his moment of irresponsibility? Jeb Stuart, without question one of the bravest and most gallant Virginians ever to fill a saddle, will—"

"Suh, they's a lady to see you—a Mizzus Southwick," his houseman said from the doorway.

Jeb tossed the magazine on his desk and hurried to the parlor to find Bessica standing by the window in a reception dress of dark pearl silk and a matching hat with a long crimson feather. She was as strikingly beautiful as he had ever seen her. She smiled brightly as he kissed her hand. "Ah, Jeb darling, I knew you would be very lonesome tonight, so I brought you a lovely devil's food cake."

Jeb grinned. "Well, how nice. I'll have cook serve some with fresh coffee."

"Just the coffee for me, my dear. Are you truly lonesome?"

"Restless is a better word. I can't wait until this darned court is finally over."

"But it was over today, with McLaws's testimony and that pathetic display of Longstreet's. They *have* to find you innocent!"

"Mosby still doesn't trust them."

Bessica sat upright on a Queen Anne chair. "I don't believe I'm listening to the real Jeb Stuart," she said. "I say you have nothing to worry about. The whole administration owes you an apology in the middle of Capitol Square at high noon!"

He laughed. "But what if they kick me out of the Army? Oh, I'd probably enlist as a private or something, but—"

"Ha! Jeb Stuart a private? Never!"

"Or I might run for office. Do you think I would really do well in politics, Bessica?"

She patted his hand. "I could have you in the governor's mansion in three years, in the Executive Mansion in eight."

His eyes widened. "Honestly? Do you actually think it would be that easy?"

Bessica laughed. "With your enormous popularity and my money, darling, it would be easy. I would begin at once, capitalizing on this terrible crime that has been perpetrated against you, and then get you immediately into the coming campaign as possibly a congressman. We could . . ."

He barely listened as he thought of himself as a civilian, as one of the selfsame politicians whom he had so often derided and had for so long detested. How could he do it? Of course, he could change his values, think about the overall good he would bring to both his beloved Virginia and the Confederacy. He could remain pure, above all of the sordid collusions of everyday politics, still be all that was noble and righteous. He laughed to himself—*never!*

Bessica got back to her feet, moved close. "You aren't even listening to me, darling." She kissed him lightly on the lips, opened her eyes into his, embraced him, then returned to his lips. Their kiss was long, sharing, stimulating. She moved more firmly against him, meeting his tongue vigorously. Breaking the kiss at last, she whispered, "Oh, Jeb, take me to bed and make love to me. Just this once, my beautiful darling." She undulated against him, kissed his cheek, his lobe. "You have no idea how much I've wanted you all these weeks. Just tonight, my darling, just take all of me and let me love you as if there isn't another thing in the world. Let me love you, darling, love you with all of my soul."

Suddenly Jeb pushed back, his face rigid. He held her arms firmly. "I can't, Bessica, I just can't. She's right there between us: Flora. God knows I want you, but I can't push Flora out of the way."

She looked into his tormented eyes and blinked. Her eyes brimmed as she sighed, straightened her hat. Finally she said, "There's my Knight of the Golden Spurs again, one of the last cavaliers. Damn you and your precious honor!" She drew in a deep breath, slowly exhaled, and found a tiny smile. "It doesn't make me love you any less, Jeb Stuart. But I'm afraid you'll have to eat your cake alone." She reached for her purse. "I have to go hide my chagrin before it shows too much."

He stood there woodenly, feeling her hurt. "I'm sorry, Bessica. I feel like such a boor."

She turned in the doorway, created another smile as she said, *"C'est du jolie!"*

★ ★ ★

JEB returned to the study after walking Bessica to her carriage. He was more restless than ever, but now guilt was playing a part. He could have stopped it before it went so far, but, oh, how he wanted that beautiful woman. Why couldn't he just make love to her and get on with life like other men—like his father?

He thought of his mother, and then of Flora. . . .

He went to the desk, opened her letter and read it, balled it up and threw it in the waste basket. His exciting Flora. They had met on the plains of Kansas and immediately he had been a goner. The vivacious young lady, fresh from finishing school in Detroit. Full of humor, a wonderful horsewoman. They took long rides and fell foolishly in love . . . the helplessly romantic second lieutenant of cavalry and the zestful colonel's daughter.

They were married that November in the post chapel at Fort Riley. He'd never forget how dazzling she was in her white graduation dress, her blue eyes glowing with love and joy for him. How they whirled round and round as they danced at the reception!

He took her to Fort Leavenworth the next day to reside in the mean quarters allotted such a junior officer. What a comedown for the daughter of Philip St. George Cooke! But she never once complained. Not one single time, even in her worst humors.

And later, he hadn't even been with her when little Flora, their five-year-old daughter, died. Nor could he get to the funeral because he was tied up in battle serving Stonewall in the Valley. And now she was lying down there at Laurel Hill in terrible misery while he was acting foolish over another woman.

He sat at the desk and dipped the pen. "My dearest Flora," he wrote,

> ... This is my second letter to you tonight because after all these years I still don't know how to explain how very much I love you, my darling. There is no way I can know because my love for you grows every single day, like the flowers in spring, like the storm clouds in the sky. This terrible thing will be over tomorrow, my dear, and I will come to you and hold your hand until you are well. And then we will run away alone to the shore and find a lovely cabin and some handsome horses to ride splashing through the surf. It will be a glorious honeymoon, and perhaps when it is over you will understand somewhat of how much I do love you, how much I have missed you. . . .

When he finished sealing the envelope, Jeb stood, stretched. He felt so much better, even though he knew he had used the letter as a catharsis. Yet, everything he said was true, he just had to quit fussing over this stupid court and appreciate his blessings.

He walked to a table, picked up a trusty old horse pistol that he had carried into innumerable fights. And Yellow Tavern flashed back to him . . . he could hear the rattle of carbines, the shouting voices, the screaming horses, the other explosions of battle; he could see the bright sunlight in the smoke and dust, Custer's bluecoated troopers, his own heroic boys in butternut, the flags waving. *"Bully for Old K! Give it to 'em, boys!"* The sudden smashing kick in his side . . . crimson blood. Falling. . . .

Why did he want to go back to Yellow Tavern—because of his nearly fatal wound, of his miracle? What pulled him back like a homing pigeon, like a nail to a magnet?

Suddenly he knew. It was clear as day! It had to be . . .

He, Jeb Stuart, Brigadier General, C.S.A., Chief of the Cavalry Bureau, was doing just exactly what he was put on this earth to do. If those people found against him tomorrow on some improbable pretense, he would challenge the decision all the way to the hilt. He wasn't cut out to be a politician, or serve in some foreign potentate's silly army. Nosireebob! The only way his beloved Virginia and the

Confederacy could get a full measure out of him was right where he was. And in the battles that were off the horizon.

He put the horse pistol down, felt warm, relaxed.

By tomorrow afternoon, his praises would once more echo through the Confederacy!

★　★　★

"**S**UH," Jefferson Davis's butler said from the doorway to his office in the White House. "They's a major here with a telegraph for you. Says it's awful important, Your Excellency, suh."

The president closed the book he had been reading, frowned. He didn't like to be disturbed this late in the evening. "Send him in," he replied.

The major was the chief telegrapher at the War Department. He saluted, handed over the message. Davis read it quickly:

> Arlington Virginia. 13 August 1866. Your Excellency. I regret to inform you that I must go against your wishes in the matter of the Stuart court of inquiry. I will be available to testify at one o'clock P.M. on Tuesday 14th August in the State Courthouse. It is a matter of honor and my decision is irrevocable. I have also informed Generals Bragg and Stuart. Signed/Robert E. Lee.

Davis stared, read the message again. "Goddamnit!" he snapped. "Sir?"

"The man's crazy!"

"Sir?"

Davis turned to the wall to hide his bursting anger. What in the hell had gotten into Lee? In just one more day the court would be all wrapped up and packaged neat as a pin. It wasn't quite as he'd planned it, but it would do. Goddamnit, now this! There was no telling what Lee might say. Always playing the white knight. It had been that way through the last two-thirds of the war—everyone worshipping Lee, not giving their president his due. Who the hell did they think ran the country, fought and scratched to keep the Confederacy alive when all the walls were crumbling? Who in the hell managed to beg, borrow, and steal the shot and shell, the rations and medical supplies, everything else an army needed to fight? Was it Robert Lee? *Hell* no! He just rode his famous gray horse in majesty and got all of the battle accolades . . . while it was he, Jefferson Davis, who made the major military decisions!

Without Lee, Gettysburg was finished. Now, it was anyone's guess. And having Lee as his running mate was an absolute necessity. Damn fool! He turned to the major. "Have you delivered telegraphs from General Lee to Bragg and Stuart?"

"Yes, sir, by messenger at this very moment."

Davis nodded, frowned. "Very well. I want a copy of this message to go to Secretary of War Breckinridge and General Beauregard."

"Yes, sir. At once." The major saluted and turned to go.

"And get word to Secretary Breckinridge that I want to see him immediately. And Ambassador Judah Benjamin, as well. No, just give the ambassador a copy of the telegraph."

Stupid goddamned Lee!

★ ★ ★

JOHN Mosby arrived at his house shortly after ten to find Spring Blakely curled around a copy of Poe's *The Gold Bug* in the parlor. He apologized, asked her if she had eaten yet.

"Yes, your Winnie was very kind and filled me up quite well, thank you. But while trying to solve Poe's cipher, I've been troubled by my own little dilemma—should I go home like a nice lady, or go find one of your nightshirts and crawl into your tempting bed?"

"And?"

"I was leaning toward the nightshirt, but then I remembered that I'm still mad at you."

"Oh, yes, that."

"And then I remembered that even *I'm* not that blasé. A lover, yes—a full time sleeper, no. That requires a certain amount of activity with a preacher, sir."

He chuckled, sobered. "What did your French actress have to say?"

Spring told him about Verita's lover.

"And you believe her."

"Yes. I led her on to a fair-thee-well, and what she said made sense."

"Did you tell her about Rawlins seeing her with that man?"

"Yes, she never blinked an eye. I honestly think she was telling the truth."

"Well, she probably doesn't have anything to do with any of this sordid affair. Probably just coincidental." He sat in a straight-back chair as his cook, Winnie, brought in a plate of cold chicken, and clucked at him about his eating habits. Moments later, with a mouth full of chicken, he mentioned his feelings about Longstreet. "You know, I hope history will treat him more kindly than I did in this court. In much of the war, he was one of our best generals."

She smiled softly. "I know, but don't get too sentimental yet. The verdict isn't in."

He looked at her sharply. "Do you know something?"

She sobered. "No, honestly."

Mosby stared at his plate, thinking about Longstreet. After a short silence, Spring said, "John, we really do have to talk about our big problem." She watched for a strong reaction, saw none, as he picked up a thigh and went to work on it. "I mean it. I can't help the way I feel about the shackling of human beings in bondage, and you must respect my opinion on the matter."

He wiped his mouth. "Spring, honey, this isn't the time. This is the first moment I've had to relax all day. Let me say this, my respect for you is limitless and you have a right to your own opinion in any matter. I—"

"Suh," Aaron said from the hallway, " 'Scuse me, but General Stuart is here."

Throwing a look of surprise at Spring, Mosby jumped to his feet and hurried out of the room. Stuart apologized for the late visit, handed him the telegraph from Robert E. Lee. Mosby read it quickly. Looking into Jeb's eyes, he shook his head and said, "Well I'll be damned."

"What do you think?" Jeb asked.

Mosby shook his head. "I don't know. I do know that court would be crazy to find against you after today's testimony, but as I said, anything can happen. When I went up to Arlington, I thought having Lee as a witness was the best solution. Now, I don't know. He covered for Longstreet in his Gettysburg report. It worries me."

"Whatever he does will be for the best."

Mosby stroked his beard. "Now, I'll have to think about how to handle him."

"Same as I told you when you went up to Arlington, John," Jeb replied with a frown, "I don't want *anything* brought up that might be detrimental to the general. He is a holy man."

Mosby's tone was patient. "He's not *holy*, Jeb—a bit *spiritual* perhaps, but not holy."

"You know what I mean." Jeb's face was getting red.

"Yes, I know, my friend. But we have to do what is best for you. We've come this far."

Jeb frowned. "We'll wait and see."

★ ★ ★

"IT WILL be no problem, my dear," Judah Benjamin said as his driver pulled up before his house at 9 Main Street. "I will just tell everyone to squeeze tighter together on the bench. I'm sure they will all be so excited about being near the celebrated Mademoiselle Jolie that they won't mind a bit."

Verita smiled. She would be right near the front of the courtroom, point-blank range from all of the targets. It would be absolutely impossible to miss! She smiled, replied, "I think it will be so exciting. I've never been in a courtroom, anywhere, in my life."

"I find military courts fascinating, so you should be quite intrigued. I once represented an officer in a murder case on one. But you have to remember, this is not a real court-martial."

They stepped down from the buggy, went up the short walk to the front door. Judah's butler was hovering just inside, looking worried and holding out an envelope. "Suh, they was a man here from the War Department. He was looking all over for you, he said. He left this here letter from the president."

They hurried inside, where Judah quickly read the copy of Lee's wire. He would have to notify Rawlins. He smiled at Verita. "Well, my dear, it seems the schedule for tomorrow is changed a bit. You're going to see a *real* star in the courtroom." He told her about Lee.

She looked at him wide-eyed. "Will they still let me in?" She could barely maintain her composure. *Lee—how fortuitous!*

He patted her hand. "Certainly, my dear. But you don't know what this means. General Lee is the most beloved man in the Confederacy."

He chuckled. "For him to appear as a witness is like having Moses come down from the Mount. Half of Richmond will turn out just to get a glimpse of him. I know the president will come to the court. Perhaps I'll be able to introduce you to him."

"Oh, how exciting! Do you really think I could meet him, Judah, really?" *Davis!*

"It will be his pleasure, darling. He was at the play opening night, you know. And he told me how much he liked you."

They went into the parlor, where he poured two brandies.

She was afraid her hand would shake with all of the excitement she was bottling up. *Lee and Davis! Everything they had dreamed of was going to happen just as if they had written it out in detail!* She couldn't wait to get word to Salmon!

★ ★ ★

SHORTLY after midnight, Verita hurried to Salmon Brown's room in the Spottswood. He was still up, having returned from Rocketts only twenty minutes earlier. She quickly relayed the news about Lee. Her hazel eyes sparkled. "Isn't that remarkable! Lee and Davis —I've been running that over and over in my head like a poem. Both of them, right there in front of us like sitting ducks!"

Salmon pounded his fist into his palm. "Yes, by God, and Amistad will flash across the heavens like a comet! I'll have to make changes, adjust the attack time. By God, we're really going to get them all! Davis and Lee, Davis and Lee—it is like a poem!"

"Oh, and talking Judah into taking me along tomorrow was no problem. I'll be right there in one of the first rows."

"Good. Everything else is in order."

"What about their suspicions?"

"Mosby's just probing. If he had anything concrete, he'd have arrested Jubilo, and I wouldn't be standing here. It's all going *perfectly!*"

"What was the letter from Higginson?"

Salmon withdrew it from his coat pocket. "Our brave ex-colonel has turned into a goddamned lackey, licking Jubilo's boots. *The bastard wants us to cancel the raid!*"

Verita just stared at him.

He hadn't told her about the minister's earlier telegraph. "In the letter, Higginson says it's all because Jubilo not only won't give us Abraham's support, but that the damn fool washes his hands of Amistad. The goddamned yellow-belly! But it doesn't make any difference because we are going to attack *anyway!*"

Verita continued to stare at him. Higginson stopping them? They couldn't hold off now—not with everything so close. How could Higginson have possibly let Jubilo sway him like that? "Did you tell the others?" she asked.

"No, I don't want any voting on this decision."

"Good. There'll never be another chance like this. God, I can't believe Higginson would do this."

"Well, he has. But once we've blown the roof off the goddamned South, he'll come to us hat in hand."

Verita grinned. "I can't wait until tomorrow."

"Me either," Salmon said, his eyes bright. He drew the big Whitney revolver from its holster and aimed it at a picture on the wall. "Did I ever tell you how much I enjoy killing?"

"No," she replied, suddenly feeling aroused. She touched the Whitney's barrel, stroked it. "Tell me."

"Did you ever smash a wasp?"

"I've killed a wasp."

"No, I mean *smash* it, grind it into bloody pulp. A wasp is an enemy, and crushing an enemy, mashing it into total destruction, is the ultimate conquest. Well, I get this feeling of utter *power* when I kill any kind of enemy. It's sort of like blasting a heavy caliber bullet between a man's eyes and watching his head blow apart . . . or something like that. I can't quite explain it."

She wet her lips with her tongue. She'd never seen this exciting side of him! His eyes *glowed* when he was like this. There was no wounded, tentative boy here. God! She had to have him! She looked at the revolver—her knuckles were white, gripping it. . . . She let go, moved her hand inside his thigh.

The sheen in his eyes suddenly turned to distress.

She found his lips, his tongue, his growing penis. "*God*, I want you, Salmon!" she said, jerking to her feet and reaching for her dress fasteners. "Hurry!"

His eyes were still troubled. "I don't know. I haven't been with a woman for—"

"I don't care! Hurry!"

He fumbled for his belt, staring as her petticoats flew over her tousled head and her erect nipples appeared.

In moments she was undulating against his full erection, and drawing it into her body.

THE LAST DAY

"**NO!**" Salmon Brown jerked up in a cold sweat from his pillow. He could still see his father, feel him, *smell* him! He had been right there in the hotel room with him, bending over the bed, shaking his long, bony finger with the dirty nail—his wild brush of hair sticking out over his pale, bloodshot eyes . . . that beak of a nose, the wide mouth surrounded by his full mustaches and the long, wiry gray beard. The foul breath. *The Old Man had just been there!*

He had strained to hear the angry words tumbling from the Old Man's lips, but there was only silence. Silence and accusatory eyes, eyes filled with hate and some of the madness, more than some of the madness.

He knew what the Old Man was saying—"You didn't come, you young weasel. You didn't have the stomach for it!"

"No, you don't understand," Salmon Brown said to the presence that lingered. "I couldn't, I knew you would dally, I just couldn't. But you just stick around for tomorrow, Old Man. I'll accomplish more than you *ever* did! You wait and see!"

Salmon swung his legs over the side of the bed, shook his head, tried to chase away the ghost. His hand trembled, his stomach was knotted, just like all those times in the past, back before he met Higginson. He used the sheet to wipe the perspiration off his face. It was just a silly dream, the Old Man coming back to scare him. The Old Man knew Amistad would put Harpers Ferry to shame, he knew it, and that was why he came.

Salmon held his big watch up to the first morning light coming through the window. It was five-thirty-nine, and the day of his fame was just coming awake.

The biggest day of his life. . . .

★   ★   ★

AARON brought in the *Richmond Examiner* just as John Mosby sat down to eat his breakfast of bacon and thick, golden hotcakes. And there it was: GENERAL ROBERT E. LEE TO TESTIFY AT STUART COURT! The story was shorter than the headline, making Mosby wonder about how much old Pollard knew. Still, there it was for the whole world to see on this already warm and sticky August morning. He looked for the editorial he knew would follow, sipped the steaming black coffee, and began to read:

> **What brings Robert Lee down from his castle on the Potomac—finally? Was it the wiggle of his master's finger from the White House steps? Or is a palace revolt a-seething? Why didn't General Lee come down in the beginning of this circus that has occupied the State Courthouse for the past week and a half? For whatever the reason, the world will finally (we hope) know the definitive answer to the enigmatic and heavily obscured puzzle of Gettysburg today when Marse Robert takes the stand. Yesterday, James Longstreet was the culprit. Who will it be today—Traveler? See you in court, Mr. President.**

Mosby had slept poorly, spinning around with guesses as to what Lee would do, and had finally decided to just ride it out with whatever might seem best. One thing was certain, there would be no artifices, nothing contrived in this upcoming session of the court.

He would just have to wait.

It was the other problem that was plaguing him the most. It had kept his head buzzing as much during the night as had the court. What possible target could this spectral Amistad be aimed at? Was it an actuality, or one grand hoax?

No, it was a reality. If anyone should know, he should. He was almost envious of the man who had masterminded the whole thing —the use of revolutionary names, the audacity. . . .

What the *hell* could they be after?

His eyes rested on Pollard's editorial.

The last line . . . "See you in court, Mr. President" suddenly stood out as if in bold print. *"See you in court, Mr. President."*

And all at once he knew!

It had been right there in front of him all the time!

This Amistad was going to hit the Stuart court!

He whistled. Sure as hell!

They were going to go after Davis and God only knew whom else!

"Mr. John, General Rawlins is here to see you!" Aaron called out from the front entry.

Mosby nearly spilled his coffee as he jumped up from the table. "Send him right in, Aaron!"

They shook hands quickly. Rawlins handed him an envelope. "This just arrived by courier from Grant."

John Mosby's blue eyes flashed. "In a minute, General. I've just figured out what the hell is going on with this goddamned Amistad! They're going to attack the court and assassinate Davis!"

Rawlins just stared.

"I know it as sure as if they wrote me a goddamned letter! What an opportunity to blow away the whole top of the Confederacy. Just think about it, think about who all is there—even without Davis. Damn near the whole cabinet, the senior generals, the ambassador to the United States, the governor of Virginia, assorted members of Congress, even the chief-of-staff of the United States Army!"

It was Rawlins's turn to whistle. "God, John, you might be absolutely right. Sonofabitch! If ever there was a chance to ignite another goddamned war, this could be it! Yankee abolitionists assassinate—" Rawlins started to cough, choked it off, wiped his mouth. *"Sonofabitch!"*

"And Lee's coming is perfect for them. I'll bet they're dancing in the street somewhere in this damned city."

"How can we stop them?"

Mosby stroked his short beard. "Lots of ways, and maybe none. I'll have to give it some thought." He remembered the envelope in his hand. "What's this?"

"Salmon Brown."

Mosby hurriedly pulled out the contents. It was a short dossier on one of the sons of John Brown, a son who did not go to Harpers Ferry. Some clippings—mostly the ones Mosby had in his office file.

The man's military record. A picture. Mosby looked at it closely. It was a small indistinct tintype of a man in a Union uniform. He was cleanshaven. In the right-hand lower corner it contained the date: 1861. "Have you ever seen him, General?" he asked.

Rawlins shook his head. "I looked at it under a magnifying glass. It just isn't clear enough, or else I've never seen him. Still, there's something about him—probably just that he looks a little like John Brown did."

"Can I have this?"

"Of course. What are you going to do?"

"Have an artist make a larger drawing of it. Get it in circulation. Probably won't do any good, but we might get lucky."

"What else are you going to do?"

Mosby reached for his hat. "Get into my office and do some powerful thinking."

"You could still be wrong."

"Yes. And they might say I got hold of some more of that bad opium, but by God, I *know* I'm right!"

★　★　★

SERGEANT Reverdy Ogg greeted Mosby at the door to the Military Intelligence Office. "Soon's I read the damned paper this morning I said to myself you were going to be a-needing me. What can I do, Colonel?"

Mosby handed him the envelope from Grant. "You know that drunken artist who draws portraits on the corner of the square? Take that picture to him and have him start drawing. About nine by twelves. Tell him he'll get paid a dollar apiece—two dollars for every one he gets done by nine o'clock."

"Anything else?"

"Get right on back here. We've got a lot to do."

"Yes, suh!"

Ogg had been gone only moments when Jeb Stuart hurried into the office, Richmond *Examiner* in hand. "I wonder how Pollard got hold of this," he growled.

"It just falls into his hole," Mosby replied. "You seen this, General?"

He handed over a note from Bragg stating that the court would not convene until one o'clock.

"Yes, he sent word to my house."

"You got any crack shots sitting around, Jeb—some unfamiliar faces?"

"Why? We going to shoot the members of the court?"

"No, *we* aren't," Mosby replied. He quickly explained his premise about Amistad.

Stuart's eyes widened. "I don't believe it."

"I'll bet a year's pay on it. That's why I asked you about the crack shots. I've got an idea playing around in the back of my head and we might want some sharpshooters."

Jeb looked at him through narrowed eyes. "You sure you know what you're talking about, John?"

"Yup. In fact, I'm going to see Beauregard right now. You want to come along?"

"No, go ahead. I don't want to talk to any of them until this is all over. You serious about those sharpshooters?"

"Absolutely."

"There are some boys up from South Carolina. Hampton's lads. Staying out at the fairgrounds. One of them, an ex-corporal by the name of Tommy Perkins, is a sharpshooter that I met one morning when I rode down to Hollywood Cemetery and visited the ghosts. I can send someone out to get in touch with them."

"I need about a half a dozen."

"Anything wrong with regulars?"

"Yes, I want strangers."

Jeb nodded. "Done!"

★   ★   ★

"MOSBY, I think you've been reading too much of Poe's junk," General Pierre Gustave Toutant Beauregard remarked over his cup of strong coffee. "You haven't got one single bit of concrete evidence that such a grandiose plot is afoot."

"I've got a dead informer who nearly had his head cut off." Mosby stood patiently before the general-in-chief's large ornate desk.

"Hell!" Beauregard snorted. "He could've gotten that for messing around with somebody's wife, you know that. They do it all the time, just like billy goats a-rutting."

"Then why did he send that name—Salmon Brown—the way he did? No, sir. That man was killed for sticking his nose in. Someone down there in Rocketts knew what he was doing."

The Little Frenchman shrugged. "Even so, that doesn't mean a whole bunch of abolitionist murderers is going to descend on the State Court House and kill everybody. Hell, man, your imagination is in a whirlpool."

"Sir, I officially request that the court be delayed until we can straighten this out."

"Absolutely not! The courthouse can be guarded."

Mosby held the general's eyes. "The risk is too great, sir. It must be recessed until we can find out who these people are."

Beauregard sighed, sipped his coffee. Finally he said, "Colonel Mosby, I don't have to remind you of the president's personal interest in this case, do I?"

"Hardly, General."

"He wants this damned court finished today."

Mosby frowned, not budging. "Sir, he *has* to know about Amistad. *Someone* has to authorize a delay."

"Watch your tone, sir!"

Mosby came to attention, his eyes slits. "Sir, I request permission to see the president."

Beauregard shook his head, played with the large curl at the side of his forehead. "All right, damn it, we'll *both* go."

★　★　★

JEFFERSON Davis had decided against going to his office in the Customs House and facing the usual day's bag of privilege-seekers. With Lee coming, he wanted to do nothing more on this day than watch the drama of the Stuart court reach its climax and die out—then get the general straightened out regarding his upcoming campaign chores. He was still furious with Lee for going against his wishes about appearing in the court, but his hands were tied. It had been quite a coup convincing the general to be his running mate, instead of running *against* him. So he could only push him so far. This damned court! He didn't care whom they crucified now, just get it over with!

He listened impatiently as Mosby spun out his tale of dread in the small mansion office. When the intelligence officer finished, Davis leaned back in his big chair, shook his head. "I simply can't believe such a preposterous plot can take place. Surely, a certain amount of imagination is involved, Mosby."

"I know, Your Excellency. I would have trouble believing it myself if I were you. But we can't take any chances."

Davis watched him through hooded eyes. "They could kill me right here, if they wanted to get me."

"Yes, sir. But if my guess is right, they want a mass attack right in front of the press."

Davis got up from his desk, withdrew a long-barreled revolver from a holster on the wall, thought back to his days of command with the Mississippi Rifles. They wouldn't dare! He turned back to Mosby, shook his head. "No, not with General Lee arriving, and the damned newspapers all set to have a heyday. No, I simply can't approve a delay. Request denied, Colonel."

"Sir, give me one day—"

Davis glared. *"Request denied, Colonel!"*

"I'll arrange adequate security, Your Excellency," Beauregard said.

Davis looked first at the general-in-chief he didn't like, and then at Mosby. His tone was caustic. "I would think you could safeguard a simple courtroom, gentlemen. Good-day."

★ ★ ★

THE fuming Mosby returned to his office to find a telegraph waiting: "Dear John. Arriving by train at 12:30 today in wheelchair. Please get me in the courtroom and do not tell Jeb. Thanks. Flora Stuart."

He handed the wire to Ogg, told him to make arrangements with the provost sergeant to provide space down front on the aisle by the windows. "Better yet," he added, "you bring her in and keep her safe in the event of trouble."

"Yes, suh. What do you want me to do about Harrison? There isn't much sense in hanging onto him now."

"No, but one more day won't hurt. Then you can pay him off and send him on his way."

"You know, Colonel, it's too bad he never joined your rangers—he is a pretty bright man."

Mosby shrugged. "Tell him to jine the cavalry—I'll use him next time around."

"I see you've been reading them Yankee newspapers. If they have their way, we'll be a-doing it all over, sure as hell."

Mosby shook his head. "God, I hope not, Reverdy. But if we don't get this Amistad thing taken care of, it might not be a bad idea to own a good horse or two." Mosby paused. "Enough of that. Now, listen closely—here's what I want you to do when an ex-corporal by the name of Tommy Perkins comes in. . . ."

★   ★   ★

C RISPUS walked nonchalantly up the steps to the entrance of the General Post Office across the street from the south side of the State Court House. He stopped, looked back toward the front of the courthouse where several hundred people had already gathered. *Lee!* he snarled to himself. They were coming out like maggots to feed on their great white hero. The *bastard!* His wartime leadership had been the major factor in keeping slavery alive in North America.

The Napoleon of the Western World, they called him, and kissed his sacred white feet. Well, before the sun set on this 14th day of August, the great general would be quite mortal—mortally *dead!*

Crispus looked around carefully. It was dangerous to come near his post office box now, but he had to find out if anyone had taken him up on the newspaper column offer. That was *his* ticket to fame, and this would be his last chance to get it. Surely someone had the sense to commission his work—the most explosive, enlightening writings ever by a negro. Surely.

He glanced around again. If they had a brain, they would certainly be watching for him to come today. But he had to take the chance.

There was a policeman at the bottom of the steps, and another by the entrance talking to a lady. Two armed soldiers were near the entrance—that was a new wrinkle. He'd noticed several armed soldiers around the courthouse. But nobody was looking at him. There had to be someone inside.

He pulled his slouch hat low over his eyes and stepped through the open door. Stopping, he drew a chaw of tobacco from a pouch and casually looked around as he chewed it into shape. The post office was crowded, probably due to the fact that everyone wanted to be free after noon, when Lee arrived. He got in the right line, kept his head down. After several minutes, he reached the window. "Box three-forty-one," he said quietly.

The clerk looked at him a bit longer than was normal, he thought, then disappeared. He would have to be ready to run for it. A poster on the wall caught his eye. REWARD! it announced, *and a drawing of Salmon Brown stared back at him!* At least it looked like Salmon Brown—younger and without a beard. It was him all right. "If you have seen this man," the lettering below the drawing read, "report directly to the City Police Department. $1,000 Reward! Urgent!"

One thousand dollars! God, they really knew!

"You have nothing, boy," the clerk said.

Crispus jerked his attention back to the window. "Thank you, suh," he mumbled. He turned, walked slowly to the door. If they had Salmon Brown's picture all over, they had to be close. Outside the door, he stood against the wall and waited. Moments later, the man he expected came out, looked hurriedly around, turned abruptly into Crispus's face, tried to pass off his look of recognition, and walked down the steps. He was wearing a brown suit.

Crispus sauntered along, passed him, headed for Rocketts. And at a discreet distance, the man in the brown suit began to follow. Crispus went down to Main, hurrying along. The man remained about a half a block behind, keeping pace. Following him by another half a block were the two soldiers. At Twentieth Street, Crispus turned down toward Libby Prison, where the Union officer prisoners had been kept during the war. It was vacant now, somber in its silence, watching the river flow by.

As the man in the brown suit rounded the corner of the building on the river side, Crispus lunged forward, knife flashing. He rammed it straight into the man's stomach, once, twice, three times, and then slashed his throat. Throwing a hurried glance up the street, and seeing no one, Crispus darted up an alley. By the time the soldiers arrived, all they saw was the dying man in the brown suit.

★   ★   ★

FOR days Verita had planned her ensemble for what she secretly called "her day in court." White was the color she decided upon—for the virtue of her mission, and for truth. The blouse was full in the sleeve and high in the neck, of white satin trimmed generously in off-white Chantilly lace, which also edged the scalloped hem of the looped silk skirt.

She picked up the single strand of pearls Judah had given her two nights earlier, tried them, decided they complimented the creamy lace. Besides, she smiled to herself, it was only fitting that she should wear his pearls when she shot him. She adjusted the hat, drew the arching brim over her forehead in a slightly rakish position, and nodded with satisfaction. Flat-crowned, of white crushed velvet, with a lace trim and a white ostrich feather trailing in the back, it gave her just the adventurous yet chic look she wanted.

She smiled again into the mirror, fluttered the off-white silk fan in a teasing gesture. Within hours she would be the most notorious woman in the world—known everywhere by those who would not accept oppression as "The Woman in White." She would be one of the most famous women revolutionaries in history; her name would make headlines in New York, Boston, London, Berlin. In Paris, the young revolutionaries would toast her to the heavens. Karl Marx would sing her praises!

Hiking her skirt up above her shapely right leg, she drew the short-barreled Lefaucheux revolver from its special thigh holster. This .35 model had specially engraved silver plating, a fitting beauty for such a very special niche in history. Returning the Lefaucheux to its hiding place, she patted the pouch on her left thigh; it contained the extra bullets.

She stood, drew herself up to her full height, ran her hands down over her breast, her flat stomach, to her pelvis, felt the erotic surge of it all, and smiled once more into her reflection.

The Woman in White.

She liked that.

Except that she would be the *black* Woman in White, because now her whole purpose in being here, her whole purpose in *life*, would be crystal clear when she announced that she was a Negro. Higginson had been absolutely right—every Negro woman in the South would hear about her, and countless numbers of them would throw down their yokes and join the Cause . . . the name she'd chosen, *Verita*, would live forever!

★ ★ ★

I N THE warehouse at Ludlum Wharf, the other Amistad members were going through the final preparations for their mission. There was little conversation. Revolvers were being cleaned for the third time, ammunition being wiped off again to remove the tiniest piece of lint or dirt that might cause a round to jam in the cylinder.

Crispus hummed the melody of "Yankee Doodle" while he sharpened the edge of his knife on a small whetstone.

"What do you think?" Nat Turner asked Cinque, more to just break the quiet than to get a reply.

" 'Bout what?"

"You know, the attack—finally getting down to it."

"Nothing to think. Just do it."

"Yeah, that's about it."

Denmark Vesey walked up. "I hear New Orleans is some kinda place."

"Uh huh. Got some fancy women there," Cinque replied.

Beecher Lovejoy slipped into the blue uniform coat of a Union infantry corporal. "Gonna be hotter than hell wearing this under a duster."

"I still think wearing these here uniform coats is dumb," Cinque growled. "The people should know we is just plain Southern coloreds with enough guts to do somethin."

"Yeah, I agree," Denmark Vesey said.

"The word come down from the man," Crispus said. "Higginson said wear 'em, we wear 'em." He laughed. "When these righteous white people see their leaders getting killed by Negroes in Union uniforms, they are going to go *crazy!*"

"Hell, war might be declared before we get out of town!" Cinque added with a chuckle.

They all laughed.

Salmon Brown came through the door, greeted them. "You all okay?"

"Just getting more and more excited about killing us some slavers, boss," Crispus replied. "You seen your picture yet?"

Salmon stared at him. "What do you mean?"

"They've got a picture of you looking at everybody coming into the general post office uptown. Pretty good likeness, minus the beard."

Every nerve in Salmon's body jumped to attention. *They were getting close!* He didn't even ask the man what the hell he was doing up at the post office. "What did it say?"

"One thousand dollar reward. Urgent!"

Salmon quieted his alarm. "Won't make any difference now. Okay, let's walk through it once more."

He reached for the uniform jacket with its yellow shoulder boards embroidered with colonel's eagles. He had toyed with wearing a sergeant's stripes—as he had during the war—but that wouldn't be important enough. Salmon Brown couldn't be a sergeant!

That picture worried him.

★ ★ ★

I T SEEMED as if everyone in Richmond was dressing for the afternoon session of the Stuart court. In the old Samuel Cooper House at Third and Grace, Jeb examined himself in the mirror. He had decided earlier that if he was going to be found responsible in any way for the outcome of the Gettysburg campaign, the world would see Jeb Stuart at his proudest. The fine gray uniform was new, had been finished by his favorite tailor just the day before. Its buttons and gold bullion braid were bright in the noontime sun that flowed into the master bedroom. Also reflecting the sun was the hilt of his dress sword as it hung on the yellow silk sash at his waist. Not to be outdone, his old cavalry boots were shined to a bright luster and were set off perfectly by the gold spurs at his heels. He tugged the new slouch hat with its fresh black plume over his forehead and patted the loaded revolver on his hip.

Smiling, he hummed a few bars of "Jine the Cavalry."

The Jeb Stuart of old was going to appear in that courtroom today, and he was ready for anything they could dish out. He thought. There wasn't anyone in Richmond who didn't know the blame belonged to Longstreet, and General Lee was just coming down to tidy the whole mess up. He thought. Of course, as Mosby said, it could still be tricky. And he could still see Lee that day when he finally rode into Gettysburg, when the general raised his fist in red-faced anger and said, "General Stuart, where have you been? I have not heard from you for days. And you the eyes and ears of my army!"

It was the worst he had ever felt in his entire life.

Could the general be remembering that and wanting to remove the stain from Old Pete and fix it on the cavalryman who loved him so much? No, he wouldn't do that, he couldn't. But with his powerful sense of honor, he just might. . . .

Well, he had to be ready anyway. In that case it would be finished, for he wouldn't fight it another iota. But the general wouldn't really do that to him . . . would he?

Huh, only a moment ago he was singing, and now he was feeling low down. Wasn't that about as stupid as he could get?

He found a short laugh.

When this was all over, he'd get Sweeney and the boys together and by George, they'd have the goldarndest, hifalutin'est ball since the war!

★　　★　　★

JOHN Mosby knocked on the front door of the Breckinridge house at twelve-twenty. He asked for Spring Blakely, and was invited into the front parlor to wait. Moments later, she hurried into the room. "Oh, John, I'm so glad you came. I've been thinking about you all morning. My uncle—"

"Yes, her uncle doesn't like the idea of her running around meeting you everywhere but at her home," John Breckinridge said over her shoulder.

"I'm sorry, sir. Things have been hectic, and I didn't think I was welcome here."

The secretary's expression was cool; it reminded Mosby of that night at Breckinridge's supper party. "You haven't been exactly my favorite subordinate lately, Colonel, but that doesn't mean I have any reason to keep you and Spring from seeing each other. Of course you may call on her here." He glanced at the wall clock. "But isn't this a rather strange time—particularly with all you've got going on?"

"That's exactly why I'm here, sir."

"You mean this Amistad scare that Beauregard told me about."

"Yes, sir. I think it would be unwise for you and Spring to be in the courtroom today."

"But I *have* to be there. This whole court of inquiry is under my jurisdiction."

"Sir, it will get along just fine without you."

John Breckinridge scowled. "As you know, Colonel Mosby, I've held some high offices, including senator and vice-president of the United States, and major general in our army. I think, by God, I'm capable of deciding where I should be at a given time."

"Yes, sir," Mosby replied. He turned to Spring. "But I don't want you there today."

Spring smiled. "I wouldn't miss it for anything."

"Mr. Secretary, will you stop her from going?"

"Now *that*, Mosby," Breckinridge said with a touch of a smile, "is something all of my importance can't control."

Mosby shook his head. "All right then, promise me this—at the first sign of any trouble, will you get down below the bench and stay there?"

"Uncle John," Spring said. "Will you excuse me for a moment?" She came close, kissed Mosby lightly on the lips. "Yes, I will. And thanks for caring. What about you?"

Mosby frowned into Breckinridge's eyes. "I'll be fine if I can just get enough people to understand how much danger is involved in that damned courtroom this afternoon."

★ ★ ★

"MR. BYRON Smith has checked out, sir. About three hours ago."

Thomas Wentworth Higginson blinked, nodded. "And he left no messages?"

"No, sir," the young clerk replied.

"Thank you," Higginson said, turning away from the Spottswood desk. Now where could Salmon be? he asked himself with a touch of alarm. The man was supposed to wait at the hotel for him. Of course, he was late—the train had been twice delayed en route from Washington—but that shouldn't have anything to do with Salmon. The letter had told him to wait. It was possible for him to have stepped out of the hotel for some reason—but to *check out?*

He pulled out his watch. Now what? Could he be down in Rocketts at the warehouse? The court was due to open in twenty-five minutes; maybe he had decided to go there. But why hadn't he waited as ordered? He looked around the empty lobby. Something was terribly wrong here, he could feel it. The letter had been absolutely clear. . . .

And suddenly it hit him—*Salmon Brown was going to go through with it despite his orders!* His insubordinate attitude, his dislike for Jubilo, the man had lost his logic. The inherent Brown insanity. But the others wouldn't follow him . . . surely not. Not Verita . . . maybe he should go to Bessica Southwick's house to check on her—no, he couldn't be connected. He nodded—it was all out of control, and just as sure as there was a hell, Amistad was going to strike!

Higginson jerked toward the door. Somehow he had to get inside that courtroom to see what he had wrought.

★　★　★

THE man named Murphy walked down the aisle of Jubilo's empty church to find the preacher adjusting his red cravat before the small wall mirror in his office. "They's all at the warehouse, Colonel," he reported. "All except the woman, and she went to the courthouse with the Jew. I looked in through a dirty window, and sho 'nuff, they's all a-wearing blue Yankee uniforms. And they's got dusters to wear over them."

Jubilo nodded. "Just as I thought." He knew damned well Salmon Brown would never listen. All he wanted was his father's glory and nothing would stop him, not even Higginson. And so here it was, the showdown. This Amistad thing had to be handled properly or he might as well be a slave back in South Carolina again. If Salmon Brown and his fanatics brought this thing off, the whole country could erupt with ineffective uprisings, burnings, killings of white people, and mass

slaughter of the coloreds. And when the blood quit running, Abraham
would be finished and his people would wear a yoke worse than
anything they'd ever known. Today was the crux. Everything that had
gone before was nothing. . . .

"Your horse and buggy is ready, suh. You want me to come along,
just in case? I got my cavalry revolver."

Jubilo shook his head, donned his hat. "No, my friend, I'm just a
spectator. For the time being, at least."

★ ★ ★

THE three military judges had been in the chambers for twenty
minutes discussing their avenues for the findings. And they
were still at an impasse.

George Pickett absently filed a fingernail as he said, "I don't care
what Lee says, I'm not changing my mind one bit. Old Pete is sick,
and what happened yesterday just proves it. Stuart deserves a court-
martial, sure as hell. Just as Old Pete says."

Hood sat on the edge of a desk, sipping lukewarm coffee, supporting himself on his good leg. He stared out the window at the
crowd, said nothing. He couldn't believe Pickett could be so goddamned stupid.

Bragg relit his dead cigar. "Well, we have to come up with a unan-
imous finding or His Excellency will be pretty damned mad. I talked
to him this morning, and he doesn't mind sticking it to Longstreet.
There isn't a soul who was in that courtroom yesterday who doesn't
know he was to blame for the actual battle."

"He was *not* to blame!" Pickett snapped.

Hood turned from the window. "You're so prejudiced you're blind,
George. Goddamnit, you weren't even there that second day. I *know*
we would have crashed into Meade's rear with such thunder that it
would have been over by noon the next day. The only bluecoats that
would've been left, would've been dead or captured."

"Lee wasn't listening to him anyway!"

"Huh uh. That's no excuse. He just flat refused." Hood shook his
head. "No, His Excellency is right."

Braxton Bragg blew out a thick cloud of smoke. "Yes, it's settled.
If General Lee comes up with something incriminating against Stuart,

we recommend a court-martial. But it's doubtful he will. Either way, we'll recommend that Longstreet be reprimanded but not tried, due to his impaired condition. We will also recommend that he be retired from the active-duty list. And His Excellency wants Stuart to be fully vindicated. It'll add just the right tone to the end of this whole damned mess."

"I'll fight it, General, no matter what."

Bragg frowned at the younger general. "No you won't, George, because that would be stupid—even for you. You're already going down in history as the leader of one of the greatest charges ever mounted. Why ruin it?"

Pickett struggled with that. "But my boys, God bless them. How can I hold up my head knowing they died in vain? You don't know how it bothers me."

Hood spoke from the desk. "Lincoln used that phrase in his Gettysburg address, you know. And a lot of people up North are reviving it. So you can learn to live with it, George."

★　★　★

MOSBY couldn't remember the downtown streets of Richmond being as crowded since Armistice Day. From Broad south to Main, from Fourteenth west to Eighth, people jammed the streets. The Capitol grounds overflowed. In the immediate vicinity of the State Court House there were so many onlookers that a buggy had trouble getting through. He guessed that some three thousand people were in that location alone. Bunting and flags hung everywhere. A second brass band had joined the one made up of ex-soldiers, and was competing at the top of its lungs. One minute it was "Nellie Gray" and the next it was "Oh Susannah." "Boots and Saddles" was sounded constantly by a slightly drunk former cavalry bugler wearing a uniform jacket with corporal's chevrons on the sleeve.

Protest signs were everywhere. And women in their finest. Playing boys somehow managed to run, dogs chased them barking, and flies buzzed in the heat. Vendors peddling everything from sausages to ice cream were making a fortune. Even a large number of coloreds mixed unmolested in the joyous, celebrating crowd.

And it was noisy!

Mosby worked his way through to the top of the steps near the entrance, where he found Jeb standing near the open door talking to a former cavalry major from the 1st Virginia. Everybody was waiting, waiting for the great hero of the Confederacy to arrive—the man who had saved the South by his brilliant generalship and inspiration: Marse Robert E. Lee.

"Is the president here yet?" Mosby asked.

"You serious?" Jeb replied. "No way he's going to come before the general."

All three of the officers touched their hat brims in a salute as Bessica Adams Southwick and her captivating house guest from Paris came up to them on the arm of Judah Benjamin. "How handsome my knight is today!" Bessica exclaimed. "I'm having a small buffet and a special commemorative champagne shortly after the court closes. You all must come." She touched Jeb's hand, smiled into his eyes.

Verita murmured, *"Enchanté,"* as they moved into the courtroom.

General John Rawlins was next, in a light gray suit and a worried look. "Any luck?" he asked.

Mosby shook his head. "Not yet."

"President McClellan has been notified."

"Good. If Amistad strikes, he'll need all of his persuasive powers."

"He needs them anyway, John. I suppose you've heard about all the unrest up North."

Mosby nodded. Reports from his widespread agents filled his desk.

As Rawlins moved inside, Edward Pollard of the *Examiner* walked up. Jeb's expression hardened immediately. "I see you are dressed for the occasion, General," the editor said caustically.

Jeb started to say something, but Mosby caught his arm. "Don't bother, my friend."

"Jeb, honey!"

Stuart turned at the familiar sound of his mother's voice as Elizabeth flew into his arms. Over her shoulder, he saw with delight that Flora was just clearing the top step in a wheelchair handled by Reverdy Ogg. He bounded forward and in a moment was bending over, kissing her, murmuring his love. "Why didn't you tell me?" he asked, holding her hand.

Her eyes brimmed. "I wanted to surprise you."

"What did the doctor say?"

"The doctor didn't need me today. You did, my darling."

"I'm going to be fine, Honey Pot." It seemed ages since he had called her that. "Just fine."

"How does it look, Colonel?" Elizabeth asked.

"We'll just have to wait and see," Mosby replied. "But another matter puts you and Flora in danger." He told her his fears about Amistad.

"Don't worry," she replied. "We'll do just as Sergeant Ogg tells us." She lifted her chin. "We're the Stuart women, you know—"

The roar of the crowd and the loud rendition of "Dixie" announced the arrival of General Lee. All heads turned toward Main, where an elegant barouche, drawn by two mahogany bays with shiny coats and arching necks had just appeared. In the back seat, wearing his uniform from the armistice ceremony, General Robert E. Lee sat erectly, nodding and smiling to the eager people cheering him with great warmth. His sons, Rooney and Custis, rode with him.

"Remember that day at Spotsylvania?" Jeb asked softly.

"How could I ever forget it?" Mosby replied, remembering the bright balloons floating in the clear sky, the hushed voices, the quiet sounds of horses and leather, the solemnity and finality of it all. Grant and his generals. But mostly he remembered this white-haired general, now slowly making his way up the street, receiving bouquets of bright flowers amid continuous rousing cheers. For this was the man, above all others, who personified not only the honor of the South, but of all America, from Canada to Mexico. Perhaps of the whole world of quality.

He turned, went inside. There was much ahead.

★　★　★

SALMON Brown wiped the sweat from his forehead, shifted his weight as General Lee's carriage stopped a few yards away. In spite of his passion for the job ahead, he felt a certain reluctance about killing this great man who was dismounting amid such fervent acclamation. After all, Lee had freed his own slaves, even before the Harpers Ferry raid—so he was far from the epitome of oppression.

Both bands broke into a loud rendition of "The Bonnie Blue Flag." The cheer that followed drowned out the music. People reached out, tried to clutch at their hero, to just capture a touch to cherish forever.

He looked closely at Lee as the general made his way up the steps. He was so close! The alert dark eyes, an amiable yet reserved expression framed by the white beard; the erect, powerful torso with the short legs—yet a certain tiredness, or was it the illness that was rumored, the heart disease?

For only a moment, it seemed the great man looked directly inside his eyes. What would Robert E. Lee think, he wondered, if he knew that John Brown's son had come to even the score for that October day seven years earlier . . . that immortal day when Lee, then a Union colonel on leave, had been pressed into command of a force sent to put down an insurrection led by John Brown and supported by his *loyal* sons. . . .

Lieutenant Jeb Stuart had been there too, had tried to negotiate with the Old Man, had taken his Bowie knife when the assault on the enginehouse that sheltered the insurgents was over.

Now it was all coming full circle.

Soon they would be just as dead as the Browns of Harpers Ferry.

Salmon Brown turned to see another carriage working its way through the noisy crowd. President Jefferson Davis, accompanied by General Beauregard, sat tall in the back seat, waving to the crowd, showing his political smile.

The biggest spoke in the wheel.

Salmon glanced around the crowd, finding Crispus and Denmark Vesey, both quite close to the steps, a few yards apart, easy to spot in their dusters. Beecher Lovejoy was further back.

They would be in position in time.

★ ★ ★

JUBILO climbed into the closed buggy behind his church, picked up the reins, and looked back at the building. Life would never be the same after today, he told himself with a sigh. He knew as sure as he knew his own name that the peace, the all too limited preparation of Abraham, was coming to an end . . . a premature end, because his people weren't ready for what lay ahead. He had thought about the return to war at great length, but never really believed it would happen. He didn't know exactly how he was going to work that out. So much depended on what happened today.

347

His church, the store, his dreams—they might all come to an end, but there was nothing he could do about it. From a personal standpoint, he was just as much a victim as those targets of Amistad. *Those damned killers!*

At least his hands were clean of this abominable act that was about to explode in the world's face. And that would be important when it came time for the Southern leaders to deal with him.

He had thought about waiting at the courthouse to watch, and he might have gotten away with that. White folks always thought all niggers looked alike. But he had to see it all. He drew the big watch out of his pocket again. Time was running down, speeding, in fact. He tapped the reins on the horse's rump and headed for the Court End of uptown Richmond.

★   ★   ★

T HE inside of the courtroom was loud also. Mosby stood at the Stuart table, glancing at last-minute notes when the cheer went up for Lee. He came to attention briefly, then smiled and nodded to the general as he and his sons took seats in the front row. For the first time, Mosby felt the excitement, the tension. He watched Lee shake hands with Breckinridge, kiss Spring's hand, speak to Judah Benjamin and John Rawlins in the row behind him. *What would Lee do?*

He glanced around the courtroom.

The side aisles were full this day, and all of those standing there weren't idle spectators. He caught Tommy Perkins's alert eye, saw his friends scattered up and down the sides. He had decided to use just four of them, what with the crowd and all. And Ogg was there. Besides, Salmon Brown and his Amistad had to first get *into* the courtroom—

"Colonel Mosby!" It was the police captain with whom he had worked on the Israel Jones death. "Sir, we have two reports on your Salmon Brown. The room clerk at the Spottswood has positively identified him as a Byron Smith from the American Import Company, Limited. But he checked out of his room this morning!"

Mosby nodded. "What about the company?"

"Another man, a real estate fellow with property down in Rocketts, identified him as the man who rented a small warehouse in the name of the American Import Company, Limited. We rushed down there, but no one was there. We did find used chewing tobacco, some food remnants, several boxes that had been shipped in from Washington City, *and a box of thirty-six caliber revolver ammunition!*"

Mosby nodded again, looked around the courtroom with narrowed eyes. "Anything else?"

"Yes," the captain replied. "Both of these men said Byron Smith is wearing a short beard."

Once more Mosby shot a searching look around the huge room, flicking back and forth to each man with a short beard. He could be anyone! No, not quite—there was the picture. "All right, Captain, I want you to put your men into the crowd outside and look closely at everyone who answers the description. Have you got a copy of the drawing?"

"Yes, sir. But do you know how many people are out there?"

"Do your best."

A loud buzz went up from the spectators as Jefferson Davis, followed by General Beauregard, strode down the center aisle to the front row where General Lee and the others sat, came briefly to the position of attention, and greeted him respectfully. The president and the general-in-chief would sit in a special box that had been installed in front of the first row.

Several yards away by the windows, Jeb turned back to his wife. "Honey Pot, I'd better get on over to the table. I guess the scene is set for whatever is ahead. We'll just have to play it out."

Flora squeezed his hand. "We'll do just fine, darling."

Jeb looked from her to his mother, who patted his other hand. "Now, I want you both to listen to Sergeant Ogg, here, in case there is trouble. Okay?"

He started to leave, but Flora pulled him back. "Kiss me," she said, not knowing why it seemed suddenly so important.

Stuart grinned. "You've just been away too long." He leaned down and kissed her soundly on the lips.

★　★　★

F ROM across the courtroom, Bessica was unable to avoid seeing the open display of affection. She felt a sharp pang of jealousy, but quickly smothered it. The shock of seeing Jeb's plain little wife in that wheelchair hadn't worn off yet; in fact, she just knew her cheeks were still burning a bright red! She might have known his Flora would do something like this . . . it was just the type of thing Bessica Adams Southwick would do herself!

She found a tiny smile as Jeb turned and walked toward his table. He was still the handsomest damned man in the Confederacy, and the final score wasn't yet in. It was all a matter of patience . . . and once he got that whiff of political power, the glimpse of himself sleeping in that White House someday . . . then she would have him. The boy-man in the red beard and cavalry boots would be hers one way or the other. . . .

★   ★   ★

M AJOR General John Rawlins tried to keep his eyes off Verita, but it was no more possible for him than for any other man in the courtroom. In her white ensemble, she was undoubtedly the most excitingly beautiful woman there. Men stared and women nervously fluttered their fans in envy. Rawlins remembered her in the covered buggy when she tempted him, recalled the taste of her lips and her soft breast. Why had she played that game with him? Was she just a foreign temptress with hot drawers, or was there some reason? He might find out sometime . . . another time, another place.

"Well, my friend," he said to Judah. "What do you think of the folly you have witnessed for the past week? Will it add to your political skills when you become president?"

Benjamin smiled. "There has been a bit of the absurd, to be sure, John. And one always learns something in the political whirlpool, but I love my Confederacy too much to be contemptuous of any of the drama of its young life."

"What is your guess as to the outcome of the court?"

"The president's purpose has been served."

Rawlins chuckled. "So it doesn't matter."

Judah chuckled. "Politics, my friend, is fascinating."

Verita glanced past Judah's profile to Rawlins's black eyes. A faint smile touched her lips. She turned her attention back to the people in the rows around her, keeping her hands tightly clasped to hide the light tremor. She had never felt such sheer overwhelming excitement in her life. She was smack-dab in the midst of the most powerful men in the Confederacy, even in the western hemisphere, and within the next hour she would take some of their lives. *Eliminate them!* God!, she could see it already, smell the gunpowder, *taste* it!

She glanced back at Bessica, smiled, a brittle smile because she had changed her mind; she *would* kill her hostess. The cold-blooded killing of a white woman by a Negro was the most despicable act in the South. Over that deed alone, the hot-blooded men of the South would rush to war!

"Have you ever seen General Lee before?" Judah Benjamin asked quietly.

She shook her head, displeased at the interruption, but glad to exhale some pressure. "No. He's a decidedly handsome man, isn't he?"

Judah nodded his head. "Decidedly."

He won't be an hour from now! she said to herself. *Why don't they get on with it?*

She unclasped her hands to feel the Lefaucheux revolver on her thigh, turned her attention to Davis. He would be her first target after Benjamin. Then—

"*All rise!*" the provost sergeant commanded.

The three members of the court entered the silent courtroom, took their places behind the bench. General Braxton Bragg glanced at the other two members, nodded in the direction of President Davis, and intoned, "This court of inquiry is again in session. Colonel Axline, please present the first witness."

The judge-advocate announced firmly, "The court calls General Robert E. Lee."

The hush that had fallen over the room on the entry of the court members was even more pronounced as General Lee got slowly to his feet and walked erectly to the witness stand. He glanced briefly at Braxton Bragg, then at Hood and Pickett. Even Axline's voice was subdued as he administered the oath. When the swearing in was over, Lee settled into the witness chair.

"General Lee," Axline said. "You, of course, require no introduction regarding your duties in the Pennsylvania, or Gettysburg, campaign. Nor do I feel it necessary to reiterate the proceedings prior to your appearing here. Would you, sir, please tell the court your side of the activities as they relate to General Stuart?"

Robert Lee nodded, looked directly at Jeb, then generally at the center of the audience. His pause was long, as if he were reluctant to begin. Finally he gathered himself like a fatherly storyteller and commenced in a firm voice. "It was decided following the Battle of Chancellorsville in May of Eighteen-sixty-three to take the Army of Northern Virginia north to Pennsylvania for several reasons, one of which was simply to give Virginia soil and crops a respite from two armies by drawing the Army of the Potomac north and away from Washington into Maryland. There were also tactical and political considerations, primary being a decisive victory over those people and the possibility of a peace move from them."

General Lee's white hair was combed long over his baldness from the side of his head, and sometimes he subconsciously touched it as if to make sure it was in place. He did so now as he continued, "The cavalry battle of Brandy Station was an unfortunate prelude to our march north, but I must say here and now that had General Stuart *not* assembled his whole cavalry corps for the parades that have been discussed in this court, the Union cavalry attack would not have met such a concentrated enemy, and might easily have had its way in my rear."

Mosby raised an eyebrow at Jeb, and smiled. "One for Stuart," he whispered.

"As the three corps of the army began the march north," Lee went on, "I found it imperative to keep the enemy cavalry from discovering the fact that our entire army was moving. It was Stuart's job to keep him away on the other side of the Blue Ridge. . . ."

★　　★　　★

JUBILO parked the buggy halfway between East Twelfth and East Thirteenth on the north side of the deserted street. His position gave him a clear view of the target down on the corner across the street at 1201. Although the columns of the portico of the famous mansion faced south, the front was still impressive. It was guarded on this day by two uniformed soldiers with rifles.

It was the Davis Mansion, the White House of the Confederacy.

Jubilo checked his watch. 1:14 P.M. He looked back down Clay to see the buckboard approaching. A moment later, it stopped in front of the mansion and two men climbed down to unload a wooden coffin large enough to accommodate a twelve-year-old. Boldly, the two men carried the coffin up to the front entrance of the White House.

"Halt!" one of the guards ordered, stepping in front of them. "Where do you niggers think you're going? This ain't the service entrance."

"We's done been told to bring this here coffin to de White House, suh," Cinque said.

The sentry scowled, glanced at the other soldier. "Well, you just load that thing right up and go on around. Here—what are you doing?"

Cinque and Nat Turner, the other Amistad member, placed the coffin on the ground, then suddenly swung up at the two soldiers with long flashing knives. The sentries never had a chance as the blades tore into their guts. Both soldiers slumped, one of them already dying, the other losing consciousness. Quickly they were pulled into nearby bushes. Picking up the coffin, the two attackers hurried inside the mansion.

Inside, they rushed to the back portico and shot the two sentries stationed there. Servants and one white male secretary were rounded up quickly. The only member of the first family to be found was Mrs. Varina Davis, the president's wife. She protested fiercely, "Now, see here, you Nigras, this is the home of the president! *You'll both hang! Do you hear?*"

They looked at her contemptuously as they tore off their dusters to reveal the blue Yankee uniforms. "If anyone is to live, you all gotta shut up!" Cinque told them harshly, as Nat Turner ripped off the top of the coffin and swiftly began to remove the dynamite.

Varina Davis stepped forward. "I won't have this—"

Cinque smashed the long-barreled revolver over her forehead, knocking her to the floor. Blood spurted from the ugly gash. "You!" Cinque barked at the secretary. "Pick her up and take her out to the carriage house. Now! The rest of you, get moving too!"

Nat Turner moved swiftly, placing charges around the walls.

Outside, Jubilo looked at his watch. It was 1:19.

★ ★ ★

ONE of the few noises in the courtroom as General Lee continued
his narration was that of the reporters' pencils scratching on
paper. Lee caught the eye of his former secretary as he said, "What
Colonel Marshall related is essentially correct. I *did* mean for General
Stuart to return from any feasible thrust into the enemy rear and
remain on my right flank throughout the march."

He looked directly at Jeb. "Unfortunately, the most vital of orders
are not always written clearly. In this case, I signed an order that was
far too ambiguous and full of license for him to know my true inten-
tion." The general smiled for an instant. "And knowing Jeb's pro-
pensity for the dramatic, I should have known better.

"Nevertheless, I believe General Stuart should have made every
effort to return directly to my side once he found that their army was
moving, in fact, was over the Potomac. . . ."

John Mosby listened closely, trying to find points to refute, or at
least challenge. But he knew it would be useless. Whatever Robert E.
Lee said would be etched in stone, and even to question it would be
preposterous, a sin. He glanced sideways at Jeb and saw his friend
nodding in agreement with what Lee was saying, even though it was
critical of him.

"It has been argued that I had some other cavalry that could have
done the job, and that is so. But when a commander has been spoiled
by the likes of a general like Stuart, he tends to rely too much on him,
to expect him there. . . ."

★ ★ ★

OUTSIDE on the steps of the courthouse, the festivities were still
going on; the music had its same zest—perhaps more, due to
the consumption of a new jug of corn whiskey by the musicians—and
the crowd continued to mill around as if at a great family reunion.
Salmon Brown watched the handful of policemen working their way
through the crowd, looking sharply into people's faces. Tugging the

wide brim of his hat lower over his face, he edged backward toward the wall. He hoped the damned dusters didn't attract their attention.

He glanced at his pocket watch. It was 1:21.

He held up nine fingers to Crispus, who watched him from the other side of the entrance.

Now if only Cinque and Nat Turner had met no trouble . . . He looked again to the guards by the entrance; they were alert, peering around carefully, looking closely at the faces near them. Each held a piece of paper with the drawing of a man's face on it. God, he wished he had one to keep as a memento! Maybe he could get one later. He laughed to himself. That would be no problem—it would be in every newspaper in the world!

He caught Denmark Vesey's eye, and that of Beecher Lovejoy. Again he held up nine fingers. A policeman spoke to Lovejoy, looked at him carefully, then moved on. Salmon sighed. Cinque and Nat Turner *had* to complete their mission at the mansion—unless the guards by the entrance were totally distracted, it would be impossible to get inside the courtroom.

He drew in a deep breath, squeezed the handle of his Whitney under the duster. His second revolver was a Navy Colt.

★ ★ ★

I NSIDE, Verita tried to quell her impatience by curling her toes. No one could see that, could have any idea of the sheer intoxication that was pulsating through her. "What time is it, Judah?" she whispered.

Benjamin didn't pull his attention away from Lee for a second as he withdrew the watch from his vest and showed it to her.

One-twenty-two, she said to herself, taking a deep breath as she felt the tension rise. Eight minutes to go. She wondered how it was going outside and at the mansion. God, there was so much that could go wrong.

But it wouldn't!

She glanced sideways at Judah, picturing him in a pool of blood.

She smiled, knowing that by killing him she would be saving men who would continue to finance the Cause for years to come. It was all going to happen so soon. Shifting around, she saw the same look of rapt attention on Bessica's face. Every one of her targets was mesmerized by that white-haired general speaking so quietly before the bench.

Eight more minutes.

Once more her hand moved to the revolver and stroked it.

★ ★ ★

ROBERT E. Lee again smoothed the hair on top of his head as he paused. "Thus, two great armies, each filled with its share of heroes and magnificent leaders, were probing their way north looking for each other. Meade was now in Union command, a fact that I learned from General Longstreet's spy, Harrison. On the night of the thirtieth, I disregarded information from one of my generals that Union cavalry was in Gettysburg.

"I didn't want to believe it because I was certain Stuart would have informed me of the imminent presence of Meade's main body. I *knew* he would come riding in any moment with information I could absolutely rely on."

Lee looked again at Jeb, sadly. His voice lowered. "I was wrong."

Lee turned to the president of the court. "General Bragg, with your permission, I would like to leave the witness stand to finish my testimony. I believe it belongs to the people of our great new nation, if not to the world, and I would like to present it from my feet."

Braxton Bragg nodded. "Permission granted, sir."

Mosby tensed as Lee got to his feet, moved to the front of the bench and faced the spectators. Touching Jeb's sleeve, he whispered, "This is it, the whole case."

But Jeb was enthralled, watching with glowing eyes the face of the man he revered.

The courtroom was as still as a tomb.

"Gettysburg," Lee began, "will be discussed as long as there is warfare. It was a great gathering of valiant soldiers where acts of heroism were so common they went unnoticed. Gettysburg was also an opportunity for the Confederacy to bring about the end of the war in Eighteen-sixty-three."

Lee's dark eyes moved around the audience from journalist to politician, from Flora Stuart to John Rawlins, from common spectator to the assistant judge-advocate. "Unfortunately, we did not win there, and many thousands of brave young men died or were maimed in the sixteen months that followed. Battles are often won or lost on the most inconsequential of things, an inspired shout, a falling flag, the toss of a coin. Specific blame can be fixed on a hundred events, or on none. . . .

"If we had taken Culp's Hill early on . . . if General Ewell had done this or that . . . if General Stuart had not ridden away." Lee turned to the bench, looked into Hood's eyes. "If Longstreet had listened to General Hood about updating the attack plan at the Round Tops." His eyes went to Pickett. "If the artillery had done a better job on Cemetery Ridge . . . if I had listened to General Longstreet."

Robert E. Lee turned back to the audience, his voice low, quiet. "These are the nails of the horseshoe, any one of which would undoubtedly have won the battle for us. They are all conjecture. It has been expedient in certain quarters to blame General Longstreet for being stubborn and slow to move. The fact is, Longstreet was *right* about the way the battle should have been conducted."

The white-haired man moved to the Stuart table, placed his hand on Jeb's shoulder, looked down softly into his former cavalry commander's eyes. "And now there are those who wish to blame Jeb Stuart. That would be a severe injustice. If I were to command a thousand armies in a thousand battles, I could never ask for a more loyal or enthusiastic leader than General Stuart. He was simply a victim of my own mismanagement."

As the tears flowed down Jeb's cheeks, Lee looked first at the members of the court, then at the spectators. "For the simple truth is that the responsibility of victory or defeat is solely that of the commander. No one else. And in the case of Gettysburg, I committed one error after another . . . tactical errors. Like Suvorov, I knew only how to attack—when encirclement and maneuver, or possibly defense, may have been the answer. . . .

"I offered my resignation later, but everyone was too busy finding excuses to place the blame squarely where it belonged. And that was directly on my shoulders."

Lee drew himself even more erect, looked straight ahead. His voice was low. "For at Gettysburg, I was simply a second-rate commander."

It was utterly silent.

The general stood there for a moment in the hush, then turned back to the witness stand. A low murmur slowly began to spread through the courtroom, then Jeb Stuart got to his feet, eyes awash. "Sir, you are the greatest general who ever walked," he said, and then began to clap his hands. "Hear! Hear!" someone in the crowd shouted, and people began to get to their feet. Mosby, too, began to applaud, then others, and soon the entire room joined in a rousing cheer, and another. Grinning broadly, Mosby pumped Jeb's hand.

"Order!" Bragg yelled, slamming his Colt on the bench. *"Order in this court!"*

★　★　★

J UBILO hauled back on the reins and jumped down from the buggy where it stopped a half block north of the courthouse on Twelfth. He didn't have to look at his watch to know it was 1:28 and that the long fuse would be burning at 1201 East Clay while the Amistad dynamiters fled the scene. He had to get next to the courthouse wall before the explosion, otherwise he would be caught up in the tide and never be able to make it to the door.

And he had to get to that door in time.

Seconds later, he reached the corner and blew out a deep breath. He turned northward to watch, knowing that his life would never be the same. Everything was out of control, mad. . . . He began to recite the twenty-third Psalm, *"Yea, though I walk through the valley of the shadow of death . . ."*

★　★　★

B ACK at the Davis Mansion, Cinque and Nat Turner hurried out the front entrance and hastily climbed into the buckboard. Cinque clucked to the horse and slapped its rump with the reins. The startled horse jumped and started off in a fast trot around the corner on Thirteenth, headed for Rocketts. Turning the corner on Marshall, they slowed in the middle of the block and looked back to watch their handiwork.

Suddenly it happened. The light was white, tinged in gold and black, crimson in places, as it flashed out and buckled the walls. The blast was enormous, with a shock wave that smashed nearby windows, and blew parts of the roof five hundred feet high. It was equivalent to the sound of a massive artillery barrage, or a ship-of-the-line's broadside. It rocked Richmond in every direction like a giant thunderbolt!

And then the flames began to appear.

The two members of Amistad looked at each other wide-eyed, then grinned. "Gawd!" Nat Turner said.

Cinque again cracked the animal on the rump with the reins. *"Go, horse, go!"* he shouted.

★ ★ ★

THE explosion from East Clay burst down the four blocks over Capitol Square, stunning the huge crowd outside the State Court House. On cue, Beecher Lovejoy shouted, *"The Davis Mansion! The Yankees have blown up the Davis Mansion!"* The word flashed around the throng and suddenly the people started to break away and run north up Twelfth, screaming oaths and becoming an instant mob. Nine of the eleven sentries stationed near the entrance looked around uncertainly for a moment, then panicked and also ran toward the sound of the explosion.

While the two guards right at the door stared after them, Salmon Brown and Crispus moved quickly in on them and rammed long knives into their backs. Swiftly, the other two members of Amistad joined them, tearing off their dusters to reveal the dark blue Union uniforms. *"Inside!"* Salmon shouted, waving his pistol and leaping through the doorway. He shot the two guards inside the entrance before they knew what hit them.

The explosion and the shots struck those inside the courtroom into a shocked silence. But John Mosby was stunned for only a moment. *Of course, this had to be it!* "Jeb!" he shouted, drawing his pistol. *"Now!"* He whirled. *"Ogg! Perkins!"*

A woman screamed, then another.

Salmon Brown rushed to the middle of the center aisle and took advantage of the sudden stillness to shout, *"I am the son of John Brown! His last written statement said 'the crimes of this guilty land will never be purged away except by blood!'"*

For a moment he stared into the shocked eyes of Thomas Wentworth Higginson, who turned from the aisle seat that had cost $200. *"You lost your nerve!"* Salmon snapped. *"You traitor!"* From five feet away he pulled the trigger, blasting the minister back against the bench.

At that instant, Verita hiked up her looped skirt and jerked out the revolver. Jumping to her feet, she shouted, *"I am Verita, a Negro from New Orleans here in the cause of freedom! Viva Amistad!"* She turned, jammed the barrel into Judah Benjamin's ribs and laughed into his startled eyes. *He would never pass on any names nor conquer another woman in this world!* She jerked the trigger. The concussion from such short range blasted the ambassador into the mesmerized Rawlins. Already Judah's eyes were glazing.

Wheeling, she swung the Lefaucheux with both hands to line up on Jefferson Davis, directly in front of her. *"Die for Amistad, you tyrant!"* she shouted.

More women screamed.

Men shouted as more shots were fired. *"Look out! Stop them Yankee niggers!"*

Verita fired once, missed, as Mosby threw himself into the president, knocking him to the floor. Just as she again got Davis centered in her sights, a smashing blow on the side of her head from John Rawlins slammed her sideways.

"You crazy bitch!" he shouted.

She recovered, firing directly into Rawlins's chest, pausing to exult over the look of startled pain spreading over his face as he slumped to the floor. The last thing she heard from him was *"Sonofabitch!"* followed by a choppy cough as blood began to trickle from his mouth.

She had to get Bessica! Swinging the pistol backward, she tried to aim at her hostess. But there were too many people in the way. There, almost, Bessica's eyes were wide, her mouth open. It was the last thing Verita remembered because the heavy fist of a man behind her crashed into her skull, knocking her to her knees. "No, not yet," she mumbled. Bright lights and darkness followed.

Gunfire filled the room in a wild barrage of shots, as Beecher Love-joy, Denmark Vesey, and Crispus—each blasting away with two pistols—took aim at their assigned targets. Mosby's defenders, hampered by panicked spectators, tried to get clear shots at the blue-clad attackers. *"Die, you white slavers!"* Crispus shouted.

More shouts and screams filled the air; spectators started trampling each other as they climbed benches and jumped toward the wall to get away from the blazing guns.

John Breckinridge went down from a bullet in the shoulder while trying to shield Spring Blakely. A woman in the third row took a bullet in her breast. Another slug shattered the cheek of a reporter standing mesmerized beside Edward Pollard in the press row. Crispus, face livid, shot Beauregard and another general before Reverdy Ogg's bullet spun him around.

The instant Mosby hollered, Jeb Stuart jerked out his big pistol and faced the crowd. He really hadn't believed Mosby, had, in fact, forgotten about this crazy radical thing in his great joy and sadness for General Lee. He aimed at the shouting man in the center aisle, but a spectator jumped, screaming, into his line of fire. Were they really Yankee soldiers? Was it a major attack of some sort? What kind of madness was this? He got a black soldier in his sights. The big LeMat *roared*, and he saw his target snap around, but stay on his feet. He tried to fire again, but another panicked spectator crossed his sights. He looked over to Flora and his mother, caught a glimpse of their wide eyes above hands that covered their mouths in unbelieving terror.

Salmon shot a civilian in the second row, then bore down on his special target—the white-haired general standing in front of the witness box. This was it, what it had all come down to. Kill this man and every soul in the world would remember his name forever! See, Old Man, *this* was the way to do it! He brought his pistol up, saw Lee's black eyes staring back at him angrily. The fool just stood there erect, as if some kind of an aura would protect him. Didn't even have a gun—what kind of a soldier was he? Now, Salmon Brown, now! *Watch, John Brown, as I blast the face off the most famous general in the world! You never did that, John Brown!*

Jeb saw the man striding straight down the aisle. He was wearing a Union officer's uniform, cavalry eagles on his shoulders, a slouch hat over intense eyes, aiming a long-barreled revolver right at General Lee! No! He fired the horse pistol, but it just *clicked!* "General Lee, get down!" He lunged sideways, throwing himself in front of the general just as the long-barreled revolver belched flame. The big slug slammed into his side, felt just like a horse kicked him, just like at—"*Stay down, General!*" Flora's scream was in his ears as he hung onto Lee, shielding him. And suddenly the shots became distant, the screams muffled. It was bright, very bright, and Lee was saying something to him, but he couldn't understand it. Flora, Flora—

Salmon Brown shoved a woman aside, tried to draw a new bead on Lee's face.

But at that moment, bursting through everyone in the center aisle, Jubilo rushed forward shouting, "*Salmon Brown—you coward!*"

Salmon turned, tried to train his revolver on the huge black man descending on him with a cavalry pistol aimed straight at his chest. Coward? *Jubilo!* How could he possibly— He fired into the black man's huge body, but Jubilo lunged right at him. How—

Jubilo's .52 slug smashed into his chest, just before the falling negro leader piled into him. Salmon Brown was dead before he hit the floor.

Braxton Bragg, finally using his Navy Colt for what it was intended, fired two rounds at Denmark Vesey before a slug from the still fighting, cursing Crispus hit him in the arm.

From where he covered the president, Mosby got a clear view of Crispus, lined up on him and shot him in the stomach. Crispus staggered, his eyes wild, firing both pistols as his arms dropped. Mosby fired again, catching him in the chest. And the former Toronto newspaper reporter crashed to the floor.

Ex-corporal Tommy Perkins shot the staggering, still shooting, Denmark Vesey for the fourth time; his friends riddled the last member of Amistad, Beecher Lovejoy, with round after round until he hung draped over the corner of a bench, his dead eyes staring out of a shattered face, his two revolvers still smoking where they lay on the floor.

And suddenly it was quiet; the people just stared through the smoke at the mayhem around them.

Flora Stuart's scream broke the spell. She fell out of her wheelchair and dragged herself forward, trying to get to Jeb.

Horrified, Mosby disentangled himself from the white-faced president, and rushed over to where General Lee was leaning over the prostrate Stuart. *No! God, no!* He leaned down, saw the blood spreading rapidly over Jeb's side, soaking the yellow sash and turning it bright maroon. Jeb was blinking, not seeing, his head in Lee's arms. "He took my bullet," the general said softly.

"Get a doctor here!" Mosby shouted, leaning close, searching Jeb's eyes. "Oh, God, hurry!"

Jeb's lips moved, barely forming the faint words, "Bully for old K! Give it to 'em, boys!"

Furl that Banner, softly, slowly:
Treat it gently—it is holy,
   For it droops above the dead;
Touch it not—unfold it never;
Let it droop there, furled forever,—
   For its people's hopes are fled.
                    —Abram Joseph Ryan

JOHN Mosby looked out at the wet early evening from the windowseat of Elihu B. Washburne's famous dining room. The rain had been falling steadily since the previous morning and showed no signs of letting up. Funerals and rain; rain and funerals, he thought. How was such a kinship ever born? Was it God's tears falling when a favored child passed on? Or was it His way of ensuring the drabness of death? He had been to two funerals in two days—Jeb's massive, tragic service at St. Paul's Episcopal Church in Richmond the day before, and John Rawlins's today.

He hadn't known Rawlins well, but he liked all he knew about the man. The man with the mark of death upon him had at last cheated the dread disease that raped his lungs for so long. He could see him now, finishing a coughing spell, unable to keep from looking at the telltale sign of coming death, and spitting out, "Sonofabitch!"

Now John Rawlins's two closest friends were mourning the man's death and John Mosby was an intruder. Congressman Washburne had known Rawlins for many years, but Lieutenant General Ulysses

S. Grant, the general-in-chief of the U.S. Army, had been like an older brother to him. At times in their years together, when John Rawlins stuck to his mother hen role, it had been the reverse.

"May I pour you some warm coffee, Colonel?" General Grant asked quietly from his elbow.

"No, thank you, sir," Mosby replied.

"It's a bad time for both of us, and I'm sorry you had to get a second dose like this."

Mosby nodded. The pain wasn't discernible in the quiet man's expression, but he knew it was there behind his sad blue eyes. "I got to talk to General Rawlins only once when it wasn't about that damned business of Amistad," Mosby said softly. "And he mentioned something about finding his niche before it was too late. I wonder if he knows, wherever he is, that his death was a major factor in holding off a war."

Ulysses S. Grant nodded. "He probably does—he always seemed to know everything else. Why, I'll bet if I'd worn a sock with a hole in it—which I did on many an occasion—he could tell me which foot it was on." He smiled briefly, took a deep drag on his cigar, and stared out at the rain.

Mosby shook his head. "How many generals do you think were killed during the war, General?"

Grant continued to look into the rain. "Don't know. Quite a few."

"And all it resulted in was two countries sitting here on the verge of going at each other's throats again. Yet, the death of John Rawlins gives us a pause to collect ourselves and cool off the hotheads. Do you think, sir, that President McClellan could have had the prescience to send him down to Richmond for some such purpose . . . to be expendable in the event of—"

"The president isn't that bright!" Grant said sharply.

"I'm sorry, sir, just some idle conjecture. Nevertheless, I can tell you for a fact that if he hadn't been there, hadn't spoiled that Amistad woman's shot at Davis, and been killed by her, our president would have had no choice but to call up his army. The Confederate Congress would have given him no choice."

Grant was more talkative than usual, possibly due to his deep grief. "And if he, as a senior Union general, hadn't been killed by Northern abolitionists in that shootout, the North would have done the same thing to McClellan. Still might, for that matter. It's been breeding hard for a couple of weeks now."

Mosby nodded. That was why he was here—not because he had been close to Rawlins, but because they had been trying to stop Amistad in a joint effort. It was Breckinridge who had decided Mosby would be the man best suited to represent the C.S.A. at Rawlins's funeral, that he could informally do the most good with Grant. "Sir," he said, grabbing the opportunity to speak boldly, "I know how it is with the people up here. And I know how it is with the press and the politicians. It's a popular thing to talk about charging across the Potomac and finishing the job with those damned slavers. I know that, sir, but a man like you can stop it. You and Mr. Lincoln. Oh, I know, I'm a damned Rebel and I'm supposed to hate both of you with an undying passion, but I don't."

Grant looked at him, took a puff on his cigar. "I'm just a soldier and Mr. Lincoln is just a civilian," he replied.

Mosby looked into his eyes. "Yes, sir, but with all this discontent with Mr. McClellan, one of you is bound to be the next president. Now is the time to use that influence, sir. We don't want to fight again, and neither do you . . . I don't think." He knew he had better stop before he went too far.

Grant stroked his beard, nodded.

"I just caught the end of that," Congressman Washburne said as he walked up. "Good reasoning, Colonel. But what if Congress, which is really the voice of the people, still decides it wants to march back into the South?"

Mosby cocked his head, smiled lightly. "Then, sir, it would be up to a powerful congressman to help that soldier and civilian . . . I would think."

Both Grant and Washburne nodded. "Well," the congressman replied, "as long as we have people like you to talk with, maybe some common sense will prevail."

Mosby reached for his hat, found a tight smile. "We've got a lot of good talkers down there, if you remember."

Grant stuck out his hand. "Come up and see me sometime soon, Mosby. Under more pleasant conditions. We'll chat some more."

Mosby stepped back and saluted.

It was all he could ask.

But as the door closed behind the Confederate officer, Washburne looked at Grant and shook his head. "It really is too bad, isn't it, Ulys? There's only one solution, and it isn't talking to *anyone*."

Grant nodded grimly. Sooner or later, this year or next . . . sometime in the not too distant future . . . an army in blue would once more have to splash across the Potomac in anger.

And then maybe those people would begin to realize how very gray their victory had been.

★   ★   ★

E DWARD Pollard held the editorial up to the light of the oil lamp on his desk at the *Examiner*. He sniffed, disliking it. But he had to write it—the whole South was ready to deify that goddamned Stuart. He changed a word: venerate. Yes, it stuck right in his craw to use the word. . . .

A Eulogy to Jeb Stuart

No braver act can a man perform than to lay down his life for another. In the case of General Jeb Stuart, he gave his life for perhaps the greatest man the South has ever produced. Now we must venerate this hero as another fine son of the South, of Virginia. And true hero he was. And victim. Yes, Jeb Stuart was a victim of a court of inquiry so evilly devised and stacked against him—surely by our noble president—that it took the ruination of a senior general, the appearance of none other than General Lee, and a vile attack by Northern killers to clear him. And cleared he is—of any dereliction, of any performance less than heroic, of any discreditable conduct. May he rest in peace in that special heaven where the great warriors go.

Pollard shook his head; he really disliked it. But he shrugged: that was the newspaper business. He picked it up to give to the typesetter and was about to blow out the lamp when an idea struck him. He reached for a pencil and began to tap it on a blank sheet of paper. He could wait a few days for the grief to sink in and lose its edge ... then he could begin a series of articles in which he might use Stuart to great advantage—play on his memory to get at Davis. After all, if Davis hadn't tried to hang Gettysburg on Stuart, there never would have been a court of inquiry for those Yankee killers to attack. . . .

OCTOBER 24TH, 1866

JUST one portion of Libby Prison had been kept open since the
end of the war. The famous old institution that had held thousands of Union officers was now reserved for the few major prisoners
awaiting trial for crimes against the Confederacy.

The warden opened the door to a small but airy cell, shaking his
head. "I'd just as soon you'd talk to her somewhere else, Colonel. You
know what a dangerous bitch she is."

Mosby nodded, smiled briefly. "I'll be careful." This was his sixth
trip to interrogate her.

He went inside, said, "Hello, Verita."

She was standing before a small cracked wall mirror, brushing her
short hair. The coarse gray prison dress hung on her like a sack, but
her rouge was perfect. She raised a disdainful eyebrow in the glass.
"Did you come to help me dress, Colonel?"

Mosby glanced at the white dress laid out on the cot, guessed that
it was the same one she had worn that terrible day in the
courtroom—with the blood washed out. That would be like her, no
looking for mercy, just open defiance. He chuckled. "From what the
big boys tell me, I guess that would be most stimulating."

She turned, ran a hand over her breast to her hip. "Quite."

"You ready for today?"

"Of course."

"It'll probably be bad, you know."

"They let me read the papers."

Mosby detected her perfume, felt a flicker of excitement as he looked into her bold hazel eyes. No wonder men like Judah Benjamin lost their heads over her. Or any man. "I might still be able to do some good," he said quietly.

She laughed. "Don't play games with me, Colonel. They want my head and no matter what I tell you, they'll have it on a pike."

"I'll go all the way to the president."

"Ha! With the election so close, do you think *he's* going to do anything? No, Colonel, I'll just appeal. After all, I'm a woman, and they haven't proven first degree."

"It doesn't matter. You're being tried as a Negro murderer in the *South*. You killed and tried to kill *white* people." Mosby frowned. "Get sensible, Verita. An appeal will be turned down in five minutes. You're right, they'll close in on you like sharks around a bloody morsel of beef—unless you make a deal. Tell me about those people up north. Just give me one name."

Her eyes hardened. "Don't be foolish, Mosby. Our great cause won't stop if they kill me, *or* those up north. Do you think Amistad died in that courtroom? Ha! It was only the beginning—a *hundred* Veritas and Salmon Browns will descend on this decadent order before it's crushed and the black folks can walk in freedom."

She moved close, her eyes aflame. "Even if you cut off the heads up north, new ones will pop right up. But it's even worse, Mosby, you folks have got the poison now. That's correct, right there in your guts are four million people who know they can get you. They can kill and burn, sneak up on your women in their sleep and cut their throats, Mosby. And just knowing that's going to happen will destroy you. By God, Mosby, you'll destroy *yourselves!*"

He shook his head. "There may be some truth to what you say, but it isn't going to happen tomorrow. You know what, Verita? The sad part of this whole thing is that brilliant, remarkable people like you don't do something constructive about the problem."

"Get out, Mosby!"

"Think of what you can do if you are alive."

Her eyes narrowed, she leaned close. "Mosby, I'll be alive a thousand years after you are ashes."

★ ★ ★

T EN minutes later, Mosby was waiting inside the main entrance of the prison when Jubilo walked toward him, escorted by a guard captain. "He's all yours, Colonel," the prison official said.

Mosby stuck out his hand. "Nice day to get out of jail, isn't it, Reverend?"

Jubilo shook hands briefly. "Good as any, I suppose."

As they were passed through the door, Mosby pulled out two thin cigars, handed one to Jubilo, and struck a match. As soon as they were both puffing, Mosby pointed to his open buggy. "C'mon, I'll give you a ride."

Jubilo nodded, crawled in the buggy. When they were a few hundred feet away from the prison, he turned around and looked at its bleak walls. He had been there since August 23rd, the day he was transferred from the hospital. At first they had questioned him daily, even while he was recovering from the terrible chest wound Salmon Brown's shot had caused—Mosby, the police, members of Congress, generals, the president's secretary, anyone and everyone who thought he might confess or lead them to the others involved with Amistad. But in the last month, it had slowed down, and finally they just let him sit there. Twice Mosby arranged for his wife to visit for a few minutes. The rest of the time, he figured he was lucky the guards didn't shoot him for some trumped-up reason—he knew how much they wanted to. It was Mosby who finally got him out, convincing President Davis that he had merely heard about the attack accidentally, and had thrown himself into the shootout just in time to save General Lee. And General Lee had thanked him personally before intervening with Davis.

"Well," Mosby said, "have you decided that place isn't any fun?"

Jubilo just looked ahead, puffed on the cigar.

"You know, of course, that you'll be right back in there if you so much as sneeze the word Abraham. And this time, they really will throw away the key. What happened two months ago is an unscabbed sore throughout this country. God only knows how many colored folks have paid a terrible price in beatings and even death since then. Do you know that, Jubilo?"

The huge Negro nodded again.

"I told you once, I'll try it again. If we're going to sort all of this out, we are going to need some strong Negro leaders with sense in their heads and patience in their hearts. I still think you are going to be one of them."

Jubilo flicked off the ashes, and turned suddenly. A tiny smile appeared briefly at the corners of his mouth. "I already am."

★ ★ ★

I T REMINDED Mosby of the circus atmosphere of the Stuart court—the line of people struggling to get inside, the women gaily attired as if for a great social event. Which it was. Men came to lust, and every woman in Richmond wanted to see this fancy high yellow who had wormed her way into the very core of their society get just what she deserved.

Verita was being tried by a military tribunal, a point of law Mosby considered wrong, since she was a civilian. But the high-handed decision had come down directly from Davis himself, declaring that the crimes of which she was accused had occurred in a military court and were part of a massive plot against the government of the Confederacy. Seven general officers and two colonels constituted the tribunal. Major General Jubal Early, a longtime lawyer before the war, was the president. Black bearded and gruff, he had held an iron hand over the proceedings since the opening statement, keeping Verita's high-priced lawyer from Alexandria tightly in tow.

It was strange that the whole Stuart court should come down to this, Mosby thought, watching General Early get ready to deliver the sentence. Early had been the one senior officer on record who openly defended Jeb before the court.

He glanced to the right, three rows ahead. Bessica Adams Southwick sat erectly, seldom taking her eyes from the defendant. While it would have been in poor taste to go formally into mourning for Jeb, she had worn nothing but severe ensembles of gray each time she had appeared in public since his death. And that had been seldom, because the newspapers had had a heyday over her involvement with Verita. Mosby made a mental note to go see her and personally express his condolences. And perhaps learn more of the connection that had sent Verita to her doorstep—the Yankee cousin who had made a hurried trip to Europe.

"It's hard to believe that I had lunch with her only a couple of months ago," Spring said with a wondrous touch in her voice. "She was so worldly and vivacious when we talked about the anti-slavery movement."

"She was what you might call 'inspired,' " Mosby replied dryly.

"Don't be sarcastic, darling. When I see her waiting there, so tragic and beautiful, I just want to cry."

Mosby said nothing further. His lovely liberal fiancée would never believe the prison cell scene.

General Jubal Early pounded his gavel. "The defendant will stand before the bench," he commanded sternly in his raspy voice.

Verita, exquisite in the same ensemble she had worn the day of the attack—including the rakish, flat-crowned hat with the ostrich feather, rose with her attorney and moved to face the tribunal. Her face was a cool mask, her air superior.

"Verita, as you choose to be called," Jubal Early began. "You have been found guilty on all charges and specifications of murder and attempted murder and acts of war against the government of this country. I would harangue you for these beastly crimes, but it would only demean this court to stoop so low. By secret ballot, with three quarters of the members concurring, you are sentenced to be hanged by the neck until dead within sixty days of this date!"

As Early's gavel pounded, Verita turned, looked fleetingly around the courtroom and finally found Mosby's eye. A faint smile touched her lips.

★   ★   ★

THEY drove leisurely west along Byrd Street, letting the horse pick his own speed. It was one of those brisk, clear fall days when the rich colors of the fallen leaves covered the ground like the wayward patches of an unfinished quilt. Only the black bare limbs of the trees were forbidding. "Do you think Poe would have written something about her?" Spring asked suddenly.

"Yes, most probably," Mosby replied. "A beautiful woman with the kiss of death on her brow. Yes, I'm sure he would have reveled in it."

She took his arm, leaned for a moment on his shoulder. "These are difficult times, aren't they? So much is new and so much is old, and the marriage of the two is so perplexing. We have just finished the most terrible war in history and yet perhaps our troubles have just begun. Where are we going, John?"

"I don't know. The letter from Grant this morning wasn't good. McClellan is finally bowing to the pressure and is calling sixteen state regiments to active duty. It may be only a political ploy, but it means Davis will have to do something similar. And sword-waving is dangerous.

"And Abraham worries me. It's beginning to wiggle and breathe like a mammoth sea serpent just coming to life. I'll have to fight it with every ounce of my energy because it is seditious, but I can understand it." He reached in his pocket, withdrew an envelope, and handed it to her. "And many of us have to get our own houses in order before we'll be able to solve our country's problems. This is my personal start."

Spring withdrew the two affidavits, read them quickly. "Oh, John," she said softly, looking up at him with suddenly brimming eyes. "They'll be so happy. Almost as happy as it makes me." She kissed him on the cheek, then replaced the freedman's papers for his two house servants, Aaron and Winnie, back in the envelope.

"Just remember one thing, Miss Blakely. I'm still a long way from being a goddamned abolitionist," he said gruffly as he turned the horse into the lane that led to Hollywood Cemetery.

"That's good enough for me," Spring smiled. "One in a family may just be enough. I'm not promising anything, darling, but if I hold my sign-carrying down to a minimum, maybe only go to one convention a year—do you think that'll be good enough to get me married?"

"I'll think on it. 'Specially since I've already given you a ring."

The lightness ended when he rounded the corner and turned down the lane that led to the Cavalry Memorial. Stopping below the statue of a charging cavalryman, he dismounted silently and reached in the back of the buggy for the new black ostrich plume. Moments later, he stood before the new grave, the one centered below the three others and covered by fresh flowers that some mourner had placed on it that morning. He stood there several moments before placing the black plume on the center of the grave, then dropped to his knees.

From the other side of the hill, he thought he heard the faint strains of a banjo strumming and the voices of a tired cavalry column singing, "If you want to smell hell—if you want to have fun—if you want to catch the devil—Jine the cavalreee!"

His eyes brimmed.

The years faded back to the summer of '61. . . .

It was another bright day, and he was lying down by the side of the road taking a break from the long dusty march north of Winchester. He was a skinny twenty-seven-year-old private and he glanced up with curiosity when a thickset man of about his own age rode up on a remarkable bay. He was wearing a Yankee undress uniform with Confederate insignia and a broad grin. He leaned down from the saddle, slapped an officer on the back, and laughed loud enough to be heard on the other side of the enemy lines.

"That's Stuart, our new colonel," someone said.

Flowing brown mustaches, a flaming beard, and merry blue eyes. Bright sun reflecting off the hilt of his cavalry saber. A yellow sash. Unmistakable confidence, strength. That was the most vibrant sign he gave off—sheer, inexhaustible strength.

There had been a great chasm between them then.

Now it had returned.

The last cavalier was gone.

P.S.

===

I T IS most intriguing to play with history in a might-have-been, particularly when one tries to adhere to the facts once the premise has been established—and inserts a number of truly fascinating real historical characters. Here is what actually happened to some of them:

Colonel John S. Mosby was the first great ranger and one of the most notorious of Rebel leaders. He practiced law after the war, eventually gained access to President U.S. Grant's inner circle, and served in various government positions. He died in Washington, D.C., on Memorial Day, 1916, at the age of eighty-two.

John A. Rawlins became Secretary of War when Grant was elected president. He died of tuberculosis in 1869. Rawlins, Wyoming, is named after him.

Salmon Brown actually did back out of going to Harpers Ferry with his father, John Brown, and was in on the Kansas murders in the '50s. He committed suicide in Portland, Oregon, in 1919 at the age of eighty-two.

Judah P. Benjamin, perhaps the most brilliant member of Davis's cabinet, fled through the Bahamas to England at the end of the war and made a name in British law. He died in Paris in 1884.

John Bell Hood lost the battle of Atlanta, which led to Lincoln's 1864 reelection, and finished the war as a full general in spite of his physical handicaps. As a New Orleans merchant he fathered eleven children in ten years, but died suddenly of yellow fever, along with his wife, in 1879. Fort Hood, Texas, is named for him.

George E. Pickett never forgave Robert E. Lee for Gettysburg and remained loyal to Longstreet all his life. He was nearly tried by Lee just before Appomattox for dereliction. He died at the age of fifty in 1875, leaving his twenty-seven-year-old wife, Salli, to write his biography.

Braxton Bragg became an engineer in Texas after the war, and died in 1876; possibly because there was no known injection for distemper. Fort Bragg, North Carolina, the Green Beret and airborne center, is named for him.

James Longstreet became an insurance executive and a Republican, later serving as Minister to Turkey—one of many political appointments. His strong criticism of the beloved Lee regarding Gettysburg led to his ostracism in the South. He died at eighty-three in 1904.

Flora Cooke Stuart survived her husband by sixty years.

James Ewell Brown Stuart died of a wound in his side inflicted by a Union cavalryman's pistol at Yellow Tavern in May, 1864.

—Robert Skimin

In appreciation to:

My perceptive editor, Brian DeFiore; my agent, Freya Manston; Louise Arnold and John Slonaker of the U.S. Army History Institute; Marijean Murray and her library staff of the U.S. Army Sergeants Major Academy; James O. Hall, who really tracked down the spy, Harrison; Samuel J. T. Moore, Jr.; the librarians of the Museum of the Confederacy and the Valentine Museum; my wife, Claudia; Martha Peters; and all the other librarians, biographers, and historians who made this book possible. Thanks, y'all!

—Robert Skimin